moonlighters

A NOVELLA COLLECTION

ANITA KELLY

contents

sing anyway

note to readers

This novella includes brief mentions of gender dysphoria and fatphobia.

For memories of Chopsticks III, and the friends who let me sing along

And for pop music, which saves me still

sam

ALL MY FRIENDS WERE ASSHOLES.

I tried to leave for the bar later tonight; I really did. I sat around my apartment for as long as possible, snacking on cheesy puffs and watching my cats growl at each other. Garfunkel always antagonized Simon and Simon always played right into it. They were both idiots.

But even after stalling for what felt like forever, I was still the first one at Moonie's. Like always.

Moonie's was technically The Moonlight Café, although nobody actually called it that. The *café* in particular always tickled me. As if we were conjuring uncomfortable chairs on the sidewalk in Montmartre, sipping tiny cups of espresso and chomping on perfectly flaky croissants. You couldn't get a croissant at Moonie's if you begged on your hands and knees.

Still, I loved Moonie's, in this pure, uncomplicated way, like children loved snow days, or cats loved tiny dots of red light. I loved its not-so-slight seediness, its sticky floors and dreadful food selection, its weird location in the middle of an industrial wasteland section of the city. Moonie's wasn't a place you happened to stumble into during a night out on the town. Moonie's was a place you went to on purpose.

And even though it didn't actually advertise itself as a queer bar, all the queers knew it was Our Place. We came here on purpose. For some reason. Some cheap liquor, excellent karaoke reason.

What I *didn't* love was having to be the one who saved our table every time, awkwardly thumbing through my phone and nursing a beer until someone else in our group finally decided to show. It was like my friends completely forgot that time we showed up and our entire favorite table —including the tables from the side we always dragged over to make ÜberTable—was taken by a sloppy bachelorette party. It had been a qualified disaster, but apparently I was the only one who cared.

Or perhaps, my friends simply *knew* I was the only one who cared. Hence taking advantage of me always being here early to save our table.

Although, okay. If I was being honest...I was also here this early for my own sake. Because if I wasn't out of the house by 8:30—the time of night I was typically already rolling into my jam jams and gleefully snuggling under my covers to watch YouTube until I passed out—then the probability of me actually leaving the house at all decreased exponentially.

Sometimes, I wondered if I'd gotten too old and pathetic for even Moonie's.

But no. I wasn't. Not yet. Because I was here now. And each time I came here, it reminded me, reassured me. That I still had the ability to break loose a little. And I needed that.

After tossing my jacket around a chair, I walked to the bar on the opposite side of the room, waited for the super unfriendly butch bartender to notice me. She was here almost every time we came to Moonie's and had never smiled at me once. I was equal parts terrified of and deeply in love with her.

My phone buzzed in my pocket.

Claire: *Harry just vommed all over the nice rug*

Kort: *truly disgusting*

Claire: *going to have to cancel the sitter*

Kort: *ugh, why are babies*

Claire: *I'm so sorry :(*

Kort: *we made poor life choices*

"You need something?"

I jumped. Fuck. Scary Butch Bartender finally noticed me while I was oblivious on my phone, which definitely meant she hated me even more now. This was an ominous start to the evening.

"Sorry, I'm so sorry. Just a Rainier."

She plopped the can on the counter and wordlessly stuck out her hand for my card. After I handed it over with what I hoped was my most charming, so-sorry-again, I-am-gonna-tip-you-so-hard smile, I slinked back to our table. Well, *my* table, currently. Should I make ÜberTable now, to make sure we had it? Except...with Claire and Kort out, that meant their weird neighbors likely wouldn't come, either, which sucked, because even though they were *fucking weird*, they reliably provided at least half of our most memorable Moonie's moments.

With a groan, I remembered Nate was out of town, too. So he and whatever randoms he normally pulled in were also out.

We might not even have to shove an obnoxious number of tables together at all.

I slumped down into my seat at my singular table, accompanied by my cold can of lager and my friend, Instagram. Which I definitely had already caught up on while I was eating cheesy puffs in my apartment.

Sigh. Twitter it was.

Things only began to look up when Kiki, the karaoke jockey, walked by on her way to her station fifteen minutes later and gave me a wave. I smiled back. Kiki was without a doubt our favorite KJ. She liked us, didn't let the same people hog the mic over and over, and was cute as hell. I was pissed Claire and Kort were missing out on a Kiki night. Their loss for deciding to raise spawn.

I'd finished off my Rainier by the time another text of doom appeared on my phone, this time from Rae: *I am so sorry, if I don't get this brief done this weekend I am royally screwed.*

So. Claire, Kort, Weird Neighbors, Nate, Nate's Randoms, *and* Rae were officially missing out on a Kiki night.

I stared at the sparkly letters that adorned the wall next to me, that had adorned this wall for all of eternity: *HAPPY BIRTH AY*, they shouted, seemingly at anyone, the *D* long missing. At Moonie's, every day was someone's birth ay. It had become a phrase of affection amongst my friends and me, particularly at the drunken end of a karaoke night, shouting it at each other nonsensically: HAAAPPY BIRTH-AYYYY!

But clearly, the likelihood of *birth ay* proclamations tonight appeared dim. With everyone else out, the only friends who remained were Steve, whom I loved but who refused to sing at karaoke, which lessened the fun a bit, and Kelsey. And you truly never knew if Kelsey was going to actually show to an event or not. Which would be annoying with anyone else, but Kelsey was so fucking hysterical whenever she did decide to show that her flakiness was instantly forgiven every time.

Even if she *did* show tonight, me, Kelsey, and Steve would be...kind of an odd group. Missing too much of the glue of everyone else. Best to bail now for the good of the order.

I stood, moving toward the bar. Man, Butch Bartender was gonna be pissed when I closed out on a $4 tab.

But then the door opened.

I was already at the bar when she walked in. I sucked in a breath.

Lemon yellow dress tonight, splashed all over with large, blood-red poppies. Her shoulders were draped in a velvet jacket the same shade of red as the flowers on her dress. Although the jacket didn't hide the neckline of said dress, which dipped low in a glorious V, framing her breasts perfectly. She laughed as her group walked to their table, and I caught a bright, brief glimpse of it—straight white teeth framed by cherry red lipstick, curving around an exhalation of mirth—before she turned away. She was wearing thick hoop earrings, sea green, just enough of a color contrast to the rest of her outfit to look clever. When she turned, I could see glitter on her cheeks, sparkling gold even under the dim lights.

She always looked good.

But fuck, she looked good tonight.

"Another?"

Butch Bartender had caught me unawares *again*. And when she held up another sweating can of Rainier, I nodded. Like the miserable human being I was.

I scooted back to my table, telling myself it was *not* super creepy to nurse another beer for the sole purpose of getting to hear my karaoke crush sing her signature opening song. I mean, I *did* put on pants and everything for this outing. It would be sad if I left before I even heard one song. Especially if it was hers.

My karaoke crush, or KC as I called her in my head—being that my brain always forgot her actual name, being that we had never actually talked to each other—and her group of friends weren't here *every* time our group was, but like a lot of other Moonie's regulars, we frequently overlapped. When she didn't show, I had a rotation of other karaoke crushes amongst the Moonie's Strangers Who Didn't Necessarily Feel Like Strangers When We Were Here, as I had a rotation of crushes for almost every aspect of my life.

I was very good at being thirsty. Less successful at the actual drinking part.

Everyone else paled in comparison to my #1 KC, though. She always wore the prettiest clothes, usually brightly colored dresses, as she was tonight. Sometimes she mixed it up, though. Last summer, during a particularly rough heat wave, she came to Moonie's wearing short overalls in this wacky checkered pattern over a tight tank top. I had never seen her show that much arm or leg before, and she looked so powerful on the dance floor when she sang that I almost passed out.

Because that's what #1 KC was: powerful. I'd overheard her chatting at her table with her friends before, and her speaking voice was surprisingly feather light and high pitched. But when she had a mic in front of her, she had one of those voices that you could tell came straight from her gut. Like the strength of her lungs could blow, blow, blow your house down. She didn't prance around the dance floor like some of these queers did—although to be clear, I was always here for a prancing queer—but moved her body in a way that mattered, in a way that made you stop and pay attention. She was big and gorgeous and whenever she sang I wanted to just...melt into her.

And then sneak into the bathroom with her and bang against the wall.

Not that that would ever happen.

But a non-binary-person-who-appeared-to-have-no-friends could dream.

Aaaand there she went. Walking up to Kiki. Putting in her first request.

I took a big swig of Rainier. Which I then proceeded to choke on. The bar was starting to fill up now, and not only was I taking up a whole table by myself, I was apparently losing the ability to even function properly.

I got a hold of myself, and moved to a small two-seater, back in the corner. As far from ÜberTable as I could get. Such was my fate.

My phone buzzed in my pocket again.

Text from Steve: *wait so is anyone making it to Moonie's tonight?? Running super late anyway, let me know!*

Kiki picked up the mic and moved to the center of the floor.

"Time to get this party started, my people! My request list is still pretty light, and you know it won't be that way for long. Bring me your songs, babes!"

With a wink, she launched into the first song of the night.

Kiki liked to kick off karaoke herself, which, considering she was going to spend the next several hours of her life listening to drunk people screech and holler in her ear, she fully deserved. She had a great voice, a cute little shimmy, and she always chose the best throwbacks.

Although when she launched into Jennifer Paige's

classic 1998 hit, "Crush"—which I would have appreciated on any other night, because, hilarious—I nearly thwacked my forehead onto the table.

Instead, I steadfastly stared around at the rest of the room, only glancing at the back of my #1 KC's head for the briefest of moments, telling myself Jennifer was right. It was just a little crush. Not like I fainted every time we touched. Not that we had ever touched. So perhaps the jury was still out on that one.

And then Kiki was back behind her little table, and shouting into the mic: "Here we go, everybody! Put your hands together for crowd favorite, Lilyyyyy!"

#1 KC—*Lily*, how did I always forget that, so pretty— got up from her table. She walked over to Kiki with a smile and took the mic. Her yellow dress swished.

And I couldn't tell if I was excited, or if I was sad. Excited, because it was going to be awesome. Sad, because once Lily sang Carrie Underwood, Kiki would let a bunch of other losers sing until she gave Lily another round. Which meant that after this, I'd truly have no excuse to be here anymore. And dammit, coming all the way out to Moonie's without getting to have a true Moonie's night was a disappointment of epic proportions.

But then Lily opened her mouth.

And okay, maybe the awesomeness beat out the disappointment. Even though I'd heard Lily sing "Before He Cheats" at least ten times before, it still kicked me in the gut as soon as she started.

I never knew what she'd end up singing later on, but every single time she was here, Lily started the night with "Before He Cheats." And I admired the hell out of it every single time, because I had to be at least six drinks in to even think about approaching a microphone, and even then, only when one of my friends dragged me with them. But to be one of the first singers of the night meant putting yourself out there to a half-full room of sober people. And it wasn't like Lily chose an easy one to start with, like a Lisa Loeb "Stay" kind of selection, one you could quietly croon while everyone else got their cheap drinks and shitty fries and ignored you.

No, Lily chose this bluesy, shit-eating country song with a chorus that used up entire lungfuls of air. It was like she needed to launch herself into this balls-to-the-wall song to get herself into the groove. Because she was a little hesitant at first, a little shaky during that very first *right now* of the opening verse. But soon she was *belting* it, leaning over when she got real into the best lines, swaying her hips across the floor during the sassy verses, and Jesus. What a star. By the end, her eyes would be sparkling, and everyone in the room would be a little bit in love with her.

Or maybe it was just me. But seriously, every time she sang about scratching her keys into the side of that dude's car—well, I wouldn't have minded if she wanted to carve her name into *my* leather seats. Or whatever. I would be one hundred percent down with whatever the fuck she wanted to do, was what I was saying.

And while I always felt this way, there was something about watching her sing tonight while I sat here alone that made the whole experience heightened. The table next to me had filled up with a bunch of people I didn't recognize, and they were all chatting loudly with each other like Lily wasn't singing "Before He Cheats," and I sort of wanted to bash their heads in. Even though Past Me had probably chatted with my friends too during "Before He Cheats." Because it was a bar, and that was what you did. And you weren't drunk enough yet to loudly shout along with every dumb song every stranger chose to sing.

But Present Me had literally nothing else to do except stare and listen to every word of it. And fuck me, but it felt like Lily was singing directly to me. And it was magnificent. Every hair on my body stood on end.

Except. Maybe Lily *was* singing directly to me.

Because suddenly, that was what was happening.

My karaoke crush was staring back.

lily & sam

THEY WERE ALONE TONIGHT, which was odd.
Maybe that was what made my eyes snag onto theirs, the
surprise of their solitude, and their eyes so intent on mine. I
had felt their eyes on me before, of course—I was good at
this, and I'd always gotten the sense from the way they
watched, from the enthusiasm of their applause after I
finished a song, that they knew I was good at this, too.

And even if you knew you were good at something, it
felt fucking satisfying to have a stranger acknowledge it.

But why were they all by their lonesome at that little
table in the corner tonight? They—and I was pretty sure
they used they, because sometimes they wore a black jean
jacket with a *they/them* pin on it—often seemed to be the
first one here of their group, but eventually their friends
would join them. I liked their group; it felt like theirs and
ours had this unspoken Moonie's camaraderie. We cheered
and danced for each other's songs, respected each other's
favorite tables if one group got here first.

But I had always secretly found this stranger, the one
currently sitting alone in a corner, to be particularly

adorable. They seemed shy; never sang by themselves, always dragged up with one of their friends later in the night. And even then, they refused to look at the crowd, staring only at their friends as they shuffled awkwardly around the dance floor with one hand in their pocket, grinning. Having fun but embarrassed, face flushed bright red. I always wanted to run up to them afterward and squeeze their cheeks.

And then maybe squeeze their ass, if they let me, just to see how they'd react.

They also consistently knew the songs, which I respected. That was the thing about karaoke: everyone thought they were safe throwing any song up, since the words were right there on the screen in front of you. But if you didn't *really* know the lyrics, the beats to come in on, the rhythm of the lines—you were screwed.

Cutie in the Corner didn't have a great voice, and might have blushed and shuffled while they sang, but they always knew the words.

When I caught their eye tonight, though, their face wasn't red, and they weren't grinning. They were...looking at me like I was the only one in the room, eyes dark and serious.

And I was almost done with the song, so the claws of Carrie's confidence were firmly implanted now. I felt sexy and strong and *good*. And their eyes on me felt right. Like maybe everyone else in the room were the real idiots, for not looking at me like that. And so I kept staring back.

And, well, damn. Singing at Moonie's was always a bit of a rush, but maintaining eye contact with a stranger while I did it was...kind of hot. And really fucking intense.

I kept thinking they'd look away. Or that I would. But I found I couldn't. Or didn't want to. Or both.

The Power of Carrie must have been strong tonight. Because while they looked at me, and I sang about getting my revenge, it almost felt real. Like I could be a star. Like I had someone waiting for me in the crowd who thought I could be a star, too.

By the end of the song, my heart was fluttering around in my chest in this hectic pitter patter, and I felt hot all over.

When I handed Kiki back the mic, my hand was shaking.

Quickly, I wiped my palm on my dress. I took a deep breath.

And I turned around and walked right past my table— oh god, my friends were going to give me so much shit— and headed straight back there to that sad little corner, and the stranger who had just made me feel sexy as hell. Because it was Saturday night. And it was Moonie's. It didn't matter if I made a fool of myself. It was safe.

I watched their eyes grow wide as I plunked myself down in the seat across from them. They looked slightly petrified, which was real stinking cute. And helped me feel a little more normal. Because some of the heat that had flared in me while I was singing cooled when I realized I was back to wanting to pinch their cheeks. Which was probably good.

"Hey," I said. "Do you mind if I sit out that embarrassing post-singing high here with you for a second? You know, when you have to go back to your table after a song and suddenly don't want anyone to look at you ever again so you have to pretend to act chill even though you're not?"

Their mouth only gaped for a second. And then they blinked and appeared to get control of themself.

"Oh my god," they said. "You should never feel embarrassed. You are *amazing*."

I bit my lip to keep myself from smiling too hard. Why had I never talked to this person before? I should have them on speed dial for whenever I needed a boost, back in the non-Moonie's real world.

Because the truth of the matter was, I *wasn't* a star. Or *amazing*. At least not in that breathless way they had said it. I was as shy as Adorable Blusher here appeared, most of the time. Or maybe shy wasn't the right word. When I applied it to myself, *shy* made me feel like a little kid. I was introverted. Quiet. Which was fine; that was who I was and how I was comfortable.

It was only when a KJ handed me a mic, and all I felt was the warmth of the lights and the dark comfort of this bar, which only ever seemed to be full of queers and freaks —my people—that I got to be...something different.

"Thank you." I cleared my throat, wishing now that I had stopped at my table to get my drink. I always needed a few good, strong swigs after Carrie. "Where are your friends tonight?"

"All bailed," they said on a sigh, seeming to relax a little. "Which would have been nice to know *before* I left the house, but, oh well."

They shook a lock of hair off their forehead. It was dark, almost black, streaked through with grey and on the curly side, perpetually disheveled. They were wearing a plain black t-shirt tonight, with a turquoise pocket. It was a smart pop of color. It also highlighted their eyes, which were blue-ish-green and...rather spectacular. Which I had always suspected was the case. But it was pleasant, seeing the evidence up close as they glanced across the table at me. They looked a bit older, their skin a bit weathered, the stubble adorning their chin flecked with grey, just like their hair. But those eyes were pretty as sin. And made all the better, I thought, by the fact that either they wore mascara or had the prettiest eyelashes known to humanity. But I was pretty sure it was mascara. Because sometimes they sported eyeliner, too, some shadow on their lids. Tonight, though, it was all lashes.

It occurred to me that, once again, we had probably been staring at each other for too long.

"I'm Lily, by the way," my brain finally kicked into gear to say.

"Right! Sorry. I'm Sam." Apologizing for no reason. *Sam.* Adorbs.

"Do you want to sit with us?" I offered with a tilt of my head, back toward our table. "You don't have to. But you can if you want."

"I—" They opened their mouth. Closed it. And then, instead of answering my question, blurted: "I like your dress."

"Oh!" I looked down at myself, as if I had forgotten what I was wearing. "Thank you. It's one of my more recent favorites. I was pretty happy with how it turned out."

Understatement. I was thrilled with how it had turned out. Like after years of working at it, I was finally starting to understand draping. And how to actually shape fabric to my hips properly.

"Wait." Sam's eyebrows furrowed. "You made that?"

"I did. Making clothes is…" I waved a hand around. *My dream.* "Kind of a hobby. It's surprisingly satisfying, making your own clothes. Especially when you're fat, and shopping for store bought stuff is such a nightmare."

"So you make most of your clothes?" Sam asked, brows still in a cute bunch, and I appreciated it, that they didn't react to the f-word, that they didn't try to tell me I was wrong.

I nodded, and they leaned back in their chair, shaking their head.

"That's...incredible. Your clothes are always so great. That's not a hobby; that's like...a fucking *skill*."

Your clothes are always so great. Like they had noticed them before.

"God," I couldn't help but laugh. "Can I just carry you around in my pocket all the time so you can keep showering me with compliments whenever I need them?"

"Yes," Sam said immediately.

And then blushed.

I was fucking glad I had come to this table.

"Uh," they said, looking away and scratching at the back of their neck. "Can I, um. Get you a drink?"

"Sure." I had a barely-drunk drink back at our table, but I was not going to object to a person who thought I was awesome getting me another one. "Gin and tonic?"

"Cool." And then they were gone, *wooshing* over to the bar Wile E. Coyote style.

I sprinted back to our table to down my already-purchased G&T in one gulp.

"*Lily!*" Preeti hissed, eyes wide, leaning over the table. "Tell me everything."

"Yeah, what the hell?" Jonny smacked my arm. "You walked right on past us like you didn't even know us. And the way you two were eye-fucking when you were up there! I didn't even know you knew that dude!"

"I love this." Bri pointed her beer bottle at me. "Y'all know Lily being bold at karaoke is literally my favorite thing in the world. I have a good feeling about this. It's gonna be a good night."

Like that, the ridiculously large gulp of alcohol I'd swallowed down sloshed uneasily around my insides.

The Power of Carrie *had* been too strong. I had overestimated. Because the *amazing* person Sam thought I was—who plopped themselves at a table, uninvited, to talk to a stranger—wasn't actually me. *Lily being bold at karaoke.* Sam had been flirting with an illusion.

And now...the idea of keeping up that illusion with Sam for only a few hours, knowing it would have to end at last call, only seemed depressing.

I didn't know what I had been thinking. I *hadn't* been thinking, was the issue. Blasted karaoke adrenaline.

"I *don't* know them," I finally said, when I realized all my friends were staring expectantly at me. "And don't call them dude. At least, I don't think." I glanced over at the bar, where the bartender was sliding two G&Ts into Sam's hands. I took another deep breath, trying to shake off the icky feeling creeping into my brain, threatening to send the Power of Carrie toppling.

This was fine. We hadn't *eye fucked*. They just didn't deserve to sit by themself all night. This was good. A totally normal thing. There was nothing wrong with keeping up the illusion of Karaoke Lily for a few hours of letting loose and getting to know another Moonie's regular a little better. I was being dramatic.

"I'm pretty sure they use they/them, and their name is Sam, and their friends all bailed at the last minute, and they like my dress—" *okay*, I didn't have to mention that part, but they had been so nice about the dress— "and I invited them to sit with us, so just be fucking cool or I'll kill you in your sleep. Hey!"

I smiled brightly up at Sam, who was standing uncertainly at the end of the table. I patted the empty chair to my right. Friendly. Bold. Moonie's normal. "Sam, meet everyone. Everyone, meet Sam."

* * *

Oh god. I had been mildly okay with Lily coming over to talk to me—HAHA JOKES, it had been fucking wild, but once the actual talking started it had also been kind of fun. I think.

But being thrown straight into meeting a whole new group of people—even if, sure, they were all people I'd seen do karaoke a bunch of times before, which was such a ridiculous, vulnerable act that we probably rated as acquaintances, at least, maybe—was upping the ante. It was hard not to feel pathetic for real, like the only reason they were inviting me into their club was because my friends had abandoned me. Because...that was the only reason they were inviting me into their club.

I sat, sliding Lily her gin and tonic. I hoped she didn't like fancy gin. Butch Bartender had raised her eyebrows at me, being that I'd never ordered a gin and tonic before, and asked "Well liquor okay?" And I had no idea what even constituted good gin so I'd just nodded. Although, wait, the pretty blue bottle I often stared at while waiting for Butch Bartender to take pity on me was gin, I was pretty sure. Dammit. I should have gotten Lily the pretty blue gin.

"Happy to have you, Sam! I'm Bri." A Black woman with a wide smile reached her hand out to me across the table. "Sorry to hear about your friends. I always love watching that short one do Bel Biv Devoe."

"Nate," I smiled. "That's his sole go-to, yeah. He's out of town. My friend Steve might show up later," I checked my phone in my pocket, to make sure I hadn't missed any more texts. "...but probably not."

"What do you do, Sam?" A guy on Lily's other side leaned forward. "Jonny, by the way."

"Hey, Jonny." I gave a dorky little wave across the table, until I realized the extent of its dorkiness and quickly aborted it. "I teach at the university downtown."

Lily turned to me, eyes bright. How did sitting next to someone seem so much more intimate than sitting across from them? It should have been the opposite. But our shoulders were almost brushing now. I could *smell* her here, some kind of citrusy perfume, and I wanted to bathe in it. So much potential for knees knocking into each other. Thighs pressing together, possibly, if I played my cards right.

Which I definitely wouldn't, because my romantic prowess was level negative three.

"You're a professor?"

I took a sip of the G&T, which wasn't half bad.

"It's not that impressive, I swear. It's more like...a job for people who didn't want to leave college and didn't know what else to do."

"I doubt that's true," Lily said. "Or else colleges would be full of a lot of shitty professors."

"Yeah, well." I shrugged. Case in point.

"What do you teach?" Jonny asked.

"History."

"Oh my god, history was my favorite subject in school!" another woman at the table shouted. "Do you have, like, a specialty? Professors always study real specific shit."

I shifted in my chair, realizing how long it had been since I'd met anyone new. I wasn't used to talking this much about myself.

"Well, I teach pretty much whatever they tell me to teach, but...my research focuses mainly on early 20th century America. Immigration in early 20th century America, specifically."

"Oh yeah." The woman who loved history nodded her head approvingly. "That's sexy shit."

"Is it?" I laughed. "I find it rather upsetting and discriminatory, actually."

"No, Preeti means the fact that you study it," Lily filled in. "You do *research*. That—" She lifted her glass, "—is sexy."

I was pretty sure Preeti and Lily were fucking with me. There was nothing remotely sexy about me, including my research. From my already-meticulously-studied chosen field to my physique, which could best be described as *chunky*, everything about me screamed *mediocre white person*. I had been told I had nice eyes, a point which I could concede, but I failed at pretty much everything else: hair product, originality, fashion choices. God, I *wished* I could make clothes that actually made sense for my body, like Lily. Or even understood how to shop for them.

I lived alone in a small apartment with two cats and more maps than any single person would ever have a tangible use for. I lacked interesting hobbies.

The only vaguely interesting thing about me was a late in life acceptance of Feeling Real Weird About Gender. And even then, *interesting* wasn't exactly the right word. I had no idea what the right word was, and had been searching for the last few years to find it. I'd take an even remotely accurate string of words at this point. But when I did find them, I'd buy a new sparkly journal in celebration.

And maybe after writing those close-enough-to-accurate words down in fancy pen on every single page, my brain would finally be able to shut up about it.

Or maybe the journal wouldn't be sparkly. Maybe it'd be a nice matte gray.

It would depend on the day, really.

"It's...no," I managed to get out, unsure about whether I should explain that half of my life was trying to get under-grads to think past the beliefs their parents had taught them and utterly failing. And grading the same papers over and over. And feeling like a tool whenever I had to meet with like, actual smart people.

Or maybe I should've just gone with the whole Lily-thinking-I'm-sexy point of view.

"What do your students call you?" she asked. "Professor...?"

"Bell," I said. "But I usually ask that they just call me Sam, because Professor Bell feels weird. Even though when-ever I ask them to call me Sam, there's normally at least a quarter of the class that look at me like they *know* I am wasting their too-expensive tuition, and they...are not wrong, probably. Anyway!" Wow, apparently my brain really couldn't go with the *pretend you're sexy* plan there. Probably for the best. "What do you all do? You know," I cast a glance at Lily, "when you're not singing and designing your own clothes, and stuff."

"We all work together, actually," Lily said, gesturing toward the rest of the table. But she totally smiled at me first, quick and small, like it was a secret. "At a veterinary clinic. Bri's one of our vets, and Jonny and Preeti are vet techs. I'm a lowly receptionist."

"Excuse me," Preeti butted in. "I think you mean to say customer care specialist."

Lily rolled her eyes. "Sure."

"Seriously, though." Bri took a swig of her beer. "Lily's job is harder than mine."

"Bri," Lily deadpanned. "You literally took out a dog's eyeball today."

"Yeah, and then I got to kill some old lady's cat and she

cried for an hour. It's a job that keeps on giving, veterinary medicine. But *you* had to deal with that asshole who made that other client cry in the lobby. And who then tried to refuse to pay for bloodwork. Even though he definitely fucking okayed the bloodwork. Anyway, you're a goddamn angel."

"One hundred percent," Jonny said.

I agreed that Lily was probably an angel. But I hated that she had to deal with assholes, instead of...being surrounded by pretty fabric all day, or whatever she actually wanted to do with her life. I had to fight a completely inappropriate urge to rub my hand over her back.

"*Anyway*," Lily said pointedly, "Some other people will likely show up in a bit. We do have some friends outside of work."

"Debatable. But yeah, my roommate Alexis will probably show up at some point," Preeti said. "And Jonny's new boyfriend that he won't tell us anything about."

"I don't even know if he's coming, and if you call him my boyfriend, I will punch you in the face."

"Wow, y'all are *feisty* tonight." Bri raised her eyebrows.

"And up next at the mic, we have Preeti and Bri!"

Preeti squealed and raised her hands in the air.

"Dammit, Preeti, what did you put my name on?" Bri slammed down the last of her beer as she stood. "I am not nearly drunk enough for this shit yet."

"You'll like it. Come on." Preeti dragged her by the arm over to Kiki.

I was close enough—Lily and her friends' table was the one closest to the dance floor—to hear Bri mutter "motherfucker" when the song came up on the screen. But she lifted the mic to her mouth to say, "You better fucking let me do the Monica part."

Preeti only had time to roll her eyes, as if this was clearly already established, and then they were launching into "The Boy is Mine."

Lily was leaning forward to support her friends, elbows on the table, but her shoulders immediately began to bounce to the beat. Her hair, dyed platinum blonde, was up in two tight knots on either side of her head. Up close, I could see how neat the part was, her dark roots exposed at the perfectly symmetrical line. I pictured her getting ready for tonight in whatever her apartment—house?—looked like, sitting in front of a mirror, running a comb expertly down her scalp. It made a shiver run all the way down to my toes.

I took another sip of gin and tonic.

And even though the night still felt early, apparently two Rainiers and a G&T were enough to loosen me up. Because when Lily looked over her shoulder at me, her chair dancing having grown even more pronounced as the song progressed, I somehow found it in me to lip sync at her, with a bit of flair, *I know it's killing you inside*, and she smiled.

Not a secret smile like before. A thrilled, mouth cracked wide open, *I approve* smile.

Against all odds, it was possible this night out at Moonie's wasn't going to be a total failure after all.

lily & sam

SHORTLY AFTER BRI and Preeti sat back down, and Jonny's new boyfriend showed up—his name was Pablo and he *kissed Jonny on the cheek* when he walked in—I spotted that the table next to us finally seemed to have abandoned The Binder. And before they could protest, I darted over and grabbed it.

Moonie's' karaoke system had nearly every song you could think of, but even though we'd been doing this for years, I still liked a good perusal through The Binder for inspiration. They also had a database of songs you could search through on this ancient laptop in the corner, but it was like, *dude you got a Dell* old. The Binder was the best.

"Here's what I'm thinking," I said to Sam, plopping it down on the table between us. "We should do something totally cheesy and classic, because we don't know each other's tastes well enough yet to choose something else."

Their eyes widened comically, as they had when they saw me approach their table. I loved it just as much this time.

"Oh," they said, sitting up. "You mean, like, singing together?"

"Obviously," I said. "Obviously we are singing together."

Their mouth formed a little O.

"You..." They scratched their forehead. "Maybe you don't remember my singing abilities, from previous karaoke nights?"

"Oh, I do," I smiled. "I know you can't sing. But I also know this is Moonie's, and it doesn't matter. And you only sing when someone else makes you, so this is me, making you."

They grimaced.

"So...something totally cheesy and classic?"

"Yes!" I beamed. "Except not like, horrifying cheesy and classic. No 'I Will Survive' or 'Pour Some Sugar On Me' or whatever."

"Oh god," Sam said. "That guy who always does 'Pour Some Sugar On Me.'"

"I know; he's the worst. But maybe like...Aretha? Or Celine. Oh, or Stevie?"

Sam shrugged.

"I've done Stevie before. Are we talking 'Superstition' or like, 'Sir Duke' territory?"

"Wait." I stopped on a page, stuck my finger on the sticky lamination. "We can do Stevie later, maybe, but *obviously*, we should start with this."

Sam leaned closer—some hair fell over their forehead— and then they started to laugh. I was obsessed with their laugh. I remembered hearing it vibrating across the room from their table in the past—my second favorite thing about them, behind their karaoke shuffle dance—but having it rumble right in my ear filled my veins with pleasure. It was a laugh that was half hiccup, half snort. It was deeply unattractive and strangely made me want to kiss them.

"Lily. That is probably the most cliché karaoke song of all time."

"But for good reason!" I protested. "It's still enjoyable, every single time! And it's so fun to sing." I poked them in the leg. "Come on."

They were still shaking their head, arms crossed over their chest. "Fine," they said, but their eyes were laughing. "Whatever."

I practically ran the slip of paper to Kiki.

Lily was only back in her seat for thirty seconds before Kiki called her name again. For a panicked second, I thought she was sending us up right away for the song Lily had just given her, the song request slip that, improbably, had my name next to hers. But it wasn't; it was another request Lily had put in earlier. It was "Today" by the Smashing Pumpkins.

And it was...damn. I liked hearing Lily sing "Before He Cheats" for the pure fun, turn-me-on factor, but this was different. Lily's voice, like Billy Corgan's, somehow went from light and sweet to dark and gritty in the matter of a breath. This song was all fuzzy guitar and irrepressible energy, optimistic and bittersweet all at once, and halfway through I was already half-hard, just sitting there and watching her. My chest felt weirdly full of...happiness, maybe.

But I completely forgot that toward the end of the song, Billy sings *I want to turn you on* over and over. And this time, when the words came out of Lily's mouth, a delicious growl, she didn't lock eyes with me like before. She merely glanced at me once and away. But that glance was enough to make my throat dry.

That glance was enough to make me wonder what the hell I was doing.

Was this simply all in my head? Were her insides also churning when she sang *I want to turn you on* and looked at me? Because it was suddenly clear I was out of my depth here. Sitting at this table was the most impulsive thing I had done in...my life?

She was the one who came to me. So maybe impulsive wasn't the right word, since I was pretty much dragged into this situation, albeit willingly. Maybe this was normal for her, or her friends? Maybe they dragged strangers into their lives all the time?

But it struck me very deeply at that moment, surrounded by that table of almost-acquaintances, watching Lily on the dance floor—a Lily who knew my name, who looked at me when she sang tonight, and not just on accident—that it wasn't normal for me.

What was the endgame here? Were we just going to sing together, and drink together, and say goodbye? And then the next time we were both at Moonie's again we could laugh and hug and say, 'Hey! How've you been?' That sounded nice. Normal-ish, maybe, for people who were better at socializing than me, who didn't hang out with the same core group of people they'd known since college and no one else.

Or were Lily and I going to end the night with one of us straddling the other's lap, our tongues in each other's mouths? That seemed like a very un-me, not-normal possibility—my tongue hadn't been in anyone's mouth since

Dan, and after Dan, I seriously contemplated whether the muscle should remain safe and sound inside my own body for the rest of my life, and had landed pretty firmly on *yes*.

But yet, it was becoming increasingly difficult to *not* picture that happening with Lily and me. Which was...exciting, obviously. And terrifying.

I knew I was veering into serious overthinking territory here. But the thing was, it wasn't just romantic prowess I lacked. Dan had highlighted in a particularly painful way how bad I was at relationships, but he came at the tail end of several decades' worth of failed relationships. I either wanted the wrong things, or wanted too much.

And so over the last year, I had decided to turn *wanting* into a game. Because I was tired. I felt committed now to wanting in a way that was safe: silently watching Lily at Moonie's all those previous nights of the last few years. Finding quiet, luxurious joy in the mornings when my favorite barista was on shift, pulling my espresso shots with those perfectly toned, artistically tattooed forearms. Understanding that my station in life wasn't likely to change at this point in the game, that I would keep teaching undergrads who seemed increasingly far away from my own life experiences with each passing year, until I could one day retire and wile away my time watching travel documentaries about places I would never be able to go.

But it didn't feel sad, necessarily. Sometimes the wanting felt like enough. Wanting gave you things to look forward to. I looked forward to Pretty Barista's forearms, to the lightning flashes of possibility at Moonie's. Thirst was a perfectly good reason to wake up every day, in my estimation. It was when you thought you actually had the things you wanted that the future loomed with inevitable disappointment and devastation. I was too old for all of that now.

But somehow, by accident, I was here. Sharing glances with a woman who made wanting—*real* wanting, a visceral escalation of quiet, secret wanting—feel easy. Justified. Comfortable and safe, somehow.

Even though the tiny voice of reason that existed somewhere in the recesses of my brain was shouting at me that none of this was safe at all. That I was doing it again. Pretending something was bigger than it was.

By the time Lily flounced back into her seat next to me, I was taking slow, steady breaths through my nose to get myself together. Trying to picture giving her a simple hug goodnight. A friendly greeting the next time we met at Moonie's.

And then she looked at me, and her brown eyes were so bright and alive that my mind went kind of melty and soft. The tiny voice of reason in the soft tissue of my brain was all but extinguished. And without thinking about it, I reached out and ran a finger over her knuckles, resting in her lap.

"Need that minute to get chill again?" I asked. "I can pretend to not want to stare at you, if it helps."

But she shook her head and smiled. "Nah," she said. "I'm good this time."

I should have left then, probably. If I didn't want the lap straddling, tongue stuff to happen. But I didn't. Instead, I stayed long enough until time slid into the blurry karaoke alternate universe. Where all that mattered was each song, singing along and laughing and forgetting that anything other than this—pop songs and nostalgia and queer people —existed.

The first song I somehow allowed myself to be pulled

onto the dance floor for was Flo Rida's "Low," which was, both the song itself and the dancing that was happening to it, absolutely ridiculous. There was no real stage at Moonie's, just the open dance floor at the front of the room, so whenever the night hit that spot, that point where all self-consciousness fled and someone chose a song that really popped, half of the room congregated up there, swarming around the singer, one silly, uncoordinated mass that tore down all borders. Including the border that should have prevented Sam Bell from ever, ever dancing to Flo Rida's "Low."

But Lily, of course, *could* get low, like really fucking impressively so, and I just sort of bounced around haphazardly and tried not to get too hard while she worked her hips and her breasts and her shoulders in an exceedingly distracting way. The only thing that saved me from combusting was the fact that there were twenty other assholes around us doing the same exact thing.

Five seconds after "Low," as we were making our way, sweaty and breathing too hard, back to the table, the next singer busted out a Lady Gaga banger that I had definitely not even thought about in at least ten years. Which meant we immediately changed course and charged back to the dance floor.

And then—shockingly, because I had almost forgotten—Kiki called our names. *Lily and Sam.*

And next thing I knew, I had a microphone in my hand, and Lily was beaming at me. And I told myself that this would be the easiest thing I'd ever done because I could let Lily carry us the entire way. But my face flushed red anyway as the words flashed on the screen attached to the ceiling above us: "Total Eclipse of the Heart."

And then the words popped up, and Lily elbowed me in

the side and said, "You're Voice 1," and fuck, I *couldn't* just let Lily carry us because this was a duet. Which I would have fully realized when Lily put it down on that slip of paper if I hadn't been so distracted by her face, and the dimples in her round cheeks when she smiled.

I had to sing the dumb "turn around" parts, and my voice cracked on the third or tenth one in—the first one that was followed by "bright eyes," because who can actually hit that pitch? No one, that's who. And Lily—put together, karaoke goddess Lily—actually *giggled* into the mic at me as she tried to get through the first "every now and then I fall apart," and it was so cute that I discovered I wasn't even embarrassed. Or maybe I was just drunk. Either way, it all felt worth it, the very probable humiliation, to be right next to Lily on that dance floor as she sang about powder kegs giving up sparks and really needing me tonight. Or, no, not *me*, per se. Forever was gonna start tonight for *someone*. But I had given myself over to this thing now, and would volunteer as tribute if she asked.

And the thing about duets was that sometimes only singing your lines alone was actually...kind of boring, but you didn't know if it was a faux pas or not to join in on the other person's lines. But toward the end of the song Lily was waving her arms at me in a 'come on' kind of gesture, so that we were both screaming all of those completely over-the-top lyrics together. And it was funny because I'd only ever been up here with a microphone in my hand next to my friends who had known me for decades; had always thought I would only be comfortable doing such a ridiculous thing with them at my side. But I had known Lily for all of a few hours, and somehow it felt the same.

When it was done, the tinkle of the piano accompanying the last "turn around, bright eyes" fading away into the night, that Embarrassing Post-Singing High Lily had mentioned earlier hit me full force. I still wasn't embarrassed, exactly, but I didn't want to break the spell. Didn't want to go back to Lily's table right now and have all of her friends smirk at us.

I put a hand on her elbow as we handed back our mics. "Drink?" I motioned with my head toward the bar. She nodded.

The actual number of gin and tonics both Lily and I had consumed had grown muddled. I only knew there kept being clear, refreshing drinks on the table garnished with likely completely unsanitary limes, and we kept drinking them. I could also tell, from the woozy way my head felt, especially after singing Bonnie Tyler, and from the way that literally every single thing that was happening seemed perfect and beautiful, that I was approaching my limit.

But I stood at the edge of the bar, elbow brushing Lily's elbow, and ordered one more from Scary Bartender anyway. She raised an eyebrow at me as she handed them over, like she had no idea what Lily was doing with me, and I shrugged. Her guess was as good as mine.

"Tell me more about your clothes," I said before bringing the tiny plastic straw to my mouth and turning my body toward Lily. It was quieter here at the bar, away from the dance floor, and I wanted a chance to breathe, to talk to her more. It was better lit here too, and I could see how her pale skin was flushed with patches of pink, either from the singing or the dancing, down her neck, toward the tops of those lovely breasts. Her hair knots were still firmly in place, but the heat of the now-crowded room had made a few tendrils near her forehead spring loose: small, sweat-soaked curls. And for a second, the wanting became acute: a flash in my veins of wishing she was truly mine.

"You really want to know?" She faced me, an eyebrow raised. "Because once I get going on this topic, I can get kind of...verbose. Or maybe obnoxious is the better word."

"I promise," I smiled. "I am here for your verbosity."

She leaned her back against the bar, elbows propped on the counter.

"Well." She cleared her throat. "It's a well-established truth that shopping as a 'plus size'—" air quotes, eye roll, "—person is a pain in the ass."

I nodded.

"Most bigger chain stores these days, like Old Navy or whatever, do have plus size options, but they only go up to 3 or 4x, if you're lucky. And even those plus size options aren't available *in store*, only online—as if our existence is too shameful to exist in public, or something—so you can't try them on. So you waste a ton of time and money and guesswork on clothes that might not even fit you well anyway."

She took a sip of her drink, shaking her head.

"Even if you find stores with bigger sizes, it's tough. Because fat people's bodies are so different, you know? Some of us have big bellies and skinny legs. Some have big hips but are skinnier up top. Some of us are short and some of us are tall. And for people with breasts, sometimes nothing seems right. I can't tell you how many dresses I've bought that made my ass look fantastic but were weird flappy bags from my shoulders to my stomach. And like, I have great breasts!" She motioned to her chest. "Work with my breasts, people!"

"Um." I realized too late that these were statements I did not need to respond to. Because Lily looked at me, eyes twinkling with what I hoped was laughter. "Uh. Yes. I agree."

Her mouth curved into a grin. She looked like she was going to say something, but then she schooled her features a bit and faced away from the bar again.

"Anyway. Eventually I was like, my kingdom for an outfit that actually fits my shoulders, my boobs, my stomach, and my hips. So I started messing around on my own. I saved up for my own sewing machine. And...it was hard, and frustrating, when I wasn't an expert designer right from the get-go. But it was also fun. Now that I'm better at it, it's really fun." She paused. "I love wearing this dress. That I made myself, that I feel 100% comfortable in, that makes me feel sexy. But most fat people don't have that, which is so frustrating to me. Society already does enough on its own to make us feel like shit. Having to suffer a lifetime of ill-fitting clothes feels like kicking us when we're already down. I wonder if most people even know what it feels like, to wear something that actually fits them, how it can be...completely transforming. For people who have never had that feeling, clothes feel like this extra burden instead of something that can make them feel amazing."

I was contemplating whether I had ever felt 100% comfortable in an outfit, and coming up with a resounding *nope*, when Lily kept going. But her voice had turned softer, less righteous, and I had to lean in closer to hear.

"Anyway, I think maybe I would have turned to making my clothes anyway, even if I wasn't fat as fuck. My grandma made clothes, too. She was the one who taught me how to sew when I was a kid, even though I was always terrified that her ancient Singer was going to cut off all my fingers."

She smiled, and I felt something in my chest open up, grateful and eager to absorb this precious Lily memory. Like suddenly I was tumbling head over heels into her life in a real way. Like with each second, she was further and further from being a mere karaoke crush.

"Going to the fabric store with her when I was a kid was one of my favorite things, this routine that was just ours. I could have spent hours running my hands over all the different fabrics—silk, all the different kinds of cotton, fleece, denim. Knowing that my grandma could take all of that and make it into something useful. And the button aisle!" Lily turned toward me again, moving a fraction closer, as if she needed to be as close as possible to fully exude the magic of the button aisle. "So many shapes and colors. The fucking best."

She turned away again, taking a sip of her drink, and I felt the loss of her heat.

"When I started thinking about messing around with clothes, when I finally got my own machine, it felt like coming home in a way, you know? It breaks my heart that I started doing it after my grandma died. She didn't like my body." I was watching Lily like a hawk by this point, so I saw the way she swallowed here, thick and slow. "But I think she would have at least respected my clothes."

A silence stretched then. I didn't know what to say. Although my brain had plenty it *wanted* to say to her grandma. If, you know, she wasn't dead.

Eventually, I brushed my fingers over her arm. It seemed to shake her awake, at least a little bit.

"I think...sometimes there are things we love as kids, and then we forget about them as we grow up, either by accident or because we think we should. And then one day we remember them, and it's like, why did I think I had to give this up? And that's how I feel whenever I go to the fabric store by myself now. I love all of the variation of fabric, patterns, designs; all of it is so...pretty and soothing.

There are even *sounds* of the fabric store that are comforting to me, like when the workers roll out a bolt of fabric onto the table when they're getting ready to cut it for you? And it's like, *thump, thump, thump*." She smiled, looking straight at me. "And the scissors when they cut it, they have this very specific snip, you know?"

I did not know. I had no fucking idea what she was talking about. But I was pretty much out of my mind with wanting to kiss her.

But...I didn't.

Because...romantic prowess. Negative three.

And because at that exact moment, a new song started across the room. A song whose opening chords I knew by heart. A song that made me want to twirl Lily back onto the dance floor, hold her close, let her see all of me. But that would have been different from Bonnie Tyler, from Gaga. Even hearing it at all right now felt like a little too much. The stranger who was singing it was killing it. Killing me.

"Are you okay?"

I looked down, and only then realized I must have been spacing out. Lily was biting her lip.

"Sorry," she said. "I'm kind of drunk and didn't mean to...ramble about the fabric store for an hour? Oh my god."

Those splashes of pink returned to her skin and I almost spilled my gin and tonic all over her in my flailing.

"No! No. I could listen to you talk about clothes and the fabric store and your grandma for hours more. Seriously. I just...this song."

Lily tilted her head, listening. "I think I recognize it?"

"It's 'This Charming Man.' By The Smiths."

"Oh." She smiled, just a little, cheeks still pink, almost looking embarrassed. Which...Lily was a rockstar who shouldn't be embarrassed about anything. I had a horrible, sinking feeling that I was fucking this night all up. "The Smiths are definitely too cool for me."

I shook my head vehemently. "No, they're really not. Or at least, this song isn't; it's only a pop song, but..." A harsh breath escaped my lips. I suddenly wished I had consumed even a tiny bit less gin.

She had shared her grandma and the fabric store with me. I could share this song with her.

"When I was a teenager, I used to lie on my bed and listen to this song for hours, literally, and feel..."

I trailed off, flailing mentally now. But Lily only looked at me. Eyes patient. Everything about her so fucking soft and strong.

"I don't know. I don't even know what Morrissey was actually singing about in this song, and everything I've learned since then confirms that Morrissey is pretty much an asshole, but when I was a kid and felt...I don't know. Like I was lonely and weird and maybe really fucking gay but maybe not? It was like his voice on this song was the only person who understood. And I really thought that maybe *all* boys sat in their rooms and listened to this song and secretly felt all these things, but it turned out I was...wrong."

I was resting an elbow on the bar now, restlessly drumming fingers against the cold, smudgy counter, unable to meet Lily's eyes and pretty much wanting to die. Lily being excited about the button aisle with her grandma had been a cute anecdote. Me trying to explain "This Charming Man" felt like the equivalent of reaching into my chest and pulling out an album of embarrassing childhood photos that you only engaged when you were really in love with someone and wanted them to see all of your most cringey parts.

But then Lily lifted a hand and trailed her fingers on my wrist, feather light and kind. My fingers stopped drumming.

"It's a beautiful song," she said eventually, her voice almost a whisper.

We were quiet as the performer wrapped up, Lily's fingers still at my wrist, my heart pounding in my ears.

"I don't know if I've ever felt transformed by clothes, like you were talking about," I said eventually, as soon as the song was over. I stared down at the bar, feeling a little shaky, but determined to get the conversation back on track. "It sounds nice. I wish sometimes that I had…" I waved a hand. "More of a fashion sense. If I could express myself better that way. But—" I shrugged and looked down at myself, at my black t-shirt and black jeans. "I pretty much only wear this."

She took her hand off mine then. She put her glass, which she had been holding with her other hand, down on the bar. And when I finally looked at her again, her eyes had changed, gone from soft and sympathetic to all sharp and assessing. I quaked a little, in anticipation or self-consciousness or both.

"I think you *do* have a fashion sense, in a way." She smoothed both of her palms over my shoulders, down the sleeves of my shirt. "I love this pocket, first of all. And I associate you with dark colors like these, with that black jean jacket you normally wear. And the fact that I can make any association in my head, of you with clothes, means you *do* have a look. Fashion doesn't have to be fancy."

Her hands traveled down my sides, toward the hem of my shirt, the waistband of my jeans. It was possible I stopped breathing.

She knew my black jean jacket.

She remembered details about me. Like she had noticed me before tonight.

One small thing clicked into place.

"Your jeans could be better, yes," she said, cocking her head, "But honestly, jeans—pants in general—are hard for a lot of bodies, for a lot of reasons, even though we're all conditioned to wear them."

I let out another rough sigh, partly because of the truth of that, partly because her hands were still resting on my sides.

"I have a hard time figuring out what to wear for work, most of the time," I admitted. "I know I should look like a semi-put together adult, and I don't...know how to do that. Khakis and dress shirts are kind of a nightmare, and I...don't know what else to do."

"So what *do* you wear to work?"

I looked back down at myself and winced. "Um. A nicer shirt, but pretty much...this?"

"Hmm. Well, first of all, you don't have to wear khakis, Sam. *No one* should have to wear khakis. You simply need to find the *right* pants and shirts, if that's what you want to wear."

She opened her mouth and then snapped it shut.

She picked up her gin and tonic again, chomping rather aggressively on the tiny straw, and stared back toward the dance floor.

I had a feeling she wanted to say something else. And that I knew exactly what it was.

And I didn't feel offended. I felt...suddenly, strangely excited.

"None of your friends have misgendered me all night," I said slowly, trying to figure out how to approach this. It all made sense now. That Lily must have seen my pin. And remembered. Which wasn't actually a small thing at all. "It's been really nice."

"Oh," she said, shrugging. "Of course."

"I've thought about wearing...other things," I said after a beat. "Just to try something different. But I don't know...how to make it not look ridiculous?"

She turned toward me again, one corner of her mouth curved upward.

"What do you mean, ridiculous?"

"I mean," I motioned toward my body. "This is never going to be a Harry Styles situation. I am never going to make that—" I pointed to her dress, "—look good. And I don't even know if I *want* that. Even though it's beautiful. I..." I frowned. Well, damn. Apparently the magic of Moonie's, and Lily, and too much gin wasn't going to make this any easier. I had been feeling hopeful there for a second.

I leaned back against the bar and let out a breath.

"I only started wearing that they/them pin a year ago," I said, deciding to go all in. I'd already almost cried over Morrissey in front of her, so why the fuck not. "The school's QSA was giving them out. I don't know if I ever would have even contemplated thinking about myself as non-binary, or genderqueer, or whatever I am, if there weren't a ton of my students who identify that way now, and other faculty, too. I thought I would...try it." I scratched at the back of my head. "Fuck, that sounds so dumb. But as soon as I started using they/them, it felt right. Like...I don't know, like what you were talking about when you wear an outfit that actually fits you for the first time?"

Lily smiled. "Yeah."

"I imagine it felt kind of like that. There was just this...*relief* at not having to be a *he*."

She nodded, eyes serious.

"When something really fits," she said carefully, "You suddenly realize how much energy you've been unconsciously devoting to not fitting."

"Yes." I breathed out. "Yes. But...some of my enby students are these like, androgynous supermodels." I kicked at the floor with the toe of my sneaker. "Which, you know, is fine. But even when they're not, they're so fucking confident in who they are. And I feel sometimes like I'm just this imposter, still trying on different outfits to see what works. And maybe, *maybe* this was all part of what I was feeling when I was a kid lying on my bed listening to 'This Charming Man.' And there are just better words for it now. But sometimes I..." I faltered. "I wonder if it would be easier to just take that pin off my jacket. I'm still not good at correcting people who use he/him, because...like, I get it. I'll probably always look like a boring old dude."

Lily shook her head. "Not boring. And not old."

I snorted.

"Lily, I'm in my forties, and all I know is that when I was a kid, it felt like my parents were perpetually in their forties, and that means I'm old. How old are you?"

"Thirty-two."

I gave a dreamy sigh. "Ah. Sweet youth."

She rolled her eyes.

"Anyway. I..." I frowned again. I'd joked, but I actually was a little caught off guard by Lily being over a decade younger than me. Even though I should have guessed this to be true. "I have no idea where I was going with this. I am...drunk."

"You were being honest," she said steadily. "Which I feel honored you trusted me enough with. *And* you were talking about the clothes you wear to work, how they don't feel good. And how you'd look ridiculous if you tried to wear something different. Which is—" She huffed, crossing her arms. "Patently untrue. Obviously."

I raised my eyebrows.

"Obviously," I repeated.

"Yes." She squared her shoulders, taking a small step closer to me, as if in challenge. "That's the thing about clothes. It's like...like picking a song to sing at karaoke. You can choose *whatever you want*. And all that matters is that you feel happy when you're singing it. It's nice when the audience sings along with you, but they really don't have to for it to still be powerful, as long as *you* feel it. You know?"

"Okay," I countered. This was what I wanted, working through this with her, but now I was feeling weirdly defensive. I should have expected it. This was how it went when I had asked Claire to help me with makeup, too, a year ago. This sense of possibility, followed by this frustration that I didn't automatically know what to do. That it didn't immediately click. Because when it came to my body, nothing had ever seemed to click. "So what am I going to wear instead? A nice blouse and a pencil skirt?"

Her eyes flared.

"Yes," she said. "If you wanted to."

I guffawed.

"You think I can pull off a *pencil skirt*?"

"Yes," she repeated, again, with feeling.

"Fine," I said, my voice a little too loud. "Tell me what would look good on me, Lily."

Her chest rose and fell. Pink splotches all down her neck.

She took another step closer.

"I think you can wear whatever the hell you want to, Sam Bell," she said, a hand reaching for my hip. "Including this shirt and these jeans for the rest of your life, if they make you happy. But I think a pencil skirt would look nice on you. And...a good V-neck, maybe."

Her hands traveled up to my chest, back to my shoulders. All the air wooshed out of me, the world going topsy turvy, any frustration about dumb gender and my dumb body melting away as the air around us changed. All that mattered were her hands on me, the closeness once again of her body heat, the power of her. All of which made my body feel the opposite of dumb. Like I could absorb some of her Lily-ness through mere proximity. Like the fact that she wanted to touch me at all meant something.

It was the most physical intimacy I'd had in a year. I hoped Scary Bartender was proud of me. I was a little proud of me.

"I would love to see you in a skirt with a snug V-neck sweater. Yeah." Lily nodded, almost as if she were talking to herself. "That would be really fucking hot. There's lots you could do, Sam. I could—"

She stopped suddenly, blanching, and took a step away.

"Sorry. If that was out of line. You can dress however you want, obviously. Sorry."

I opened my mouth to say something. To ask her to go back to that part where I could be *really fucking hot.*

"You don't have to be sorry. I asked."

"I know," she said, face pink again, "but I hate when people give me advice about *my* body, like I haven't already thought about every possible option myself, so. Sorry."

I wanted her fingers on my wrist again. Her palms on my shoulders. Instead, I shoved my hands in my pockets. Considered what to say.

"I don't know if I've thought about every possible option for my body, honestly," I said quietly. And then, "I just still can't believe you think I could fit into a pencil skirt." Like, she had seen my stomach.

Her eyes warmed, like the last embers in a fire sparking back to life.

"I really do," she said sincerely. "Pencil skirts don't have to be confining."

"Well," I said, feeling awkward, but not in a bad way. It had been my choice, to get overly vulnerable with her. And I think I felt...okay. "Thank you."

"You're welcome." And then she actually smiled. She was still so, so close. If she so much as took a deep breath, her breasts—her *great* breasts—would smoosh right into my chest.

She bit her lip.

I got that topsy turvy feeling again.

"I don't care what you wear. But I cannot believe you think you're boring, Professor Bell."

The way her mouth curved, the glint in her eye when she said *Professor Bell*.

Take a deep breath, Lily, I thought.

Instead, Kiki's voice from across the room made her turn her head, take a step away.

"Oh, wow," Lily said. "I can't believe Jonny's actually singing, with Pablo here." A pause. "He must really like him." She turned back to me, a look on her face I couldn't read. "I have to go support him; is that okay?"

"Oh my god, of course." I pushed off from the bar, and it felt like waking up after a dream. "SWV is way more important than this conversation anyway."

"Don't say that." She put a hand on my chest again, for just a moment. I wondered if she could feel my heart beating under her palm. She looked away. "Jonny does slay 'Weak,' though."

He did. And it was sweet, watching Pablo's smile as he watched him, back at their table. It felt safer in general, back at the table in front of the strobe lights of the dance floor. Something had shifted at the bar, and I knew it was my fault. The wanting I could never stop myself from feeling had supercharged when Lily stepped too close to me, when she wasn't just a stranger with a strong voice and a swagger I admired. When she became someone with bittersweet memories, someone who listened to me ramble my nonsense and looked at me with all of her focus. Something had gone downhill when Morrissey came on and my heart, for some reason, decided to bleed all over the floor at her feet, a floor I would never want to look at too closely in the bright light of day.

I didn't know what I was feeling, honestly. If I was ready to go home and forget all of this, or if I had stumbled into something miraculous.

Either way, it was better here, where it was dark and loud and all I had to focus on was my recall of lyrics from songs I used to love. Where the syllables that fell from my mouth needed to be short and sweet, spoken in a shout into the soft shell of Lily's ear, and all she needed to answer with in return was a smile.

lily

WELL, I was fucked.

Sam Bell was supposed to be an experiment for Bold Karaoke Lily, an impulsive decision that would merely add to a fun night out at Moonie's. But even though I had stopped drinking after that last gin and tonic at the bar, I kept getting drunker on Sam anyway, like they were seeping steadily into my bloodstream with each open admission of vulnerability, each shy smile, each horribly belted song.

And I was definitely going to be hungover.

Things got back to karaoke-normal after our stint of oversharing at the bar. My confessions and theirs had made my insides feel all fizzed up, like a bottle of soda dropped on the floor. But back on the dance floor, this night was understandable again. Music, laughter, a bit of lust. Just another night at Moonie's.

Sam and I danced to more songs, from the frenzied hilarity of Reel Big Fish's "Sellout," which was essentially all of us jumping up and down a lot while screaming, to Madonna's "Like a Prayer," which was probably the most animated I'd seen Sam. My friends and I were all dancing in a circle for it, surrounded by the rest of Moonie's—everyone emptied their seats and barstools for "Like a Prayer"—and when the choir part came in, Preeti grabbed Sam's hand and Sam went with it, grabbing her other hand, throwing their head back and lip syncing together, and I felt so deeply happy. It was like the power of Madonna suddenly taught Sam how their hips worked. They looked so relaxed as they twirled and sang along with the rest of us, so far away from the frustration that had momentarily worried their face back at the bar. Under the lights, the blaring speakers, they were just...free. Like an angel sighing.

Their friend Kelsey showed up at one point, slipping into our circle as we danced to Nelly.

"I have friends!" Sam shouted to me excitedly after introducing us.

"I know," I laughed.

Shortly after that, Kelsey sang exactly one song—Michelle Branch's "Everywhere," which brought the house down—and promptly disappeared.

I made Sam sing one more song with me, Dolly's "Jolene," which made them laugh even harder than when I had suggested "Total Eclipse of the Heart." But like the first time, they were a good sport about it, giving it their all, grinning at me over the microphone. Which, by "Jolene," was almost too much for me. No, their scratchy, off-tune voice wasn't made for Dolly—or anything with a melody, maybe—but as I suspected, as they had proven with every other song I ever saw them open their mouth to sing, they knew every single word. Were on beat, line for line. Barely had to glance at the screen for the lyrics. And I had never wanted to fuck anyone harder. When we handed Kiki back our mics, it took everything in me not to grab their hand and stick all of those knobby knuckles into my mouth.

I settled for landing heavily into my chair as we sat back down for a breather, egregiously pressing my thigh into theirs. Their hand reached up and scraped across the back of my neck, brief but burning, making every nerve on my scalp tingle.

"God, you're beautiful," they said, and I wanted to take them then and there. Instead I curled my fingernails into the palm of my hands, dug them in until the pain reminded me that this was temporary, that Moonie's Me was just that. That the more carried away I got, the more I was letting Sam fall for a Lily that wasn't fully real.

It was well past midnight by then, and soon Jonny and Pablo took off, hand in hand. I felt tired but happy, a little loopy, my throat sore from hours of singing. Like always after a night at Moonie's, my voice would be a dry husk for the next twenty-four hours.

It felt like a blink, but soon Kiki was announcing last call, the bar slowly but surely emptying out. I was leaning against Sam, my head on their shoulder, their hand making absentminded circles on my knee. It had just sort of seemed to happen, our bodies drifting closer and closer together throughout the night. My eyes drifted closed, the lights of the dance floor hazy flashes of warmth against my eyelids, and it felt remarkably natural, falling asleep against Sam. The only other people left at our table were Preeti and Bri, and I was sure they were making faces at us, like they'd probably been making faces all night. They were going to give me hell on Monday morning at the clinic.

But right now, the clinic felt so far away. That jerk client, who had yelled at me about bloodwork for his dog, bloodwork that his dog needed, and that I knew he could afford—the ones who couldn't afford it never yelled—seemed like a distant dream. Everything felt unreal except for my own heart beat, Sam's breath falling lightly onto my forehead, tickling my eyelashes. I wanted to actually fall asleep here, rest right here in this moment forever, and never have to think about what would happen tomorrow, and the day after that, and the day after that.

I didn't, of course. Because the bar was about to close.

And because Kiki was saying my name.

I sat up, pulling away from Sam, blinking and confused.

"...that is, if she's awake enough to close out the night for us," Kiki said into the mic, smirking.

Sam nudged my shoulder, made a shooing motion toward the dance floor with a sleepy, encouraging smile.

When I turned toward the screen, I gulped. When had I even requested this song?

I hazarded a glance at Sam, who was sitting with their chin propped in their palm, that calm smile still on their face, and I remembered. After Sam had told me about their favorite song from when they were a teen, that Smiths song, I had put in *my* favorite syrupy song from my youth. And god, I couldn't even remember the last time I'd heard it, but as soon as the first notes of The Bangles' "Eternal Flame" came on, I understood Sam's stricken look at the bar when they heard Morrissey. Because it took me there immediately, back to my childhood bedroom, lavender walls covered with posters of bands I idolized, listening to this song and wondering if anyone would ever love me.

Little Lily was so misguided about so many things, was so consumed with things she wanted to change. Too big and too small all at once. And almost everything that Little Lily didn't know what to do with, Grown Up Lily now loved. Grown Up Lily now knew all those things were strength.

But no matter how put together grown up me was, my voice still couldn't quite hit that slightly breathy, high, sweet vulnerability of Susanna Hoffs. When I started, my voice was rough around the edges from over-singing, but I made my way, shakily, to the first chorus.

But even then, I sounded a little warbly. Normally when I could get loud, stretch out the strongest lines, I was at my best. But this wasn't even just because my throat was scratchy. This was because this song was too fucking earnest, and I was feeling too many things, and was too strung out to be able to hide any of it.

And through all of it, Sam kept looking at me, like they had been looking at me all night. Gentle and admiring and pure. I felt so grateful for them at that moment, no matter what happened next, for giving me this night. For making me feel like I was the most interesting person in the room. For being such a comforting presence, for gifting me with their honesty, for granting me so many precious, casual touches throughout the night that made my skin heat and my belly burn. I felt strangely bared to them in this nearly empty bar, in the middle of what could have been a very ordinary September night, like they were the only one I had ever wanted to sing for. Like their friends abandoned them on purpose, giving me room to find them.

And when I asked, in the song, *Do you feel my heart beating? Do you understand?* I felt like they did. Like they really, really did.

In the middle of the last chorus, while never breaking eye contact, they stood. They walked around the table, leaned against it. Waited.

Kiki came to me, took the microphone out of my hand.

"Go get 'em, tiger," she said with a wink. Gave me a small shove.

They met me halfway. I only took a few steps, and they were there, green eyes dark and serious, although their mouth was still smiling. They cupped both hands around my face. Rubbed a thumb over my cheek.

I heard a high whistle that I instinctively knew was Bri.

And then Sam closed the gap and kissed me.

sam & lily

THE SEPTEMBER NIGHT air was chilly when we stumbled outside, waking me all the way up. We waved goodbye to Preeti and Bri as they stepped into a cab. They had been thinking ahead, had called one ten minutes ago.

I continued to take the Not Thinking Ahead At All path when Lily tugged my hand a second later, led me to the side of the building, and shoved me against the wall. It was hard and a little shocking and the complete opposite of Lily's lips on mine again, which were soft and plump and hot, and the combination made me dizzy.

Until, suddenly, she was gone.

"Sorry." Lily huffed out a breath, hands on her hips. I did my best to not flail wildly and crash into her breasts.

"Sorry," she said again, shaking her head. "I didn't think I'd have to do this, give this preamble before we make out, but...my head's gone a little weird, and I really like you, and I don't want you to suck. So. I just need to make sure you're not secretly grossed out by me, and/or that you don't have a fat girl fetish. Even though you're not skinny, either, but you're not capital-f fat like me; you're just...adorably thick.

But I've learned that all shapes and sizes of people can be shitty, so." She took a deep breath. "I just have to be sure."

I froze, slack jawed, stuck between horror that Lily was saying any of these things, and weirdly proud about being called *adorably thick*. While it was clear to me that Lily was confident as hell, I had always felt considerably less so, whether due to a possible tiny smidge of dysphoria or the fact that my body shape seemed to be confined to *shapeless blob*. Which had probably been clear to her when we were discussing pencil skirts.

But Lily thought I was *adorably thick*. Two little words, and I couldn't even explain why I liked them so much. Maybe it was just the fact that they came from her. But suddenly I felt...the closest to sexy I'd ever felt. No matter what happened tonight, I was going to carry that phrase with me for the rest of my fucking life.

"Lily." I tried to gather my thoughts, running a hand through my hair. "I mean it when I say you are genuinely beautiful. But...if it makes you feel any better, or can convince you I don't have a fetish, the last person I dated was a skinny ass dude named Dan. Who was really great at sex stuff but sort of bad at...liking me. And you probably didn't need to know any of that, but I'm not objectifying you. Or, like, I am, but just because...you're pretty and I like you."

Romantic prowess: negative six.

But surprisingly, Lily's shoulders relaxed, her face gentling out, like her defensive shield had retracted.

"What do you mean, he was bad at liking you?"

"Oh, you know." I scratched at the back of my head. "Bad at like...asking about my day or wanting me to ask about his, or like...caring about me?" I shrugged.

"So, he was an asshole."

"That seemed to be my friends' conclusion."

She studied me for a moment.

"Did he ever come to karaoke with you?"

"Once, yeah. Why?"

"I'm just picturing myself retroactively booing him."

I huffed out a small laugh. "Well, he didn't sing, so."

"Of course he didn't. Even easier to boo at him, then."

I shuffled my feet, beginning to regret bringing up Dan.

I knew he probably was an asshole. No, he was definitely an asshole. But in bed, no one had ever made me feel so attended to, so...thoroughly debauched, in such an exhilarating way. It seemed hard to believe that someone who treated my body with such care, who made me feel so *good*, physically, couldn't care about me even a little, emotionally. Nate told me this was naive. But that only made me feel even shittier, so I stopped talking about Dan to Nate, or to any of my friends really, after that.

"You know," Lily cocked her head, "I've always been worried that I'm only okay at sex stuff. Like, how do you *know*, really?"

This shocked a laugh out of me.

"Me too. Although, well." I scratched needlessly at my hair again, face flushing. "Dan did teach me some stuff."

"Wow," Lily breathed. "I really hate Dan."

I smiled at her. The night was still cold, but warmth was sliding back into my blood.

"I would really like it if we stopped talking about Dan now. Do you believe me? That I want you?"

"Oh, yeah. I'm sorry. I knew you did. I just...got freaked out. Sorry. Although..."

"Yeah?"

"It was really cute watching you squirm."

She grabbed my shirt and pulled me back to her.

"I would very much like to have mediocre sex with you, Sam," she whispered into my lips, which made me laugh, so it took my brain a second to catch up with the fact that finally, she was kissing me again, and her tongue gliding past my lips was just as sweet as I'd imagined.

I fell back against the wall and she came with me, parting my legs with her thigh, her hands weaving into my hair, fingernails scratching at my scalp. A noise escaped my throat, raw from karaoke, and she growled back, pressing her body into mine. And everything about it felt right, comfortable and satisfying: transformative. The perfect fit.

* * *

God, I loved kissing this adorable nerd.

It was embarrassing, that I'd shown my insecurities in asking those questions—I shouldn't have to do that shit anymore, and it had been obvious all night that Sam liked me. Was attracted to me. But when the door of Moonie's shut behind us and we were out in the cool, quiet night, away from the contained safety of the bar, I got scared. I wasn't ready for Bold Lily to disintegrate, for this bubble to burst. And I was still a little fucked up from "Eternal Flame." So, yes, I was freaking out.

But then Sam had called me pretty.

Do you believe me? That I want you?

People had used *beautiful* with me, plenty of times, until it almost became this conciliatory, meaningless thing, this unnecessary reassurance that fat can be beautiful. Like a sunset is beautiful, or a Christmas tree, or a rainbow. Generic and safe. A different kind of safe than Moonie's safe: safe as a means of hiding messier truths.

55

Somehow, though, *pretty* sent shivers down my spine. *Pretty* felt specific to my skin.

And *want* reflected everything filling up my gut, using the strength of my body to push Sam up against this wall outside of Moonie's. I never wanted to back away from this wall, because I feared that once I did, once we stepped into a car and drove away from this place, the spell would be broken. I would go back to quiet, ordinary Lily. But here, with Sam's tongue in my mouth and their hands on my body, I was made of want. And I felt like a queen.

And so I made my decision. As long as Sam's body was touching mine, it would be like the magic of Moonie's was still watching over us. I could still be the person Sam thought I was, for a bit longer, until the dawn broke.

And I would make it worth my while.

I tore my lips away to pull in a few ragged breaths. The light from the huge white sign out front, shouting *The Moonlight Café* into the middle of nowhere, as if you could miss it—the only other things out here were train tracks and dusty excavators—cast a pale glow on Sam's face. Their eyes looked dark, heavy lidded. My bright red lipstick was smudged all over their mouth. I didn't have the kind of excess cash on my receptionist salary for high quality lipstick, but at the moment, I was grateful for it. It made Sam look sexy as fuck. Heat pooled between my legs, between my lungs, in the pulse of my fingertips, and I desperately wanted Sam to feel as sexy as they had made me feel all night. But I wanted to do it right.

"Honest question," I said, brushing a curl off their forehead. "If I am thinking really filthy thoughts about your body—say, your dick in particular—is that a form of misgendering you? Because I'll stop if so."

Sam closed their eyes for a moment, a shudder passing over their shoulders.

"It's...complicated," they said. "For other people, yes. Probably. I don't know. For me, almost all of my fucked up feelings about gender are..." They waved their hand in circles in front of their face, and then their chest. Their heart. "Here."

And then, almost a whisper: "I want to turn you on. My body is yours, Lily."

I put a hand there, over their heart. Felt its strong, steady rhythm.

And then I put my other hand between their thighs, over the bulge in their jeans, and I gave a small squeeze.

Sam made a sound that sounded something like, "Mmmnergh," and dropped their forehead to my shoulder.

"Can I ask," they spoke into my neck, their hot breath on the exposed skin there warranting them another squeeze from my hand, "what filthy thoughts you were having about, uh...me?"

"Oh, mainly that I need you inside of me, like, *right now.*"

My hand slid up, fingertips skirting their soft belly. Tried to slip my hand down between their jeans and their briefs, but it was too tight. Dammit, Sam, you deserved better jeans. I went for the button and zipper instead, my other hand falling down to help.

"Lily," Sam breathed. "If you go much further, I'm going to fuck you against the wall of Moonie's."

"And?"

"And I really don't want to do that. It's probably very dirty, for one thing, and your clothes are very pretty."

Oh. Well. They had a point there.

"Then call a fucking car, Sam," I huffed out. And with a

shaky laugh, they pulled their phone out of their back pocket, and they did.

"My place okay?" they asked.

"Yes." My place was an absolute mess at the moment, which I hated, and I didn't want Sam to see it. I bet their place would be nice and neat, full of interesting artifacts from around the world, whatever kinds of things history professors collected.

Professor Bell. I remembered the way their pupils had widened, back at the bar, when I'd called them that. I made a mental note to make plentiful use of the phrase over the next few hours.

When the car was requested, Sam stuck the phone back in their pocket, mumbling, "Ten minutes," before reaching their hands around my backside and pulling me fully back to them. Their mouth went to my neck this time, sucking on my earlobe a bit, which had always been my very favorite thing, and I let myself make a purring noise as I ran my fingers through their hair. I couldn't believe I had been nearly asleep twenty minutes ago. Every corner of me buzzed alive now, and Sam was exploring every one of those corners, with their mouth, with their hands over the thin fabric of my dress. And fuck, I spent two weeks getting this dress right, but how I wanted to rip it off right now so that those hands could make contact with all of my skin.

I could count the people I'd been physically intimate with on one hand, but even of those, there had been at least two who seemed happy to kiss my mouth but were strangely hesitant to touch my body. As if touching my fat rolls would unpleasantly highlight their existence. But none of my rolls or my curves or my dimples seemed to present a roadblock to Sam's hands, and by the time our car pulled up, I was panting and aching for them.

"Fuck," I said when Sam stepped back. "This is going to be the best hookup ever."

Sam froze. They were still only a foot away from me, so I saw the confused look on their face, the way their eyes clouded over, a crease forming in their brow. It was only a second, and then they seemed to shake it off. "Yeah," they said, distractedly, and turned around to walk to the car. My heart sank.

I didn't know why I'd said it. I was turned on beyond reason and wasn't thinking clearly. It sounded silly and flippant, and I hoped Sam knew I didn't feel flippant about any of this.

But maybe it was good that I said it.

Because we had only truly known each other for a few hours. And most of those hours had been spent dancing and singing. We barely knew each other, and now we were going to go fuck each other's brains out. It seemed pretty clear. Sam had to know this had all the markings of a one-night stand, right?

Of course, I'd never actually had a one-night stand before. But it seemed like a practice Bold Lily would be able to handle.

And a one-night stand could still be meaningful. Right?

God, I didn't want to hurt Sam.

I tried to take deep gulps of air before I opened the car door and stepped in. But even then, I had to work on not making my labored breathing overly obvious to the Lyft driver as the wheels of her car crunched over the gravel parking lot, before it pulled onto the bypass and left Moonie's behind. Sam and I sat silently on either side of the backseat, and even though they were right there, their absence made my heart flutter, a little pulse of panic. I hated the awkwardness I had just injected into the air between us, and the real world crept in with each rotation of the car's tires.

Touching, we had to be touching. That was what I had promised myself.

Stay in the moment. Hold on to the night. Sam was an adult; they knew what they were getting into. This could still be magic.

I reached my hand over, leaned in a bit, rested my palm on the inside of Sam's thigh. Their leg dropped open immediately for me, and I smiled, the ache in my chest loosening as my hand moved slowly upward. Until Sam hissed out a "Lily" in whispered warning, and I stopped. Instead, I coached their arm to rest on the seat between us, palm up.

And until the car stopped at Sam's apartment many minutes later, I ran my fingers in small circles along that palm, around their wrist, up their forearm and back, listening closely for how their breath hitched, feeling the slightest shivers tremor beneath their skin, feeling more like Bold Lily than I had ever felt. It was even better than the power of Carrie or Dolly, feeling the goosebumps rise along Sam's arms. Knowing I was the one who had put them there.

sam

I DROPPED my keys on the ground. Kicked the front door shut. And pushed Lily against the wall, Lily with her featherlight fingers that had made me so hard in the Lyft I could barely think straight. And I was feeling pretty good about myself, honestly—that was some damn good romantic prowess, the door kicking and everything—and thought Lily felt the same, being that she took my lower lip between her teeth and *tugged*, but a second later, she leaned away with a frustrated groan.

"Listen, I love the urgency, I really do, but we already did the wall thing at Moonie's and my feet are killing me. I need a bed, like, pronto."

I nodded. "Done and done."

As I led her into my bedroom, I was grateful my tiny apartment was relatively clean, that I had wasted away this afternoon until I could leave for Moonie's doing the dishes and going through my stacks of junk mail and sorting through the clothes I inevitably left in a pile on my floor each week, to later be separated into "should wash" and "eh, could wear again."

Not that Lily seemed to be paying much attention to my apartment.

She slipped her velvet jacket off her shoulders as soon as we entered the bedroom, and looked like she was moving to take off her dress, too, until I quickly interfered.

"Wait." I walked behind her to the zipper. "Can I?"

"Fine," she huffed, that same frustration in her voice as she'd had outside of Moonie's. It drove me wild. "But don't be all slow about it. I'm dying here."

I grinned, nestling my nose between her shoulder blades, the curves of her back, as the dress slid off her hips, as I got to work on her bra. She released a heavy, happy sigh when I worked it off her shoulders, mumbling "goddamn devil underwires" as it fell to the floor. I slid to my knees, lips skating down her spine until they reached her underwear, all the while trying to breathe her in, take the heat of her skin into my own, squeeze this moment for all it was worth.

Because, as she had reminded me back at Moonie's, this was a hookup.

Which...was one of those words I had always found to be a little nebulous, honestly.

Maybe I could have asked Lily for more details about what she meant, but I felt, instinctually, from the way she had said it, that I wouldn't like the answer. That I already knew it. That the tiny voice of reason in my head was dancing on some squishy piece of gray matter somewhere, shouting, *Told you so*.

And if I had asked, it might have ruined whatever happened next. And now that we had gotten to that *next* part—I loved the shake of Lily's hips as she helped me wiggle her underwear down her legs—I was so very glad to be here.

Even though every fiber of my being felt like this was the farthest thing from a *hookup* I could imagine.

I smoothed my hands over those hips, down those wonderful thighs, intent on blocking the word *hookup* from my brain and focusing on the moment. Which I did by planting an open mouthed kiss over Lily's left butt cheek, pressing my tongue into the dimples.

"Sam," she said after a minute, her voice raspy, "Come on. I want to see you."

Fair enough. But I gave her butt a good bite, for good measure, smiling at her hiss before I stood back up and twirled her around. She smacked my shoulder, eyes full of fire.

"You are...*ugh*." And then she was kissing me, hard and ruthless, her hands yanking at the waistband of my jeans. "Just—fucking—get them off," she said into my lips, and I was pretty sure her voice was all hoarse like that mostly because of karaoke, but there was also lust in there, for *me*, which was completely illogical but I'd take it.

The lust dropped away a bit, though, a second later, when she leapt away from me and screamed.

I had my pants halfway down my legs and almost fell straight on my face.

"Oh my god," Lily wheezed. "It's just," wheeze, "a fucking cat. Sorry." Her hand was still clutching at her chest. "It," wheeze, "startled me."

I looked down. And watched Garfunkel lovingly twining his way in and out of Lily's legs, purring against her ankles.

"Goddammit, Garfunkel." I yanked my jeans back up and quickly scooped him into my arms, tossing him unceremoniously into the living room. "Where is Simon," I

63

muttered to myself, looking around until I saw him staring at me from the top of the fridge. Obviously.

"You monsters behave yourselves," I said before slamming the bedroom door shut.

I turned back to Lily, desperately hoping my cats had not ruined the moment, because if they had, I swear to fucking—

"Strip," Lily said, arms crossed over her chest. There was an amused look on her face, but that raspy voice was serious.

Alrighty then.

I yanked my pants off, and my underwear, and then my shirt, and hopped around for a second getting my socks off, because there was nothing more humiliating than being naked except for socks, and I was sure it was all very undignified but Lily seemed satisfied by it. Because when I stood back up, fully naked, she said, "*Finally*," and pointed to the bed. "Go."

And holy shit, I liked being bossed around by Lily. It was like every fantasy I'd ever mildly contemplated while watching her sing "Before He Cheats," but a million times better. Because I knew how soft she was now. How patches of pink bloomed on her neck and her chest when she thought she had said too much. How fragile she looked when she sang that last song in an almost empty Moonie's, how I had wanted to sink to the floor with her, wrap her in my arms and never let her go.

I scrambled under the sheets and she came with, and I jumped on top of her with a level of glee I knew my body would pay for later. I had gotten the picture by this point that she was impatient, so I tried to be quick with exploring her body with my mouth, making my way down to her thighs, but damn, I wanted to be more thorough. Maybe she'd let me be more thorough later.

I had only ever been with a couple of women before, and both had been a long ass time ago—and one had turned out to be a lesbian—so I felt a little nervous as I settled in between Lily's thighs, hands tracing up the tender skin there. I wanted to be good at this for Lily. Because I didn't actually want to have mediocre sex with Lily. I wanted to blow her mind.

"Professor Bell," she rasped, and it was like those two words by themselves somehow forced pre-cum to ooze out of my cock. Fucking A, I was *really* never going to let any student ever call me that again. "I don't know what you're staring at down there, because I've seen it and it's honestly not that exciting, but if you don't put your mouth on me soon I'm going to lose my mind. Just as an FYI."

I laughed, and it loosened my nerves.

I opened her up with my fingers, and she was so wet, so slick on my fingers and my tongue, that it gave me all the confidence I could ever need, and it was easy. So easy to lick her where she needed to be licked, to hum my pleasure against her clit when she voiced hers. I loved how she tasted, the intimacy of oral, how it brought you to the earthy, carnal realness of sex, the weird wonderfulness of our bodies. That our pleasure centers were these odd fucking aliens but there were so many ways to make them feel good, so many ways we could make each other feel good, no matter what kind of body we had. Which was why I increasingly hated the entire concept of gender the more I let myself think about it.

We were all just aliens. We all fit together.

There were probably so many ways to fit together that we hadn't even thought of yet.

"Sam." Lily's voice was oddly high pitched, and it made me pull away in alarm.

"You okay?"

I had been sort of involved in my clit-labia-alien world down there for a while, and I blinked up at her, taking in that her chest was rising and falling in heavy gusts, that her forehead was damp. She grinned at me, eyes sparkling, and I tried, for about the fortieth time in her presence tonight, to not combust.

"Yes. But come here." She motioned limply with a hand and I followed, my knees aching as I readjusted, locking my elbows at her sides. "Just give me a second." She ran her hands over my shoulders, down my chest. "I'm not good at multiple orgasms. I don't want to come yet. Want to come with you, when you're inside of me."

This sounded hot and vulnerable all at once, and I rested my forehead on hers, taking in some needed breaths of my own.

"Okay," I said. "We can make that happen. Just tell me when you're ready."

Her hands kept traveling over my chest, my stomach. I tried not to wince. Even though I loved how it felt.

"You don't like your body," she said, so softly, and I wanted to die a little. Although, as if to soften the blow, she reached down and gently cupped my balls, and honestly, it helped. "Is it dysphoria or something else?"

"I don't know," I said, honestly. I opened my mouth again to say more, to say that I mainly just thought my body wasn't all that attractive, but then I closed it again. Because maybe dysphoria did play a small part. Maybe it always had and I just didn't know. Which felt...I don't know. Embarrassing. But maybe it shouldn't be. Maybe it was okay. "I don't know," I repeated.

She nodded. Brought her hands and her eyes back up to my face. Her hair knots were ever so slightly akimbo now, her cheeks flushed, eyes soft.

"Well. I think you're gorgeous, Sam Bell," she whispered, and something inside me felt like it cracked. A touch of pain, but more openness left in its wake.

"I'm ready," she said after a steady minute of me staring at her, once again not knowing what to say. "God, Sam." She touched my hair. "I am so ready for you to fuck me."

And so I did. It was like I was barely conscious for the putting on of the condom, for the rearranging of limbs, but when I slid into her, still so slick and tight and *present*, I was aware of everything. How incredible it felt. The way Lily's mouth dropped open, the way her eyes almost closed but didn't, keeping a hazy watch on me the whole time as I thrust into her, how it made me feel like a god. Or a goddess. Or some ephemeral genderless being full of heat and light. How the thickness of her thighs caged around me made me feel so fucking safe and close to her. How our skin felt, sliding against each other, the softness and friction of it.

"Sam," she said, when I could feel she was close, when I was starting to lose my own grip on things, "Talk to me."

The words fell out of me, nonsensical and ridiculous, and I realized as my own orgasm started to claw its ways into my toes that I wasn't even sure who I was talking to, her or me or both of us at once, that we were both beautiful and hot and good, and the cry she made when she came, her eyes finally squeezing shut, was the best sound I had ever fucking heard. It sent me tumbling over the edge seconds later. It felt endless, this tight spiral of bliss, like our bodies were infinity, like we were born to feel only this.

But of course, we weren't infinity; we were mortal little

aliens, and I collapsed onto my elbows as I came down, breathing heavily into Lily's collarbone.

"Fuck," I said.

"Same," she replied. She made little circles with her fingertips on my back, and I closed my eyes, skin tingling everywhere, drinking it in. Until finally, regretfully, I had to pull out, and creakily make my way to the bathroom. When I got back, Lily was already half asleep.

"I should go pee," she mumbled as I wrapped my comforter around us. "But. Mmm. Tired."

I kissed her temple. "You do you, Lily." Even though she was right. She should definitely pee. But she only smiled, eyes closed, and blindly threw an arm around me.

Within minutes, she was asleep.

lily & sam

HOURS LATER, I woke to weak light filtering through the sole window in Sam's bedroom. It was still early, far too early to be awake on a day after karaoke. My head ached; my throat was a desert. Maybe it was the unease of being in a different bed that awoke me; maybe Sam had shifted in their sleep and surprised my system.

I looked over at them, resting next to me, and they looked so peaceful. Their hair was delightfully tousled, the whiskers on their chin that had scratched my skin last night more defined. We had drifted in the night, but one of their ankles was still hooked around mine. It was hard to look at them, their loveliness yanking on my gut like an anchor, making me doubt everything: what we had done last night, what I was going to do next. Making me want to stay.

So I looked at the walls instead. I had barely comprehended anything about Sam's apartment last night, other than it was small and neat and had lots of nicely framed things on the walls. But now, in the dim light, the lust drained from my system—not completely, with the heat of their body still so close to mine, the preciousness of their sleeping face, but enough that I could think more clearly—I realized I was completely surrounded by maps.

Straight ahead, the wall opposite the bed seemed dedicated to maps of subway systems: mazes of angular, brightly colored lines and interlocking zig zags. London. Tokyo. Boston. Paris. New York. Seoul.

To my left, next to the window, there was a large map of National Parks of the United States.

I craned my head, tried to see what was above Sam's headboard. Something sepia toned and historical looking, a spider's web of patterns and boundaries and landmarks.

Finally, I took a deep breath and looked at Sam again. They were so quiet, the in and out of their breathing the most soothing, gentle thing. I wanted to meditate to it, let it work itself into all of my sore spots.

Instead, I leaned over and pushed their shoulder.

Later, I would wonder why I did it. Why I didn't just get up, quietly gather my things, and leave.

At the time, something about it made sense in my head. The dawn might have been breaking, but we were still touching, technically. And they had asked me something about myself, back at the bar at Moonie's, when we'd talked about clothes. Something that made me happy. I'd never had a chance to ask them something back, about what brought *them* joy. I needed to finish the circle, before I untangled my ankle from theirs. Before the night was officially over.

"Hey," I whispered, shaking them again. Their eyes blinked open, and they lifted their head, looking confused. They stared at me for a second, the blurriness in their eyes clearing just a bit, before they smiled and dropped their head back to the pillow.

"Hey," they said. And ugh, that satisfied, half asleep smile. Kill me. "You okay?"

"Tell me why you love history," I said. "And subway systems maybe."

"What?" They laughed, but it wasn't their weird snorting laugh. It was more like an amused breath.

I nodded to the maps surrounding us.

"History. Why do you teach it?"

They blinked a few more times. And then they rubbed a hand over their face.

"Um," they said. "This isn't quite the postcoital conversation I'm used to? Not that I'm really used to postcoital anything, these days."

"I want to know," I insisted. "Just tell me one thing."

I think...I was searching for a souvenir. One thing I could take with me. Something that would always make me remember Sam Bell.

They looked at me for a long moment, brow slightly furrowed. And I knew whatever they ended up saying, the souvenir was always going to be this. The way they looked at me. From the corner of a dark room. While they were inside me. Half awake in a dimly lit room, their eyes sleepy and thoughtful.

Taking me seriously, every single time.

"Well, as for subway systems, they are incredible," they said matter-of-factly. "We built trains? *Underground?* What, and I cannot stress this enough, *the fuck*?"

I laughed. Which was the worst. If they kept making me laugh, I'd probably end up crying.

"And subway *maps* are the best, obviously," they said.

"Obviously."

"Look at them!" They waved a hand. "All the patterns

71

and different colors. So satisfying. I feel like that's something you understand, yeah?"

They looked at me, eyes bright, and I nodded. I understood it so well.

It felt like they were inside me again, but in a different way, a way that made me ache even more.

They turned their face toward the ceiling.

"As for history..." They went quiet, their face serious. "It makes me feel calm. The fact that we can collect these little pieces of the past, and put them together in a way that makes sense. In a way that sounds logical. Because so much of what happens in modern day, current life feels so messy, so awful. It never makes sense, as we're living it. It makes me feel better to know that someday, years from now, some nerdy historian will collect pieces from this moment and write a paper that says, *This is what happened at this moment in time, and this is why it happened. This is what we've learned from it.* Even if what that ends up being is that we fucked everything up, I have to believe some person out there in the future will be able to talk about it really eloquently, at least. And be like, wow, those Americans were dumb. Let's examine all the ways the American experiment went wrong from the start, in neat bullet points and timelines that everyone can clearly understand."

They paused. Another laugh-breath.

"It is maybe weird that that thought soothes me."

"It's not weird at all," I said. Or, more accurately, croaked. I desperately needed a glass of water. "I wish I could watch you teach."

"Oh, god. You really don't." They turned back toward me and shrugged their shoulder that was now facing the ceiling, the tiniest bit of color creeping into their cheeks. "I don't know if I'm any good at it, but it's where I've ended up. Sometimes, though..." They drifted off, and I nudged them again.

"What?" I grinned. "Say it. I want to hear you compliment yourself."

They laughed, and it was almost a snort. The color in their cheeks darkened.

"Sometimes—not as often as I should, probably, but still sometimes—I actually get to see a kid have a breakthrough. Of like, fuck, this is all so much more complicated than what I thought I knew. And that realization is like...*it*, you know? That's all history is. Knowing that you know nothing, but being stubborn enough to still want to try to learn *something*, if you can."

I hoped I always remembered the way their eyes looked right then, so very green and smart and sexy and good.

"Did any of that make any kind of sense? I'm still half-asleep here."

"It did," I whispered. "Thank you for telling me all that, Professor Bell."

Their mouth curved, a soft crescent.

"And I like maps in general because I'm a nerd. I've always wanted to travel the world, but I'll never be able to. So I like to make believe."

"What do you mean you'll never be able to?"

"Because I wracked up a ton of student debt and then ended up in a job that doesn't make a ton of money." Another shrug. "It's okay; it's my choice. I could choose another, better paying job if I wanted to. And I've tried. It just turned out that I was really bad at everything else. So...I collect maps instead, and daydream. And milk my memories of that one semester I did in Rome over twenty years ago. And watch a lot of YouTube. It's almost as good as plane tickets. God, I am talking a *lot* for barely being awake.

Do you want coffee or something? Or should we be making out? I can definitely brush my teeth if you're up for that. I'm up for that. For the record."

I snuggled further into the pillow. I found myself dangerously close to wanting to know everything. About the other jobs they'd had. About their semester in Rome. About all the places they wanted to go. I would listen to it all.

I also *was* up for making out. But no.

The night was almost over.

The sun was creeping higher into the sky. Real life Lily had things to do today, to prepare for the work week.

So instead I asked the most innocuous of all the questions in my brain.

"What do you watch on YouTube?"

"You seriously want to know?"

And even though their voice was incredulous, the look on their face was so eager. Like I had asked the right question. It was adorable, and my heart almost cracked in two.

"Yes," I whispered.

"Well, in that case." They grinned. "Lily. I watch *so much*."

* * *

I reached over the side of the bed to grab my phone from the pocket of my jeans.

"There are a million travel vlogs, obviously," I said, clicking on the red and white app. "And seriously, the museums of the world are doing *amazing* work on the Internet these days. But—" I clicked through my subscription list, "—what I've been really into lately? Are the trains."

"The trains," Lily repeated, a hint of a smile in her voice. I looked over at her, just to double check that I wasn't going too hardcore nerd here, that the tone of her voice was affectionate and not a thin veil for oh-my-god-shut-up-and-let-me-fall-back-asleep. Which I wouldn't be opposed to either, honestly. I had no idea what time it was, but I was exhausted.

But even through my dazed semi-consciousness, I was a bit exhilarated from talking about my life with Lily at Whatever Unknown Hour of the Morning. It felt a bit like when I was a mere youth in college, and would spit out my best papers at three a.m. Or maybe the papers actually weren't that great, but I definitely had some *great* conversations at three a.m. with my friends.

Actually, scratch that; I bet the conversations were probably the worst, too.

But they *felt* like the best, and that's what talking to Lily right now felt like. Like maybe I actually *had* gotten the answers to her questions right. The way she looked at me, slightly entertained but her eyes all twinkly, too, made me feel like something was going right. The fact that she had even woken me up to ask me such questions was—well, kind of weird, but also kind of sweet.

And the fact that she snuggled onto my shoulder when I brought up the first train video instead of raising a skeptical eyebrow—could've gone either way, in my estimation—felt like something was definitely going right.

After we watched a few minutes of train footage, I'd move the conversation back to her. Ask her more about her job, how long she'd worked there, if she wanted to keep making clothes as a hobby or if she'd ever thought about doing it professionally. Kort ran her own small business, pounding copper in a rather violent fashion into surprisingly delicate jewelry; maybe she could give Lily some advice.

Or maybe we shouldn't talk about work at all; maybe we should just get breakfast and talk about our favorite breakfast foods. Or I could make us tea to soothe our throats and then we could have lots more sex.

"This guy's in Serbia a lot," I said into her hair as the video started. "There's no commentary, just the country-side going by. For hours. So it really feels like you're there. It's weird, but whenever I'm feeling anxious, a train video always calms me down."

Lily hummed into my chest.

It was the last thing I remembered.

The next time I woke up, the sun was higher in the sky, harsher against my eyelids. My phone was facedown on my chest.

And I must have been wrong.

Things must not have been going right after all.

Because Lily was gone.

sam

FOR THE SMALLEST MOMENT, a lick of hope flared in my chest when I picked the phone up and saw the notifications for new texts. Before my bleary eyes comprehended that they were from Claire and Kort.

I realized then that I had never actually gotten Lily's number. Hadn't even thought about it.

I didn't even know her last name.

Romantic prowess: negative five hundred.

I closed my eyes, took a few breaths in and out before I stood—damn, I was sore—and did a cursory sweep of the apartment.

But as suspected, Lily had not left a note.

Claire: *omg Sam! Is it true nobody showed to karaoke?? But you always get there so early; don't tell us you were there alone :(*

Kort: *SERIOUSLY SAM IF THIS HAPPENED I WILL DIE*

Claire: *text us back ASAP to tell us what happened & tell us you don't hate us*

Kort: *but I mean if you did I would understand, personally*

I threw my phone on my dresser and flopped back onto the bed.

I allowed myself twenty minutes to curl into the tiniest ball I could. Squeeze my eyes shut. Breathe in the scents barely still present on my pillows—citrus perfume and sex—and feel what I wanted to feel: complete devastation.

My brain was a torpedo of Lily. Her voice slicing me wide open. Her hips swinging as she sunk herself low, low, low on the dance floor. The ghost of her thighs pressed tight against mine, warm skin against warm skin. Her hands curving over my shoulders, my chest, my hips when we were at the bar, telling me I could look sexy. The echo of her laugh, tingling in my ear, sinking down to my toes. The comfort of waking up next to her, ankle hooked around mine, mouth full of questions. Wanting to know me. Making me feel like I was interesting and worthwhile.

She had come to me, back at Moonie's. She. Had come. To me.

I curled myself inward. Clenched my fists. Let the sadness flow over me like a wave.

And then I took a deep, ragged breath. I drank a full glass of water and took three ibuprofen. I fed Simon and Garfunkel. I brushed my teeth.

I steeled myself for the day, and for tomorrow, and the day after that.

I wasn't going to be dramatic about this. I was not.

And I wasn't, for a while. Because, well. I fell back asleep.

And was only woken up hours later by a loud, jolting pounding on my door.

I would have ignored it if I could, but I had this neighbor Agnes who was older and got confused sometimes. She definitely shouldn't be living by herself, but I didn't know what to do about it, other than open the door when she knocked and answer her questions about the weather report, and assure her that the truck that backfired last night in the street had *not* been a gunshot, and listen to her talk about Jackie Onassis sometimes.

Anyway, it wasn't Agnes.

"What are you doing here?"

"Nice to see you too, friend." Kort pushed past me into my apartment, and I couldn't even block her because she was carrying a small human on her chest.

"Have you been checking your phone? We were worried."

I closed the door behind Claire, who was my oldest friend. Who was going to make me talk about my feelings. Fuck.

"Uh. No. Hold on."

I escaped to my bedroom and picked up my phone.

Claire: *Sam, can you respond?? I want to make sure you're not dead*

Kort: *no, she's just feeling guilty and thinks you hate us*

Kort: *but I hope you're not dead, too, for the record*

Claire: *also Harry stopped vomiting and Kort really wants to get out of the house*

Kort: *a legitimate cause for celebration*

Claire: *Can we come over? I feel like we haven't hung out in a long time and I really am sad about missing last night :(*

Kort: *okay bitch, you never responded so now claire actually thinks you hate her, good job*

Kort: *we are coming over to make sure you're not dead*

When I walked back into the living room, Kort was bouncing Harry on her chest, and Claire was sitting at the edge of my favorite chair, frowning.

"So are you okay? You look super tired."

I flopped onto the couch. "A night at Moonie's does that to you. You know that."

Both Claire and Kort's eyes went wide. In like, the exact same way. Lesbians.

"So you *did* go?" Claire asked.

"Oh my god," Kort grinned, "Did you really go and sit by yourself in a corner for like five hours? Because I can totally see you doing that, actually. This is kind of amazing."

"No, I did not sit by myself in a corner," I said sharply. At least, not for *hours*.

"So what happened?" Claire asked.

I draped an arm over my eyes. Tried to hold in a dramatic sigh.

"Okay. So you know that other big group that's there a lot, that sits at the table right next to the dance floor?"

"Of course." I could picture Claire's nod, the trying-to-understand look of concern on her face. "They seem like good people."

"Oh, and there's that woman in their group you have a crush on," Kort said, almost casually. I raised my arm to stare at her in dismay.

"How do you know that?"

"Come on, Sam. You're always spellbound when she sings. And there was also the fact that the last time we were at Moonie's, at the end of the night when you were really drunk, you kept talking about how you wanted her to step on your face. Or something. I don't remember the exact phrasing, but it was entertaining."

"Oh." I stared at the ceiling. "I do not remember that." And then, covering my face again: "Iamsuchanidiot."

"Waaaait a second." And now I could picture the look on *Kort's* face: predatory. Gleeful. "Sam. What. Happened. Last. Night."

I thought I knew, I thought.

But right now, in the cold, hungover light of day, I felt at a loss.

"Well. The, uh, woman who I wanted to step on my face invited me to sit at their table, so...I hung out with their group all night."

"She invited you to sit at their table?" Claire repeated.

"It was fun," I said weakly. It had been. I was relatively confident on that point.

"Hold up," Kort said. "Are you telling us you made new friends?"

"Aw!" I could picture Claire's eyes lighting up. "Sam, you made new friends!"

"I don't like it." I moved my arm to see Kort shaking her head. "You're not allowed to make new friends. Only us."

"You're the ones who abandoned me!"

"*Vomit.*" Kort said. "*Projectile.*"

"Your choice to reproduce."

Kort opened her mouth. Then nodded and resumed bouncing. "Yeah. That's fair."

"So is that the only reason why you haven't been answering your phone?" Claire pushed. "Because you stayed out late at Moonie's and were hungover?"

I *could* have said yes. But I was bad at lying. And it was Claire.

I covered my face with both arms this time.

"Fine. Lily—the one who invited me to their table—and I kind of...clicked. I thought we clicked really well, actually. So we sort of slept together?"

Claire gasped and hit my side. Kort let out a low whistle.

"This," Kort said, "is incredible. I can*not* believe we all missed this."

"Kelsey did show up at one point," I remembered. "I

was pretty drunk. Don't know if I introduced her to Lily or not. She sang one song and left."

Kort laughed. "Of course she did."

"Sam," Claire gushed, "I'm so excited for you! This is the first person you've slept with since Dan, right? And she doesn't even seem like a gigantic asshole, from what I can remember of her, anyway. Personal growth, Sam!"

"Yeah, well."

God, I wished Claire hadn't mentioned Dan. Because everything I was feeling felt remarkably, horribly Dan-ish.

Like I had thought something special had happened to me—that the wanting between us had been the same—and then I woke up and discovered I must have had it all wrong from the start.

It was hard not to feel like last night had been the nail in the coffin. How many times could I do this to myself?

Even though it had truly felt like it was different. But wasn't that how it always felt, at the start of something? Maybe it was merciful, to have whatever existed between Lily and me not even get past the beginning.

Back to the plan, then. Fully commit myself to a life of Crushes Only. A future of eternal pining. Fantasies that could never hurt me.

I really didn't think it would be that bad.

After I got over Lily.

Or more accurately, after I got over the possibility of her.

"Yeah, well, *what?* Good god, Sam, lower your arms. You look like a pouting teenager." Claire yanked on an arm and I let it fall away. "What happened?"

"She...left."

"So text her," Kort said. "Tell her you want to hang out again. You deserve someone good, Sam."

Oh no, Kort was being nice to me. I must have seriously looked rough.

"I...didn't get her number? Anyway," I waved a hand, "She made it pretty clear that it was just...you know." I couldn't bring myself to say the word. A *hookup*.

"Nevermind," Claire said. "I take it back. She *is* a gigantic asshole."

"No," I said immediately. "No. She's not. She's...*blergh.*" I blew out a breath.

"Oh, Sam," Claire said softly. "You really like her."

"Of course I do," I said. And horrifyingly, even though I knew it would happen, I blinked back tears. I felt an awful urge to lean into the pouting teenager bit, explain to these two people who were so wonderfully in love and had their lives together that it didn't surprise me, that Lily left. That she didn't want me enough for more than a hookup. No one ever did.

Well. I think you're gorgeous, Sam Bell.

I closed my eyes to block out the memory. Block out my friends' worried faces. They made the steel spine I had been trying to build feel more like a paper house. I wanted a greasy breakfast sandwich and hot chocolate and to maybe go back to bed for the rest of the day.

"You need to find her somehow," Claire said after a long moment, her voice determined. "There's no way you can sleep with Sam Bell and not be a little in love with them."

I managed a weak laugh.

"You don't have to pump me up, Claire. I'll be okay. I'm sorry I worried you."

"No, I'm serious!" she said. "I know you, Sam. You don't take relationships lightly. You should at least try to contact her, if you really like her, and see what she's thinking, too. Did she say anything to you before she left?"

"No. I just woke up and she was gone."

Kort sucked in a breath. "Ouch."

"Yeah," I agreed.

Claire frowned. "Do you know where she works or anything?"

"A vet clinic. Of which there are only, you know...a million, approximately, in this city."

Claire rolled her eyes. "There are not a million. And vet clinics have websites! That probably have employee pictures on them!"

"She's a receptionist," I said. "They probably don't have pictures of them." A pause. "Even though their jobs are really hard," I added.

Although, they had said Bri was one of the vets, right? They probably had pictures of the doctors.

The only thing I knew was that it couldn't be Simon and Garfunkel's vet, because I definitely would have remembered seeing Lily there.

I didn't say anything else. But mentally, I knew I was probably going to stalk every vet clinic within a thirty mile radius later tonight on my phone. Possibly over a pint of Ben & Jerry's.

"Alternately," Claire said, "We can just go to Moonie's *way* more than we have been, and wait to run into her. And ask her what the hell she was thinking."

I groaned. I hadn't even contemplated the possibility of running into Lily at Moonie's again one day. Why hadn't I thought about that? I truly was an idiot.

"My body feels like it's been hit by a truck," I countered. "You know our old asses can only handle Moonie's once every like, three months."

Claire pouted. "But I miss it. And I want to meet Lily."

I reached out and took her hand. "I'll think about it.

And keep you updated. For now, can we talk about something else? Please?"

She squeezed my fingers. And then, because she was my best friend, she leaned back and said, "Sure."

And we did. And they made me laugh for a while, and I started to feel almost human. I was almost about to ask if they wanted to binge watch K-dramas or something, like we used to. And then Harry, who had been sleeping against Kort's chest this entire time except for a brief episode where he woke up and sucked on Claire's boob for a bit, woke up again, for real this time. Loud and *mad* at the world, and honestly, I could relate.

Claire grimaced.

"We should probably head out."

"Yeah, of course," I said quickly. Totally fine. I got it.

"But we'll hang out again soon?" she asked hopefully, and I could see in her face, that she knew I was disappointed. Or maybe she was disappointed. But this was what happened, when your friends all grew up better than you.

"Definitely." I actually lifted my body off the couch. It hurt. "Let me get a Harry hug before you go."

Kort handed him over, and he screamed in my face as I held him up, his little mouth so pink, his eyes so full of fury. I laughed and squeezed him to my chest anyway. He kicked me in the gut.

I knew I gave Claire and Kort a hard time about deciding to have kids. But sometimes, I really felt like Harry and I understood each other.

They all left then, and the apartment felt too empty, too quiet.

I ordered a pizza for myself and curled back up in bed. Garfunkel sank into the empty space next to me, where Lily had been last night. He was warm, and soft, but it wasn't the same.

I got out my phone.

I tried to empty my brain the best way I knew how. I watched a train make its slow way through the German countryside.

NINE

lily

I SERIOUSLY CONTEMPLATED NOT GOING to work on Monday morning. I rarely called in sick. I deserved it.

But I knew it was simply delaying the inevitable. Jonny and Preeti and Bri would give me a hard time on Tuesday, instead. Best to rip off the Band-Aid. And I actually felt better, putting on my scrubs, doing my makeup, brushing my hair, like it was any other day. Like I had not spent all of yesterday afternoon in some kind of fugue state, my head and my heart trying to reconcile what I had done.

I couldn't tell if I was consumed with guilt, or with mourning. Or both.

Like most Monday mornings, it was busy at the clinic. Animals to help check in for surgery, phone calls to answer. Emails to respond to, records to send. A woman came in for a morning appointment with two new kittens, little black and white furballs we all got to cuddle and coo.

It wasn't my dream job, but it wasn't all bad, sometimes.

If luck was on my side, I would have been on a different

lunch schedule today than everyone. But when I was finally able to collapse onto the saggy couch in the break room, Jonny and Preeti were there, finishing up their lunches.

"Girrrrl!" Jonny practically screamed.

"I'm dying, Lily." Preeti sat up in her chair. "DYING."

"I can't believe I missed the kiss!" Jonny moaned. "I am never leaving Moonie's early again."

"So did you bang?"

Jonny hit Preeti's shoulder.

"Preeti. Be decent." He leaned toward me. "But you know you could tell us, if you wanted to."

"I mean, *obviously* they banged," Preeti said.

I sighed. This was mortifying, but honestly it would be easiest to answer. Other than customer care, oversharing was our clinic's top skill. "Yes, we did."

Preeti squealed.

"When are you seeing them again? God, you two were so precious."

"Oh." I dug my lunch out of my bag. "I'm not, probably?" I stood to busy myself by the microwave.

"What do you mean you're not?" Preeti sounded aghast.

I pressed the timer on the microwave and turned around, leaning my palms on the counter.

"Come on, you guys," I said. "You know Moonie's Lily isn't me. It was a special night, yeah. But it wasn't…" I shrugged. "Real."

They both frowned.

"What do you mean, it wasn't real?" Preeti asked. "I saw the way they looked at you all night, the way you looked at them."

I turned back around, trying to find a clean fork. They didn't get it.

And seriously, what the shit ever happened to all the forks in this place?

"Lily," Jonny tried, his voice sincere. "We all really liked them."

"Yeah," Preeti said. "We really did. They were fun, and sweet."

They *were* fun and sweet. And kind. And sexy.

I thought of their maps. The train videos. The way they looked at me at Moonie's.

And I thought they were also more full of longing than anyone else I'd ever met.

It made an ache form in my chest.

Maybe because it felt familiar.

Or maybe I was just upset because I didn't know if I'd ever be able to return to Moonie's again. Which broke my fucking heart.

"It was just an impulsive hookup," I insisted, stirring my noodles.

"But a *good* hookup, right?" Preeti asked. "Or was it not good?"

I shoved a forkful of noodles into my face.

"Very good," I said, mouth full, irritated.

"Lily!" Preeti shouted. "A good hookup with a fun, sweet person is a hookup you want to see again! Do you know how rough it is out there? I feel like I'm losing my mind right now. Back me up here, Jonny."

"Oh, you are fully backed up here. Lily, they were super into you, and super cute. Did something happen?"

I stared down into my bowl. *Did something happen?*

I couldn't keep on with this conversation. I knew how cold I sounded right now, how cruel and illogical it seemed like I was being.

But something *did* happen. And I didn't know when it

happened, if it was when we sang "Jolene," or when I watched them dance with Preeti to "Like a Prayer," or if it was when they were taking off my bra and kissing down my spine. Or if it was when they answered all my prying questions half-asleep, and I wanted to stay curled up with my head on their shoulder, watching the boringest YouTube videos I had ever seen in my life, forever.

What happened was that I liked Sam Bell too much.

Extricating myself from them when they drifted off to sleep that morning, their phone falling onto their chest while that slow train still chugged through Serbia, was one of the hardest things I'd ever done. I had felt like a monster, leaving without a trace.

It was strange. I'd spent the first however many years of my life worrying that people would be so disgusted by my body that they would never love who I really was, *inside*. But I knew Sam wasn't disgusted by me: they had made me feel worshipped, desired, sexy, all night, both at Moonie's and in their apartment.

But what if it was the *inside* part that was actually disappointing?

How would Sam feel when they learned that the Lily who loved to sing and dance at Moonie's actually spent most of her time silently working at her sewing machine or reading a book? And even the sewing and reading days were good days; they were the days I wasn't so exhausted from the clinic that I could do something other than sit on the couch like a lump.

I imagined Sam would be sweet, and kind, and sexy, all the things they were now, for a while. I would, inevitably, fall for them even harder than I already had after only a few hours together. And then, eventually...they'd get bored. How wouldn't they? They wanted to travel the world; I barely made the rent in my shared apartment. They were full of dreams and I couldn't contribute in any way to fulfilling any of them.

It would break my heart, disappointing Sam Bell.

"Nothing happened," I said. "Look, can we talk about something else? Please? I don't mean to be a jerk; I'm just tired. Can we talk about Jonny and Pablo instead? Jonny SWVed for him, and then they left early! They obviously banged, too."

Jonny smiled slyly, twirling a bit in his swivel chair.

"Indeed."

Preeti rolled her eyes.

"Please, I already got all the deets from Jonny yesterday."

"He thought my performance was *sexy*," Jonny grinned.

"Of course he did." I smiled, genuinely, for the first time since walking into the room. "It *was*. It always is."

Preeti shoved her empty Tupperware back into her bag.

"And *Jonny* has another date with Pablo for next weekend. Because he doesn't hate happiness."

"All right, Preeti." Jonny gave her a look. "Let's leave Lily alone."

"Sorry, sorry." Preeti came over and squeezed me into an aggressive hug, almost knocking my noodles into my lap. "I just love you, Lily Bo Bily, you know?"

"I know." I patted her forearm.

"Either way." She stood with a sigh. "We *did* have an impressively high banging ratio this weekend."

Jonny nodded, taking his silverware to the sink. "We did."

"Go us!" Preeti pumped a fist into the air. "Maybe next time y'all can pass on some of your banging mojo to me."

"You can have all of mine," I said. "Although considering this weekend was the first time it worked, I can't make any promises."

"Banana nana fo Fily." Preeti shook her head at me on her way out the door. "You are chock full of banging mojo. Everyone knows it but you."

Jonny kissed my forehead. "But I think you do know it," he whispered, before following Preeti back into the treatment room.

I shoved two more bites of noodles into my mouth.

And then I threw the rest in the trash. My appetite had been off since Saturday night. Maybe I'd never drink gin again. Maybe this was an opportunity to better myself.

I spent the rest of my lunch break walking around the block, kicking away leaves with my sneakers, listening to nothing but the wind whistling through the trees, surrounded by the sure safety of silence.

But in between the quiet, all I could hear was a scratchy, off-key voice singing *turn around, bright eyes*.

It was ridiculous. And I could say what I wanted to Preeti and Jonny. To myself.

But no matter what I did, I couldn't get it out of my head.

Three days later, on my drive home Thursday night, it happened. Finally, another song barged into my consciousness. Finally, another song forced me to wake up.

"This Charming Man" was on my radio.

While I *had* vaguely recognized it at Moonie's on Saturday night, I couldn't remember the last time I had actually heard it for real. It piped loudly into the quiet confines of my car, just me and the dark night and Morrissey. And while I wasn't a superstitious person, I couldn't help but feel it was a sign.

I turned the volume up even louder and allowed myself to think about teenaged Sam listening in their bedroom. It was melancholy and beautiful. A lump formed in my throat.

I realized it all at once, listening to that song. I had been correct, essentially, in my assessment of Saturday night. Sam and I barely knew each other, and then we slept together. It was a hookup.

But even though there was so much I didn't know about them—what was their family like? Had they grown up here? What was their favorite movie, favorite childhood memory?—maybe, somehow, in those few hours at Moonie's, we had been able to see the essence of each other. Through the music we loved, the way our bodies moved and touched, how easy it was to talk about the things that mattered. Like through a few pop songs we were able to understand who we had been, who we dreamed of being, and the possibility of who we could be now—at least who we could be in those rare, important moments when we let ourselves go.

And maybe holding that night tight to my chest forever, because I was scared of what would happen if we tried to pursue anything further, could be beautiful in its own bittersweet way. Romantic, even. One perfect night preserved in memory, untamed and untainted.

But maybe I deserved more. Maybe Sam—both the person who had listened to The Smiths too much, and the person who collected maps and made me come so hard I almost blacked out—deserved more, too. Maybe we could fill in the details later. Maybe when someone saw the essence of you, it would be wrong to let that go.

When I got home, I almost frantically Googled, my

heart pounding. It was so easy to find them. They popped right up on the university's website. Sam Bell: Current Class Schedule. Office Hours. University email and phone number.

And a picture. Those eyes. My stomach flipped.

Office Hours.

That could work.

Without even taking off my scrubs, I turned on the desk lamp over my sewing machine. I got out my sketchbook. And I began to plan.

Maybe Bold Lily could, for the first time in her life, attempt to make an appearance outside of The Moonlight Café. In broad daylight, at least once.

I thought about—for perhaps the hundredth time that week—what it had felt like to sing "Jolene" with Sam, how much raw joy had filled my veins.

Go for it, Lily.

It was what Dolly would do.

lily & sam

THE FOLLOWING TUESDAY, I stood in front of a plain wooden door and took a deep breath. And then another. I stared at the placard in the window: *Sam Bell*. The letters made shivers run down my arms. So they hadn't been a figment of my imagination. Good to know.

The whole time I'd been walking through the halls, up the stairs here to the third floor, I'd expected someone to stop me, tell me I didn't belong. But no one had even looked at me. And now I was here.

And I was terrified.

Okay. *Okay*. I was doing this.

I brought my hand up, made a fist, practiced. I wanted it to sound strong.

KNOCK

KNOCK

KNO—

The door opened before I'd even finished my practiced number of knocks, my knuckles suspended in midair.

"Hey Eric, did you for—"

Sam's mouth hung open, their eyes widening as they

took me in. Realized I wasn't Eric. My breath got stuck in my throat.

"Lily?"

I barreled inside before I could lose my nerve.

I dumped the bag in my hand into the empty chair in the corner, the only seat other than the one at their desk. There was barely enough room in here for us both to stand; if someone actually sat in that empty chair while Sam sat at theirs, their knees would knock together. Coming to office hours as a student must have been terrifying.

Even when you weren't about to make a potential romantic catastrophe out of yourself.

"Hi," I said, turning around to finally look at them.

And oh. *Oh.*

I had been so preoccupied the last several days working on what I'd brought here today, practicing what I was going to say, convincing myself I could do this at all. Focused on the task at hand. I always liked having a project.

But now that Sam was actually in front of me, everything came rushing back.

The first moment our eyes locked across the room at Moonie's. Their hand on my knee under the table. Shoving them against the wall in the parking lot. Their mouth on my earlobe, their mouth on my back. Their mouth on my clit. How it felt when they finally pounded into me, over and over and over, so full and right.

I had expected their office to be sterile. A cubicle, maybe. But the only light in the room emanated from a lamp on Sam's desk, casting everything—casting Sam—in a warm, golden glow.

I wanted to climb them like a tree.

"Hi," they said, shoving their hands in their pockets. "Um. Why are you here, Lily?"

I blinked. *Focus, Lily*.

And after a few more vigorous blinks, I truly took in Sam's face.

I had been ready for a look of confusion or surprise. But what threw me was the wariness I found there instead. Their face had been relaxed and happy when they'd opened the door expecting Eric, but now, it had closed off completely. Like they couldn't wait for this to be over.

My stomach sank down to my toes.

"A couple things," I said, trying to sound upbeat, normal. Like I hadn't been thinking about this moment for days. Like my palms weren't sweating.

I glanced quickly at the walls around us as I tried to gather breath—and courage—into my lungs. The maps here all seemed more old-time-y than the majority of the ones at Sam's apartment, mostly of the Eastern seaboard, Europe. But they were nicely framed, neatly arranged on the wall, just as at their home.

I thought about how when Sam talked, they made it sound like they were a mess inside. *Bumbling through*, I remembered them saying at Moonie's.

But all of the hard evidence that surrounded them suggested that in reality, Sam Bell treated their life with extreme care.

"So. I made you some clothes." I nodded toward the bag. "I had to guess on your measurements, so they might all be shit anyway, but..." Another deep breath. "It was fun for me. I like making clothes for people, and I liked making clothes for you. Sitting at my sewing table, where I feel safest. Thinking of you."

I swallowed.

"But, after they were done, I realized they might not be the nice gesture I'd thought they'd be. Clothes are personal,

Sam. You should always have the right to wear what makes *you* feel good, and it's entirely possible one conversation wasn't enough for me to know, accurately, what makes you feel good. So, I, um. Brought a backup gift, too. If you don't want the clothes."

Sam eyed me levelly, leaning their palms back against their desk. There was an uncomfortable moment of silence.

"You made me clothes," they said slowly.

"Yeah." I swallowed again. "I'm sorry. You really don't have to take them."

Another long pause. I forced myself to not melt into a puddle.

"I...I'm sorry, Lily. But why are you bringing me gifts?"

"I wanted to explain myself. And thought if you didn't let me, which would be within your rights, I could at least leave something with you. For you. As a thank you for a truly wonderful night."

They stared at me a minute more. And maybe my own eyes were going wobbly, but I thought their face softened, just a tiny bit.

"I'd like to see the clothes," they said eventually, and I about fainted with relief.

I moved to the bag and took out the sweater.

"We could start with this," I said, turning around, the fabric soft and reassuring in my hands. It was 10% cashmere. The most I could afford. The feel and weight of it leant me confidence I desperately needed, being that I was starting to doubt myself more with each passing second.

And then I looked up and actually processed Sam's outfit.

It was like my brain could only take in Sam in bits and pieces today, or something, but—

"Oh *no*, Sam," I couldn't help myself from blurting. "That shirt's awful."

Sam blinked and looked down at themselves. And then nodded their head, once.

"I know," they said.

It was a short-sleeved linen button-down shirt, a boring pale plaid, and it might have been fine, if it wasn't a size too big and wrinkled as shit.

I took a step forward. I was pretty sure I was shaking a little. But this was my one shot. Bold Lily had to try.

I raised my hands to the first button, my fingers an inch from their chin.

"Can I?"

I looked up. Watched Sam suck in a small breath.

And after an excruciating moment, they answered, almost in a whisper: "Yes."

Oh thank god. My heart beat harder with each button, but I rid Sam of that horrible shirt. Resisted the urge to run my hands over their skin.

And then I lifted the sweater over their head.

"Oh, damn," they said, pulling their arms through the sleeves. "Soft."

"Yes," I whispered, and I gave in to the urge, like it was acceptable now that there was new fabric there. I ran my palms over their shoulders, down their chest, rested them on their belly. The sweater was dark purple, the perfect amount of fuzzy, and actually fit Sam's body, so you could see their curves. "Soft."

We stood like that, practicing our best move—staring at each other too long—until I removed my hands and turned back to the bag.

"We don't have to do the next part," I said, holding the folded up leggings and skirt. "You can take them home and try them on later. And then burn them. Whatever you want. Your decision."

Sam looked at me, then at the clock. They reached over and locked the door, checked that the blinds were pulled tight.

"Office hours are over," they said. "Let's do it."

When they pulled their jeans down, I saw the angry red lines they left on their skin, and I bit my lip. I knew this entire exercise was perhaps more for my benefit than Sam's. That not everyone cared about clothing, put so much emotional investment in it as I did. But I could not wait until Sam's skin was covered with soft, stretchy, rayon-cotton blend instead, a fabric that held their body in with care instead of punishment.

I handed over the bundle of clothes. Watched quietly as they pulled on the forest green leggings. The charcoal grey pencil skirt, dotted with small white polka dots.

I had to bite back my pride. My guesswork on fit had been even better than I hoped.

They looked divine.

But Sam only looked down at themself and sighed.

"Oh," I said, blinking back sudden tears, feeling absolutely ridiculous that they had appeared at all. "It's okay Sam! It's okay if it's not transformative, if they don't fit. I'll take them back. You can keep the sweater, it's—"

"Lily," they interrupted, shaking their head. I thought maybe they were smiling, just a little, but my brain was panicking too much to fully believe I wasn't making it up. "Stop. Okay? Breathe. It's okay. I like them. They feel good. It's just...as I thought."

They ran their hand over the top of the skirt, where it hugged the soft bottom of their belly.

Oh. Okay.

My brain recalculated, and I couldn't help myself. I reached out, covered their hand with mine.

"I like that," I said. "That's your body, Sam. That's just how it's shaped. There's nothing wrong with it."

Their eyes met mine. My own body felt overly aware of everything: the pulse in my fingertip, pressing against Sam's knuckle. The slight unsteadiness of my breathing. The way Sam's lips were just barely parted. How small their office was, that glow from their lamp. It felt like we could have been a tiny pod, rocketing toward outer space, no one else around but us.

I stepped back.

Trying to steady my breath, I turned around and reached once again into the bag.

"I brought an alternate, though."

I brought out a different skirt: same charcoal gray, although this one was patterned with little pink lightning bolts. The cut was still simple, but more free flowing, with an asymmetrical hem.

I could tell as soon as Sam slipped it on that this one felt better to them. They swung their hips a bit. They were staring down at themself, and the light was dim. But I was pretty sure they were blushing.

"Swishy," they said. "Fun."

I exhaled. Swishy seemed promising.

I still wasn't entirely sure if this was going well, or if everything was awful.

But time to stop messing around now.

I took a tiny step forward.

"Sam," I said. "I'm sorry."

They looked up, and there was a spark there, in their eyes—did they truly like the clothes? But whatever it was faded. Their eyes were steady on mine as hurt came to the surface instead.

"You said a few minutes ago that you had a wonderful night," they said quietly. "So why did you leave?"

I closed my eyes. *Here we go.*

"You got to know me under false pretenses, Sam," I said, snapping my eyes back open to look at them. "The person you see at karaoke, who dances and sings loudly and confidently is...not me. She only exists at Moonie's. The truth is that in my everyday life, I'm..." I shrugged. "Quiet. Kind of boring. I didn't want you to actually get to know me and... be disappointed."

Their eyes narrowed.

"Wait a second," they said. "I thought you yelled at *me* for calling myself boring."

"You're *not*," I said defiantly. "You're a *professor*. You have this badass little office." I waved my hands around to make my point. "I would kill to have a little office like this, all to myself."

"You make your own clothes," Sam countered. "You knew how to make *me* clothes."

"You studied abroad in *Rome*," I shot back.

"You have this *voice*," Sam said. "This voice that..." They faltered. "Slays me."

My breath caught. I blinked, a gap of silence stretching a moment too long.

"You have two cats named Simon and Garfunkel," I managed. "Which is really fucking charming."

"You have cool, interesting friends who love and support you," they said.

"And my middle name is Marie!" I threw my hands in the air. "Why are we shouting facts about each other?"

"I don't know," Sam said, but they were smiling. I was

sure now. It was possible they had been smiling this whole time. "Although I'm pretty sure you started it. My middle name is Anthony, by the way. After my grandfather on my mom's side."

Ridiculously, I felt like crying again.

"Well," I said. "Well, that's nice to know. I want to know stuff like that. I just..." I shook my head, trying to get back to the point. "Saturday night was intense. And my past relationships have not always been awesome, and it felt like...things could potentially be awesome, with you."

"Yeah," Sam said, face sobering. "We're agreed, there."

"And it's...scary," I ended, and wow, that sounded twenty times more embarrassing coming out of my mouth than I had anticipated. And I had anticipated it being pretty fucking embarrassing. "And I don't want to be scared. So I just want you to know who I really am, that I'm not actually Karaoke Lily, before we go any further. If you want to go any further."

There. I didn't know if I had said anything exactly how my heart wanted to say it, but I'd said enough.

I felt suddenly tired.

Sam released a small sigh.

They pushed off from their desk and took my face in their hands.

"Lily," they said affectionately, running a thumb over my cheek. "Of course Karaoke Lily is who you are."

I started to protest, but they put a finger to my mouth.

"I mean, if we were all who we are at Moonie's all the time, we'd all be exhausted." They smiled that gentle smile. "You can't fake who you are when you're up on that dance floor with a microphone in your hand, Lily. It wouldn't turn me on so much if it was fake. It might not be who you are seven days a week, but that doesn't mean it's not still a part of who you are." They studied me, their eyes serious. "Look. Right before you came in here? This freshman, Eric, who's only taking my intro class to fulfill an elective requirement, who thought it'd be an easy A, stopped by to tell me how much more he was enjoying the class than he thought he would."

They paused, brow creasing.

"Okay, and to ask me for an extension on his next paper, because his grandma died. *But* he also had all these questions about the Dawes Act, which is understandable because the Dawes Act was fucking wild, but the fact that he was asking the questions, outside of class, that he *felt* something about injustice in 1887—"

Sam was still holding on to my face, and I didn't know if they even noticed that they started squeezing my skin tighter as they talked, but—well, I liked it. A lot.

"Anyway." They huffed out a breath. "Moments like that are *my* Moonie's moments, you know? And they only happen every once in a while. I wish I could be a brilliant professor for them, for you, all the time, but I'm not. I know, though, at this point, that if I don't let myself feel a *little* proud of Eric de la Rosa being real pissed off about the Dawes Act, I won't have the energy to keep going."

One of their hands caressed down my neck. Involuntarily, my eyes fluttered closed.

"Sorry," they said. "I'm still running on a slight high from Eric. I just meant...we have to take our wins, Lily. You at Moonie's?" I felt them lean in, their breath hot on my cheek. "You simply wouldn't be able to sing like that if that voice wasn't yours."

What would Dolly and Carrie do? I asked myself.
What would Karaoke Lily have done, Saturday night?

And I thought—maybe—they'd all want me to look at Sam, and believe them.

"Plus," Sam murmured into my temple, "You weren't very quiet at my apartment, either."

I flushed.

"That was different, too," I said, weakly.

"Mm." They kissed my forehead. "Either way, I find it very hard to believe that you will disappoint me. Show me your quiet parts, Lily. You have no idea how much I would like to be maybe-a-little-boring together."

They kissed my nose. It was sweet, and tender.

But at that moment, I did not feel like being very tender at all.

* * *

Lily leaned her head back to look at me. I thought—I hoped —I saw something like possibility there in those brown eyes. Something like trust. Something like want.

And then she reached up and kissed me with a ferocity that made my head spin.

Her arms were suddenly around me, clawing at my back, and I stumbled half a step, until my butt was fully pushed back against the desk.

Just like last time, as soon as her lips were against mine, our bodies aligned, it was like we just...fit. Like our bodies were meant to be together: my softness next to hers; her strength bleeding into me. And within minutes, my entire system buzzed with need.

Although it was possible I'd been buzzing with need ever since she walked in the door, considering she looked so ridiculously fantastic. Her hair was down today, and she was wearing a leggings-skirt combo too, although her skirt was long and pale and floofy and made of...what was that fabric? Tulle? Almost opaque but not quite, a little magical, like fairies had concocted it in an enchanted forest. It was offset by a faded Sinead O'Connor t-shirt, tight against her chest, and a thick cardigan sweater. A cozy infinity scarf wrapped around her neck. A perfect picture: Lily in the Fall. I wanted to cuddle her to death.

Except when she first walked in, I told myself I didn't. Because I had spent the last week and a half convincing myself this was over, that *all* of this was over: Lily and everything she represented. I had gathered all my strength, and decided to *not* virtually stalk every veterinary clinic in the metropolitan area. I had caught up on all my grading, instead. Apparently taught the shit out of the Dawes Act. Smiled extra hard at my barista. Told myself I was fine.

And I was. I would be. Because I would always have my friends. Claire would take care of me when I was old and fragile. We'd already promised each other, years ago. And if Claire died first, I was sure Kort would take care of me, albeit more grudgingly. Or if all else failed, Harry. I'd make sure he knew his responsibilities, once he was old enough to talk. In any case, I didn't need...need.

But when Lily started to explain that the reason she walked out of my apartment two Sundays ago was because of *her*, and not *me*...it knocked the wind out of me a little. I didn't know why I had been so surprised. Maybe I was a little self-absorbed. Or maybe my head was still more fucked from Dan than I realized. Because Dan made it pretty clear that it was me. That it was always me who had misinterpreted things. Who wasn't the right fit, who wasn't enough.

The fact that Lily might think *she* wasn't enough had honestly never even occurred to me.

It made all of my not-so-stable walls crumble immediately.

Because it was going to be the most fun I'd ever had, proving her wrong.

I pulled away from her mouth to 1) breathe, and 2) remove that scarf from her neck. The collar of her t-shirt was ripped and loose, and a growly sound escaped my throat, pleased at all that newly exposed, available skin. I attacked it with my tongue, with my teeth, and she wove her fingers into my hair, grabbing and pulling with a delirious-making amount of gentle pressure.

"Lily," I said into her shoulder, my own hands roaming under her sweater, and then under her t-shirt, for which she rewarded me with a gasp, "I thought I'd never see you again."

"Sam," she whispered, and I thought that was all. I was seconds away, myself, from whispering her own name, over and over, for no other reason than wanting to say it. But then, a minute later, just as I was about to suck her earlobe into my mouth, she added: "I missed you."

For a fraction of a second, I froze. And then, without really thinking about it, I found myself gathering up all that magical tulle in my hands, until my fingers could reach between those wonderful thighs. She shifted her legs, opening for me, and I pressed my fingers against her, and she was so hot there, even through the layers of thin fabric.

"Yes," she whispered, tilting her hips toward me, "Please, Sam. Touch me."

I always was a good listener.

Using both hands, I separated her leggings and underwear from her skin, navigating one hand down, down, and *oh*. I sucked in a short breath when I felt how wet she already was. Her underwear was some type of satiny material, smooth and cool against my knuckles, contrasted against the heat of her. She made soft, breathy sounds against my neck, and I wanted to swallow them whole.

After a few minutes of circling her clit, I slowly slid one finger inside her. She ground against my palm.

"Sam," she whispered, "That's perfect."

She had sort of collapsed into me, so it was hard to see her face, but I leaned down to plant a kiss at the edge of her eye, where a few locks of hair had fallen forward and gotten stuck on her mascara. I moved another finger inside, and then another. She moaned, one of her hands tickling up my side, underneath this soft, soft sweater. This sweater she had made for me.

I didn't quite understand what I had done to deserve any of this. But maybe now wasn't the time to overthink it. Maybe now was the time to do what I always tried to do at Moonie's: let myself go. Feel grateful as hell to be alive in this moment, right now.

And let everything else fall away.

Lily was leaning back, mumbling something incoherent: "I need—I can't—"

She grabbed my plaid linen shirt, which was crumpled on the desk behind me. The shirt that I knew was ill-fitting and too wrinkled, that I really wished I had not worn today. Not that I could have anticipated Lily showing up at my office door.

But then she shoved her face in the shirt to muffle her cry as she tightened around my fingers and came, the same cry I remembered so well from that Saturday night, somehow feral and pretty all at once. And on second thought, maybe I would frame the shirt.

She dropped it to the ground as she came down, leaning even more heavily into me. I extricated my hand and used my other to draw small circles on her back. We were quiet a moment. Absently, I rubbed my thumb against my forefinger with my free hand, feeling her slickness that was still there, taking the time to really absorb it, along with the general warmth of her body against mine, the slight scratchiness of her sweater on the fingertips of my left hand. So many pleasurable sensations, so many different textures. So many ways to be in a body.

A bit shakily, Lily pushed herself away from me. Silently, she repeated the same actions to me that I had done to her.

She lifted up my skirt, rumpling it up on my stomach. She gave me one small squeeze through my leggings, and I was so riled up, that was honestly almost enough to send me over the edge. But I got a hold of myself—or rather, Lily made quick work of pulling down my leggings and briefs and taking hold of me.

For one brief, glorious moment. And then she was gone.

I opened my eyes, which apparently I had closed at some point, probably when she lifted up my skirt. But it was a good thing I opened them again, because I got to witness Lily reaching underneath her own skirt, and...rummaging around in there for a second, before bringing her hand out again. She grabbed the base of my cock again, this time semi-lubed with her own release.

She looked up at me and laughed a little. Probably because the look on my face was likely...something.

"Better than spit," she said.

"That it is," I concurred.

"Shut up," she said, blushing suddenly, and for some reason it was that blush that made me remember we were in my fucking *office*. Holy shit.

I forgot again two seconds later. Because she reached

her other hand into my hair and brought me down to kiss her as she rubbed me to oblivion. And that *mouth*. Those hands. That tongue, that—

"Lily." I broke away. It was getting to be too much, so fast. So fucking dirty and good. I felt out of my mind. "What's your last name?"

"Fischer," she huffed, looking down in concentration.

I was able to get out, "I missed you, too, Lily Marie Fischer," before—

"Oh *fuck*. Wait. Fuck." I gripped her hand, stopping her. She gave me a quizzical look. I had to pant a few times before I was able to explain. "Don't," huff, "want to ruin," huff, "the sweater."

It occurred to me later that I could have just taken off the damn sweater, but it was fine. Because with a smile, Lily sank to her knees instead, and then I wasn't able to form words. To be honest, her mouth had barely even covered the head of my cock when I exploded. I didn't need a shirt to scream into—my entire system always seemed to freeze when I came and I could only get out the faintest groans; I was slightly jealous of Lily's ability to make such a joyful sound—but it seemed to last forever. I felt almost bad. But Lily appeared to be doing just fine. She leaned her head against my thigh when I was done, and we both took a breather.

I really had missed her, I realized. I had spent every day since she'd left my apartment convincing myself I didn't. I tried so hard I believed myself. But now that she was here, it was like rediscovering something I had held once, however briefly, that made me feel so very light, so full of joy. Something my entire being had been longing to find. And I wasn't going to let go this time.

I pulled up the leggings, readjusted my skirt. Lily stood to meet me again. I glanced at her.

"Um." I hesitated. "We're probably doing things a little backwards here, but...would you want to get dinner with me tonight?"

Her face cracked into a smile. She relaxed against me.

"Yes," she said. It was possible my heart soared.

"Tacos?" I asked. She snuggled even closer.

"Tacos," she agreed.

I ran my fingers through her hair.

"Perhaps not *so* boring, you and me," I murmured.

"Maybe," she said. But there was a smile in it.

"Although I do have to admit this wasn't quite typical for my office hours."

She muffled a half-laugh, half-hum into my shoulder.

The memory of today might actually prove to be a problem. I would have to work on not getting turned on every time I entered my office now. But that was a problem for Future Sam.

"Hey," I said, some of her words from earlier poking through my post-orgasmic haze. "Hey. Didn't you say you had brought a backup gift?"

She leaned away. "I did."

"Can I have it?" I asked, feeling eager and happy in such a blissfully simple way. Like somehow, for some reason, Christmas had arrived early for me today, out of the blue: love and light and gratitude. And presents.

Lily cocked her head, considering. "Will you buy my tacos?"

"Of course."

She grinned. "Okay. But don't get too excited or anything."

"Well, now I'm *really* excited." I pumped my fist. "*Back - up - gift! Back - up - gift!*"

"Okay, okay." She disentangled herself from me. "But, uh. Can I wash my hands first?"

"Yeah." I smiled. "There's a bathroom right across the hall." I leaned over to unlock the door. I probably should have washed my hands too. But some perverse part of me wanted to keep Lily's scent on me a little longer.

As I waited for her to come back, I stared at the walls of my tiny office, taking a deep breath. I swished my skirt a few times. It was nice.

I would need to wear it more, to figure out if I actually liked it or not. If it truly fit. But I was glad to have it as an option. Maybe some people were able to figure everything out on their own. But someone showing me different options had always been so helpful to me. Even if it took me a while to grab onto the things that made sense for me, that felt good, until they actually felt like my own.

They were small things, in the end. Pronouns were such tiny words. A dab of makeup, when I felt like it. A different piece of fabric.

But it was so nice. Having options.

When Lily came back, she walked immediately to her bag again without looking at me. She lifted something out and hid it behind her back.

"This might be dumb," she said, biting her lip.

"Lily," I said. "New rule. No more trashing your gifts before you give them to me, okay? It sort of dampens the whole experience a bit."

"You're right. You're right. Okay."

She took a step forward.

"I made you a map."

She handed me the frame.

It was small, maybe 8x10.

I couldn't stop smiling. I felt it lighting up my face, unstoppable.

The Moonlight Café, it said at the top.

She had included all the best parts, with neat little labels. Of course she could draw; of course she had wonderful handwriting. All of those parts of the brain that I could never get to light up were bright and beautiful in hers.

Behind the bar, there was a small figure labeled *Hot, Scary Bartender*. I laughed.

"You think the bartender is hot?"

"Oh yeah," Lily answered, with feeling, and shivered a little.

But I couldn't even feel jealous. Because while the map was mostly drawn in black pen, there were small red hearts drawn in every spot that had mattered the most on Saturday night: *Sad Sam Table*, as she had labeled it, in the corner. The spot by the bar where we had talked about clothes and Morrissey. The middle of the dance floor, next to the microphone.

"I love it," I said.

"Yeah?" Her eyes were wide, hopeful.

"So much." I had never loved something this hard in my goddamn life.

"I know it's not, like, a work of art or anything."

"Lily. It's the best. *The best*. I already know where I'm going to put it."

She opened her mouth, and I knew she was going to say something else self-deprecating. But instead, she only said, "Okay," and smiled.

"Thank you." I let out a breath. "I don't know if anyone has ever been this nice to me in my life."

Lily frowned. "Well." She turned around, picked up the empty bag and her purse. "We are going to have to fix that."

I picked up my black jean jacket from the hook on the wall. Threw my own bag over my shoulder, shoved my jeans and old shirt inside. I smoothed my hands over my skirt and then joined Lily where she waited, in front of my office door.

"Oh my god," she breathed, looking at me. "Sam. Your jacket."

"Yeah?" I looked down, worried I had accidentally put it on inside out or something.

"It's perfect. It makes the whole outfit—"

She moved her hands around rapidly, and actually *squealed* a little, bouncing on the balls of her feet.

"Gah!" she eventually shouted. "You look so good!"

I laughed. And held the Moonie's map to my chest.

"I might change for dinner," I said, hoping that wouldn't disappoint her. "I don't know yet."

Lily reached over and squeezed my hand, the one not clutching the best present ever.

"That's fine by me. As long as you throw out that other shirt."

"Oh, no. You screamed into it when you were coming. I'm never getting rid of it now. Anyway, this is probably the bigger deal than dinner, wearing this down the hall right now," I rambled, thinking out loud as it hit me. "My colleagues or students could see me. Which...actually doesn't feel like that big of a deal, now that I think about it?"

Lily waited patiently.

"And since I was very recently sexed, there's not much threat of sporting a woody in these leggings—which *are* very comfortable, by the way—so that's good."

Lily made a choking sound.

"A woody?"

"I know, I know, I'm feeling kind of loopy and it just popped out. My grandpa used to call them that."

"Grandpa Anthony?"

"Yes!" I smiled. "He was a very dirty old man."

"I do think plenty of people with penises wear skirts and dresses every day and manage just fine, Sam."

"You're right. I'm being weird."

"No. You're processing. And being cute."

"Yeah?" I opened the door. "How cute? Like, invite-me-back-to-your-place-after-tacos cute?"

Lily bit her lip. "My place is a mess, and I have two roommates and thin walls. I like your place better."

"You *do* have to see where I put my newest map," I conceded. "Although I want to know more about your roommates. And, you know, everything else about you."

We walked into the hall. No one even looked at us, which was strange, because I was pretty sure we were both glowing.

"Did you drive?" I asked. She shook her head.

"No, I took the bus."

"Cool." I gave her hand a small squeeze. "I could drive you home, if you wanted? And we can meet back up in a few hours?"

"Yeah. I'd like that."

"Holy shit, I cannot wait to see what your taco order is."

She laughed.

"I'm serious," I said. "But don't tell me. I want it to be a surprise."

She made another little giggly noise, and I looked over at her. She was looking down at the ground, shaking her head. And smiling.

Romantic prowess: not bad, actually.

"Hey," I said as we exited the building, headed to the employee lot. "Serious question."

"Shoot."

I stopped in the middle of the sidewalk and turned to face her.

"Would you sing for me sometimes? Like, if I continue to be cute enough to get you back in my apartment?"

Her cheeks went pink, her eyes surprised.

"Like...just hanging out in your apartment, singing? A capella?"

I shrugged, tugging her a little closer.

"Yeah. You know, when we're in bed, or making hot chocolate in the kitchen...maybe you'd sing 'Dream a Little Dream of Me' and I'd boop some whipped cream onto your nose. Or something. Not that I have fantasized about this or anything."

She covered her face with her hands. But I could tell she was still smiling.

"I don't know," she said through her fingers. "I might have to work up to that."

Oh my god. She hadn't been lying. She was...shy.

And it was absolutely, thrillingly adorable.

"That's okay." I stepped back. Gave my skirt a little twirl. Because I was feeling full of possibility, my body a tiny bit more free. "No pressure."

She dropped her hands and we kept walking.

"I *am* okay with one thing," she said after a minute.

"Yeah?" I looked over.

"Singing along to the radio." She grinned. "The inside of a car is definitely the best place for singing, outside of Moonie's."

"Oh my god." I grabbed her hand again and started jogging toward my beat up Corolla. "Let's fucking go."

"Okay, okay," she laughed as we got there, out of breath. "But I get to choose the station. And warn me next time you're going to make me run like that; my boobs are angry at you now."

"You're on, Fischer."

I unlocked the door and threw my bag in the backseat.

"And I'll make it up to your boobs later," I added as I put the keys in the ignition.

She snapped her seatbelt into place.

"Deal."

I turned the engine.

And then I waited for Lily to sing me a song.

our favorite songs

note to readers

This novella includes mention of parental death from cancer, brain cancer specifically, as well as one line referencing self-harm. Please treat yourselves with care.

For Lou
who listened to Radiohead with me &
helped me feel a little less alone in high school

& for the OG Anita
you are missed

1.

AIDEN

"OF COURSE," Kai Andrews said as he sat down across from me. "It's you."

Kai Andrews.

Just sat down.

Across from me.

I did a quick memory check to make sure I wasn't high.

Alas, the only depressant I'd consumed tonight was this just-okay IPA in front of me. And Kai Andrews was definitely still sitting at my table, snug against the back wall of Moonie's, next to the sole window in the building. Like most squat buildings containing exactly one window, Moonie's—or The Moonlight Café, if you wanted to be technical about it, and nobody did—wasn't a particularly fancy place. A fact only doubly confirmed by said window being mostly obscured by black bars and a large neon sign advertising Bud Light.

But still, it was my shitty bar, my barely-a-window window, my slightly crooked table. Where I was supposed to be meeting Penelope, my best friend, for our semiannual   let's-get-drunk-and-laugh-at-people-doing-karaoke Moonie's invitational.

Which my high school nemesis had definitely never, ever been invited to.

Kai laughed. Or half-laughed. It was one of those charming, head-shaking kind of quiet chuckles that only truly attractive people could pull off.

"I take it Pen didn't tell you she invited me."

My mouth, which I presumed had been gaping like a fish, snapped shut. I grabbed my smudgy pint glass and drew my just-okay beer closer to myself, as if it could protect me.

"Yeah, that'd be a *no*."

Of course Kai was laughing. Of course he thought this was funny.

He tilted his head. A strand of shiny russet hair shifted on his perfect forehead.

"Wow. Aiden. You are like...seriously pissed. I didn't know either, that you'd be here. If that helps."

"It's fine," I said, even though it wasn't; it was *weird*, so weird, that he was here, that Pen did not run this by me. But *it's fine* was what normal people said in these kinds of situations, and I was totally going to be normal about this. I was not freaking out. "What are you even doing in the city? Don't you live down south somewhere now?"

Kai shook his head, brought his own pint glass, full of something clear and bubbly, to his lips.

"Not anymore. Just got a job at the port."

"Oh. What are you doing, building ships or something?"

Kai placed his glass carefully back on the table, clearing his throat.

"Welding on them. Yes."

Let it be noted, for the record, that I did not disintegrate into goo here, even though I wanted to.

Of course Kai Andrews was building ships. It helped explain the fact that he was more built than ever. He was currently hiding most of his bulk under a thick hoodie, considering it was approximately ten degrees outside, but I could *tell*. His shoulders were even more lumberjack-y than they had been in high school. I didn't want to think about what his biceps looked like under there.

His face was the same. Almost. It was probably point-five degrees more handsome. Which was infuriating.

"So. What are you up to these days, McCarstle?"

Waiting for Penelope to show up and explain herself to me.

"I'm..." I faltered, the gears of my brain still struggling to shift from first to second. And anyway, I truly could not think of anything I wanted to do less at this moment than tell Kai Andrews, Ship Builder and Owner of the Perfect Face, about my MFA. "I'm in grad school." *And walking dogs on the side. I don't know how I'm existing, or how I even afforded this beer, to be honest. Aren't I impressive?*

"For writing?"

"Yeah." I scowled.

Kai's face actually lit up with a smile. Like he was proud of me.

"That's awesome. What are you writing these days? Still..."

And because we lived in a reckless, cruel world, the earth did not swallow me up into a pleasant dark hole when I said, "Poetry. Yeah."

Kai's smile stretched wider. His skin was flawless, his teeth straight as sin.

"Awesome," he said again. "I can't wait until I can buy

your books at Barnes & Noble one day and say, hey, I knew that guy once."

We had known each other, once. Barely. We knew each other because, for whatever reason, Penelope loved both of us, and we loved her. Because Penelope was the rarest of flowers, a tropical bird: grace and blinding colors, a magical ability to flit between all social groups and leave everyone somehow better in her wake.

Kai Andrews, though, solidly fit into one box. Star soccer player. Handsome, polite. Didn't overload on AP classes like me, but still made the honor roll. He was the kind of teenager teachers would bring up in the staff room whenever he won his latest accolade, pointing at each other and saying, "Kai Andrews? Now, that's a good kid." Top Candidate for Goodest Kid.

I was pretty sure Kai had done an apprenticeship after high school. Like it was the fucking 1800s or something. That was the level of pure he was.

And I was the gangly queer boy who scribbled poetry in the margins of all of my notebooks. Who detested extracurricular activities, mainly because I was never brave enough to join one. A mid-tier candidate for Smart Awkward Kid We'll All Forget About in a Year.

And now, five years post high school graduation, somehow we were sitting at a tiny table together at The Moonlight Café. If there was anywhere I pictured ever running into Kai Andrews again, it certainly wasn't this odd, queer karaoke bar in a deserted corner of the city. His presence made me feel off kilter, like the filter on the world had just changed and my eyes were still adjusting. His knee brushed against mine and I nearly jumped.

"Don't hold your breath," I eventually mustered. About the finding me in Barnes & Noble thing. Which had been a very Dad thing to say, like he should have been ruffling my hair as he said it. Kai Andrews was a built, hot dad, and having him in front of me made me feel like a teenager again. Running a little too hot, not knowing what to do with my hands.

And then, thank god, my phone rang.

Penelope was FaceTiming.

Which, I realized with a sinking feeling in my gut, was not a good sign—her face should be here, at Moonie's, and not inside the cracked screen of my phone—but I swiped to pick up anyway.

And saw my best friend sitting in a hospital bed. With a big white bandage on her forehead.

"Hey! Hey hey hey hey," she said, fast, before I could even open my mouth.

"Pen?" I frowned, leaning in to hear her over the din of Moonie's. It was still pretty dead in here, but she sounded too tinny and far away anyway. "What happened?"

Kai leaned over the table, trying to see her too. Which brought his perfect face entirely too close to mine. I tried to position the screen at the center of the table between us, to prevent any further leaning on his part, but it didn't seem to help matters.

"So, little thing, not a big deal, I promise, just—oh, hey! Kai! You made it!"

Her face burst with a smile, bandage shifting as her eyebrows catapulted.

"I did. Can you tell us why you, on the other hand, appear to be at the hospital?"

"Well, okay, I was on my way there, I swear, but did you all know the rain turned into snow? And apparently there was black ice? And my tires did a wee little whoopseedaisie and

—" Kai and I both leaned in even closer as she paused. His hair almost brushed my cheek. "And I might have had a slight run in with one of those signs that flash at you how fast you're going over the speed limit? Which, if you think about it, is kind of funny. Like I was finally just like, 'fuck you, sign!'"

Kai, the heathen, actually did laugh, another soft chuckle. I frowned, increasingly concerned about Pen. Glancing out the window, I could just barely see, through the bars and the back of the Bud Light sign, a smidge of the parking lot, where—huh—snow was indeed funneling through the air, highlighted by the bright spotlights of the lot.

"Penelope," I said. "What happened after you hit the pole?"

"Well, first, this woman stopped and was like, 'whoa,' and I was like 'I know,' and it really is true, you know, how when bad things happen, the helpers are always there, or whatever Mr. Rogers says, and—"

Penelope paused again. I could see, even through my cracked screen, her lip begin to quiver.

"Pen," I said, trying not to grow frustrated, being that she had a big bandage on her head.

"He was so good, you know?" She wiped at her eyes. "He was such a good man. We need a new Mr. Rogers. Like, right now."

"I know we do," I soothed. "But Pen, what happened to you after that? Are you okay?"

"Yes, I'm fine, honestly. My knee's a little crushed and I guess I bonked my head and I have a tiny bit of a concussion. And my ribs hurt a little? But seriously, I'm lucky I was just going down Division and not, like, 405."

"Hey, Penelope?" Kai cut in. "I love you, and I'm glad

you're feeling okay, but I'm pretty sure you're not supposed to be using screens, if you have a concussion?"

"Oh, right, absolutely. Mikey's on his way and he'll do his growly thing if he sees me doing this. But I knew Aiden couldn't be truly mad at me if he saw my poor concussed face on video."

I opened my mouth to defend myself.

"Well," I said.

Master of Fine Arts, right here.

"I'm so sorry I didn't tell you Kai was coming!" Penelope yelled, all her words running together, and I didn't know if this frenzied shout was because of the blunt trauma to her head, or a practiced effort to make me less upset.

"I knew Kai wouldn't care if you were there, but I was worried you would say no. I decided to not say anything, in case the night fell through anyway, but...I've been trying to meet back up with Kai since he got back into town. And I haven't seen *you* in like, three weeks, either, Aiden, and I miss you, both of you, and I had all these ice breakers in my back pocket I was going to use, and—was he mad, Kai?"

"Oh, yeah," Kai grinned. "Like, *super* mad."

"I was *surprised*," I clarified, glaring at both of them. "A reasonable response, I think."

"Anyway," Kai said smoothly, "I really think you should go before Mikey, or the nurses, yell at you for being on Face-Time. Can you ask Mikey to text one of us when you get home?"

"Aye, Captain." She saluted. "And listen, I really am sorry for causing this cluster, but maybe you should both just head out? Get home safe? You know our city doesn't know how to handle snow."

"Yeah," Kai said. "We'll take care of ourselves. Love you."

"Love you, too." A pause. "Aiden?"

Oh. Right. "Love you, too."

Penelope blew a kiss, and was gone.

I flipped the phone screen down on the table and sat back in my chair, blowing out a breath. I stared out the window. This city of rain really was a mess when it came to snow. The fact that it was snowing at all right now was so typical. Snowstorms forecasted for weeks never materialized; snow no one expected shut down the city for days.

We should go.

Except...I was feeling embarrassed, somehow. I loved Pen, and clearly she knew me too well, but—*I knew Kai wouldn't care if you were there, but I was worried you would say no.* The fact that she had to keep it from me, and then call me on FaceTime, while concussed, to make sure I wasn't too mad. Which was a smart move, but still.

I wasn't a child. I could be a grownup about this. Kai and I were hanging out now. This was fine. And the snow wasn't even sticking yet. Or at least, I didn't think so. It was hard to tell what the outside world actually looked like through the Bud Light haze.

I looked at him. He had leaned back in his chair too, a much more acceptable distance between our faces again. I realized the silence had probably been stretching too long. He had an eyebrow raised in question, and it was super hot. Were my facial muscles even capable of quirking a brow like that? God.

"Well," I said again, my newest favorite word. I steeled my spine a bit. I could handle this. "We're already here. We might as well finish our drinks."

Kai stared back at me for a moment. It was possible I could actively feel my pits sweating, during that moment, but that was a plus of being at Moonie's. It already smelled kind of weird in here.

"Sure," he said eventually, wrapping his hand around his pint glass, all of his calloused fingers, his wonderful, knuckley knuckles.

I had this sudden flashback. Junior year of high school, I had overslept and was incredibly late to school. I was rushing to first period and my backpack just...broke. Like the zipper just fucking broke, out of nowhere, and my shit went everywhere.

And of course—*of course*, like it was a dumb teen movie—Kai Andrews was there. Somehow having chosen that exact moment to step into the hall on his way to the bathroom. So we were both scrambling to pick up all of my papers and books, and I couldn't believe it was actually happening the whole time. We kept reaching for the same things at the same time, so our hands kept bumping into each other, fingers brushing, knuckles knocking, and it was simultaneously the most mortifying and erotic experience of my young adult life. It probably took five minutes to clean up my stuff, but it felt like an hour, at least. And at one point, Kai shook his head and said, almost under his breath: "God, you're such a mess."

It was possible I went home and cried. And then maybe wrote a poem about Kai Andrews's knuckles.

He picked up his glass now and gave me a small smile.

"Sounds like a plan to me."

2.

KAI

I HATED how relieved I was, when Aiden didn't want to bolt at the first opportunity. It was snowing; Penelope was in the hospital. There was no reason to be here.

And yet.

I was glad Aiden didn't want to leave.

Which was...annoying.

I didn't know why this guy still irked me so much. Why it *mattered* that he still clearly hated me. Or maybe he didn't *hate* me. Was irritated by me. Actively disliked me. Did not want to be bothered by my presence.

And for some reason, even though I hadn't talked to him in five years, I still wanted him to change his mind.

It really hadn't been a surprise to me, when I walked in and saw the back of his head slouched over this table, that tightly curled black hair as unkempt as ever, the pale stretch of his neck above his sweater so oddly familiar. I knew he and Pen were still close. She would mention hanging out with him in our texts, or he'd pop up on her Instagram sometimes. Half of me maybe even expected him to be here.

But when I actually saw Aiden McCarstle in front of me, I felt almost...excited. That maybe he'd see me this time, years later, and for once in his goddamn life, he'd smile. Hold out his hand and say, "Hey, man. How's it going? Good to see you."

But of course, he'd only scowled. Exactly like he'd scowled every time I even glanced his way in high school.

I just didn't *get* it. I was always nice to him. I tried to be nice to everybody. I didn't think it would have bothered me if he was simply a jerk, another snooty smart kid rolling his eyes at the jock. Who cared.

But I knew Pen, and she wasn't friends with jerks. She loved Aiden McCarstle with her whole being.

There was also the fact that I'd read every poem he'd ever published in our school's literary magazine. And there was that time we were in pre-calc together senior year and sat next to each other, and I might have glanced at his notebook sometimes. Because he was always scribbling something. And somehow still easily managed an A. I worked harder than I'd ever worked at anything in that class to muster by with a B-. Aiden spent half of every class writing stanzas in his notebooks that had nothing to do with logarithms or exponential functions, and still kicked my ass.

Point was, his poems were always really good.

It made me inordinately happy, actually, that he was still working on writing stuff. That Aiden McCarstle hadn't turned into an accountant or something. Not that there was anything wrong with being an accountant. If pre-calc was any indication, he would have been good at that, too. It just wouldn't have felt right, for him.

Anyway, it was just...weird. That he wrote all these pretty things, but still scowled at me so much.

Even though he wasn't scowling at me anymore. He had

been kind of curled into himself, after he'd hung up with Penelope, in that way he always used to sit, staring out the window and unconsciously messing with a loose string on the sleeve of his sweater. It was black and white striped, the sweater, a little loose on Aiden, who was as skinny as ever. His face was a little leaner, a little sharper. His eyes a little older. But otherwise, he looked exactly the same.

He straightened now, tall and severe in his seat. Really *looked* at me. Like he was ready to do this now. Whatever *this* was.

And only then did it finally, finally occur to me.

I had to fight to not laugh.

Ever since I'd realized I was bi a few years ago, I'd been going through old memories in my head, trying to figure out when I should have known. All the things I'd hidden from myself. Realized I had probably been half in love with my co-captain on the team, Lars, for years. That really, a large majority of my entire soccer career from my first middle school camp through senior year had been slightly homoerotic.

McCarstle had never even crossed my mind.

But I saw it now, as I looked at his ratty sweater and those dark eyes staring me down from that assessing, intelligent face.

It had always bothered me that Aiden never liked me because Pen loved him and because he wrote really beautiful words. But I'd only just received the last piece of the puzzle, the one I hadn't been ready to admit to myself in high school.

I'd always thought he was kind of cute.

Oh my god. I was a shallow jock, after all.

I'd been pretty damn positive about the bisexual thing for at least three years now, but man. Rewriting the history you thought you'd known never ceased to be mind-blowing. And *hilarious.*

All this time, I'd had a crush on this guy and never even knew.

I leaned back and took another sip of my Sprite to hide my smile.

Moving back home had been harder, and weirder, and lonelier than I'd expected. I was going to let myself enjoy this night.

"So," I said. "We should probably figure out what we're going to sing."

Aiden's Very Serious Exterior he'd been giving me broke suddenly, a slash of panic crossing his face.

"What? No, you must've misheard me. I only said we'd finish a drink. We're not...I don't sing."

I tilted my head at him.

"You hang out at a karaoke bar, and you don't sing? Still trying *that* hard to not have fun, McCarstle?"

He frowned, forehead creasing.

He opened his mouth, and then snapped it shut. Full on glared at me. Which tickled something in my gut, made me want to laugh again. Did I *like* it when he looked angry with me? I guess I had needled him a bit there. Attraction was confusing.

Abruptly, Aiden stood and stalked across the room. He talked with the cute girl who had recently moved behind the high table in the corner, stationing herself behind a laptop. It was hard to tell from here, and Aiden only paused at the table for a minute at most, but I was pretty sure he smiled at her, his shoulders relaxing an inch as she smiled back.

Okay, no. I definitely still wanted him to smile at me.

When he returned, he threw a few small pieces of paper, along with two tiny golf pencils, onto the table.

"Fine," he said. "Let's do this. But I have a proposition. We get to choose the song the other person has to sing."

I smiled, grabbing a paper and one of the pencils.

"I'm game. So are we choosing songs the other would hate? Or think was funny, or something?"

"Yes," Aiden said, hunched over, already scribbling on his, one hand covering the paper, as if this was a school quiz and he thought I might cheat. He added, "Or whatever you want."

"And we don't tell each other what we chose."

"No." He flipped over his paper and sat back in his chair, crossing his arms over his chest.

I tapped my pencil against the slightly sticky tabletop. Suddenly, the options seemed limitless. There were simply so many songs Aiden McCarstle probably hated.

After a second, Aiden left the table again. I liked watching him march across the room, in those skinny dark jeans and that sweater that was definitely too big for him.

He plopped a huge black binder on the table.

"If you need inspiration," he said, before grabbing his beer and staring out the window again.

I flipped through the plastic pages, and holy shit, the options actually *were* limitless. This was more stressful than I anticipated. But then my eyes landed on something in the Cs, and it just seemed right, for Mr. Tortured Artist over there. It was a good song. And yeah, he'd probably hate it.

I wrote it down. Without looking at it, Aiden snatched up both pieces of paper and brought them up to the cute girl. He sighed when he sat back down.

"I might need more alcohol for this."

"I'll grab the next round," I said, standing. "What kind of beer are you drinking?"

I expected him to scowl again in protest, but he only nodded. "Whatever IPA's on tap. That'd be nice, thanks."

Having survived another visit with the intimidating butch bartender I'd met when I first walked into the bar, I returned to the table with two more pint glasses. I had been trying to think, the whole time I waited at the bar, of conversation starters that would help Aiden McCarstle not hate me. If Pen hadn't been concussed, I might have texted her for some of those ice breakers.

But before I even had a chance to try, Aiden surprised me.

"I heard about your mom, last year. I'm sorry."

I blinked.

"Oh." I took a sip of my soda. "Yeah. Thanks."

It had been a brain tumor. She'd been totally fine, preparing to retire and live her best life. And then within a year, she was gone. Just like that.

It was part of the reason I'd moved back home, to deal with the house. Aunt Tina had done a little bit, but I'd offered to do the rest. It was too much for Dad. And I wanted to do it.

I just didn't know why I hadn't done it sooner. The truth was, I'd wanted to turn around and come back home pretty much the moment I set foot in Klamath Falls five years ago. But I was learning so much at the forge down there, where I apprenticed, and they kept promoting me, and…I don't know. I learned how easy it was, sometimes, to get stuck in a place.

I should have moved back the moment Mom got the diagnosis. I came back a lot for visits, to check in during treatments, but I kept going back to Klamath Falls to "wrap things up," even though wrapping things up usually meant staring into space after work, rubbing my dog Jack's ears, and doing absolutely nothing. And then she was gone. I finally came back for good then.

For some reason, I came back after she'd already died. And I'd never be able to explain why.

"Sorry if that was weird, to bring it up," Aiden said, shifting in his seat. "I just remembered, all of a sudden, Penelope telling me about it."

"No," I said. "It's okay. I'm glad you did. Most people I know simply pretend it never happened, so. It's good, to acknowledge that it did."

"Yeah." Aiden nodded.

And all of my conversation starters had disappeared out of my head, now. But I felt oddly more comfortable. I meant what I'd said; I actually was glad Aiden had mentioned it. It brought us a little more up to speed with each other, in the here and now of our post-high school realities. And it made me feel a little better about him, that he cared enough to remember Pen telling him about it, that he cared enough to say something.

In general, I'd learned I could always breathe a little better, whenever someone did mention Mom. Like the grief moved partially out into the open air instead of existing solely in my brain. Always hurt more, but still gave me more space to breathe anyway.

"So Mikey," I said, after another long sip of my drink. "I haven't actually met him yet. He a good guy?"

"Oh." Aiden's eyebrows lifted at the change in topic, but his shoulders relaxed, like they had when he'd talked to the karaoke jockey. "Yeah. He's great, actually. They met that summer when Pen worked at Trader Joe's?" A small wash of pink graced the tops of his cheeks. "Sorry, you probably know that already."

"No, it's okay." I shook my head. "I haven't been around; it's different. I only get the texted version of things, or the Instagram version of things. I want to know."

"Yeah. Okay. He's kind of goofy. Like, would gladly wear those Hawaiian shirts even when he wasn't at the store, you know?" Aiden shrugged. "But I don't know; he's really sweet. Loves Pen a lot."

"He sounds perfect for her."

"Yeah." Aiden grinned a little into his beer, and my stomach swooped. It was the first time his lips had curved that way, at least in front of me, since I first sat down. And it was lovely.

"All right, friends who have endured this fine wintry mix out here to join us tonight!"

The cute KJ boomed over the room on the mic. My head swiveled automatically toward her and the large dance floor next to her station, a disco ball shining neon lights onto its empty surface.

"Time to get the party started with everyone's favorite Moonie's performer...Lily!"

A woman wearing an aqua colored dress decorated with large purple polka dots walked to the dance floor, taking the mic and launching into a rather impressive rendition of "Before He Cheats."

She made me smile, all of her bright colors and her swagger.

Her joy also made me start to doubt my song choice for McCarstle.

Aiden made an *a-ha* sound in his throat, and I turned back to him, an eyebrow raised in question.

"Oh, sorry. I just realized something. It's not important

at all. But this woman's partner, over there." He pointed with his chin toward a person sitting along the wall, who was staring at the blonde woman singing Carrie Underwood like they wanted to eat her. "They've looked kind of familiar every time I'm here, and it just clicked. I think they're a professor at my school. I've never had them, but I've seen them around. Anyway. Now I know where they get their fashion sense."

I could see what he meant. The professor wore a skirt that wasn't as colorful as Lily's dress, but still chic in its own way.

"What school do you go to?" I turned back toward Aiden.

"Oh, just the university downtown." He slumped back into his chair again.

"And...grad school," I said slowly, realizing I knew absolutely nothing about grad school. "Is that a full-time thing? Or do you work somewhere too?"

He ran a hand over his face, like even the mention of school exhausted him.

"Yeah, it's pretty full-time, but I do...um. I walk dogs, on the side."

I almost choked on my Sprite.

"You walk dogs?"

He blushed fully now, and it was so pretty, that heat filling the sharp lines of his face.

"Yes," he said, sounding distinctly irritated again, and I seriously had to stop being turned on by that. "I don't know if you remember Amy Bishop, from school? She runs her own dog walking business, and..." He shrugged. "It helps pay the rent. Sometimes."

God, I was tickled by this. I wondered what McCarstle's favorite kind of dog was. I pictured him holding a wiggly, snot-nosed puggle up to his serious face, and I couldn't even hold in my smile.

We watched two other people perform. The first chose an old Blink-182 song, which made me laugh, while the other shouted a slightly cringey version of "Single Ladies." We continued to make small talk. I was beginning to feel pretty good, like maybe Aiden McCarstle didn't completely hate me, after all.

And then the KJ called his name.

3.

"HURT."

As written by Trent Reznor. As performed by Johnny fucking Cash.

Otherwise known as the most depressing thing ever fucking recorded.

Who even performed "Hurt" at karaoke? Someone who was able to sound like Johnny Cash, maybe, but let me tell you, that wasn't me, and otherwise it was only awkward. I was already up here, and I had a mic in my hand, and I had promised myself to act like a fucking adult, so I wasn't going to stomp out of the room like a pissed off child, even though I was definitely pissed off.

So I sang. If you could count trying to get through this miserable song as singing, which I didn't. It was elongating syllables in the most painful way possible. In front of a room full of strangers. It was possible I'd never be able to return to Moonie's again.

I had no idea what song I'd thought Kai would choose for me, but I definitely hadn't expected *this*. Did he think I was that much of a cliché? Did he think I still sat in my room listening to shit like this and smoking clove cigarettes?

And to think I'd actually started to feel a little soft toward him, after I'd remembered his mom had died. After we'd managed twenty minutes of acceptable conversation. After he started looking at me in this way that was...faintly intriguing.

Of course, I hadn't seen the guy in five years. Maybe I forgot some details about him. Maybe that was how he looked at everyone.

Not that it mattered how Kai Andrews looked at me, anyway.

In any case, I felt like a dumb joke for every excruciating minute of that song, and I'd been wrong. Kai Andrews wasn't the goodest kid. He was an asshole.

I returned the mic to Kiki without looking her in the eye and stomped over to the bar. I still had half of my beer back at the table, and I didn't know if I could truly afford that many more drinks on my own tab, but the bar was as far away as I could currently get from Kai. Plus, the bartender here was the best. Maybe if I had a minute of being surrounded by her badass, cold-as-ice vibe it'd help me put myself back together again.

"Another?" she asked.

"Yeah." I pushed my palms against the edge of the bar.

"That was a weird song choice, man."

I shook my head, sighed.

"Yeah."

"I liked it."

I met her silver-blue eyes over the taps. She nodded and shoved the beer my way. As soon as I grabbed it she turned back to her till, dismissing me.

Yeah. That had helped.

I took a sip off the top before squaring my shoulders. Nothing for it.

I fell back into my seat across from Kai. Who at least had the good sense to look chagrined.

"Hey," he said immediately, leaning forward, "Aiden, I—"

"And now, good folks of The Moonlight Café," Kiki sang into her mic. "Help me welcome up to the stage...Kai!"

Kai's lips set into a fine line before he stood.

I leaned back in my seat, downing the rest of my beer(s).

Maybe watching Kai also humiliate himself would make the night a bit better. And then I could go home, and pretend this had all been a strange fever dream.

But of course not.

Because while Kai's face still looked tense as he walked onto the dance floor, soon, the dulcet tones of Miley Cyrus's "Party in the USA" burst out of the speakers. And Kai's face morphed into an easy, relaxed grin.

He jumped into the first verse right on beat.

He got more into it with every single line. Started boogying around the floor, his smile somehow perpetually growing. He...seemed to know every word? Like, he was barely looking at the screen. He rubbed his stomach, hunched over his shoulders when Miley talked about being nervous, homesick. During the first chorus, he threw the hand that wasn't holding the mic in the air, waved it around like he just didn't care.

He was having the time of his life.

Fuck me.

I didn't know why I thought it would be funny to watch him sing a song like this. The only song I knew for certain that Kai Andrews loved was a real weird one from the '70s or '80s or something, so I thought a solid 2000s pop tune would be a decent choice for prime embarrassment, especially for someone like him. Someone made of bulging biceps and knuckles that made me shiver. But of course. Of course Kai Andrews was the one all-American boy somehow bred without a shred of toxic masculinity.

And the crowd was loving it. Well, if you could call it a crowd. The bar was half empty, probably because of the snow. Still, everyone else present, except for me and the bartender, emptied their seats, the butterflies flying away for all of them, nodding their heads like yeah. Kiki jammed behind her table. The blonde with the killer voice, who worked at the veterinary clinic I brought clients to sometimes, and her professor beau got down at the edge of the dance floor, beaming at each other and laughing. I felt weirdly jealous of both of them, their ease with each other, with their own bodies. The joy that was palpable between them.

It was almost as embarrassing, somehow, sitting in the dark corner of the bar by myself as it had been when I'd been standing up there singing Johnny Cash. But I couldn't make my feet get up and join the dance floor. Even as Kai waved a hand at me, beckoning me to do just that. Even as Kai fucking *winked* at me. Which made me feel like this wasn't merely a fever dream; I'd actually entered some bizarre alternate universe. But I just...couldn't.

Kai dropped his hand, shook his head at me. Still smiling, he turned his attention to a guy who *was* winking back. Who was slinking around the dance floor, weaving closer and closer to Kai with each hip shimmy. He was wearing a too-tight t-shirt, which, come on; he knew there was a blizzard outside, right? Maybe he was good looking. I didn't know. It was hard to tell at Moonie's, sometimes, who was a creep and who was awesome. There was this dangerous, queer edge to this bar, where it felt like things could implode into a fantasy or a disaster at any moment. Which was why I loved it, of course.

But it was *my* weird escape. Not Kai's. He didn't fit here.

Except, according to the dance floor, he did.

And Kai was...Kai was smiling back at the maybe-hot/maybe-a-hot-mess guy. They circled around each other as Kai sang, came dangerously close to touching.

And wow, I hated it.

My jealousy had a bitter taste in my mouth, like it knew it was illogical but was fully ready to poison me anyway. And that cemented it. This had been a fun experiment and all, reigniting an old, hopeless crush for absolutely no reason.

But I needed to find an exit from this night, and soon.

KAI

IT WAS OFFICIAL.

Karaoke was *the best.* All caps: BEST.

I couldn't believe I'd never done it before.

I bounced back to the table, and I knew, somewhere in my brain, that Aiden looked like he wanted to punch something—my face, probably—but I was still too full of adrenaline from the Miley dance party to be overly put out by it this time.

"Well," he said, reaching behind him for his coat before my butt had even hit the seat, "This has been great, but—"

"Wait!" I practically shouted, my smile sliding fast into a frown. "Wait. You can't leave yet. Hold on." I grabbed one of the extra slips of paper and a pencil. "I have to make it up to you, the 'Hurt' thing. I misplayed the game, obviously. I'll do better this round, okay? One more round."

Aiden hesitated, still turned in his seat. He bit his lip, which he always used to do when he was deep into scribbling in his notebooks, truly lost to the outside world. The fact that I had noticed this lip biting, that I remembered it in precise detail, made my new bi-memory smack the inside of my brain and chuckle.

"Come on," I pushed. "You still have most of that beer left."

He let go of his coat. Rather obviously reluctant, but still, he let go of his coat.

"You won't choose a song that people listen to when they're contemplating self-harm?"

"No." I shook my head emphatically. "Promise."

He grumbled, but he reached for a slip of paper, too.

"Fine."

More lip biting. And then he wrote something down. I wrote something too, something better, and grabbed both sheets of paper and ran them up to the KJ, whose name I'd learned was Kiki, which was the absolute perfect name for her. I couldn't wait to get to know her better. Miley had inspired confidence in me. I could make Aiden have fun with this night, too; I knew it.

"That guy was flirting with you," Aiden burst out when I sat back down, surprising me once again. Maybe I should keep leaving the table, keep seeing what he'd say next, each time I returned. "During your song. You were flirting back."

I nodded, slowly.

"You shouldn't do that." He frowned. "It's not nice."

"Ah." I took a sip of my soda, cleared my throat, the Miley adrenaline replaced with that now-familiar *here we go* feeling roiling through my gut. I'd learned it was best to get it out of my mouth quickly, whenever an opportunity presented itself, before I lost my nerve. "I guess I should tell you. I'm bi."

Aiden froze, like a deer caught in headlights. It was cute, this look on his face, but I was also surprisingly uncomfortable. I worried, suddenly, that this admission would somehow make Aiden mad. One more reason for McCarstle to hate me, even though I knew that wasn't a rational fear. But maybe he wouldn't believe me, think I was playing him. Or...I didn't know. I was still relatively new at this.

"So," he said, forehead bunched in confusion. "You're not with Mei anymore?"

At this, I laughed, my nerves soothing a little.

"No. Mei and I broke up before graduation, Aiden. Pretty sure she's been engaged to her college boyfriend for like a year. Although," I added, "I could still be bi even if I was still with her."

"I know," Aiden said quickly, covering his face with his hands for a second. "I know. Oh my god. I can't believe Kai Andrews is mansplaining queerness to me."

I laughed.

"You kind of asked for it."

"I know. I'm just...processing. Were you always—"

"No," I said. "I wasn't closeted in high school or anything. Or, well, maybe I was, to myself." I played absently with one of the golf pencils. "For the record, I do not recommend discovering you're bisexual while living in Klamath Falls."

Aiden winced.

"Yeah. That sounds...bleak."

I nodded solemnly. "That's a good way to put it, yeah."

"So are you seeing anyone now?"

Aiden's face flushed after he said this, and he quickly sat back in his chair, fidgeting with his phone. Like he hadn't meant to say it, and it had just slipped out somehow.

"I mean," he said, "Not that it's any of my business."

I stared at him for a minute.

Interesting.

"No," I answered. "Are you? You never really dated anyone back in high school, from what I can remember."

"No." He shook his head. "I mean, I *have* dated people. I'm not a total loser. But I—" He wrapped his hands around his beer. "No."

"I don't think you're a loser," I said. "I never did. You know that, right?"

His eyes flicked to mine, one quick, lightning bolt glance.

"Let's not talk about high school," he said, staring out the window.

"All right." I shrugged. And thought a bit more about what he'd said. "Although you know, I just have to say, I don't think dating history has anything to do with being a loser or not."

He leaned forward, covering his face with his hands again, keeping them there this time.

"Ugh," he mumbled through his fingers. "*Fine*, Mr. Magnanimous. You are right. We are all wonderful rainbows."

I wanted to pry his fingers away from his face. And then kiss him, maybe.

Instead, I laughed, in sort of a helpless way. And then I just fucking asked it.

"Why do you hate me so much?"

Aiden froze again. Peeked at me through his fingers.

He dropped his hands and leaned back in his chair.

"I..." He looked down at his palms. "I don't."

And then Kiki called his name again.

5.

I FELT RATTLED as I took the mic once more from Kiki.

Why do you hate me so much?

I guess I should tell you. I'm bi.

There weren't enough people at Moonie's tonight. Kiki was cycling through our songs too fast; I wasn't ready to be back up here again. I didn't want people looking at me, didn't want *Kai* looking at me under these bright ass lights. It felt like he'd already looked at me too much tonight.

I had whiplash from all the different things pinging around in my brain, all the different things I'd felt in…what? The hour, less? That I'd been hanging out with Kai Andrews. I was probably being an asshole to him, and I didn't want to be. I wanted to be like the blonde woman in the purple polka dotted dress. I wanted to be the badass bartender who didn't give a fuck. I wanted to be Kai, singing Miley, getting everyone to their feet. I wanted—

Oh. I didn't have time to think about everything else I wanted, because "I Knew You Were Trouble" was on the screen. And I had about five seconds until I'd have to open my mouth and sing.

Kai had given me Taylor Swift.

Did he...did he know? That I had always secretly been a Swiftie? Was this a gift? Because now I felt kind of bad, about the next song I'd chosen for him. I—

Damn, okay, here came the lyrics. And—oh god, I loved this song.

Still trying that hard to not have fun, McCarstle?

This was my chance, then. To stop being what Kai Andrews thought I was. To stop retreating back into my high school self just because I was suddenly confronted with my high school nemesis/crush. Who was apparently bi now. Whatever. Time to prove I was an adult. By...singing the shit out of Taylor Swift.

And I did. I *did*.

Fun Dress woman, her professor with the skirt, they got to the dance floor first. Kiki came out from behind her KJ station, shook her hips at me. With me? No, I still didn't really know how to shake my hips. But I was moving, a little. I was having fun, dammit.

This song was a fucking *jam*.

I let myself glance at Kai once. He hadn't moved from the table, but I wasn't bothered that he wasn't on the dance floor. It almost felt...respectful, like he was letting me have my moment. But that was probably me projecting. He was smiling, though. I could tell, even from up here, even though he had his fist over his mouth. Like he was trying to hold in an even bigger smile from escaping.

I liked that. I liked being the focus of Kai Andrews's smiles. Maybe that was why I was so angry at him all the time in high school, not just because he was so perfect and so different from me. But because his smiles were always directed at other people. And I wanted them all for me. As illogical, as selfish as that was. And maybe it was only happenstance, that I was alone with him at this bar tonight, that he happened to be smiling at me now.

But he was right. Like he was right about everything. I had spent an inordinate amount of time in my life holding myself back from things. Although, in my own defense, I didn't always see it like that. I wasn't holding myself back from the world; I was simply better at standing in the shadows and observing it. I was *good* at it, observing the world. Writing it down.

It wasn't *sad*, or this tragic way of being; it was just...different. I always liked coming to Moonie's and sitting in the back with Penelope, listening to everyone else sing all their favorite songs, off-key and enthusiastic. It didn't matter that I didn't normally pick up the mic myself. I could still feel it. I still showed up. I was still a part of it, in my own way.

And yet.

Maybe I should take advantage of opportunities when they were presented to me. Like gorgeous men's smiles. To accept the invitation to the dance floor, to put down the pen, to step out of the comfortable shadows. If only just for a little while.

I didn't know what to do with my own smile, though, when the song finally finished and I returned to the table. It was embarrassing, but I couldn't quite keep it off my face. And I apparently wasn't quite brave enough yet, to throw it directly at Kai. Like he had done for me.

"That was a better choice, then," he said. And even though I couldn't make eye contact right then, I could *hear* the smile in his voice, and that was somehow worse than seeing it.

"Yes," I answered. "I, uh. I love Taylor."

Kai chuckled, and it was low and rumbly and extremely pleasing to my core.

"Good," he said.

And before I even had the chance to fully regain my breath, Kiki said Kai's name again.

"Oh," I said quickly. "Kai. Uh."

I had made him promise to not choose any more sad sack songs for me. But I hadn't made that promise in return, for him.

He looked at me as he stood, raising an eyebrow again.

Shit.

"I'm sorry," I said, biting my lip. "In advance."

6.

KAI

I BLEW out a breath as I stared at the screen.

Well. This wasn't fair.

But then again, I'd given Aiden "Hurt." Maybe this was completely fair.

From the corner of my eye, I saw the blonde woman in the bright dress—Lily—stand from their table, reach for her jacket. The idea popped into my head, and I had approximately ten seconds to pull it off.

I rushed to the table and whispered my plea. Lily hesitated, looked over at her partner. They nodded at her with a little smile. She turned, squeezed my shoulder, and walked up to get the second mic from Kiki.

Thank god.

So when I had to start singing about secret chords and David pleasing the Lord, about minor falls and major lifts, at least I wasn't alone. Her voice next to me was gentle and strong, and I focused on her kind face as we made it through the verses. I had learned, over the last few years, that it often was strangers who made the best saviors.

To be clear, I loved "Hallelujah." There probably

wasn't a soul alive who wasn't moved by Jeff Buckley's singular voice. I loved "Hurt," too. Sad men covering sad men. I hadn't been completely trying to make fun of Aiden, although it occurred to me, of course, once he had started singing and scowling through it, that he probably thought that was my sole intent. But just like this one, "Hurt" was a beautiful song. And Aiden deserved beautiful songs.

Although, yeah, probably not necessarily in karaoke form.

I hoped I was making it up to him now, even if I'd grabbed assistance to do it. It was weird, adjusting to this melodic lament after Aiden had just rocked so hard to "I Knew You Were Trouble"—which, damn, had been an amazing thing to witness—he was *so, so* close to smiling at me, I could tell—but Lily and her wonderful voice helped me get there. And soon, I didn't feel awkward at all, standing in the middle of this half-empty, run-down bar in my hometown and singing this sad, sad song. I only felt...every little bit of it.

When it was over, and we handed back our mics, Lily walked over to her partner. Who had been leaning against a wall near the door, watching intently the whole time. They handed her her coat, and wrapped their arms around her shoulders. They kissed her forehead. And then they both turned and left.

And I just stood there, at the corner of the dance floor, watching this small, tender moment.

And I suddenly missed my mom so much it took my breath away.

I turned, walked toward the opposite corner of the room, away from our table. I thought I'd seen a door back here, by the restrooms—yes, there it was. A crooked arrow was hand drawn on a piece of notebook paper, taped to the wall. *PATIO*.

The icy air hit my face as soon as I stepped outside, a welcome shock. I walked to the edge of the small wooden platform, past the picnic tables with frozen ashtrays, their heaps of ash and cigarette butts dusted with snow. It was a covered patio, but the powdery flurries and harsh wind blew through anyway. I stood at its furthest edge, staring out into the distance.

The snow was sticking now, probably had been for some time. There was really nothing else out here. What a funny place for Penelope and Aiden to hang out. I stared at the snow stacking up on a vast lot full of construction vehicles behind the bar, behind a barbed-wire fence, their industrial forms like robotic ghosts.

We should go home soon.

I took a slow, deep breath, the cold almost painful in my lungs.

This moment didn't make much sense. "Hallelujah" had nothing to do with my mom. Although she had always loved music, hummed random snippets of random things all the way until the end.

I had started kissing her on the forehead like that, though. Like Lily's professor had kissed her, before they walked into the night.

Leaning over the hospital bed. Resting my mouth on her forehead for just a moment. It felt like a safe way to say I was sorry, that I wasn't there enough, that this was happening at all. Both of our eyes closed, my touch focused on one part of her that hadn't been worn away, that still felt warm and soft and good. Squeezing her hand, feeling how frail it had gotten, always felt so much scarier.

It wasn't ideal, that this was hitting me now, here, but

I'd learned grief never was ideal. Never did make much sense. It hit you when you least expected it, but when you most expected it, too. It was always sort of there. You just didn't have control over when it got loud.

But when it did, I'd decided to hear it. And right now that meant getting some air, even if it was fucking freezing, and simply waiting for it to eventually turn back into a whisper.

The door creaked open behind me, slammed shut.

"Hey."

I glanced back once, to see Aiden lean against the wall next to the door, cross his arms over his chest. He pulled his sweater up over his hands, shivered.

"Hey." I stared back into the snowy wasteland. "Sorry. Just needed a minute."

"Yeah, of course. It's fine."

And then he only stood there. Giving me space. Letting me be quiet.

It was nice, actually. Which was a little surprising. He had definitely wanted to hit me, or bolt, or something, when I first walked into this bar. But I had this gut instinct, right then, that Aiden McCarstle would stand out on this dark, dilapidated patio with me in the snow for an hour, if I wanted him to.

And I found I wanted him to. Or at least, I didn't mind. I was feeling kind of confused, in general, about Aiden McCarstle. But it felt okay that he was out here.

My shoulders drooped. My breath was a white cloud in front of me.

"She went so fast," I said eventually. "We knew the diagnosis wasn't good, but I still didn't expect her to be gone so fast. I think maybe that's why it feels like it's still happening, sometimes. Like my brain's still catching up."

I looked down at the splintered boards under my feet.

"I wish I had moved back before she died. But I didn't. And now I'm just...here, and she's not. I've been wanting to come back home for forever and now that I'm here, I just feel...off. Like maybe I don't fit here anymore."

Aiden took a long breath behind me.

"That sounds really hard, Kai."

"Yeah." I kicked at a patch of ice. "Sorry. The song just...got to me."

"Understandable," Aiden said. A pause. "I'm sorry."

"Don't be."

"I think...I think you fit here, though. It probably feels different, being here now. But that's all it is. Different. Not wrong."

I wiped my knuckles against my eyes.

"Yeah."

We stood in silence a few minutes longer. I blinked, a lot, and made some kind of weird noises, between my chest and my nose, until I was sure the tears were at bay.

And then I squared my shoulders and turned, finally walking toward him, where he still stood under the one spotlight attached to the outside of the building, shining weak and yellowish onto the dark patio.

He straightened as I approached, stuffing his hands in his pockets.

"We should head out," I said. "It's starting to stick out there."

Aiden swallowed. I watched the bob of his Adam's apple, half of his face in shadow.

"Probably, we should," he said, slowly, like he wasn't one hundred percent certain of what he was about to say. "But...I have one more proposition."

Now, I knew, I knew, that Aiden McCarstle likely did not

mean *that* kind of proposition. But something about when he said it this time—maybe it was the fact that I had just gotten overly honest, and he had been kind of nice about it. And the fact that we were the only ones out here, and even though everything around us was pretty objectively ugly, it also felt a little bit holy, with the snow and the silence and the shadows. Or the fact that we were simply probably standing too close, and the wind was blowing one of his curls over his forehead, and he looked so cold that it felt vulnerable, like he wanted me to wrap my arms around him to keep him comfortable. Or I just wanted to do that.

Whatever the reason, something felt charged between us. Like something had shifted. Something brought in on the dry, icy wind. Something that begged for warmth.

"One more round," Aiden said. "We still pick each other's song, but...we pick something we know the other one loves. No more of..." He waved a hand. "Whatever this was. Just our favorite songs."

I studied him. I still felt a little fragile, wanted to make sure he wasn't fucking with me. I didn't think he would, especially after this, out here. But still.

"You think you know one of my favorite songs?"

He nodded, quick, sure.

"Yes." And then, "If you can't think of one for me, it's okay; I can—"

"No," I said. "I got one."

"Oh," he said, a little surprised. "Okay. Then, yeah."

He bit his lip.

"All right," I said. "One more round."

7.

AIDEN

THE BAR HAD EMPTIED out even more when we stepped back inside. The place felt barely alive at this point, and I almost panicked, worried we'd be shuffled out before I could make it up to Kai, and we'd have to leave with only the memories of this weird, kind of mean game I'd created. Where I'd made him sing a song that made him sad about his dead mom.

"Hey," I said to Kiki. "Can we still put in a couple requests?"

"Yeah," she nodded. "If you want. But I think we're closing up shop here soon, so make it quick."

I hurried back to the table, scribbled Kai's final song on a slip of paper.

"I'll take them to her," Kai said, and he snatched my paper and walked back to Kiki's table. Where he proceeded to talk with her for longer than it should have taken to drop off our last song requests, especially if they were in a hurry to shut the place down. Kiki typed something on the laptop; Kai leaned over the table to look at the screen. He smiled, nodded; she gave him a thumbs up.

What the hell.

We were quieter when he got back to the table. I sucked down the rest of my beer; he sipped on his vodka soda, or whatever he was drinking. Things felt different, more tense between us, but not necessarily in a bad way. Just in a way that made me itch, wanting to find the right words to describe whatever it was that was happening. Maybe we were friends now. I didn't know. Maybe I'd figure it out later, tomorrow, tonight when I got home, whenever I could get a pen in my hand. I often couldn't actually figure something out until I was physically in the act of writing it down. Then, somehow, between my brain and the paper, I found it.

Hollywood got up to sing an Al Green song. I didn't know what Hollywood's actual name was; that was just what everyone called him. He was an old Filipino man who showed up at Moonie's sometimes, always by himself, always in a full three piece suit. He'd stroll in, sing some random oldie, absolutely kill it, and then immediately leave.

And that was why Penelope and I loved Moonie's.

I hoped Hollywood got home safe tonight, in the snow.

And then Kiki said Kai's name.

I exhaled as he got up to the mic. For the first time all night, I felt truly nervous. Maybe he wouldn't be up to the song, after getting down about his mom; maybe—

"Oh, *fuck* yeah," Kai said into the mic as the song came onto the screen.

And he laughed.

His eyes looked so, so happy, the chocolate of his irises shining under the lights, that my chest expanded with this feeling, like maybe I had done the exact right thing for the first time in my entire life.

It was called "Mr. Blue Sky" by ELO. The Electric Light Orchestra. And when it started, it didn't matter that there were only three other people left in this bar. Kai performed it like he was looking for an Oscar nomination. Or maybe, more accurately, a Tony. He used the entirety of the dance floor, kicking his feet around, pumping his shoulders up and down in rhythm with the steady, persistent percussion. He spread his arms out at one point and swooped around Moonie's like he was a bird about to take flight. A really buff bird, in a lavender colored sweatshirt, singing about...well, I had no idea what this song was about. It was a strange song.

During a brief break between a verse and a chorus, Kai pointed toward the bar and grinned. I followed his gaze, and to my actual shock, saw the butch bartender nodding her head along with the beat. She rolled her eyes when Kai pointed at her, but it didn't even seem to be in a particularly grumpy way. When the song dived into another verse, as she continued drying off empty pint glasses, she sang along under her breath.

I had never seen her sing along with *anything*.

It took me a second to move my focus back to the dance floor, where Kai was still almost-floating, almost-flying, a glowing island in the middle of this dark, crummy, wonderful little bar.

There was one point where the vocals got kind of robotic and synthesized, and Kai froze, holding his hand over the mic as he sang in an attempt to imitate it, and it was so deeply dorky that I was honestly flabbergasted.

The last minute of the song was only this high-pitched choir making random noises, and Kai just kept bouncing around the dance floor through it, smiling, looking like he was super stoned, until he eventually threw the mic back at Kiki before the last piano notes had tinkled away.

He sprinted back to the table.

"How," he demanded, still grinning. "How did you know?"

I shrugged, suddenly self-conscious.

"It's your pump up song."

And now I was blushing.

"I *know* it's my pump up song!" He hit the table. "But how did *you* know that?"

"Um." I wiped my palms on my jeans. "You gave us a ride, that one time. Me and Pen."

"I did?" He frowned, forehead creasing. I tried to sink further down in my seat, horrified he didn't remember this very important moment in our non-relationship, when I so clearly did.

"Yeah. It was before one of your games. So..."

I used to give Penelope a ride home back in the day, on the rare occasion she didn't have some activity after school, French Club or GSA or running tech for the school plays. And of course, on one of those rare days junior year, my ancient Volkswagen Jetta wouldn't start. I couldn't remember now, what had even been wrong with it, if it had been the battery, or the starter, or a flat tire. There was always something wrong with it; every cent of my paychecks from the dog boarding kennel I worked at part-time during high school went back into that piece-of-shit car. But it was my one piece of freedom, that car. So I loved it like a child.

What I *do* remember from that day is the moment Penelope's eyes lit up as she saw Kai walk into the student lot. Before I could stop her, she was waving both arms at him.

"Kai'll give us a ride, I bet," she said.

And I had to turn, and watch him wave back, and walk toward us in his soccer uniform, the laces of his cleats tied and slung around his neck. Those soccer shorts always seemed an *inch* too short, showing just slightly too much of Kai Andrews's sculpted quads for my poor, extremely gay teenaged system.

"I would," he'd said. "But I have a game. Have to be on the pitch in ten. Could give you both a ride home afterward, though?"

No one calls it a pitch here, I thought.

But Penelope had nodded enthusiastically.

"I always mean to get to more of your games anyway! You're not busy, right, Aiden?" And then she'd shoved my shoulder, the traitor. "Let's go watch some futbol!"

Kai had used the five minutes it took to drive from our high school to the soccer field, a few blocks away, to blast "Mr. Blue Sky." His pump up song, he'd called it. And then Penelope and I had watched him play soccer, and it had been a beautiful fall day, and he had scored two goals, and I had been miserably jealous of all his teammates who got to hug him.

He drove us home afterward, as promised, and I sat silently in his back seat, surrounded by the smell of him— sweat, and grass, and glory—and tried to hold it in my lungs for the rest of the night.

"Huh." Kai sat back in his chair now, took a last sip of his gin and tonic or whatever it was. "That makes sense then. God, I haven't listened to that song in forever."

He flicked his eyes to mine, and they looked darker and sparklier all at once, somehow, than they had all night. Like stars in a midnight sky.

"Thanks for that, Aiden."

"And it looks like this next one will be our last song of

the night, folks," Kiki shouted, and I jumped. "Aiden, get back up here! Everyone else, make sure you get home safely tonight!"

I clutched the mic to my chest after Kiki handed it to me, blinking as I turned to face the screen. A bittersweet feeling was fizzling through my veins. This night had been weird as hell, but...well, I was kind of sad to see it end. I wasn't one hundred percent positive, but I was pretty sure I was glad it had happened.

And then I saw the song on the screen.

I stopped blinking. Simply stared.

Oh...my god.

I hardly had time to process before the first frenzied guitar chords smashed into my consciousness. I didn't think they even had this song available as a choice for karaoke. No, I *knew* they didn't have this song; I'd tried looking it up in the binder before, but—

Here it was, on the screen. "Aside" by The Weakerthans.

My favorite fucking song, from when I was in high school.

I didn't have time to even begin to wrap my head around the fact that Kai knew this, a fact that made no sense, being that I had hardly talked to Kai Andrews about anything in high school, and certainly not my favorite song. I had never driven *him* home in my Jetta; he had never sat next to me and listened to these lyrics curl around him like they had always curled around me, sure and snug and true.

God, I barely had to look at the screen. I knew them all by heart.

And in a beat, I was time traveling.

Every line hit me in the chest, just like they always had, but there was this part where John Samson sings about being lonely and unconsoled and then, in the same breath: *I am so much better than I used to be.*

It was so easy, looking back, to be who you were supposed to be in high school. To slip inside a certain mold. To be angry, to be lonely, to be viciously full of feeling. I knew what was expected of me: the grades, the quiet, the constant, barely contained, unnameable heartache. Knew it was all just this test I had to get through, and then I'd get out.

It felt easy to hate Kai in high school, to hate him and be a little in love with him all at the same time. Because it didn't matter. It was so easy to believe that nothing mattered, as long as you got through.

And then you graduated, and the real world crashed in.

And it wasn't enough anymore. To simply hide behind your favorite songs, in the shitty poetry you scribbled on every blank surface you could find. The life you'd been waiting to escape into for your entire journey through the public school system was suddenly just *there*. And it turned out you had to...do something with it.

I had spent the last five years of my life trying to do something with it, but never knowing if I was doing it quite right. Maybe not exactly failing, but flailing. Waiting for a clear, understandable path that never appeared. A ship without an anchor.

But on the dance floor of Moonie's, singing along to my favorite song, somewhere around the first chorus I let it all go. My uncertainty about my life choices. Whatever had happened in this bar tonight. Everything else disappeared, and I let myself love the frantic, painful youth of this song again, its relentless joy. And inside its fuzzy guitars and fast drum beats, I let myself love myself a little, too, the Aiden who had loved this song at seventeen, and the Aiden who loved this song still, now.

Because I *was* so much better than I used to be.

Sure, I hated grad school. I hated that I was in grad school at all, that I knew I would hate it but applied anyway, because I hadn't known what else to do. And *attending grad school, pursuing my MFA* was at least a tangible thing I could tell people—my parents, my friends, Kai Andrews—when asked what I was doing with my life.

But I had still lived, these last five years, more than I had let myself back then. I still preferred the shadows, when it came to things like karaoke. I still mostly felt anchorless. But I had grabbed hold of life how I could, in my own ways. I had taken long road trips, up into the Olympic rainforests, down the Pacific Coast Highway, down to Baja California. I had stood underneath the shelter of redwoods. I had felt the ocean cover my toes. I had fallen in love.

It hadn't worked out, in the end, with Niall, but I had still been in love once, something that had felt impossible to me back in high school, and that counted for something. I had had poems published in Tin House, in Ploughshares, in Lambda, in The Iowa Review, and I knew poems weren't exactly the same as building ships with your bare hands, but they meant something to me.

I wasn't a child. I *had* tried to have fun. I had been something, in the brief but long space between now and the last time Kai Andrews knew me. I couldn't explain out loud, exactly, what that something was—only the words in my notebooks could—but a wild part of me, just then, wanted to tell Kai Andrews about some of it, the memories I had managed to make for myself. Or at least try to tell him some of it. Because maybe he would listen. Maybe he would smile, just for me.

Not right now, though. Because this moment, these lyrics and this song and this feeling, were all mine.

Even though it was there, in the periphery of my mind, the whole time.

The knowledge that this moment was one Kai Andrews had given me.

When it was over, I handed the mic back to Kiki and walked to our table, feeling raw and open now that the song was over, unsure what to do next.

But Kai was on top of it. He stood as I came near. Handed me my coat.

"Let's cash out," he said.

At the bar, it felt like we were standing too close.

"Okay," I said when the bartender turned to run Kai's card. "How did *you* know? About that song?"

Kai drummed his fingers on the bar.

"Senior year, we were in pre-calc?"

I nodded. As if I didn't remember sitting next to Kai Andrews, feeling his presence, every damn day of that year.

"You were always writing the lyrics of that song on the cover of your book." He shrugged. "And it was—"

He paused. I turned my body toward his, gave him my full attention.

"It was different, when you wrote the lyrics, than when you wrote your poems. When you wrote poems, you were all—" He scrunched his shoulders up, hid his chin in his chest. "But when you wrote the lyrics you seemed relaxed, like you weren't even thinking about them." He un-scrunched. "And there were certain lines you wrote over and over. So I looked them up one day, and found the song."

"And you remembered the name of the song, five years later."

He shot me a quick look, before looking down and signing his receipt.

"You remembered mine," he mumbled. Which was weird, because Kai wasn't a mumbler. "It's not that hard to believe."

"And you made Kiki look it up?"

He snapped the pen back on the counter, slid the paper toward the bartender.

"Yeah, she said she can look up pretty much any song on YouTube, if it's not already in their system."

"Huh," I said.

"*Huh*," he repeated, in a weird little voice, like he was making fun of me, like we were ten years old.

And then he threw on his coat and walked out of Moonie's.

Quickly, I scribbled my own signature on the line and chased after him.

"Hey."

He stopped, turned. I caught up to him, breathless from the cold air hitting my lungs again. It was snowing even harder now, already resting on Kai's brown hair, brushing down the tip of his nose. The entire parking lot was covered in white, and it all seemed shockingly bright after the darkness of the bar, the night lit up by the harsh floodlights of the lot, the flurries above Kai's head highlighted in the glow. The lot was practically abandoned, waiting only for Kiki, the bartender, the last lonely souls of Moonie's. It felt like we were all alone again, in this strange, pretty plain of concrete and snow.

He was wearing this nice grey peacoat, and it looked both funny and perfect on top of his purple hoodie. And I knew, with certainty, that if I didn't do this now, I never would. So I reached out with both hands and grabbed those lapels. They were warm and scratchy on my fingers, and I pulled, but Kai was already pushing toward me, my efforts for naught. I had barely angled my chin toward his when his own hands reached up, gripped the back of my neck, so rough and strong, and I had imagined the feel of those hands, just like that, so many times, that I think I may have let out an embarrassing little sigh before our lips even met.

And when they did, it was all open mouths and tongues from the start, like we were both hungry.

God, it was so good.

His mouth was so hot, the skin of his chin so warm and prickly, this blazing kiss caught in the midst of the blizzard around us. The unexpected heat of it stole my breath, my inhibition, my ability to feel anything but *him*, no longer the boy with the mouthwatering thighs and erotic knuckles, but a full-blown *man*, who built ships and felt things and knew all the words to "Party in the USA."

Who still knew my favorite song.

A swell of emotion caught me in the throat like a right hook, and I was seized with a kind of terror, that the kiss would end, and the magic of the snow and the songs and the night would be over, when I had just figured out that I needed it. And even though I could literally barely breathe, and needed to break the kiss, I found myself pressing into him more, harder, so that he stumbled. I moved my hands to wrap around his back and pull him close, as close as possible, so he wouldn't leave, and this wouldn't be done.

But eventually, of course, Kai tore his mouth away from mine, on this kind of guttural moan that almost broke me.

"Fuck," I breathed, leaning my forehead against his, gasping the freezing air back into my lungs. "Fuck."

Kai didn't say anything, only stood there with his hands still in my hair, catching his breath with me.

"I have a proposition now," he said at length, nudging his nose against mine, each word a gust of warm breath on my skin. "Come home with me, Aiden."

I wanted to swoon against him, like a half-dressed lady on an old school romance cover.

Instead I merely stood, frozen.

"I live nearby," he said when I didn't respond. "We can take the bus. You shouldn't drive home anyway, in this. Did you drive?"

I nodded, barely, my skin brushing against his.

"Okay then. Come on." He stepped away, tugged at my hand.

I let myself be led to the bus stop right in front of Moonie's. Let my hand slip inside Kai's. Let myself be pulled to Kai's chest, his arms wrapped around me now, rubbing circles on my back, keeping me warm. I felt his nose sink into my hair, felt more than heard his sigh.

I closed my eyes and counted to ten. Made myself be very quiet.

I always felt more grounded, when things were quiet. And with each minute that the cold air seeped in, with each minute we lived further and further away from Moonie's and the temporary magic of our favorite songs, I began to finally freak out.

A song, really, is nothing but a fantasy. Real life wasn't lived in chords and pretty melodies.

I couldn't quite imagine myself, anymore, telling Kai about the time I went to Baja. About Tin House and Ploughshares.

I could imagine myself kissing him again, of course. And whatever else was going to happen next. I could imagine doing many things with Kai Andrews, being that I'd already imagined them.

Fuck, that kiss. I shivered in Kai's arms, and he squeezed me tighter. That kiss was going to be seared into my memory for the rest of my life.

But if anything, we knew each other even less now than we had back then, were even more of strangers to each other. What right did I have to want to comfort him about his mom? None. I had no right to want any piece of him. And I could still barely fathom what Kai thought of me, what he had ever thought of me, why he didn't walk right back out of Moonie's tonight when we learned Penelope wouldn't be coming.

But whatever picture he had of me, it wasn't accurate. It wasn't accurate, because I didn't even know what an accurate picture of me was. I was better than I used to be, and maybe for a few moments back there I had felt okay, but I was still a mess.

We still didn't fit, Kai Andrews and me. I had fit with Niall. But this...this didn't make sense. There was a reason Kai had only ever been a fantasy for me, back in high school.

Best to understand, now, if we were going to do this, what was actually happening here. In some funny twist of fate—otherwise known as Penelope Vossey—Kai and I had met again tonight. We had gotten caught up in some dangerous mixture of nostalgia and alcohol. And now we were possibly going to fuck, and it was probably going to be good.

And then we'd wake up and go back to our lives. Obviously. Our very different, unconnected lives. And it would be...fine. If anything, I should be grateful this was happening at all. How often did we actually get to live out high school fantasies? Maybe I'd been good this year after all. Maybe this was the best gift Santa had ever brought me.

I just had to be careful. Because part of me already felt a little hollow as the feelings I'd felt inside Moonie's faded. How vulnerable it had been, singing in front of each other, the horrible song choices and the good ones. How he'd let me witness a little bit of his mourning, out on the patio. The way my stomach churned every time he smiled, and when he'd been so fucking happy during "Mr. Blue Sky." Parts of it already felt far away somehow, a memory, something I was already over-romanticizing in my head.

Kai's lips grazed my jaw. His tongue pressed down the side of my neck, and *nnrrrgghhh*, that felt good. I stopped hiding my face in his shoulder, stopped this mental spiral. I shoved him back against the plastic wall of the bus shelter, took his face in my hands and smashed our mouths together again. Felt the slide of his tongue against mine again. This was carnal, and there was absolutely nothing nonsensical about that. Grab hold of opportunities when they presented themselves, right? I wanted this man. I could let myself have him, for a night.

If I was careful.

He released another low moan, reverberating against my lips. Kai was vocal, apparently, and it was going to drive me out of my mind. He grabbed my hips, pulled me flush against him. It was honestly a bit uncomfortable, the hot urgency of our bodies clashing against the cold night, my pants too tight for this. I needed to get inside somewhere, anywhere, needed to get through all these layers of distracting clothing, needed to just *touch* him and then I'd be able to lose myself again, like how it had been during the songs, able to forget how perfect he still was, how much it hurt to even let myself imagine a future where we weren't totally incongruous. Where a person like him could be mine.

He broke away again when we needed to breathe.

"McCarstle," he rumbled, shaking his head. "Who fucking knew."

He reached a hand around and squeezed my ass, and I yelped a little. My brain was apparently acquainted enough with his mouth at this point—soft, hot, aggressive but not too sloppy, absolutely acceptable—but Kai Andrews squeezing my ass was still a shock to the system.

"Andrews," I said, truth spilling out. "God, I want you in all the ways."

Kai's lips parted, and he stared at me. It was darker here at the bus stop, outside of the glow of the floodlights in the Moonie's parking lot, but I thought I could see the heat flare in his eyes anyway. Approval. Desire. For *me*.

Teenage Aiden had come at least twice already. Electrified in my subconscious, constantly whispering *holy shit* in my ear.

Sex. That was all this was.

It was already feeling easier to convince myself. That this was a fine idea.

Because sex was incredible.

I moved in again, ready to suck on his lips some more, or maybe his neck, or—

A loud, crunching noise behind me made me jump back, my heart thrumming in my ears.

The bus sighed as it opened its doors. I squinted at the bright lights of the interior. Shit.

I fumbled in my pocket for my phone, my fingers cold and slow, my eyes blurry as I tried to find the right app. I'm sure the driver had seen worse, picking up people from the Moonie's stop in the middle of the night on a Saturday, but I still felt slightly mortified.

"Sorry," I said to the driver, who looked bored and probably did not care that I was sporting a ridiculous hardon, just that I was slowing down his route. In the snow. "Sorry, sorry."

Finally, I found the app, and hallelujah, I had a few bucks on it. I heard a strange muffled noise behind me, and looked back as I swiped my phone on the reader.

Kai was laughing at me.

This asshole.

I scowled.

As soon as we were alone again, I was going to use teeth this time.

8.

AIDEN PRACTICALLY RAN to the back of the bus. I followed more slowly, trying to calm both my erection and the goofy smile on my face, as the different shades of Aiden McCarstle tumbled through my head.

I was fascinated by the Aiden who had been so clearly happy on the dance floor for that last song, this Aiden I'd never been allowed to see before, open and real. I was turned on as hell by the Aiden who grabbed hold of my coat and pushed me against the bus shelter, who kissed me with such focused, unabashed passion.

I had wanted to kiss him so badly, all night really, and especially after our last songs. But I didn't know if I had the courage to make the move myself. I had never had the courage, really, to make moves; almost all of my previous relationships were usually initiated by the other party, and I was even more nervous around men. Still felt too new and insecure at this to show what I wanted. But the moment Aiden reached for me, it was like he granted me permission, and it had felt so freeing, and so...hot. And beautiful, some-how, underneath the falling snow.

But I could tell, as soon as the squelch of the bus had broken Aiden out of our makeout reverie, that he was feeling antsy again. He crossed his arms over his chest and stared resolutely out the window as I sat next to him on the back row of seats.

And this Aiden, this Aiden who almost dropped his phone at least five times trying to bring up the public transit app, who was bouncing his knee next to me as the bus rumbled away from the stop, who had scowled at me across the table back at Moonie's—this Aiden, I knew.

And god help me, but I could fully admit it now.

I adored this Aiden.

I remembered this time back in high school, when I stepped out into the hall one morning and Aiden was there. His backpack had split wide open, and all of this stuff had fallen everywhere. It was almost comical, like he was playing a caricature of a teenage klutz in a TV show, the way he was frantically trying to shove everything back into his bag. And there was just so *much* of it, so many disorganized papers and half falling apart notebooks. He'd been so flustered, so pissed, that he'd barely been able to look at me as I'd helped him. I mean, he barely looked at me, in general, but it seemed more pointed that time.

I'd spent the rest of the day thinking about it—the flush of his cheeks, all those wrinkled papers—and smiling to myself.

I rested my elbows on my knees now, steepled my fingers loosely in front of me. Looked over, watched Aiden's jaw click back and forth as he kept staring out at the snowy night.

I didn't know if I could pinpoint it, exactly, what it was about Aiden McCarstle that made me feel a little giddy inside. It was this kind of restless, irrepressible energy, this quiet intensity. Like he was constantly buzzing inside, like he couldn't keep all of his feelings inside his skin. It was why he was always hunching over, sinking down into his seat, bouncing his knee like he was now. Like if he let himself stand fully, actually stretch out his spine and let it all out, he'd explode.

I placed a hand on his knee, and he stilled. Finally moved his gaze from the window down to my knuckles.

I caressed his knee over his jeans with my thumb, once, twice.

And because I couldn't help myself, because he'd given me permission in the parking lot to be bold, I dropped my head to his neck, darting out my tongue to the tender skin there. I moved closer, shoving my leg against his.

"Kai," he said, voice low, a little annoyed, a lot sexy. "They have cameras on here."

Involuntarily, I let out a snort. Moving my head, I looked around the bus. I'd normally be anxious about this kind of thing, too, but there was exactly one other passenger, up at the very front.

"Aiden. Do you think the bus driver is going to call security on me—in the middle of a snowstorm—for getting you hard?"

Aiden closed his eyes, let out a slow, dramatic breath.

"I hate you."

I looked down at the bulge in his pants.

"Doesn't look like you do."

But I moved my hand away from his leg. Shifted back to my seat, leaving a few safe inches between us again. And looked out the opposite window, grinning to myself.

"How much further until your stop?"

I tried to deduce where we were. The bus had its snow

chains on; we were moving through the seemingly abandoned city at a glacial pace.

"Only a few more. Five, ten minutes."

"Okay."

I glanced back over at him. He kept his legs still now, his eyes closed, like he was meditating. Angry meditating. Until I reached over him to grab the cord for my stop. At which point his eyes popped open and he looked down at my arm, stretched over his chest, and sucked in a small breath. I caught his gaze, held it for a moment, before lowering my hand back to my lap. His cheeks were pink from the cold, his lips a tad puffier, redder, from our kisses.

I want you in all the ways.

Same, McCarstle. God. Fucking same.

We departed the bus, barreled through the snow for the block and a half it took to walk to my building—the wind had really picked up—and walked through the parking lot to the elevator in silence. I swiped my card and hit the button, my insides fizzy with nerves.

My building was less than a year old, one of those new steel-and-glass monstrosities of the inner East Side that was, according to most people, ruining the city. Taller than anything else around it, sparkling and out of place. I lived in the epitome of gentrification. And it only occurred to me now, as we rode the elevator toward my floor, that Aiden would absolutely hate it.

Aiden probably lived in some gorgeous, rambling Craftsman further out on the East Side. I imagined him sharing the house with other artists, other poets. Painters, illustrators, people who read essays and graphic novels. It was probably full of plants and natural light, worn floorboards, someone always baking something delicious while someone else played an acoustic guitar. Dried herbs hanging in the kitchen window. All of the furniture from vintage thrift stores, bright and quirky and homey. Maybe they owned chickens.

The truth was, I wanted my own falling apart house someday, out in the country. Close enough to the city so that I could still easily visit, far enough away that I could own a decent plot of land. Where I could spend my days fixing up the property, adopting dogs and letting them roam free. Where I could grow a garden worthy of a spread in the *Sunset* magazine my mom always subscribed to. Where I could sit on a porch, watch the clouds drift over Mount Hood. Wake to quiet sunrises.

But when I'd moved back here a couple months ago, something about the sharp, clean lines of these shiny new apartment buildings appealed to me. They were the opposite of the house I'd grown up in, the opposite of all the memories that still awaited me, looming, in that house. I wanted something new, to make this move home feel different, so I knew I wasn't moving backward.

And...I didn't want to be alone. My place down in Klamath Falls had been pretty isolated. I thought maybe living in a place like this, where I could hear neighbors banging around behind their own walls, where I could smile at them in the mailroom, would make me feel a little less alone.

When I'd toured this one, and seen the view from this floor—the city below, and then expanding clear across the river, to the foothills beyond—it'd clinched it. I had felt safe. At peace.

At work, I spent so much time trapped in dark, hot, dangerous places, confined by my heavy protective gear. And I loved it, most of the time; it was its own sort of peace.

But whenever I came back here, walked in and saw the view, I felt light and free again.

Aiden walked over to that view as soon as we walked inside the apartment.

I tossed my keys on the kitchen counter, put my coat on the hook.

Cautiously, I walked toward him, leaned against the back of my couch behind him. Looked at the planes of his shoulder blades as he stared out the window. I wanted to reach my arms around him, slide my hands under that frayed sweater, kiss the back of his neck.

But the air between us felt fragile, now that we were here, and I didn't want to do the wrong thing. I'd lost the taunting confidence I had on the bus. I wanted him to take charge again, the way he'd pushed against me in the Moonie's parking lot. To turn and knock me down onto the couch, or command me to strip, or grab my sweatshirt and twirl me around, kiss me against the glass.

"It's a nice view, actually," he said eventually. I smiled a little. The *actually* gave him away. He did hate it.

Finally, he turned.

"Are we just drunk?"

My stomach sank. Oh god. He hated my apartment, and he hated me, just like I'd always thought. He was going to leave.

I shook my head.

"I...don't drink. I was drinking Sprite at the bar."

His eyes widened.

"You were drinking *Sprite?* Oh my god." He covered his face with his hands again. "Of course you don't drink. Alcohol would ruin your perfect specimen of a body. You probably don't eat carbs, either."

I laughed a half-laugh.

"No, no, it's just...alcohol doesn't settle well with me, I've learned. That's all."

"*Sprite*," he repeated after a minute, shaking his head. "That's so..." He dropped his hands. "Fucking cute."

And then he was on me, and I actually did almost fall back onto the couch, but he caught me, his hands digging into my biceps. His tongue clashed against mine again, that intensity he'd hit me with at Moonie's resurrected, his hands moving to slip under my sweatshirt and the t-shirt underneath.

"Off," he tore his mouth away to say, tugging at my sweatshirt. "Take these off."

My skin buzzed at the command, and I complied immediately, throwing both t-shirt and sweatshirt onto the couch behind me. Aiden ran his hands over my shoulders, down my chest, rested them on my stomach, his eyes following the path of those hands as they traveled. His fingers were long, slender and cold. I put my hands over his, still resting on my stomach, to warm them.

"Jesus," he said.

And then he leaned in, and *bit* my neck where it met my shoulder, like a fucking vampire.

I gasped in surprise and pain. And moaned when he ran his tongue over the point of impact.

"Sorry," he murmured into my sternum.

"I liked it." It surprised me, but I really had. And now I tugged at his sweater. "Your turn."

His sweater and black t-shirt underneath joined mine on the couch, and I studied his pale, narrow frame, the jut of his collarbones, everything about his body as sharp and precise as his face, just as I had imagined it. Taut. Powerful, in his own way.

I reached around him, scratched my fingers up his back,

brought him back to me. Kissed him again. And as our mouths danced, my hands drifted downward, fumbled with the button, the zipper of his jeans. I felt almost frantic now, feeling his skin against mine, like I needed to touch him immediately, make sure he didn't get away. And so I did, reaching inside those jeans as soon as I found the room, grasping him over his briefs.

His breath stuttered, his mouth pulling away from mine.

He groaned softly, a light exhalation against my cheek.

"I can't believe this is happening," he said, staring down at my hand. "I've dreamed about this for so long."

I paused.

"You have?"

His eyes flicked to mine for just a second, face flushing, and I wondered if he'd actually meant to say that out loud.

"Well." He gestured with an impatient hand toward my chest. "I mean. You know what you look like."

I grinned.

"You think I'm hot?"

Aiden only sighed through his nose, clenching his jaw. After a second, he gritted out, "Yes."

And then he kissed me again, most likely to shut me up, but I couldn't stop smiling. He grunted his displeasure into my lips.

But this was a revelation to me.

I pushed him back with a hand on his chest.

"Okay, wait," I said, feeling like I was about to burst with glee. "Did you ever jerk off while thinking about me, back in high school?"

Aiden rolled his eyes. "Of course I did. Seriously, this cannot be a surprise to you. Can we just get back to—"

"Oh my god." I pressed my fingers into my temples.

"This is absolutely a surprise to me. I thought you hated me, Aiden. Thought I was just some dumb jock."

"Well." He sliced a hand through the air. "Masturbation isn't exactly deep, Kai."

I frowned. The giddy feeling inside me froze immediately, sank like a stone into my gut.

I stood from the back of the couch, pushing him away.

"So you did think I was a dumb jock. You still probably think I'm a dumb jock. This is..."

I shook my head and stalked into the kitchen.

This was bullshit, was what it was.

It wasn't that I was anti-meaningless sex. Okay, so maybe I never thought sex was completely meaningless, but I didn't need someone to be my soulmate to sleep with them.

I just hadn't known that was what we were doing, here.

I had thought things between us tonight felt different.

Being only a hot body to Aiden McCarstle was about the most demeaning thing I could think of. It made me feel small and slightly nauseous, like I had misinterpreted everything. And I had spent too many years figuring out who I really was, already felt too old, to put up with that.

It also made me not like Aiden McCarstle very much.

And for whatever dumb reason, I still wanted to like Aiden McCarstle.

I grabbed a glass from the cabinet, filled it with water from the sink. My mouth felt too sticky sweet from all that soda. I needed to clear my head.

"Kai." Aiden leaned against my kitchen counter, arms crossed over his bare torso. "Look, sorry. I don't think you're a dumb jock. But..." He sighed again, eyes stormy, staring at some spot near the floor behind me. "Can't we just fuck?"

"No." I crossed my arms too, leaning back against the wall. "I need to know why. *Why* we're about to fuck."

He glared at me, clicking his jaw back and forth. And this time, I didn't think it was cute.

When he didn't say anything, I accidentally exploded.

"You know why I want to fuck *you*, McCarstle?" I pushed away from the wall, pointed at his infuriating face. "Because I think you're brilliant. Because I read every poem you wrote in high school, at least the ones you published, the ones I saw you write in your notebooks in pre-calc."

Aiden froze, face blanching. His jaw dropped open a little.

"But you know what?" I threw my hands in the air. "It's not even that. You could be a brilliant writer; who cares. You could also be an incredible asshole. And I think you've always *tried* to be, at least to me, for some reason. But I know Penelope wouldn't love you so much if you were an asshole. And I don't think the guy I actually had a really good time with tonight was an asshole. It's like…"

I put my hands on my hips, staring past him, trying to explain it to myself as much as to him.

"It's like you only show who you are sometimes. Like you're scared of it. Or maybe you only show it to the people you trust. Which is fine, but you never, ever let me see it in high school. Until tonight, when you did surprising things, like sing karaoke, and…kiss me." I took the briefest of breaks to lick my lips, swallowing, before I kept going. "And when you let yourself go, you're so…bright, and funny, and interesting. And it makes me want to crack you right open, so I can see that all the time. I bet when you fuck, you let yourself be like that. So *that's* why I want to fuck you."

I crossed my arms again and retreated back to my wall. My entire body felt warm, like I was blushing all the way to my toes. I was exhausted, suddenly, and almost wanted McCarstle to just go home at this point. Enough humiliation for one evening.

Aiden, at least, must have been suffering from the same body heat affliction I was, because his face was bright red, even though it was actually pretty cold in here. I should have turned up the thermostat when we came in. He dropped his arms, crossed them again. Opened his mouth, closed it. Looked everywhere but at me.

Until eventually, he closed his eyes. Took a deep breath through his nose. And when he opened his eyes again, they never strayed from my face. He uncrossed his arms and walked toward me, slow but steady, like a predator. I swallowed again, trying not to squirm, until he was so close I could feel the warmth of him, smell his body wash, or cologne, or whatever it was, that I had inhaled when he'd first kissed me—something surprisingly floral, light and clean, like daisies and jasmine, a gulp of spring air after a sudden storm.

He reached a hand out and ran his fingertips over my left shoulder.

"Tell me about these," he said softly.

I looked down at his hand on top of my tattoos. It wasn't what I expected him to say; it was not an apology or an explanation. And I was a little annoyed I was the one who had to keep doing the emotional labor here. But I suppressed my sigh and answered him anyway, like the pushover I was.

"That's my mom," I said, pointing at the *Carol* in cursive script, although I thought he should have been able to guess that. "And her favorite flowers."

Boldly shaped, pastel colored peonies wrapped around my shoulder, interspersed with smaller, crisper purple asters and twining branches of a cherry blossom. They surrounded my mom's name, drifted down to surround the head of a dopey, pure hearted shepherd mix on my bicep.

"And that's Jack."

"Jack?" Aiden raised his eyes from my shoulder to my face.

"It's what they named him at the shelter." I shrugged. "Didn't want to change it, in case he'd gotten used to it."

He smiled a little, the tiniest uplift of the corner of his mouth, and he looked back at my shoulder again.

"Was he your dog when you were a kid?"

I shook my head.

"No, I got him when I moved down south. It was, um." I shifted on my feet. "A little lonely, moving to a brand new place by myself. Jack was pretty much my best friend in Klamath Falls."

Aiden moved his fingertips down the length of my arm. Rubbed his thumb against my wrist.

"He died about six months ago," I added, my mouth seeming to move independently of my brain. I didn't know why I was telling Aiden this, right now.

"I'm sorry," Aiden whispered. And then, moving his hands to my stomach, which made me shiver, "It must have been hard, losing your mom and then Jack."

I looked down at his hands, fluttering around my skin. I was having a little trouble keeping my breathing steady.

"Is that why you want to fuck me? Because I have a dead mom and a dead dog?" I managed to get out. "Because I have to say, that doesn't feel great either."

He shook his head, slowly, as slow as his fingers were moving.

And that was what made me start to crumble, I think. Everything up until now had been fast, hard, hot, wet.

But the tiny circles he was making now—on my stomach, on my shoulders, across my chest—were so slow and gentle. Butterflies whispering up my ribs. It melted me.

"No," he said. "I don't want you because of those things. Thank you for telling me about them, though." He paused, his eyes still focused on my shoulder. "And you were never just a dumb jock to me. I'm sorry for making you think that."

He sighed, but it was quiet, almost helpless sounding.

"Kai, I want you because you're good." He stared at me then, eyes steady and dark. His fingers grazed their way to my chin. "You are so, so good."

I stared back. It shouldn't have surprised me, really. That he could make the world vibrate in one little word. Somehow imbue everything I couldn't with simplicity. I felt it so deeply, somehow, let my chest puff up with pride. And I wanted it so badly. To be good for Aiden McCarstle.

I didn't think about it. Felt myself doing it more than understanding actionable thought. Never breaking eye contact, I slid down the wall, put my hands behind my back. And I waited there, on my knees, for Aiden to tell me what to do next.

9.

HOLY FUCKING SHIT.

I stared down at Kai Andrews, on his knees, for me.

Okay, I did not see this one coming.

I had pictured *myself* on my knees for Kai Andrews, plenty of times before, but this...

I scrunched my fingers into my hair, recalibrating.

I think you're brilliant.

All right, so there was a lot going on in my head, right now, but I could handle this. I could handle Kai and his soft, pretty tattoos on his sculpted body, and all those...things, he had said, and the way my heart was taking flight in my chest, freakishly fast and breath stealing, like a hummingbird.

Yes. This was fine.

I breathed out, nodded to myself, my hands still fisted in my hair. These were all good developments. It could still just be sex; it'd just be *better* sex than I had even anticipated, knowing that Kai was hot and charming *and* sweet, and—

And oh my god. The fucker was laughing at me again.

"Hey." I dropped my hands, frowning. "Hey, you're not supposed to be on your knees and *laughing* at me. That's not how this works."

"Sorry." Kai schooled his features, but barely. His hands were still clenched tightly behind him, but his eyes were glinting, smiling up at me. "Sorry. I'm new at this. You're just really...is this okay? Are you okay?"

I stared down at him, and weirdly, I felt a little bit of Moonie's seep back into my system. How that woman had sung "Hallelujah" with him, how unashamed Kai had been to ask for her help. It had felt like cheating, when I saw him go ask her to sing with him, but as I looked at him on his knees now, it only felt...honest. To ask for what you needed.

"Bedroom," I said, and my voice sounded rough even to my own ears. A little of my own honesty, seeping in. "And take off the rest of your clothes when you get there."

He listened very well.

Not five minutes later, I was in Kai Andrews's bedroom, staring at him laid out on his bed, naked and waiting for me.

It was a nice bed. I focused on this, and not Kai's naked body, because that was still—my brain was still processing that.

His bedroom had the same ridiculous view as the living room. It had surprised me, that Kai lived here, but he had filled the sterile space with nice things, things I imagined him making himself. Like the rough hewn wooden headboard behind him. High school soccer star turned into hunky bisexual lumberjack. I imagined him in Klamath Falls, chopping wood whenever he wasn't welding, crafting classy furniture with his bare hands while Jack slept at his feet.

Or maybe he'd bought it all on Wayfair. What did I know?

Sex. Focus on the sex.

I stripped off my own pants, underwear, socks. Felt him watching me. Crawled onto the bed, crawled over him. I touched the mark on his neck where I'd bitten him earlier. He didn't react, just kept watching me. Waiting.

I sat back on my heels, examined the headboard more closely. It wasn't ideal, all abstract, no good posts or rungs to hang onto. But there was a reading light screwed into one section, a nice industrial touch, the contrast of hard metal against the warm wood. I lifted one of his arms toward it, and he understood, raising his other arm willingly, adjusting himself so he could reach. It was a touch too high, so that he wasn't completely lying down or completely sitting, his neck arched awkwardly, likely a little uncomfortable.

"This okay?" I trailed a hand down his chest. Fuck, it was a good chest.

"Yeah."

"Good."

I leaned back again, settled myself over his thighs. His body looked extra long and graceful with his arms raised above his head like that, if you could consider all those muscles and all that dark hair—under his arms, across his chest, trailing down his stomach—graceful. Which I did.

And while I wanted to do very rough, animalistic things with Kai Andrews, kneeling over him while he was like this —so pretty, so patient, so willing—I still couldn't quite believe he was giving this to me. A gift. It felt exactly like it had when I'd picked up the mic from Kiki and saw that he'd chosen "Aside" for me. Like he was giving me permission to...how had he put it? Crack myself wide open.

I had never fantasized about it happening quite like this. But it happening like this—Kai waiting for my instructions, wanting me to take charge—made me feel calm. Like my brain had never been brave enough to envision it this way, but it immediately felt right. Everything in my universe right then felt palpable and honest—him, me, this room—no longer a surreal dream. He was no longer the unattainable golden boy I could never have. We were just two people.

And I realized it wasn't a gift, actually, him submitting to me. Not exactly. Because it was shared. Like the moment he slid to the floor in the kitchen, we had started an intimate conversation. Like wordlessly, we had become partners.

I touched a long, raised scar on the underside of his forearm, the line too smooth under my fingertips.

"Dumb mistake from my first year at the forge," he said after a minute, his voice quiet.

I couldn't stop looking at that scar. And thinking about what he had said back in the kitchen, about how living in Klamath Falls had been a little lonely. Kai Andrews—the kid everyone loved, who had always seemed surrounded by friends, last I knew him—living alone with his dog, gathering scars.

I examined the rest of his arms more closely, the spiderwebs of evidence of smaller past hurts that criss crossed his skin. They made something stir in my gut, his weathered arms. Arousal, but also something…protective. Concerned. Something sharp and unexpected.

A gust of wind rattled against the window, breaking my concentration. I glanced outside at the flurry of white crashing against the panes.

I bit my lip and looked back at Kai Andrews.

Maybe, just while we lived in this snow globe of an apartment, I could pretend I actually could be his partner. Someone who got to examine his scars, who got to worry about his dangerous job, his mental state. And then I could lock it away in my memories, like Baja, like the Olympic rainforest. An epic adventure I'd gone on once. Something to write about, one day.

It didn't sound like such an awful idea, in the moment.

I leaned down and kissed him.

I was utterly obsessed with Kai's lips by now, so soft and full, erotic little pillows. I licked across his bottom one, tugged at it with my teeth before delving my tongue into his mouth again. His arms fell from the lamp to wrap around me, and I smiled.

"You really are bad at this," I said against his lips. I sat up to remove his arms from my back, returning them to the headboard.

"Sorry, sorry," he breathed out.

"Do you have any ties or anything? If, you know. You're okay with that?"

"Yeah. I am." He cocked his head toward the closet to my right. "Over there."

I jumped off him and opened the closet, a spike of adrenaline coursing through me at getting to rifle through Kai Andrews's stuff. His closet was neat, pretty spare, mostly full of t-shirts. Sneakers and boots were lined up on the bottom, sweaters and sweatshirts folded up top, and— *yes*—some flannels and Henleys hanging next to the t-shirts. He was absolutely a bisexual lumberjack in his heart and maybe I'd make him try some of those on for me later.

Almost hidden, over to the right, existed an exceedingly small selection of formal wear. Including one hanger with exactly two ties.

"Wow. What selection."

"I don't dress up a lot," he huffed out. "I don't, you know, have to wear a suit to work under my PPE."

"You have to wear PPE to your job." I considered both ties. "That's hot."

"Is it?" he asked. "It's more just hot, like, literally."

I decided on the coral pink tie—obviously I did—and climbed back over Kai on the bed.

"You sure about this?" I asked, holding the tie in my fist and searching his face. I was new at this, too, but I knew I could hurt him if we didn't do it right. "We don't have to do any of this."

"I want to," he said. "I promise I'll tell you if it doesn't feel good."

I liked everything about this sentence. Promises. Feeling good.

I closed my eyes briefly. Focused. And began.

Wrapping the silk around his wrists felt like such a precious thing. I gave him some slack, which allowed him to sink back onto the pillow just a bit more comfortably. Did my best attempt at knotting it firmly around the base of the lamp. It was possible I'd watched a few YouTube videos about knots, at various points in my life. I silently cursed myself for not having more practice—I wanted Kai Andrews to think I was brilliant at this too—but I thought I did a decent job.

I locked my elbows around his chest. Stared down at him.

"Kai," I said. "What do you want?"

I watched him swallow, the lovely angles of his throat.

"Isn't this about, um, what you want?"

"Yeah," I answered. "And I want what you want. To start with."

He licked his lips. Hesitated.

"I want you to tell me," I reiterated. In what I hoped was a half-commanding, half-affectionate kind of way.

"Okay." Another gorgeous swallow. He closed his eyes before he said, "God, I want you to suck me off, Aiden."

My dick reacted to that exactly as I thought it would.

"That's acceptable. Only if—" I leaned down toward his mouth again, "—you keep talking to me. I want you to tell me every single thing that feels good, Kai. I want details."

"Oh god." His eyes scrunched closed even tighter, and I was both a little worried I was pushing him too far, and a little distracted by how cute it was. "I'm not always good at..." He cut himself off, blinking his eyes back open, his face smoothing into determination. "No. Okay. I'll try."

I ran a hand over his stomach, and he twitched.

"You don't have to do anything you're not comfortable with. Seriously."

"No, it's good. Just...don't laugh at me."

"I won't."

I sealed my own promise by giving him one last kiss on the mouth.

And then I got down to work.

* * *

I wanted to touch him so badly.

Which was the point of all this, the tie wrapped around my wrists, and everything. It probably wouldn't have felt so impactful, being deprived of something, unless you really wanted it.

But as Aiden made his way down my body, and—oh, *fuck*, he didn't waste any time, *god*—I wanted to shove my hands in that curly hair. I wanted to caress my thumb down his cheek. And—

"Talk to me, Kai," he pulled off to remind me, which felt torturous, since he had just started, and it had felt so incredible. But, right.

I released a puff of air I'd apparently been storing up in my lungs.

"Well," I tried. "Your mouth feels really fucking good, McCarstle."

He hid his face in my thigh. I realized he was muffling a laugh.

"Good start," he lifted his head to say. "Maybe try to sound a little less aggravated next time, if you could."

Oh.

My.

God.

I had just made him promise not to, and he'd broken that promise immediately, but...I had made McCarstle laugh. I had *finally* made him laugh, and it was...by being so horribly inept at dirty talk.

The worst part was, I *wasn't* aggravated. Or, okay, at least not in an annoyed way. Any hint of annoyance bled out of me when I decided to slide down my kitchen wall. When he wrapped this tie around my wrists, the silk smooth and taut against my pulse points.

I wasn't annoyed. I was overwhelmed with how...sexy I felt. With how free I felt, laid out like this at Aiden's feet, all the control in his hands. I felt hyper sensitive, turned on as all get out, like I could explode at any moment—and more deeply at peace than I'd been in years, all at the same time. It was...it was a lot.

And I didn't want to fuck it all up by sounding like an idiot.

It didn't help that the man who had just had my dick in his mouth was a fucking poet. He could probably make a blowjob sound majestic. I wasn't sure I'd ever made *anything* sound majestic in my life.

"Hey." Aiden leaned up on an elbow, looking at me with a hint of concern. His other hand was still wrapped around the base of my dick, and he rubbed his thumb along the side of it, almost absentmindedly, which was both oddly sweet and far too excruciating a sensation, especially for how on edge I was right now. I wanted his mouth back there, hot and encompassing and obliterating. "Kai, sorry. You don't have to talk. Or do any of this at all, really. I can untie—"

"No." I swallowed, and my head began to clear. All I had to do was talk. It didn't have to be deep. It didn't have to be sexy. I could do this, for him. For me. "Don't you dare. And I'm not aggravated. This is...wonderful."

His hand stilled, his face softening.

After a few seconds, I added, "But you're going to have to go back to what you were doing, or I might die."

His mouth twitched, and something sparked to life behind his eyes. They looked...mischievous. It was a good look on him.

"I don't know. I might have to take my time, now that you said that."

I groaned, tearing my gaze away from him and banging my head back against the headboard. But he moved his hand, his whole fist this time, thank god, and stroked me slowly, carefully, perfectly.

I took a few deep breaths and closed my eyes. Swallowed. And I talked.

"I've never had someone tie my wrists like this before. *Ugh*, your hand feels so good when you—yeah, like that. Shit. Anyway, I like it, the tie, even though my neck feels a little awkward. It feels like...something I shouldn't want, but it actually feels amazing, like such a relief, like—"

His mouth was suddenly on me again, and I hissed, my hips bucking involuntarily.

"Sorry," I babbled. "I might not be able to control that. The fucking your face thing. Is that okay? It just feels so good. I don't know—"

Aiden's hands gripped my hips, hard, his fingernails digging into my skin, sharp little crescents. I gasped, opening my eyes and looking down at him. My hips bucked again at the sight of him there.

"Fuck. I don't know if that means yes or no."

He moaned around my dick, and I...was going to take that as a yes.

"Okay. Fuck." I sunk against the headboard again, fisted the ends of the silky tie in my hands. I didn't know how to summarize out loud how I felt about what he was actually doing. Other than: *God. Yes. Uuunnnnggggggghhhhh good.* And Aiden McCarstle deserved better words than that. So I opened my mouth and tried to remember what I had been saying.

"I like it, like this, the way we're—*oh*. That. *Aiden*. God." He did this swirly thing with his tongue, and I closed my eyes. Tried to focus. "Being like this, it makes me feel like I'm...yours."

Aiden paused mid-motion. Didn't make a peep. Which I probably should have expected. Good lord. I had to start saying different things, so he wouldn't pull off again and walk away into the snow.

"I like your hair," was what came out of my mouth next, which probably wasn't any less embarrassing, but it was the first thing that sprung into my mind. "And your collarbones. And your mouth."

He resumed his movements, a little more aggressively this time, and I shivered in relief.

"You are...very good at this," I managed. God, sentences were hard.

And then, as if to prove to me that he could be even better, he dropped his hand and took me in deeper. I felt myself hit the back of his throat.

"Oh shit, Aiden," I almost yelled. "I don't want to hurt you. I—" Oh, but I was fucking his face again anyway. His hands gripped my hip bones again, where he'd dug into me before, but now he just held on, pressing into their hurt, firm and reassuring.

"Damn. Damn, Aiden," I whispered. "You can't stop doing this, ever." And soon, "I'm close. I'm so close, Aiden."

He swiped a thumb over my skin, as if telling me it was okay. And that was all I needed.

There were sparks behind my eyelids, relief everywhere else—the back of my thighs, the crook of my toes, the crunch of my shoulders. I hadn't come so hard in a long time, and it felt almost surprising, like it was a new sensation. My back arched off the bed, arms clenching around my head, my brain a peaceful blender of waves. I didn't talk then. Didn't want to. Wanted to just sink here inside these feelings as they expanded around me, stretching into my fingertips, wrapping around my chest.

I felt Aiden pull off, felt him kiss the inside of my thigh, and I liked that, wanted him to keep doing it. Wanted him to cover my body with his, so he could share in my afterglow, so I could spread it from my skin to his.

Instead he crawled over me and fell over onto his side on the bed. I could barely see him anymore, since my arms were in the way. But I could hear his heavy intake of breath, in tune with my own.

We lay there a moment, two.

And even though my body felt light and tingly, my brain still recovering, the next words I spoke felt heavy somehow, like they were wrenched from my gut.

"Tell me something real about you, Aiden."

10.

AIDEN

I COULD BARELY SEE his face, just that otherworldly sculpture of his shoulders, his triceps framing his head. I was pretty out of my mind with desire, a kind of deliriousness creeping up my spine, so it took my brain longer than it should have to even register that Kai had said something. I only kept hearing him say *I like your hair* inside my head and wanting to dissolve into euphoric laughter. No one had ever been so cute during an erotic moment in their entire life.

"I'm feeling kind of like I've said a lot of things, and..." Kai tried again when too much time had elapsed without me saying anything. I tried to sober myself up, focus. Except then his tongue reached out to lick across his bottom lip, and I stared at it too long, still in a bit of a daze. I had always liked looking at Kai Andrews, but looking at him now, up close and personal, all the little details bared to me, it felt a bit like I had discovered a new species. Every single thing he did was interesting. "I don't know," he finished. "I want to know something about you."

This was completely fair, of course. And it was probably

just the adrenaline in my system, and the fact that most of my brain cells had migrated to my dick, but I didn't even feel that mad about it. Kai had already given me so much. We were in the snow globe. I could tell him things.

"I hate grad school," I said.

"Yeah?" He tried to turn his head to see me, but he was mostly still looking at his own armpit. I laughed a little.

"You doing okay?"

"Actually...my arms are kind of falling asleep?"

I sat up immediately. Untied him. His head hit the pillow with a satisfied grunt as his arms fell limply to his sides. Eyes closed, he rolled his neck a few times. And then he simply laid there and smiled.

"Tell me if they don't feel back to normal again soon, okay? And your neck's all right?"

"Yeah. It's good. And I will."

"Oh shit, Kai," I said, the realization hitting me. "We should have maybe established a safe word? I think?"

Kai laughed, but a jab of embarrassment punched through my sex-haze bliss. I was apparently pretty bad at this, too.

Kai's laughter faded as his face turned thoughtful, a comfortable moment of silence stretching. He chewed a bit on his lower lip before he said, "Is it dumb or weird to choose Jack?"

My heart did a little flippy flop thing. Of course Kai would choose his old dog.

"I always felt safe with Jack," he added.

"Absolutely," I said. "Not dumb or weird at all."

I settled back on my side and wrapped the coral tie around my own hand, like I was a boxer getting ready for my next punch. Trying not to think too much about

Klamath Falls Kai. About Jack. Trying to hold on to the sex haze. I held my wrapped fist to my mouth.

"Why do you hate grad school?"

Right. We were still talking about this, then.

I thought about where to start, how to explain it to Kai.

"Well, I'm not very good at it, for one." I grinned into the silk, my daily misery suddenly seeming a little funny when I looked at it from here, naked in Kai Andrews's bed. "I've started at least five different theses and...I don't think any of them are great, or groundbreaking, or even unique. Like—" I grinned even harder. "Who cares? I'm not solving world hunger or anything here."

This had become a mantra, something I chanted to myself on the days when I felt particularly angry and disenchanted, with school, with my classmates, with myself.

Who cares? Who cares? Who cares?

"I don't think you have to solve world hunger to still be doing something meaningful," Kai said. I ignored him, because I had already moved on to the second worst part of grad school.

"And I have to teach." I started laughing in earnest now. "I have to teach undergrads and..." I shook my head. "Kai. I am *so bad* at it."

He had been staring at the ceiling as I talked, which was great; it made talking easy. But now he turned toward me again, a frown on his perfect face.

"I'm sure you're not as bad as you think you are."

"Kai." I looked at him over my fist. "I am awful. Legitimately. Which is especially dumb because a lot of writers get advanced degrees so they can *keep teaching*. But I get so nervous before every class, and then when I'm actually in front of the room, I only feel like an asshole up there, and I just…it's bad. It's so bad. I am not built to lead other human beings."

He cracked a smile at that. A very small smile, but still.

"Why are you there, then?"

I sighed, my own grin fading. Another fair question.

I flopped onto my back, taking my turn to stare at the ceiling.

"Because it seemed like a good idea. And I didn't have any other good ideas. I kept thinking, as senior year of undergrad rolled around, that I'd figure it out, what I was supposed to do next. I got an internship at Tin House, and I thought that would help, or give me connections or something, but…" I wondered how dumb and self-important this was all sounding to Kai. "I still needed more money to start paying student loans. So I started working at this bakery, along with the internship, and I thought…I'd figure it out when the internship ended, if I wanted to go into editing, or something, or I'd get an agent and they'd tell me what to do next, but…soon I was just, you know. Working at a bakery."

"Did you like working at the bakery?"

"Yeah. It was a nice break, actually, just going somewhere and doing hard work and then going home and not worrying about…you know, being more of a genius than all the other geniuses."

"That makes sense."

"But it started to feel, last year, like everyone else was moving forward and I wasn't." For some reason, much to the consternation of my dick, I was still talking. "And I could tell any time I talked to my parents that…they weren't judging me, exactly, but were sort of like, okay, we let you get that writing degree; now it's your turn to get a real job. And…maybe I, like, don't even know what a real job is."

Shit. I was starting to sound messy. And like a child again.

"So I applied for grad school because it was what the writers I knew and admired most were doing, and it felt like something I could say to my parents, to people who asked what I was doing with my life. I'm pursuing an MFA. It's...something."

"Something you hate," Kai said.

"Yeah." I shrugged. "But I'll get through it."

An awkward pause lingered between us.

There was more I could have said. About how I thought, as with my internship, that grad school would bring me connections, bring me into this world of bright, interesting people, that I could be a part of something.

And maybe I had made some connections. Maybe I was doing fine.

But I couldn't help feeling like nothing felt like I had thought it would. That I felt weirdly disconnected from everything and everyone. And I couldn't tell if it was because everyone else were assholes, or because I was the asshole. Either option made me equally depressed.

I was meant to be moving *forward* with my life. And yet, the only people who I felt truly understood me, who I only ever wanted to be around, were Penelope, who had known me since I was a seventh grader who made extremely poor fashion choices, and Niall, who I'd broken up with a year ago, who I hadn't talked to in six months.

"Anyway, that all probably sounded really whiny," I said, feeling a little horrified, wishing more than ever that I had stuck to my Only Sex plan.

"No, it didn't. It sounded honest."

"Yeah, well. Now you know. I'm not actually brilliant. Just...scared of everything."

Another beat of silence, just as horrifying.

I was right on the cusp of opening my mouth to say, "Anyhoo, let's go back to fucking," when Kai said, "You're also a dog walker."

A laugh that sounded more akin to a bleating sheep escaped my chest.

"What?"

"You said when people ask what you're doing with your life, you can say you're pursuing an MFA. But you're also a dog walker."

I covered my face with my hands to quell my laughter.

"Oh my god. Getting burned by Kai Andrews. Adding that to my list of things I didn't expect to happen over the last twenty four hours."

"It's not a burn! I love that you walk dogs. God, that has to be stressful sometimes, right?"

"I..." I shook my head in disbelief, feeling like a sillier human being than ever. "Yes."

I should have led with dog walking, actually. There was no reason why I should have told Kai about my grad school angst, but I could have told him about the time Mitzi almost lost an ear from an off-leash dog at Thousand Acres, how there was still a blood stain in the back seat of my car from when I'd rushed her to the emergency vet. Or the time Stanley Tucci slipped his collar and almost ran straight onto Powell Boulevard and I'd thought, this is it. This is the day I kill a dog and have to give up on life. Or when Buster knocked over some trail mix from the kitchen counter in his excitement of seeing me and I had to tell the owners I had no idea whether he'd consumed any raisins or not.

Kai probably would have cared about those stories more than my internship at Tin House. But what was done was done.

He didn't make any other ridiculous comments, and I counted down the minutes until it felt socially acceptable to bring up fucking again, when he spoke.

"I'm scared of my mom's house."

Now I turned to him, and he faced the ceiling again.

"I'd always wanted to come back home, eventually, but when she passed away last year...I have to clean out her house. My old house. When the job came up at the port a couple months ago, it gave me the final push to finally quit my job in Klamath Falls and come back. But..." He blew out a breath. "I've only been inside it twice since coming back. I've driven by it a lot more than that, but I keep making excuses. I needed time to get settled into the apartment here, get used to the new job. But I know I'm just avoiding it."

Jesus.

"Is there anyone else helping you? Does it need to be cleaned out right away?"

Kai shifted one of his arms to rest behind his head. I tried to not focus on how incredibly sexy this pose was, considering he was telling a much more important story than any of the junk that had just fallen out of my lips.

"My aunt's helped a little, and she's offered to keep helping. But she's also gently told me it's my job, that I'd regret it eventually if I didn't do it. I know she's right. And Dad moved to Bend after Mom died. He..." Kai's lips thinned, his forehead creasing. "He's actually doing okay, I think, or as okay as he can be. But he knew he had to leave, find somewhere new to grieve. He took what he wanted to take from the house, and now I think he's...done."

I knew absolutely nothing about Kai's dad, or his aunt —or about his mom, for that matter—but something hot flared in my chest. It didn't seem completely fair, that Kai would be left to this monumental task all alone.

"And you don't have any siblings or cousins or anything that could help?"

"Yeah, no siblings. Only kid. I do have some cousins...huh, I actually hadn't thought to ask them before. Maybe I'll do that, if it truly is overwhelming. And Pen has offered to help. But...I actually do kind of want to take it on by myself. I just need to find the courage to, you know. Do it."

We were in this weird space where I had just shoved his dick down my throat, and yet...I didn't know if I could hug him.

It probably wasn't a good sign that I really, really wanted to, though.

"Anyway." He turned his head to me. "I feel like it's my turn to do something to your dick now?"

A strangled laugh escaped my throat.

This was a weird fucking night.

"If you're up for it."

"I am. Sorry if I ruined the vibe."

"No, I started it." I thought about this, and shook my head. "Actually, you started it by asking me to talk. Now you know what a bad idea that was."

"I disagree." He smiled at me, and it was a little sleepy, his eyes half closed. My chest squeezed. "But yeah, maybe you should punish me."

I closed my own eyes. This was quite a step up in dirty talk, from his *I like your hair* beginnings. But I wasn't sure, exactly, what Kai meant by punishment, if he had actually meant it that way. I had liked tying him up. Applying small pressures here and there. Hearing him gasp. But...whatever he was imagining didn't feel right, right now.

"I just want to fuck you," I said. "If you're okay with that."

He inhaled a quiet but sharp breath.

"Yeah," he said. "I'm okay with that. Only..." He hesitated. "I don't want to be on my knees, if that's okay. I want to see you."

I breathed out, a worrying patch of tenderness flaring underneath my sternum.

"Yeah, that's okay, Kai. Do you have lube? And condoms?"

"Yeah. Top right drawer of my dresser."

I hopped to, and good god. I stared at the lube sitting among his rolled socks, and...Kai Andrews actually did have lube. I didn't know why this surprised me. I also did *not* want to think about whoever else Kai Andrews had used this lube with.

"Do you want to tie me up again?" he asked as I crawled back between his legs. And while my erection had flagged during the whole I'm Bad At My Life/Kai Has to Clean Out His Dead Mom's House discussion, my dick perked back up at the question. Which he had asked so innocently, so genuinely. Kai Andrews was too pure for this world.

"No." I shook my head. "But—" I shoved up his knees. "You're going to hold these."

"Right," he said, grabbing hold immediately, and...fuck. I didn't move an inch for a good minute, just staring at his thighs, at his whole body, exposed to me. And his face looked so goddamn *calm* about it.

When I had pictured fucking this man, back in the Moonie's parking lot, and all the years before that, I always imagined it rather frenzied, hard and dirty, hot and desperate. But now that the moment was actually occurring, all I wanted was to be gentle.

And before I could get too in my head about it, I gave it my best try. I leaned forward and planted a kiss on the inside of his thigh. I moved my hands anywhere I could touch him, from his ass to the space behind his knees, to his hips, his stomach. I left dumb little kisses everywhere, all before I'd even popped open the cap of the lube. And when I did lube up a few fingers, I was nuzzling his balls, his thighs, like he was a very precious puppy. I was being ridiculous, basically, but I couldn't seem to stop myself.

Either way, we were both pretty worked up by the time I removed my fingers. Without the pressure of having to talk, Kai's body had relaxed, and he'd been emitting all sorts of noises—sighs, moans, grunts—with every touch, every shift of our bodies, that made me feel like I was out of my head. Breathing deep to steady myself, I took my time getting inside him. Watched his face for any sign of discomfort. Watched his face just to watch his face, really. Waited for him to adjust. Absorbed the spine-tingling, barely-there little groans he was making now.

And when I finally slid out and back in, I moved almost excruciatingly slow. Wanted to savor it, stretch it like taffy.

Again, I was being a bit ridiculous. But I imagined every slow, deep stroke somehow soothing the hurt he'd shown me on the patio at Moonie's. Easing the burden of painful responsibilities he bore.

Which, of course, was pretty much the complete opposite of Only Sex. But Kai Andrews deserved to be soothed.

And I'd obviously already lost the thread here a while ago.

"McCarstle," he eventually ground out, his face dewy, cheeks stained the most delicious shade of red wine, "You're killing me. God."

"Something you need, Andrews?"

His fingers were starting to slip on his thighs. He threw his head back onto the pillow with a groan.

"Fuck, Aiden. Fucking *fuck me*."

So apparently Kai *could* get bossy.

But the man made a good case.

I shoved his hands away, taking over, shifting his knees up even further, adjusting my own stance. And then I did as he asked. It took me embarrassingly little time, in fact, to get back to stark carnality, to fast and sweaty and loud and inelegant and so, so fucking good. I was too close to coming, too fast.

So to make sure he came first, I gritted out the only command I'd uttered in this whole sequence: "Touch yourself."

He did, almost before I'd even finished speaking, crying out in relief when his hand made contact. He came within a few strokes, making a mess of himself, and being able to truly study him, his beautiful open mouth, was both everything I'd ever dreamed of and like nothing I'd ever actually expected. I felt this rush of so many things: gratitude, for being able to witness it, and a touch of shame, like I didn't deserve this moment of intimacy with him. Sorrow, that this was probably the last time in my life I'd ever get to see it. Words were crashing through my brain, the exact right words I would use to describe everything about this, if I had pen and paper, if my hands weren't otherwise occupied with Kai's skin. I was low-key mad I knew I'd never be able to write them down in time, before I forgot, before they flew out of my brain.

Seconds later, I was gone.

Usually I came down pretty fast, especially if I was by myself. And to be real, by myself was the only action I'd gotten in a long time. Within minutes, I could be back to watching TV or reading a book, like nothing had even happened, like my orgasm had merely been a passing yawn.

But tonight, even after the last shudders of my release faded, even after I'd pulled out, it felt like I was still half in it. I walked to the bathroom, disposed of the condom, got a towel to wipe Kai down. And the whole time, my body was still buzzing, my mind still in a cloud, floaty and overly aware of every single sensation. Like if Kai so much as brushed my skin I might come all over again.

Except he didn't. By the time I slid under the covers, he'd moved over to the other side of the bed, his body barely covered with a sheet, eyes closed, arms resting like dead weight at his sides. He looked conked out, and when my body weight shifted the mattress, he didn't move to curl into my side, or wrap me in his arms. Which I appreciated. I often felt claustrophobic and overwhelmed by too much cuddling, right after—it had caused some hurt feelings, more than once, with Niall—and especially with the weird, tingly, overstimulated haze I was in, it probably would have made me implode.

So instead we simply lay on our backs, side by side, and waited for our heart beats to return to normal.

At least, that was what I did. I was pretty sure Kai was asleep, had probably been asleep since I'd crawled back onto the bed.

But then I heard him shift. Felt his hand glide along my palm. And next thing I knew, we were holding hands.

And it was perfect.

"Shit," he said. "I feel like I could sleep for a hundred million years."

"Yeah," I mumbled. "See you then."

Before I lost consciousness, I tried to think of what I'd say tomorrow morning. I felt alarmingly tender toward Kai now, and didn't want to be a total jerk about it, the fact that me and Kai Andrews as a *thing*, as a unit outside of this bedroom, still didn't actually make any sense in my brain. No matter how wonderful—and weird, and a little confusing—this night had been.

Maybe I'd just say that. *This was wonderful. Let's never do it again.*

And for all I knew, maybe Kai would whole-heartedly agree.

Except as my body sunk further into the darkness, I had a harder time remembering why, exactly, that was what I wanted.

Maybe my brain just needed to work a little harder. Maybe this *could* make sense.

After all, Kai had said it himself. Even though I'd been trying to forget it ever since he'd said it, because it had felt like such an outlandish thing to say—

Tonight, Kai Andrews had been mine.

All I had to do was believe it.

I could be better, braver than I was in high school. Right?

I fell asleep before my brain found the right answer.

11.

KAI & AIDEN

IF IT WEREN'T for Aiden McCarstle's bony elbow jabbing me in the side when I woke up, I would have sworn the previous evening was a dream.

It was still snowing. And now that there was daylight behind the grey-white clouds, the world outside my window seemed overblown, too bright, filling the bedroom with an ethereal glow. Like maybe it *was* just a dream.

But then McCarstle moved, his elbow jamming into my ribs a bit deeper, and yeah. Nope.

His head was turned toward me, the arm that wasn't stabbing me curled up under the pillow. I let myself stare at his face for thirty seconds—I actually counted, inside my head—at the way his curls fell over his forehead, at the smattering of freckles across his nose that were so faint I wasn't sure I had ever noticed them, until now. He looked peaceful when he slept, skin smooth: not even a hint of scowl lines.

I crawled quietly out of bed when my thirty seconds were up. Anything more than thirty seconds seemed foolish. Even those thirty had probably been ill-advised.

Last night was the first time anyone had stayed over in this apartment with me.

And I had liked it, waking up with Aiden McCarstle's elbow in my side.

I grabbed my phone from the side table and padded over to the window.

The world looked so quiet out there, everything a blanket of white. No tire marks on the roads, no footprints on the sidewalks. Not a soul around.

Aiden wouldn't try to leave in this. Right?

A low groan sounded behind me, the shifting of sheets. My pulse pounded, and I googled frantically anyway.

It hadn't *seemed* like just a night of fucking, last night. But I still couldn't trust my gut completely when it came to McCarstle. He was too stubborn, too skittish. Even though my heart kept floating around my body in a dumb soup of hope every time he looked at me in that intense way he looked at me sometimes. Every time it seemed like he had lowered his shields. Every time he used my name in casual conversation—*Kai, I am so bad at it*—like we were friends. Every time he touched me. And he was really, really good at touching me.

Still. It would not surprise me if he *did* try to leave in the middle of a blizzard and I never saw him again.

I scanned the local headlines on my tiny screen. My hope soup swirled around my veins in triumph. I opened my mouth as soon as I heard him roll off the bed, before he reached me, before he had a chance to speak first.

"The buses aren't running."

I turned to see him rub a hand over his face as he approached me at the window, eyes still half asleep. He garbled out some indecipherable, rusty sounding syllables, which I think amounted to, "Say what?"

"There was freezing rain earlier this morning," I explained. "And now more of this—" I gestured behind me, to the furiously falling flakes of white—"which means snow on top of ice. It sounds like the roads are impassable. The whole transit system's not running until it at least warms up some."

"Oh." Aiden looked dazed, like his brain was still processing what I'd said.

But—*but*—he didn't look disappointed. Or upset that he was stuck here with me. At least, not yet.

I had to do something, before his face changed. Because suddenly my mind was whirring, excitement racing along my skin at the prospect of all I could do with a day of being snowed in with Aiden McCarstle. If he didn't close himself off again. If we could only continue what we had started last night. Not just the sex, but the talking, too. The laughing.

He just needed to stay.

I couldn't wait for his command this time.

I dropped to my knees, and without preamble, grabbed the base of Aiden's morning erection in my hand, gliding my mouth over the tip.

Aiden startled, leaning a hand onto the glass of the window to steady himself.

"Jesus, Kai." He sounded more awake, now.

But he didn't push me off.

So I kept going, even though it was completely lewd, doing this right in front of my window, two minutes after he'd woken up. But I didn't think anyone could actually see us up here, and the rest of the city was still cooped up inside anyway, and...the world just seemed so pretty, right then, everything hushed and pure. I had been desperate to keep him here when I started, but the more I went on, it felt right, somehow, just our bodies and the whiteout outside, the quiet only broken by Aiden's harsh breaths.

He threaded his fingers through my hair, curled his fingers around the short strands until I felt the tug at my scalp. The gentle pressure of it felt so good that I had to pause for a moment, my eyes fluttering shut, a small moan escaping my mouth. Which only made Aiden tug harder.

Dizzy, I took in a few breaths before I continued, my want mounting with each passing second. Remembering the command Aiden had given last night, that had almost tipped me over the edge through words alone, I moved the hand that wasn't wrapped around the base of Aiden's cock to my own erection, moaning again as I touched myself.

"Kai," Aiden breathed. "God."

I let his approval wash over me, shivered a little in its glow.

He said my name again a moment later, his command broken up by heavy breaths: "I want you to come," *pant*, "same time." *Pant*. "Wait until I'm there too."

I stilled both of my hands, taking my own minute to breathe.

"Yeah," I whispered. "Okay."

I was already on the edge, unsure if I'd actually be able to hold myself back much longer. I upped my speed on Aiden's end, and soon—

"Now," Aiden wheezed.

My vision was a blur of Aiden's skin and the bright world outside, dancing against the black that hovered at the edges of my mind. And then—fuck—I

I was choking, tears streaming down my face. I coughed, my throat making embarrassing sounds as I struggled for air. I tried to apologize, but I couldn't make my vocal cords work, and—

"*Shit.*"

Aiden sank onto the floor, pushing me down with him, so I was suddenly against the window, the cool glass against my back soothing. Aiden ran a thumb across my cheekbone as a few errant tears leaked out, his face creased in concern. It would have been sweet to see, if I wasn't still trying to recover from being a mess.

Apparently I wasn't able to swallow while in the throws of my own orgasm. Which I likely would have realized from the start, if I wasn't so ready to do whatever Aiden McCarstle asked.

"I'm so sorry, Kai. What a dumb thing to—I'm just still half asleep, and—"

"It's okay," I managed, blinking, airways seemingly cleared.

His thumb moved down to the corner of my mouth, and I became aware that—oh god—his spunk was definitely all over my face. And neck. And mine was—who knew. I was trying to decipher whether this was all horrifying or sexy when Aiden leaned in and kissed me.

It was the opposite of how our first kiss had been last night. This kiss was slow, but purposeful, his hands cradled around my head with surety and command while his tongue worked lazily inside my mouth. It was this gentle, languorous exploration that felt...decadent, almost. The way morning kisses should feel.

The panic I'd felt when I first awoke, sure he would try to leave, bled away, the ache in my chest from my choking fit subsiding. I pulled him to me, stretched my legs around him to keep him there. Rubbed circles on his side. And even as he continued to kiss the hell out of me, I swear it was like he...softened. Like all of his sharp angles became more malleable, an easiness he hadn't yet let me see. A funny kind of kitten, purring in my lap. Bony, lanky, but a kitten nonetheless.

"Shower?" I asked once he finally pulled away, once I recovered my breath.

"Together?" Aiden sat back on his heels. A part of me wanted to reach out and bring him back to my lap, but I knew I shouldn't press my luck.

I nodded, and he shook his head.

"Showering with other humans is always a bad idea."

I frowned.

But I knew the day was going to be okay when that was all it took—just one frown from me—to make Aiden sigh and say, "Fine. But I get to say I told you so when it's the worst."

And, okay. Maybe it was sort of the worst. One of us was always cold, and anything I thought would be sexy only turned out awkward, water splashing into our eyes and our mouths. And I'd had enough choking for one morning.

Still, it was worth it. To feel clean, and to see Aiden smile, which he did a lot, every time he got to stand under the showerhead and watch me shiver.

We toweled off, and I threw on some sweats and an old t-shirt. Noticing him standing uncertainly in the corner, I rooted around my dresser and offered him the smallest set of clothes I could find. He scowled.

"Those are going to be too big."

I shrugged. "You can wear your Moonie's clothes again, if you want."

Grumbling, he took them from my hands.

Giving him privacy, I padded to the kitchen, yawning as I went. I turned on the coffeemaker, rooted around the fridge. Brought out eggs, a block of cheddar, bacon. I'd just put the frying pan on the stove when I heard Aiden enter the room.

I slid a mug of coffee his way as he slumped onto a stool at the kitchen island.

"Shut up," he said, followed immediately by, "Thank you." He wrapped his hands around the mug.

I managed to keep it together—mostly—until I turned back to the stove.

The clothes *were* too big on him. And I loved it. The sight of Aiden McCarstle, sitting at my kitchen island, wearing my clothes, unexpectedly made me want to explode. I hoped he couldn't tell from the back of my head how big I was smiling, that the cheesy scrambled eggs I cooked were the only ones to witness my sheer delight.

We ate in a comfortable silence, other than the satisfied groans Aiden couldn't seem to keep inside when he first chomped down on a piece of bacon, first shoveled the eggs into his mouth. The happy hum as he refilled on my coffee. I just sat next to him, trying not to glow too much.

I took our plates when we were done, ran them under hot water. I was rinsing the frying pan and thinking about what we should do next—Aiden probably wouldn't want to go out into the snow and, like, make snow angels, or anything, but maybe I could carefully pressure him into it —when suddenly he was behind me, arms wrapped around my stomach, mouth at my neck.

The pan slid out of my hands.

Almost involuntarily, I sunk back into him, my entire body doing this *woosh* thing that I was learning happened whenever Aiden was too close and it wanted him to take over. One of his hands snuck underneath my t-shirt, the other traveling lower, palming me over my sweats while his lips dragged over my neck, and god. I shuddered, everything suddenly running hot in my system, burning to the surface of my skin. I was so lost to him like this. He had to know.

"Kai." His breath tickled the back of my ear. "I want you to fuck me."

Okay. Well. Right. Okay. No snow angels then, for now.

I turned off the tap.

* * *

Kai turned. I pushed my hips against his, gripped the sink behind him. Everything in this kitchen was so new. Shiny and flawless.

"I've, um." He blushed, staring at my mouth. "Never done that."

It was especially cute seeing Kai this bashful right now. Like he hadn't sucked me off when I was barely still awake, whilst vigorously jerking himself off, a mere hour ago. Like he hadn't been practically gleeful about me tying his wrists to his headboard with his own tie last night. Like he wasn't remarkably free with his body, in this fascinating way that was both shy and confident all at once.

It must have been a combination of the morning orgasm and the breakfast he'd just made me, which had tasted like the best thing I'd ever had in my goddamn life, that made me so...okay, right now. More than okay, actually.

I was stuck in Kai Andrews's apartment, a pair of his too-big sweatpants tied around my waist, one of his faded t-shirts slumping around my collarbone. The snow appeared to have no intention of stopping. I had no idea when I'd be able to leave.

And I wasn't freaking out at all.

It was like any desire to fight against this had swiftly disappeared in the muted, early morning light, in the blizzard that closed us in here together.

Maybe it *was* the blizzard, actually, that was magically calming my brain. It wasn't just Kai Andrews's mouth, or his cheesy eggs. I no longer merely had to imagine we were living in a snow globe.

This was a full blown snow day.

And responsibilities didn't exist on snow days.

I understood why Kai liked ceding control to me. Like he was right now, practically limp in my arms. It was freeing, not having the option to leave. I felt weightless, trapped in time.

I didn't have to decide jack shit about anything, as long as it was still snowing.

"I would tell you what to do," I told Kai now. "But it's okay if you're not into it, seriously."

"No, no." He reached around me, grabbing my ass, like he'd done at Moonie's last night, losing some of his shyness. "I want to. Tell me what to do."

I kissed his nose.

I was a nose kisser, apparently, on snow days.

"Take off all your clothes and wait for me on the couch."

He did as asked, in good haste, as I was coming to expect. He listened to all of my rough instructions, changed positions easily when requested, until I could truly feel the power of those soccer star thighs, those welder's shoulders, and it was so good I nearly lost consciousness.

He laid his head on my chest afterward, while our bodies cooled down. I didn't mind the contact, for now. I felt tender and bruised in all the right ways.

"Wow," he said. "That was…"

"Fantastic," I finished.

"Yeah."

"Thank you for that. And for breakfast," I added. "And, you know, the stuff before that."

He laughed a little, a puff of air dancing across my nipple.

"Snow days are the best."

"They really are," I agreed. This was even better than when I was in high school. Apparently non-stop orgasms with a remarkable person beat out reading alone in my room and listening to Radiohead. Who knew.

"Aiden?" Kai asked after several minutes had passed. I blinked, realizing I had been spacing out, watching the snow out of his living room window. His voice was tentative, and for the first time all morning, I tensed. "Can you read me one of your new poems?"

"Oh," I laughed. That wasn't what I had expected, at all, but the answer was easy. "No."

He pushed off of me. Leaned down to pick up his t-shirt from the floor. Sighed as he pulled it over his head.

"Yeah." He reached for his underwear. "Figured that'd be the answer."

Shit. I scrambled up into a seated position, startled at how sad he sounded. Or disappointed, or something. Which was not at all how he should sound, after what we'd just done. It kept ringing in my ears with wrongness.

This had been a fucking excellent morning. If I had somehow ruined it, before we even hit lunch, I'd actually hate myself.

I thought about him sneaking looks at my poems during pre-calc. Talking about looking for me at Barnes & Noble. My stomach twisted. He kept...doing this. Saying things that pulled me in different directions. Routes I didn't know how to navigate.

I had a bunch of poems on my phone, and several more memorized. I knew it was nice, that he cared about them. But it felt like too much. It felt like when I'd stared a little too long at the scars on his arms last night.

And workshopping poetry was what I did out there, beyond this shiny, window-filled apartment, in ugly classrooms filled with ambition and harsh lighting. I wanted this one timeless day outside of all that, where I didn't have to worry about metaphors or cadence or meaning or worth. Where I could just be.

I didn't know how to explain all of that to Kai without hurting him.

He stepped into the bathroom. Awkwardly, I waited for my turn, cleaned myself up, put his t-shirt and sweatpants back on. He had left a new toothbrush on the counter for me to use. I stared at it for at least three beats too long.

When I returned to the living room, Kai was in the kitchen, brewing another pot of coffee, so I perused the bookshelf in the corner. It was half full of books, half full of framed photos, trinkets and mementos. The books were mostly mysteries and non-fiction, a bunch of manuals on welding and construction and woodworking.

"Coffee's fresh, if you want more."

I turned. He stood a few feet away, blowing on the top of his steaming mug, his other hand in his pocket. He looked casual, and fine—and hot, because he always looked hot—not hurt or sad or disappointed anymore, but a weird pressure to be a good person pushed at me from behind my ribcage anyway.

"I could read you other people's poems," I blurted. "If you wanted." I lifted a hand, let it drop. "I could tell you about some of my favorite poets. It's...easier, sharing someone else's words."

Kai looked at me over his coffee. A corner of his mouth curved steadily up.

"I would love that," he said, and my stomach danced a needless little jig. *He didn't fuck it all the way up!,* it shouted to my spleen.

I opened my phone and did a quick Google. And then I read him an Ocean Vuong, right there, while we stood across from each other in his living room.

When I was done, he said, "Thank you."

And he walked over and kissed me.

His phone rang a minute later—his aunt calling, making sure he was safe in the snowstorm—and as he walked away to take it, I went back to nosily looking around his apartment. Pretending the moment hadn't shaken me, hadn't felt overwhelmingly intimate.

Easier to keep staring at his bookshelves, the art on the walls, that view out his window. By the time Kai returned, shoving his phone in his pocket, I almost felt normal again.

Almost.

12.

AIDEN

WE WERE SITTING in front of the window, passing a bag of pretzels back and forth and talking about snow memories.

"We've never been particularly close, Jackson and me," I said, passing the bag back to Kai. "But whenever there was actually a good snow day, when we were kids, he'd pull me through the neighborhood, right in the middle of the street on this old sled."

Jackson always felt a little bit like Superman to me on those days. Pulling me just fast enough to be thrilling, not scary.

"I think it always felt so wild because the street was this dangerous space every other day of the year, where you had to look both ways, that you couldn't cross without grownups. But on snow days, it was ours."

The time for lunch had approached and fallen away. We'd discovered Kai had little in his kitchen that *wasn't* bacon and eggs, so we'd decided to simply wile away the day with constant snacks.

After a few moments of comfortable quiet, Kai said, "I *still* can't believe you've lived here your entire life and have never been skiing."

I shrugged, grabbing a pretzel. It didn't surprise me that Kai was a skier. Even if a true snowstorm like this in the city was rare, Mount Hood, a skier's paradise, was only an hour away. But it had always seemed like a hobby reserved for the cool, rich kids, and I struck out on both of those qualities.

"I didn't say *never*. Pen's family took me once, freshman year."

"And?"

"And I don't see the appeal of purposely hurtling yourself down a mountain. And it was fucking cold."

Kai grinned in delight.

"It's also fucking *exhilarating*."

He went on, recalling his favorite Mount Hood stories, gesturing with his hands, smiling and relaxed. I simply sipped my water and watched him, my own dopey smile on my face. Talking about my older brother had left me feeling weirdly sentimental.

It must have been the sweetness of that nostalgia that pulled my brain away from the details of Kai's story, about the time he and his friend Dylan, who I vaguely remembered, had tried snowboarding and "almost died approximately fifty times." While Kai laughed at his memories, my focus faded away, consumed instead with this vision: sitting inside a ski lodge, Timberline maybe. Writing and reading around the fireplace, sipping hot cocoa. Surrounded by strong pillars of warm timber, Pendleton rugs, deep, ancient chairs. Waiting, content, for Kai to wander in, cheeks rosy from the slopes, snow clinging to the tips of his wind whipped hair. His lips would be cold against mine as he leaned in for a kiss hello.

And then we'd sit together for a while. I'd buy him his own hot cocoa. And eventually, he'd go back to the great outdoors, and I'd crack open my book again.

I blinked. Kai was still chuckling to himself, shoving a pretzel in his mouth. I hoped his story was over. I hoped I hadn't missed any cues where I was meant to jump in with a response.

Either way, enough storytelling for now.

I stood, scratching my elbows.

"Do you have any games?"

Kai looked up in surprise.

"Oh. Um, yeah, actually. I think."

Brushing pretzel dust off his hands, he walked to a closet in the small hallway by the bathroom. I peered over his shoulder.

"I have—"

"Boggle." I reached over him to grab the square, dented box from the top shelf. "We are totally Boggling, Andrews."

He sighed.

"We both know you're going to kick my ass at that."

"Maybe."

I did, in fact, kick his ass, most of the time. I spent the first half hour trying to tamp down my excitement about the Boggling, lest I appear too much like the hardcore nerd I obviously was. Or maybe the happiness coursing through my veins was simply relief at having something to focus on that made sense. Like letters and words and beating Kai Andrews. Fuck ski lodges.

Kai did, to his credit, triumph a few times. He looked so proud each time that it was difficult to keep myself from catapulting across the table to cradle his face and pat his hair.

Still, after over an (incredible) hour of Boggling, he flopped back against the couch, hands over his face.

"Aiden," he said into his fingers. "I know you're enjoying this, but if I have to Boggle with you one more time, I may scream. Just to let you know."

"Cool." I stood, stretched out my back, and promptly picked up the coffee table we'd been playing on. I moved it to the side, revealing the lush rug underneath it that I'd been tickling my toes on all day. "Take off your clothes and lie down."

Frankly, beating Kai at Boggle had gotten me rather riled up.

He let out a small gust of air when I pinned his arms above his head. He had been smiling to himself as he undressed, but when I looked down at him now, like last night, his face was a picture of perfect calm. Like he was at home here, with his wrists trapped underneath my fists. Like he trusted me.

And right then, I felt the same. My Boggle adrenaline bled out of my system, and I only felt fucking serene.

I ran my fingers over his scars again. I had made him tell me, earlier, more about exactly what it was that he did at the port, even though I knew I wouldn't understand a word of it. He'd shown me some videos of him doing welding stuff real good. They were all super dark and looked like nothing but random moving pieces of hot metal to me. It looked dangerous, and difficult. Kai looked very excited about all of it. It had been super dreamy.

I leaned down and nipped at his nipples. He sucked in a breath. I loved making Kai suck in a breath.

I decided then to take my time. Because time was the one thing we had today. Because I wanted to.

Slowly, meticulously, I licked and bit my way around his skin. Touched, listened. Caressed all the way down to his toes. Learned him, better this time than I had before. His hardness, so much muscle and bone, but his soft places, too. The inside of his thighs, right above his knees. His hips, where they curved into his ass. The sweet spot where his neck met his ears. His mouth.

It felt like the closest I'd ever come to physically manifesting a poem.

"Aiden," he eventually whispered, voice ragged. "Please."

He had never moved his arms from where I had originally pinned him, not even once. He was getting so much better at this. I was, too.

But when I paused to really look at him, he looked wrecked. Mouth open, taking in these shaky gasps of air. Eyes glassy. Like he was barely keeping it together.

I wanted to eat him alive. I rested my forehead on his chest instead, took a second to compose myself.

And then I took him in my mouth.

He came to pieces in minutes.

Thank god we still had lube and condoms nearby from earlier, because I was pretty incoherent with need after that. It was fast, and hot, and Kai was just so good and open, and I had no words at all in my head, this time. Only raw sensation and connection. It was like I forgot myself entirely, and...I couldn't remember the last time I forgot myself entirely. That I hadn't been consumed with trying to find the right words. It felt like free falling. Too much, and just right.

I was shattered, afterward.

I barely had enough energy to tap his wrists. And then I curled myself on top of him, my head on his chest, a leg draped over his thighs.

"McCarstle," he whispered. "Thank you." I felt his nose nestle into my hair.

I knew, then, that the line I had tried to draw in my head was blurred for good. The line where we were just two people stuck inside, enjoying each other. His hand ran absently up and down my shoulder. I listened to his heart beat.

It didn't feel like just a snow day, anymore.

We lay there for a long time. I listened to his breathing return to normal. I tried to find equilibrium.

I grasped it, finally, when I felt him shift, the arm that wasn't around me going behind his head. I realized suddenly that I knew what was coming next, could practically feel whatever question it was making its way from Kai's brain to his mouth, and it made me want to laugh. Which helped me get out of my head.

Kai just really liked asking probing personal questions after orgasms. Like spilling secrets around a campfire. Camp Sex and Share. It was very Kai.

"What's the one thing you want most?" he asked. "If you could accomplish one thing, the rest of your life."

I turned my head even further into him, to hide my grin in his chest hair. Helplessly, I squeezed my arm tighter around his side.

Surely, he knew my answer to this one. It seemed so obvious—and so annoying—in my own head.

"I want to publish books," I said.

Kai just kept rubbing my shoulder.

"Tell me more. About what your books would be like."

Ugh, Kai, I thought. Grinned a bit more. But I gathered

my courage. Wanting, for some reason, to be a good camp participant.

"I've had poems published here and there. But I want a whole book full of them, where I could organize them by theme. And someone could have it on their shelf and open it up to a random poem whenever they wanted, and then put it back on the shelf until the next time they needed another one. I want the pages to be slightly yellowed. Something soothing and nature-y on the cover. A really good serif font."

I almost laughed at myself, once I finally shut my mouth. Except I didn't want to laugh at myself. I only felt like I should. And I knew Kai didn't care either way. So I didn't.

"And...I want to travel more. See more of the world to write about."

"Mmm," he hummed, a rumble on the side of my cheek.

"What about you?" I asked back. "What do you want?"

"I want a house," he said, without hesitation, "with a view of Mount Hood. A decent amount of land. Maybe out in Estacada or somewhere."

"That sounds nice," I said. Because it did.

I imagined his port job, with the risk of all that hot metal, probably paid well. I imagined a house with a view of Mount Hood was actually realistic for him.

My chest squeezed, not exactly in jealousy, but in admiration, maybe. For having dreams that were actually accomplishable. I couldn't wait for him to get that house. To be happy.

"Yeah. I'll have to figure out something at some point, about what to do next. I can't do my current job forever. It's too physically and mentally demanding. I've seen the guys who've done this for too long. I don't want to...break myself."

Immediately, almost unconsciously, I tightened my hold on him even more.

"But I'll figure something out. So I can still get the house, one day."

I almost dozed off once silence settled over us again. Thinking about Kai's house. Thinking about my bisexual lumberjack, traces of gray in his hair—fuck, he would look so good, even more weathered—rocking gently on a porch swing.

And then he said, "You should quit grad school."

My eyes blinked open.

"It's...not that easy," I eventually got out.

"I think it probably is, though."

I tried to picture going home for Christmas in a few weeks, telling my parents I'd quit school. That I had no plan.

I wanted to go back to my lumberjack Kai dreams.

"I need the loans to survive right now," I managed. "I can't exactly live on dog walking pay."

"So get another job. Go back to the bakery. You can work at the bakery and still write."

I was quiet.

"Sorry," Kai said after a minute. He blew a breath into my hair. "I don't have the right to tell you what to do with your life."

"It's okay."

I pushed off him, though, finally.

I walked into the kitchen. Filled a glass with water from the tap, drank the entire thing in one go. Found some tortilla chips.

When I walked back into the living room, Kai hadn't

moved. He was still lying on his back on the rug, a small, concerned crease between his eyes.

I sank onto the couch. I didn't know how to explain it to him. Or even to myself, really. That his suggestion that I quit school wasn't an inappropriate thing to say. I wasn't angry.

But it felt scary when Kai said it because he'd had the courage to say it out loud before I did. And now that *someone* had said it out loud, it was going to live in my head forever.

One thing I did know was that I wanted Kai to stop looking at me like that. Like something had just gone wrong, like he thought I was mad at him. Because it wasn't him I was mad at at all. So I got back up and looked around for my phone. I finally found it in the bathroom.

And I read him a Mary Oliver, to be nice.

* * *

For dinner, we had cheesy eggs again.

And it was, honestly, perfect.

Hours had passed since the grad school conversation. Hours spent sharing odd little high school memories. Sharing more poems. Staring out at the snow and the darkening sky, doing nothing. Pen had texted, assuring us she was home and doing fine. I felt so warm and content by dinner that afterward, I suggested watching a movie. Kai chose some Captain America thing, something safe and full of loud noises. I curled into his chest on the couch, let him play with my hair, because...because it felt good. Because I had lost the line. I hadn't been careful at all. I had stopped being careful, probably, the minute I first touched the scar on his arm last night. The snow was starting to taper off, but the world outside was still quiet. I fell asleep halfway through.

Kai jostled my shoulder during the credits. He leaned down to grab the remote from the coffee table, clicked off the TV. It was so dark and still then, both in the apartment and in my head, the glow from a small lamp on a side table the only thing lighting the room.

Kai stood, reached out a hand. He led me out of the living room.

There was something about walking toward his bedroom this time, the second night in a row I'd be resting my head on his pillows. We'd mostly lazed away the hours today in the living room and the kitchen, so going back to the bedroom felt...it was silly, and hard to describe, but it felt both special and familiar all at once. Like this was our routine now. Retiring together. Like lovers.

We were halfway there when the power went out.

The kitchen light clicked off, all of the shiny appliances whooshing a quiet sigh as they powered down. The snowy night outside Kai's windows, which had been illuminated in the street lights, went dark, too.

We froze. After a second, Kai turned and kissed me. It felt like the most romantic moment of my life, and I was glad we were standing in the pitch dark, because suddenly I felt deeply embarrassed. About just how carried away I'd let myself become.

After stumbling around for a bit with his phone's flashlight—I didn't dare try to use mine; the battery was almost dead—Kai unearthed one of those big candle jars from somewhere. Lit it and put it on his dresser. It was something cinnamony, rich and sweet.

I swear I meant to seduce him some more. Fucking Kai

again by candlelight probably would have been a pretty fine way to finish off this day.

But it turned out my body had had enough of that. I remembered getting under the covers, Kai murmuring something in my ear about going to the bathroom, being right back.

And then, by accident, I fell back asleep.

13.

KAI & AIDEN

I KNEW, instinctively, the moment I woke up and realized the space beside me on the bed was cold.

Everything was cold, really. I could hear the heat humming to life, but the power must have only come back on recently, because it was freezing in here.

But nothing felt quite as cold as Aiden McCarstle, sitting on the opposite corner of the bed, pulling on his socks. His black and white striped sweater was back on, his dark jeans. The clothes he'd borrowed from me yesterday were neatly folded and stacked on my dresser.

He stood, and I could feel it even before he turned to look me in the face. That restlessness was back. And when I did get to see his eyes, they were wide, slightly panicked, like they had been when I first sat down at Moonie's two nights ago. Like they had looked almost every time I ran into him in high school.

"Right. So," he said, clearing his throat.

He turned and left the room.

Dammit.

I hissed when my feet hit the floor—shit, it was cold—

and threw on a pair of sweats before following him to the kitchen, before he could leave without saying goodbye.

Even then, within the space of however many seconds it took me to do that, he'd already put on his coat and shoved his feet into his sneakers.

Dammit dammit *dammit.*

"Aiden. I don't think it's even safe to go out there yet."

He took his phone out of his pocket and waved it at me.

"Just checked. Buses are running, with chains."

I leaned against the kitchen island, crossed my arms over my chest.

"You could at least stay for breakfast." Except, wait, I'd used the last of the eggs last night. "Or a cup of coffee, at least. We should talk."

"Yeah, um." He ran a hand through his hair. "No thank you."

I swallowed to silence my growl. I knew there was probably no point even trying to argue with him. His shields were back up. He'd let them down for a precious twenty four hours with me. Had let himself be happy for a day.

And now, he was as closed off as he'd ever been.

But I didn't find his cageyness charming anymore.

He held all the control here, and I knew it. But this wasn't a control I had granted. This was a control that wasn't fair.

"Look," I sighed. "I know this—" I made a gesture toward my apartment, toward the winter world outside the window, "was intense. And probably not a totally normal way to start a relationship, but I—" Aiden's face went entirely blank at the *r* word, but fuck it—"I'd like to see you again, Aiden. I..." I faltered, wondering exactly how much I should put myself on the line here, how much of my heart I should give him when I knew, rationally, that he didn't want it.

But the irrational part of me wanted to tell him anyway. That I'd hoped moving back home would help me heal, finally, after Mom's death, but I'd only felt out of sync ever since I came back. And that I hadn't felt truly at home here —in this apartment, in this city again, in my own life— until Aiden let me sing ELO. Until he kissed me. Until he stayed here with me, and read me poems, and kicked my ass at Boggle, and treated me like I was important. Like we were important to each other.

"I had a wonderful time," I finished.

Aiden looked away, closing his eyes for a moment.

"I did, too," he said eventually, voice strained. "But I'm sorry; that's all it was, okay? A wonderful time. I got to live out a fantasy—"

"I'm not a *fantasy*, Aiden," I bit out, anger flashing in my veins. "I'm a human fucking being."

But it was like he didn't even hear me.

"And you got..." He went on, waving a hand limply through the air. "You got another notch on your bisexual belt."

I sucked in a breath. An awful, tiny moment of silence transpired before I could respond.

"That's a really shitty thing to say, Aiden."

"Yeah, well." He ran a hand through his hair again and sighed. Like he knew it was. But he'd said it anyway.

"Bye, Kai."

And he left.

I watched him walk through the door. Watched the lock snick shut behind him.

Felt the loneliness swoop back into the apartment,

filling it from corner to corner, before Aiden had even made it down the hall.

I breathed in through my nose in bitter frustration. Pressed a hand to my neck, where he had bitten me two nights ago. I had looked at it in the mirror yesterday, the purple mark unmistakable. Knew Alice at work would give me shit on Monday. It still felt tender under my fingers.

I knew there were other patterns left on me, down my arms, my sides, my hips. The scrapes and indentations of his fingernails, his teeth.

The asshole got to walk out of here scot-free.

But I'd be carrying his bruises for days.

* * *

I hadn't been prepared for the sun.

It had been so bright when I woke up, the sky so shockingly blue.

I had looked over at Kai's slumbering body, his skin golden in the light, his hair rumpled, his mouth slightly open as he slept. He was more perfect than he'd ever been.

And all I felt was wrong.

I slipped and stumbled on the melting snow, the surface beneath my feet icy and uneven. The world was still quiet out here, everyone else still wrapped in the safety of their homes, no sidewalks shoveled yet. Just walking the block and a half to the bus stop was a journey that left me out of breath, a freezing damp seeping into my sneakers, my entire body uncomfortable and clumsy.

It'd take the city days to dig out from this. My car was likely still buried in the Moonie's parking lot. Even if it was accessible, I wouldn't trust it to make it through these messy streets. I'd have to bus it all the way home. Which, especially if the buses were chained, would take forever.

Forever to sit with my wet feet and my sad brain. I didn't even have a book with me to read. And I'd used the last 1% of battery life on my phone double checking the buses were running.

I was almost to the bus shelter when I bit it. One wrong step and I was on my back on the ice, almost smacking my head on the corner of a bench.

Ow.

I laid there a minute, blinking into the sun, the breath knocked out of my lungs.

I pictured Kai leaning over me, reaching out his hand. Wrapping me in his arms. Warming me up.

I already missed him.

And suddenly, simultaneously, as the sun bore into my irises, I missed Niall.

I always missed Niall, in a way.

I pictured what Penelope would do if I told her. *I think I'm in love with Kai Andrews. But instead of telling him that, I said some real mean stuff and then ran away.*

"Aiden!" She would say, eyes flaring, smacking me in the chest. "You march back in there and make it right *right now.*"

Niall would look at me and laugh. "Of course you did, you sad bastard."

And then he'd help me up and we'd go nurse some cheap beer and feel sorry for ourselves.

With a groan, I maneuvered to my side, managed to push myself to a sitting position.

Falling in love with Niall had been so easy. We met in college, when I had been able to reinvent myself. To only show him the parts I wanted. When I had felt, for the first time, understood, seen. Surrounded by people like me, people who had always felt different, who had never fit in high school, who had yearned to break free and live a life that was new and uninhibited. Where we could all be ourselves, all of our incongruent parts, our wild, unstable minds.

We had gone to art gallery openings together, me and Niall, poetry readings, had stayed up too late, fucking and getting drunk on cheap wine. On road trips, we took pictures of each other with an old film camera he'd found in a thrift shop in Seattle. On the way to Baja, we'd sat on his friends' roof in LA, stared through the hazy night and pretended we could see the stars.

Looking back now, so much of our relationship had been a cliché. But it had felt beautiful, at the time. It had felt like I was finally alive.

And now, I was in stasis.

And while being wrapped in Kai's arms again would feel incredible, it also felt so much more complicated. Our lives were still so far apart. He was clearly dealing with his own, much more serious shit. And Kai didn't know the me Niall had been able to see. He only knew gawky, socially inept Aiden McCarstle from high school, when I'd been crawling out of my own skin every day. He only knew the Aiden McCarstle he'd met at Moonie's two nights ago, inexplicably angry and disillusioned with his life. He only knew the worst parts of me, and I didn't understand why he'd still given me so much kindness. God, I was exhausted with myself half the time. It seemed cruel to subject a shining light like Kai Andrews to that exhaustion for longer than a day.

Except...I hadn't really felt exhausted with myself, yesterday.

The bus rumbled up to Kai's stop. I stepped on, clinked the change I'd scraped from the bottom of my bag into the payment box, since my phone was dead. I dropped myself into a seat up front. My body felt heavy, tired.

I leaned my head against the window.

Penelope was going to be so mad at me.

I suddenly, desperately wanted to go back to Kai's apartment and do it differently. I didn't know why I'd said anything I said, especially that bisexual belt bit. Jesus.

Except...I did know. I had needed to be the worst version of myself, say the most hurtful things, so that he'd stop being so wonderful. So he'd let me go.

But as the bus made its way through the slush and ice, regret soured in my stomach, warring against everything else already muddled there.

I didn't want Kai to think I was a shitty person. Even if I was. Even if it shouldn't matter what Kai Andrews thought of me.

I wanted everything to be different.

God. I could lose myself in him, probably.

The only problem was, I already felt so lost.

If I lost myself in him without finding myself first, I might disappear completely.

* * *

Penelope blew up my phone the next day.

Aiden Logan McCarstle. What did you do to Kai Andrews???

He just texted me that you and him probably shouldn't hang out together anymore

?????

Look, I know it was shady, not telling you he was going to come to karaoke, but he's been going through a hard time lately, and needs friends, and...I don't know, I always thought you two would get along

Even though I know you were always so weird about him in high school, but I thought that was just because you had a massive crush on him

But I thought we could all be cool now that we're adults!!??

Were you a jerk??

Did you at least get home okay?? Kai says he's safe at home but I know your car can't handle this shit

Sigh. Okay fine just text me back to let me know you're okay

I'm officially unconcussed, by the way. At least I think so. Not sure if that's the official term. Anyway I'm free to text is what I'm saying

I love you, even if you were a jerk

But you should text me back, you jerky jerk

KAI & AIDEN

I HAD to give Aiden McCarstle credit for one thing.

He helped me get off my ass and actually start taking responsibility for myself.

Even if it was just because I could hardly stand to be in my apartment the following week. Every room reminded me too much of that day. It even still smelled like sex the whole next day, and like him: constant reminders of all the places we had let each other in, literally or otherwise.

As soon as the roads were clear, I got the hell out of there.

My mom's house smelled the opposite: dusty and stale, a space lost to time. Except it felt a little less stale, and I felt a little less sad, each time I went back. I made a plan: one room at a time. Made to-do lists and notes on my phone. And I made piles. So, so many piles. So many trips to Goodwill. Ran my truck back and forth to the dump.

Guilt seized the back of my neck with each one of those trips. Would she have approved, that I got rid of that gravy boat? That stack of paperbacks? Almost every single item of clothing? Would Dad have been okay with it?

No, I knew Dad trusted me. Which was why he'd left it all to me. I knew she would have trusted me, too, but it was just as hard as I'd imagined it'd be, at least some days. Not being able to ask her.

What here was important, Mom? What do you want me to keep?

Some things were obvious. The photo albums, the kitchenware and pottery and jewelry I knew had been passed down. The quilts she had made by hand.

And then there were the piles that weren't just hers, but my own memories that lingered in this place. These decisions should have been easier, but I felt her presence even more, sometimes. Like when I threw away almost all of my soccer trophies. *Kai Andrews!* I imagined her saying, slapping my hand. *You worked hard for those!* I laughed when I discovered, in her bedroom closet, a box full of almost everything I'd ever made in shop class in high school. I winced at the rudimentary joints, how sloppy the weld beads were. But then I smiled, remembering what a badass Mrs. Robles had been, how instrumental she'd been in getting me my apprenticeship. How supportive she'd been of me feeling pretty positive that I was done with academic schooling once high school graduation hit. That I was meant to work with my hands.

A week after I met Aiden at Moonie's, I sat in my childhood bedroom and finally texted a couple of my old friends. I knew Lars and Dylan were still in town, or at least in nearby suburbs, but we had lost touch over the years. And it was an awkward thing, trying to re-establish relationships that maybe weren't even viable anymore.

But Lars had texted back immediately.

FUCKING ANDREWS, it's been FORFUCKINGEVER
Come play with us Sunday night, 6:00

We kick a ball around on the old Meadows field every week
Muddy as shit at the moment but still worth it
FUCK can't wait to see you dude

* * *

Muddy as shit was probably an understatement. Because even though the rain had returned, washing away most of the snow, it was still December, only a couple of weeks away from Christmas. So it was more like muddy ice, which was brutal.

But god, it felt good to kick a ball around again.

There were some guys I didn't know, friends of Lars and Dylan they'd found in the years since we last saw each other, but they all thwumped me on the back and welcomed me onto the field. I couldn't even quite remember, honestly, the last time I'd put on spikes, but I was wheezing within ten minutes. My feet were soaked, my legs streaked with mud even faster. I was shit, basically. And the guys let me know it.

I hadn't felt so happy since, well. Since McCarstle. But happy in a different way, a simpler way. A soccer field would never let me down.

Still, I kept thinking about Aiden, as the night wound down, as I sat on a cold metal bench with my old teammates to switch back into our sneakers, as we caught up on each other's lives. Maybe it was something about the adrenaline of the night matching the adrenaline I'd felt on the dance floor at Moonie's, or something about being around other people from high school. But if these guys were actually going to be my friends again, I suddenly wanted them to know.

"Hey," I said, grabbing a small towel I'd thrown in my

bag, wiping down my face. "I want to tell you guys something."

"Shoot." Lars slicked his white-blonde hair away from his forehead.

"I sort of figured out something about myself when I was living down in Klamath Falls."

Dylan turned fully toward me, propped his chin on his fist, grinning.

"Do go on," he said.

I rolled my eyes, but laughed a little. "I'm bisexual." I shrugged. "Just wanted to let you know so it wouldn't freak you out, if I start dating a dude or something."

"*Have* you dated dudes?" Lars asked.

I shrugged again. "A little."

Lars let out a whistle.

"Damn," he said. "Impressive."

"Okay, so I have questions," Dylan jumped in. But then he frowned. "Wait. Am I allowed to ask questions? I'm trying to be less of an asshole."

I shoved his shoulder.

"Dylan. You were never an asshole. And yeah, you can ask questions."

"I know you said you only recently discovered this, but did you have any hints or anything, when we were in high school? Or like—" He licked his lips, motioning with his hands. "Was there anything we could have done as your friends that would've helped you feel more comfortable to discover it?"

"No, man. You were good. I was pretty clueless. I think that was all on me."

"Okay. It's just, Dakota's only two, but I want to make sure...I don't know, that he's comfortable being whoever when he grows up, you know? I'm trying to be less hetero-normative."

I smiled.

"I think if you're using the phrase 'trying to be less heteronormative' you're doing okay, Dylan."

"All right." Dylan breathed out, but he didn't necessarily seem reassured. God, being a parent seemed stressful.

"It is weird, though," I ventured. "Looking back at when we were younger, now that I know more about myself, you know?"

Dylan and Lars both gave knowing nods. Even though I didn't think either of them was queer, I guessed this strange sense of revised nostalgia might have been a universal feeling.

"I really don't think I knew it at the time, but now..." I swallowed. Tried to sound chill. Maybe getting this out would help somehow. "I think I had a little bit of a crush on Aiden McCarstle."

And Lars, but no way in hell I'd ever disclose *that*.

Dylan's eyes went wide. He leaned back, smiling again.

"Thank you," he said, holding out his hands. "This is the juicy stuff I was hoping for."

Lars's forehead creased, as if he was trying to remember. "Smart kid? Kind of a loner? But hung out with Penelope?"

"Yup," I affirmed. "That's the one."

"Wait." Dylan smacked my arm. "Andrews! I'm pretty sure that guy's still living around here! I see him on Pen's Instagram sometimes. Well, you probably know that too, I guess, if you and Pen are still close."

"Yeah, no, I know."

"Dude! You should ask him out! Oh my god. This is exciting."

"I think I'm good," I laughed. "But I appreciate your support."

And I was good. I mean, I was still a little mad at him. But it wasn't my job to make Aiden McCarstle grow up. If he wanted me, he could get my phone number from Penelope.

But until then, if the last year had taught me anything, it was that life was short. I had a house to finish cleaning, a life to pay respect to. And then I had to figure out, when I was done, how to put my childhood on the housing market.

My work was demanding. And now, I had guys to play soccer with a few times a month. I was contemplating getting a new dog soon. Something small and yappy and annoying, maybe, something the opposite of Jack. A dog that would make me laugh, a dog to make new memories with.

If whatever I had glimpsed with McCarstle never went beyond memories of the night I went to Moonie's and Penelope got a concussion, and the snowstorm afterward, so be it. It would be a good memory. And I wouldn't let Aiden's cowardice at the end of it all ruin it.

Because even when somebody left you, your memories were still your own to keep. You got to choose what to do with them.

* * *

When the roads cleared the week after I stumbled out of Kai's apartment, I finally got my car back from the Moonie's parking lot and tried to go back to normal life. Went back to school, workshopped a new poem, taught a string of horrible classes. Had trouble sleeping, sat up too late on my couch trying to push out words that wouldn't come. Watched my neighbors put up Christmas decorations, my block awash in sparkling lights and festive cheer. Walked by the tree in Pioneer Courthouse Square. Watched the snow melt.

Missed Kai the whole time.

On Friday, I took Stanley Tucci and Buster to Chimney Park. I didn't usually take my clients to dog parks; they were too risky. But Chimney Park was the best dog park in the city, open and spacious, plenty of space for the dogs to run, less possibilities for fights.

I told myself Tucci and Buster deserved an afternoon at the park. It was a cold but beautiful day.

Another part of me, though, knew why I was making the drive all the way to this industrial part of the city, far from my own neighborhood.

If I went a certain way, it'd take me right past Moonie's.

I stopped on the way back, when the dogs were good and tuckered, their heads resting on their muddy paws in my backseat.

I crunched to a stop in the gravel lot. It was the middle of the day; Moonie's wouldn't open for hours. I was the only one here.

I stared at the excavators in the distance. Blinked into the sun.

Finally, taking a deep breath, I plugged in my aux cord and thumbed through my phone. And then I played it. "Aside" by The Weakerthans.

The first blast of the guitar felt like stepping into a hot tub. That initial step always a degree hotter than you expected, shocking no matter how you braced yourself. And then you adjusted, let yourself sink in, bit by bit. Realized you couldn't remember the last time your muscles had felt like this: indulgence and care.

I listened to it all the way through. Listened to it again.

And then I searched for ELO.

Stanley Tucci made a snuffling sound when the drum beats of "Mr. Blue Sky" kicked in. Glancing over my shoulder into the backseat, Tucci looked me right in the eye before opening his jaw for an enormous yawn. He proceeded to flop his head onto Buster's butt and promptly fell back asleep.

I laughed. I laughed because Stanley Tucci was cute, and I loved him. I laughed because the memory of Kai Andrews dancing around an empty Moonie's dance floor, hands flying out at his sides, made me laugh. I laughed because it was a funny song, and I loved that this was Kai Andrews's pump up song when he was a teenager, instead of something more hip or current or more...anything, other than what this was.

I laughed because it was one of those moments where everything seemed suddenly clear.

And dammit, I was an idiot.

There had been these puzzle pieces floating around in my head all week, constantly in the background as I went through the motions of my daily life. As I quietly processed everything that had happened during the snowstorm. As I kept on, annoyingly, missing Niall. As I dreamed about a Captain America with brown eyes and soft floral tattoos and a dopey grin. As I avoided phone calls from Pen.

And in the Moonie's parking lot, all the puzzle pieces clicked into place, crystal clear and certain.

I finally understood that all of the puzzle pieces were my fuckups.

But that maybe they were okay.

Maybe failing at grad school was okay. Maybe it was okay to fail at some things. Maybe I needed to learn that doing a thing because you're scared of doing anything else is likely never going to be the right choice.

I didn't think falling in love with Niall—and eventually, falling out of love with him—had actually been a fuckup. But I understood it better now, sitting in the dusty Moonie's parking lot. It had been easy to fall in love with Niall because we had been so alike. Both full of the same big dreams.

I kept thinking, this last week, about reading poems to Kai in his apartment. Just him and me and the snow. We had never done anything like that, Niall and me, even though we both loved poetry. We would have found it corny, probably. Too earnest. We were so invested in being important in undergrad. Being the ones to change the world, to find the story that hadn't been written yet. Too stubborn and young to admit that it was the stories that repeated themselves, the ones you'd already heard before, that were the important ones, in the end.

I had needed Niall back then. To find somebody who saw me. To know I wasn't alone.

And it was possible, I realized now, that I had been comparing every relationship I'd even danced around since then to him. To that first big love.

But maybe what I needed now—no, what I *wanted* now—was someone who wasn't actually like Niall—or me—at all.

Maybe the differences between two people were actually the best parts of all of this. Maybe being different was the point.

And maybe loving someone wasn't about understanding everything about them. Maybe it only required loving their heart.

And I thought—I hoped—that maybe Kai Andrews didn't actually only know my ugly parts. Maybe *I* only saw my ugly parts. Maybe, like Penelope, Kai had in fact always seen me, even if I couldn't. Not just the gangly queer kid, or the insecure poet. Maybe he just saw me.

And maybe I'd never only seen the soccer star. Or the man who built ships with his bare hands. Maybe I'd seen that Penelope loved him, that everyone loved him, because he was so fucking lovable. Always giving everything and everyone his kindness and his generosity, even boys who scowled too much at him, and families who should have helped him better shoulder the burden of grief.

He had been right, of course, that morning. He wasn't a fantasy. He was better.

Maybe leaving Kai Andrews that morning was the biggest fuckup I'd ever done. The entire center of my puzzle. Without him, my pieces were merely an empty frame.

But maybe I could fix it.

Maybe I could strive to be the person Kai saw. The person he believed I could be.

Maybe I *could* be braver than I was in high school. Better than I used to be, but for real this time.

I unplugged my aux cord. Put the radio back on. Gave one more look back at Stanley Tucci and Buster. One last glance at Moonie's.

And then I put my car in gear and drove out of the lot.

* * *

The next week, I showed up everywhere I was supposed to show up. I got to campus on time every day. Graded my last final. Wished my students and my classmates a happy winter break.

And then I walked to the registrar's office.

And I quit.

15.

KAI

I'D MADE it to the attic.

Or more accurately, I had become irritated with the last bits of the kitchen—how many objects could one relatively small space possibly contain?—and decided to take out my frustration in the attic. For some reason I thought all the stuff up here would be old and boring, easy to sort mostly into the *For the Dump* pile. I could barely remember ever coming up here more than five times in my life; what could actually be that important?

Clearly, I wasn't very bright.

Because I'd only made it through one corner and already I was stumped. I sat on a dusty trunk by the tiny circular window and stared, dejected, at the box upon box of Christmas decorations scattered around me.

I thought I had been doing so well. Each day, the house looked less and less like a morbid time capsule, a museum Carol Andrews wouldn't have wanted, and more and more a simple, empty space, ready for someone else to fill with their own life.

But yet, here I was. Frozen by the most basic string of

Christmas lights. I wondered if it would be this, my mother's chipped collection of porcelain angels, that would truly break me.

I was so lost in thought I didn't hear the intruder until they were already clomping up the attic ladder.

In my startled haste, the only weapon I found in the near vicinity was a large wooden candy cane. I wielded it at my side like a sword, ready to use its cheerily white and red striped protection in whatever manner I had to, when Aiden McCarstle's curly black head of hair popped into the musty air of the attic.

"Jesus *Christ*."

I dropped the candy cane to the floor, leaning my hands on my knees.

"McCarstle." I breathed heavily. "What the fuck."

"Sorry."

I glanced up to see him blushing, blinking furiously.

"I knocked, but no one answered, and I figured that was your truck, and..." He scratched at the back of his head. "Your door was open. I'm sorry. Again."

I glared at him, my heart still thudding in my chest.

Except now I couldn't figure out if my heart valves were working overtime because he'd scared the hell out of me, or because now that he was suddenly in front of me again, I couldn't figure out what I felt. If I wanted to pummel the guy, or kiss him so hard he fell over. Because god help me, my blood was thrumming at the sight of him again. Maybe if I kissed him, I could conveniently knock his head on something on our way to the floor.

Whatever I wanted to do, it felt violent. And that surprised me, even though it shouldn't have.

"Why are you here, Aiden?"

"Um." He looked down, at where he was clutching a

folded up piece of paper in his hand. And oh, geez. I knew, instinctually, that whatever was on that piece of paper would probably wreck me. Whether it was an apology or a declaration of undying love. Whatever it was, I wasn't ready for it.

But instead of handing it over, or explaining why he was here, he looked back up at me and said, "I quit school."

"Oh." I blinked, standing fully. "Okay."

And suddenly, the scales of my brain tipped much more firmly into the *just want to pummel him* column.

This was profoundly unfair, telling me something that he knew would make me feel proud of him, when I was still so mad at him. Because I knew now, that I had been lying to myself over the last two weeks. I had never felt non-violent toward Aiden McCarstle at all. I had simply shoved him away to the recesses of my brain so I could focus on other things, like this house, like getting my life back together. And now he was here, and I wanted to shake him.

What did he expect me to do, run toward him and wrap him in a hug? Pat him on the back for finally listening to himself?

"Anyway," he said, casting his eyes away again. "I just wanted to tell you that. And say sorry for what I said, before I left your apartment. You were right; it was a shitty thing to say. And I wanted to give you this." He shuffled forward and placed the slightly crumpled piece of paper on top of a box of Christmas tree ornaments. "And this."

And to my actual amazement, he pulled a flower out of his back pocket. A light pink peony. My mom's favorite flower. A perfect match for my tattoo.

That he had somehow procured in the middle of fucking winter.

He placed it on top of the paper. I couldn't stop staring at it.

Aiden stepped back, put his hands in his pockets.

"You can read it later, or never, or whatever." He swallowed heavily, staring somewhere in the direction of my feet.

And then he backed up, and left.

I heard him slither back down the ladder, walk down the hallway. Distantly, a minute later, I heard the front door click shut.

"What the *fuck*," I said again, out loud, to no one.

For too many long minutes, I stood there, motionless. Frustrated at myself that I hadn't stopped him before he'd slinked away, or at least said something more to him. Like "Hey," or "Stop," or, "Whatever's on that piece of paper, read it to me out loud, you coward." Or, "I missed you."

I blew out a breath and stalked to the window. Stared outside at the grey, miserable day.

Finally, I turned around and snatched up that dumb piece of paper. Sat heavily back on the trunk.

Our Favorite Songs, it said at the top.

And right underneath: *for you.*

I closed my eyes and breathed in through my nose. His handwriting was the same, a slanted scrawl. It made my lungs seize.

Once I'd reassured myself I could breathe, and wasn't going to have a panic attack over a single poem, I opened my eyes again. They raced over the paper, my brain working double time, the way it did whenever I got an important assignment back in high school, or another email from Mom's doctors, when she was sick. Rushing too fast to the end, uncomprehending, snatching words and phrases here and there.

And every single snatched word and phrase on this piece of paper melted my foolish heart.

Just as I knew it would.

At the bottom of the paper was a phone number. Next to that, an address for Sweetness Bakery. *Tuesdays through Saturdays, six to noon*, he'd written. And then, even smaller: *Get the sour cream strawberry muffins.*

I took another deep breath, fingers shaking, and started again from the beginning. I made myself read every line slowly this time. Made sure I took it in.

I read it through one more time.

And then I picked up my phone.

16.

what the fuck, McCarstle

why did you leave?

> you mean this time, or the time I left your
> apartment two weeks ago like a real
> jackass?

this time.

> right. Well, I wasn't sure if you'd want to
> talk to me. I wanted to give you time to read
> it, if you wanted, and then decide what you
> wanted to do next.

I read it.

and I would've liked it better if you'd
stayed.

thank you. For the poem, and the flower

> thank you for reading it. It's the first part of
> my ten step grovel plan

oh?

yes. The other nine steps are surprises

actually, no, the second step was, if you
didn't hate the poem, asking you to dinner
on Friday night

but the other eight are surprises, I swear

I like surprises. And dinner.

I'm sorry, Kai.

yes, you said that in the poem

It might take me a while. To be better at
this. I'm still...kind of learning. How to be
better at this.

I think we all are, Aiden.

the house is looking really good, by the
way. I can tell how much work you've done.

thanks. Always nice to get compliments
from your home intruders

the door was open!!

actually...I had just gotten kind of stuck,
before you intruded. I've been sitting here
staring at these Christmas decorations for
like an hour.

I don't know what to do.

anyway I hope at least three of the steps of
your grovel plan are sex stuff

wow way to ruin the surprise

I was planning on the last five but we can
negotiate

but maybe, kai...you should put some up?

264

the decorations I mean. like for one last
time.

and maybe that'll help you figure it out.

or maybe that's dumb.

I could help though, if you wanted.

it's not dumb. A little weird maybe,
decorating an empty house, but not dumb.

I would like that.

just tell me when.

I don't know if I'm ready. At least not today.
But soon. Obviously. Since Christmas is in
a week, and everything.

do you remember George Lyman's
christmas party, sophomore year? Pen
dragged me along. You probably don't
remember that I was there. But I remember
you wore this wreath of holly on your head,
and your cheeks were all red from the
bourbon in the eggnog, and you were
wearing this very nice, classy Christmas-y
sweater, the color of cranberries. You were
the prettiest Christmas decoration I'd ever
seen.

fucking a, mccarstle

I...do not remember that. I wish I did.

I mean I remember Lyman's Christmas
parties, but I don't remember ever seeing
you at one

I wish you had talked to me more in high
school, Aiden. Maybe it wouldn't have
taken me so long to realize I had a crush
on you

lmaoooo KAI

there is no way you had a crush on me in high school stfu

the fact that we've had sex now is clouding your memories

no! I did!! I realized it practically the minute I saw you at Moonie's

My Bi Memory-Clarifying Muscles kicked in & I realized I'd been pining for you all along

LOOOOLLLLLL

KAI ANDREWS. you were dating Mei Qiang and winning state trophies for soccer; you were NOT pining for me omfg i'm dying

okay, SUBCONSCIOUSLY pining for you

THAT IS NOT A THING

well excuuuuse me, Mr. Always-Known-I-Was-Gay High & Mighty!!!

fuck you're cute

i can't

god i'm glad you don't hate me

at least i don't think you hate me

McCarstle

hey

I'm proud of you for quitting school.

thanks.

me too.

It's gonna make for some fun Christmas dinner conversation.

What are you doing for Christmas?

Going to see my Dad, in Bend

oh, right

I'm driving down on Tuesday. At least this is the second Christmas, without her, you know. I'm hoping it's at least a little easier than last year. But I don't know. Maybe it won't ever be.

damn. yeah.

you & your dad can start to make new traditions though

yeah. We'll get there.

anyway sorry I won't be around for any groveling plans that might have involved mistletoe or something

psh please. I can do better than mistletoe

I'll be back for new years, though

yeah?

i would love to welcome in the new year with you, kai andrews.

if you're not busy.

and if i don't fuck up anything too hard before then

it's a date.

:)

omg

i can't believe you just smiley faced me

if you had told me five years ago that aiden
mccarstle would be texting me smiley faces
I wouldn't have believed you

shut up

i can emoji

can you though

i mean it's a little weak, but acceptable

wow

if i was there, i would enact plan #9
right now

which is more about you groveling than me,
but i think it would work out for both of us

well, maybe you should be here, then

come back, mccarstle.

AIDEN STOPPED in the middle of the sidewalk.
Pulled his coat closer around himself. Stared at his phone
for a long, heart-fluttering minute.

...yeah? Right now?

yeah. Right now.

Kai picked up the peony and made his way down the
attic ladder.

okay.

shit. okay. Turning around.

see you soon, andrews.

Kai grinned when he reached the kitchen, glad now he hadn't packed the whole thing yet. He found a small vase, filled it with water, stuck the impossible flower inside. Put it on the empty table.

It made the house feel like it belonged to Carol again, if only for one day more.

Kai walked to the front door. It was freezing outside, but he opened it anyway, leaning against the frame.

He waited until he saw Aiden McCarstle round the corner, curls flying in the wind.

His irritating poet.

Keeper of his favorite song.

He watched Aiden half-walk, half-run down the block, and he could see it, even from far away. The curve of McCarstle's lips, slightly crooked, like a secret unhidden. Better than a Mount Hood sunrise. Better than a snow day.

Kai watched and waited as Aiden made it to the porch, as he looked up at him from the bottom of the stairs, biting his lip. Restless. Buzzing with energy. A Christmas song: full of ringing bells and unbridled hope.

Kai met him on the second step. Took McCarstle's face in his hands.

And swallowed his smile whole.

wherever is your heart

For all the butch bartenders
Thanks for taking care of us

ONE

Miracles, as a whole, had never had much luck in finding me.

But tonight, when I walked into a jam-packed Moonlight Café and found my seat open—

Well, all right. Maybe it was only a small miracle. But damn, I'd take it.

The Moonlight Café, or Moonie's, as it was known to us regulars, was often hit or miss in terms of crowd size. It was a dive on the north edge of the city, a funny joint out in the middle of nowhere. The queers liked it here. And queers were flighty. Some nights it was fully alive: drunken, frenetic bodies crammed onto the dance floor. Folks with far more energy than me singing their hearts out, for better or worse, to karaoke.

Some nights, it was half dead.

I liked it either way. Because Mal was always here.

Tonight, though, was Saturday night during Pride. And Moonie's was guaranteed to be packed to its rainbow-glittered gills at Pride.

Yet, even knowing this full well, I had left my house

275

later than intended, changing my outfit three times like a damn teenager. Like it mattered what I wore. All my outfits looked the same anyway, and Mal didn't seem like the type of woman who cared about whether the flannel I wore was maroon or forest green.

But even though I showed up late, even though Moonie's was already pulsing with a live-wire energy by the time I arrived, my favorite seat—at the far end of the bar, close to the door, where I had the best view of the room, where I could watch what was happening on the dance floor and watch Mal at the same time—was empty amidst the crush of people waiting at the bar for their drinks. Like it was waiting for me, a beacon in the gay desert.

I sunk onto its cracked leather like a stone.

Guess I'd have to go through with it, then. Or, you know. The universe would be mad at me. Or whatever.

Or I'd simply have to go on for the next 365 days again, knowing I was a coward.

Only a second after I made myself comfortable in my possibly-miraculous seat, Mal turned toward the door from where she stood at the till and caught my eye. The left corner of her mouth tilted up the tiniest fraction, barely noticeable, the wrinkles around her eyes deepening for a blink.

Mal was a formidable woman. Her blonde hair, streaked through more and more with silver-grey each time I saw her, was almost entirely buzzcut, and I had never seen her wear anything other than black, with the occasional exception of a dark-washed, boot cut pair of jeans. Her eyes were steel, both in their arresting icy-blue color and the way she used them—like lasers, ready to cut down anyone who dared come at her with even a hint of bullshit.

Even when the bar was busy, like it was tonight, even when I knew we wouldn't get many opportunities to talk, it was still always worth it to come to Moonie's whenever I was home, if only for the opportunity to watch all the patrons approach this bar and quake in their boots at the sight of her.

Nothing in the world turned me on more.

Except when she looked at me and gave me that mouth tilt.

Because Mal didn't smile. I had only ever seen her move her lips that way for me.

It was possible, of course, that there were other women she tilted her mouth for, on the countless nights and weeks when I was on the road and someone else occupied this seat. But I didn't like to think about that. My life was one of small, simple pleasures, and pretending Mal Edwards looked forward to the nights I showed up at Moonie's as much as I did was the most shining of them all.

"Hey." Mal rapped her knuckles on the bar in front of me, same way she always did. Her voice was low, a rumble of decadence that rang through the high-pitched excitement of the room, that pitched straight to my gut. "Good to see you."

"Likewise. Happy Pride."

Mal snorted.

"Your usual?"

"Yeah." Unconsciously, I shoved my thick glasses up my nose. Which I tended to do when I was nervous. Dammit. "Burnside. Thanks."

I always nursed a whiskey, neat, when I came to Moonie's. At other bars I stopped at on the road, I usually just got a beer, but at Moonie's, with Mal, I wanted a slow burn, something to hold on to, to keep my stomach warm. I switched up which brand of whiskey I got sometimes, which was why tonight I wanted Burnside, something local. Something to ground me here, to this town, where I only spent half my time but which still felt like home anyway, by now.

Mal slid the glass tumbler across the smudged countertop.

I reached out. Our fingers brushed for a moment—the tip of my forefinger against the side of her thumb—before she withdrew, wiping a rag resting in her other hand across the counter.

This was another thing I thought she only did with me. Left her hand on the glass a little too long. In my mind, Mal would never willingly touch anyone she didn't want to touch.

It was only half a second, a few times a night when I was here, when she brought me another, when she brought me the glass of ice water she always had on hand after the second one. But for those combined seconds, Mal chose to touch me. Or I chose to touch her, and she let me. Either way, it felt like a gift. A moment of softness between us, two not very outwardly soft people. A zap of electricity that got through, short but shocking, like the moment your lungs seized in a gasp. And by the time you exhaled, you couldn't even quite remember if it had actually happened.

"Back in a bit." Mal motioned with her head toward the crowd still clogging the bar. I nodded, brought the tumbler of whiskey to my lips as she turned away. Felt the amber liquid as it slid down my throat, biting and cool. Waited for it to do its magic. Tried to convince myself my hand wasn't shaking, just the tiniest bit.

I was too old for this shit.

I didn't want to be nervous around Mal Edwards.

Worrying about my outfit, unable to control my body. Christ. This was all a horrible idea.

There was no reason to ruin this easy thing we had between us. How many years had I been coming here at this point? Enough to make this shabby little bar feel like comfort: consistent, reliable. Important, in its own strange way. There was no reason to muck it all up now.

Except.

Fucking *signs*.

Like my seat being open tonight.

Like my damn GP a month ago, when my fiftieth birthday rolled around and inspired me to schedule an exam. The way she'd raised a careful, beautifully sculpted eyebrow and told me my body couldn't take my lifestyle much longer. Like I didn't already know my body was falling apart. Had been for years.

I had considered switching from long-haul to regional trucking enough times. Even local. Every over-the-road trucker did. Practically everyone I knew had told me enough times to switch. But I'd tried regional once, five years ago, and spending all my time on the same godforsaken stretches of I-5 over and over made me feel trapped. Underwater. The exact feeling I came to this career to escape.

Anyway, I knew plenty of truckers who'd been driving OTR far past fifty.

The number had been haunting me anyway. *Fifty.*

It was just a number. Meaningless. I knew that.

But it kept whispering its existence in my ear, intrusive and irritating, nonetheless.

Apparently the simple fact of being alive for a half century made a person introspective.

Made me think seriously about what I wanted to do

with my second half century, while I had it.

A nervous throat clear jolted me out of my thoughts.

"Gin and tonic, please." I turned to look closer at the scruffy-looking white kid who had squeezed in beside me. Who definitely wasn't a kid, but Mal always called her regulars kids, and it rubbed off on me.

"I like your skirt," I said to them when Mal, who had drifted her way back toward this end of the bar, turned to make their drink.

"Oh!" They jumped slightly, as if surprised I'd talked to them, and looked down at said skirt. They wore a plain black t-shirt, but the skirt was patterned with what appeared to be the New York City subway system, colorful curves and right angles against a white background. With a shy grin, they said, "My partner made it for me."

Mal returned with their drink then, pushed it across the counter quick and smooth. Without even a single chance for finger touches.

"Happy Pride," Subway Skirt said to me, another small smile gracing their face, before giving an adorable little wave and heading back to their table.

Mal leaned back against my section of countertop, crossing her arms, that secret mouth tilt live on her face again.

"I scare the shit out of that one," she said.

I smirked, picking up my whiskey once more. Mal always loved the regulars who were afraid of her the most. It was almost funny to me, how no one else could tell she was all growl and no bite. Or, okay, perhaps more accurately: mostly growl, little bit of bite. Or, all right, if you were an asshole...all bite. Anyway, what mattered, what I could see, was that for the good ones, behind that icy gaze and her hard edges, Mal was, in fact, nothing but soft.

Watching her track her regulars now, always scanning the room to make sure everyone was good, made my chest swell with familiarity and want. Reminded me why trying to shoot my shot tonight could be worth it.

Because when I was honest with myself, all I had ever wanted, since the first time I walked into this place, was to be hard and soft with Mal Edwards.

"Their girl has a hell of a set of lungs on her, though." Mal motioned with her chin, and I turned to finish watching Subway Skirt make their way through the room. They sat next to a big girl with blonde hair tied in a high knot, in the middle of a full, rambunctious table right next to the dance floor. She wore a form-fitting, low-cut white dress patterned with cherries, and turned to smile at Subway Skirt as they slid into their seat.

"Oh yeah, that one." My nerves started to settle, somehow, when I recognized her. My back slouched, the tension in my shoulders easing. "She sung anything yet?"

This was what we did, me and Mal. I filled her in about my favorite stops on the road since the last time we saw each other. She filled me in on her regulars.

It might have seemed like surface level stuff. But sometimes, it didn't feel that way. The road was what filled most of my days. Mal's regulars filled hers.

Sometimes, it felt like this woman who I only saw once a month knew me better than anyone.

And like maybe I knew her, too.

"Not yet." She jutted her chin again, toward the back corner behind me this time. "The best act you've missed so far is that broad back there. Did 'All Along the Watchtower.' One of the best things I've ever seen."

I shifted on my stool, twisted my neck to see a large, bald Black woman in a thin tank top drinking a beer at the table along the wall. I released a low whistle, turning back toward Mal.

"No shit."

"Spectacular," Mal confirmed, deadpan. "Anyway." She knocked her knuckles on the counter again. "Best taco."

I spun my tumbler of whiskey between my hands, a slow rotation right, left, while I attempted to hide a smile.

"Tiny truck next to a gas station in Reno. Didn't have a name."

Mal nodded. "Those are always the best ones."

I took a picture for you, I thought.

I always took a picture, these days. To remember, for my next trip to Moonie's. For the next time I got to play this game with Mal. *Best taco. Best truck stop. Best night's sleep. Best breakfast. Best scenic viewpoint.*

Just as I couldn't remember exactly how long it had been since I'd started coming to Moonie's for the simple act of pining over Mal, I couldn't remember how long it'd been since I'd started taking pictures for her. Marking things down, making little lists in this journal I'd bought one day at a Flying J in Missoula. Preparing for the superlatives she'd ask me about next time I saw her.

"Carnitas?" she asked.

"Always carnitas," I answered.

I wondered sometimes if she knew. How much better the game had made my life on the road. How it made me more observant, more on the lookout for new things. More willing to veer off the interstate, find hidden gems where a rig like mine typically didn't go. Because it was hard to fit my rig most places, and because the suits would have my ass if they knew I was wasting miles trying to find the best plate of pasta in Tulsa for Mal Edwards.

But I was good at my shit. Had been a loyal employee for decades. And every company in the nation was desperate for drivers these days. The suits could handle a few out of the way routes every now and then. To find the best hash browns in the Twin Cities. To take another picture. Add to another list.

I didn't pull out my phone to show Mal the photo of the taco truck outside Reno, though. Because she was still busy tonight, even if she was making time to start the game, and anyway, it was embarrassing. I'd only shown her the photos once. A year ago, during last Pride. When Mal had actually had ample backup. Time to talk more. When I'd had a dangerous third whiskey.

When it had seemed like something shifted. When we'd talked about more than her regulars, my favorite stops on I-80. It had still started with my stops, though. I'd gotten out my phone to show her the view from this truck stop in Idaho, and she'd leaned further across the counter than she ever had before, our elbows locked next to each other, my screen lighting up her face. And then I'd swiped to another photo, and another. And she'd brought out her phone, shown me some of her own photos of her life. Her sister, her cats. Her garden. It had felt...

Well, it didn't really matter how it'd felt. Foolish, probably. A little silly. Sharing photos on our phones like we were at camp. Showing my ass, probably, that I documented my life for her.

And then I'd left.

Because shortly after last call, I'd remembered I had nothing to offer her.

"Back in a bit." Mal glanced over her shoulder. "Get ready to tell me about the weirdest roadside attraction when I get back."

As she walked away, I was reminded of the problem. I'd already seen all the weird roadside attractions.

I was on the road more often than not. Mal deserved something better than that. A partner who would actually be there.

I had pictured it more than once. What it would be like to touch her, to hold her. To sleep at her side.

And immediately after allowing myself the frivolous luxury of these fantasies, I would picture her getting hurt. Something happening to someone she loved.

And I would be thousands of miles away, delivering TVs to a Costco in Culver City.

"All right, friends and family," the karaoke jockey, a cute little thing named Kiki, crooned into the mic. "Welcome to the stage...Preeti!"

A woman at Subway Skirt's table stood and made her way to the mic. She started singing "It Ain't Over 'til It's Over," and I drank more whiskey.

All those reasons why I didn't deserve Mal still rang true, at least as of now. Even if my body was falling apart. It wasn't like I was planning on retiring tomorrow.

And even when I *did* retire—

Fuck, I had no idea what I would do with myself when I retired. I didn't know how to be still, in one place, forever. I hadn't been still for thirty years. Being in motion suited me. It healed me.

Part of me worried that once I finally stopped, all those bandages and scar tissue that being on the road helped me build would start to unravel. Sutures coming unglued.

And so it was possible that even when I *wasn't* gone half the time, I'd have even less to offer Mal.

Yet. *Five* and *zero* continued to haunt my brain. Dr.

Singh haunted my brain. Her smart, sympathetic explanations of all the ways my back was fucked.

Half a century gone.

Every day since I'd walked out of that medical office, I could feel my future rolling away from my feet, curling unseen into the distance.

In short: I was scared as shit.

And I hated being scared.

The only thing that scared me more than my future was finally telling Mal Edwards that I loved her. Because even though I knew it probably sounded ridiculous, I was pretty sure I did. I'd never treated love lightly—didn't have a ton of it growing up, had never handed it out freely—but sometimes you just knew. That a person was made of the same stuff as you. That you never felt quite as at ease around anyone else. That even after knowing them for years, the first sight of their face every time you walked into The Moonlight Café still made your heart squeeze.

Half a century gone. Might as well start with one scary as fuck thing. See how the rest went.

Mal hadn't brought it up, that last Pride when I'd shown her the photos and then snuck out before last call, in all the times I'd made it back to Moonie's since then. I sure as shit didn't, either. I'd wanted to kiss her—well, wanted to kiss her more than usual—the next time I came in last summer and she'd slid me a whiskey, asked me about the best donut I'd found since my last visit. Like everything was blessedly normal.

But here I was again. In my favorite chair, in my favorite flannel. During another Pride. Ready to blow normal apart. If I kept my courage.

After all. If you couldn't tell a butch you loved her during Pride, when the hell could you?

TWO

"ALL RIGHT." I rapped my knuckles against the bar again. Even though I'd already done that too much tonight. Shit, June was going to notice I was being weird. "Best cup of coffee."

Another slow smile rounded her lips—she had the gentlest smile, June Davis; it always made the left side of her glasses shift up, closer to the edges of her short dark hair—and I had to look away. She smiled like that every single time I ever asked her anything. Most people who entered this place either ignored me outright or acted like I was the Dykey Witch of the West. And I was good with that role. Had cultivated it. But for some reason, I barely had to say boo to June to make her look at me like that. Like I was very cute and had just told a very clever joke.

It unnerved me every time.

Over the years, though, it had also become familiar. A balm. This bar was part of my bones now, but there were nights when things still got to me. Particularly screechy karaoke singers. Particularly rude assholes who thought the world belonged to them. Who gave me attitude for not being able to serve five people at the same fucking time. The owner, Lou, being particularly more useless than usual.

On the treasured nights when June showed up, that smile always smoothed any ragged margins. Sunk down into my chest like honey.

"That one's a repeat, unfortunately," June said with a grimace, as if this would actually disappoint me. "There's this little diner in Redding. Rosie's. Don't know where they get it, but they have the best damn coffee. Fairly decent pie, too."

"Coconut cream?" Coconut cream was June Davis's top flavor of pie. Followed by blueberry, followed by banana cream.

"Not this time, sadly." June lifted her tumbler to her lips. "But an apple-raspberry that was pretty respectable."

Motion from the other side of the bar caught my eye.

"Back in a bit," I said, the sorry refrain I had to say too many times to June, often right when we were getting into something good.

But this time, I actually didn't mind moving away to refill vodka tonics and rosés. The more distracted I could get by my actual job, the less I'd have to think about the two tickets in my back pocket.

Because every time I thought about those tickets, I felt like a bit of an idiot. And wanted to punch my sister.

"So," Britt had said during Cam's barbecue a few weeks ago, bumping my hip too hard as she sat down at the table, like she always did when she was going to say something annoying. "Pride's coming up soon."

I'd lifted a brow.

"And? You gonna ask me to wave rainbow tassels from my tits at the parade?"

"No, no." She waved a hand. "You know Cam and I do

287

that without you. I was just thinking—" She took a slug from her beer, "—about what you should do if June Davis shows up."

I scowled. Fuck me for telling Britt about June and last Pride. How I had finally been ready to jump into June's lap and do whatever the hell she wanted. Until I'd turned and she'd been gone.

"Serve her a whiskey and finish my shift without wanting to strangle anyone with a rainbow Bud Light banner?"

Britt just looked at me and sighed. I pointedly looked away, over Cam's tangled backyard.

"It's been almost five years since Olivia left."

I'd looked at her then.

"What the fuck, Britt."

I was aware how many years it had been since Olivia left. But you know what, it really didn't matter how long it had been since Olivia left. Because I had been fine. Olivia leaving had taught me some shit, and then I'd gotten over it. What I *didn't* understand was why Britt was bringing her up now.

She stared back, irritatingly uncowed by my fuck-you stare.

"I'm just saying, Mal. In those five years, the only other woman I've heard you talk about is June Davis."

I rolled my eyes, turning away again.

"June's just a regular."

Except it felt like a betrayal when I said it. The *just*. The *just* was dishonest, and I didn't consider myself a dishonest person. So I amended it immediately.

"My favorite regular, yeah. But still a customer."

I'd been tending bar for near twenty years now. My body was pretty well broken from it at this point—apparently spending most of my life on my feet wasn't great for me—but I was good at it, and I followed the rules. Such as: don't fuck your customers.

Because then they came back. Expected more. And it wasn't like Moonie's had security. I was the security, basically. And Lou probably wouldn't see me having fucked someone and it being awkward now as a good enough reason to bounce them. If some woman came back looking for me, I was trapped behind that bar until she decided to leave.

A nightmare, essentially. The truth was, I rarely had the desire to fuck anyone anyway, but still. It was a mistake I'd only made twice, and not since my early thirties.

Except I had a feeling if I fucked June—or expressed a desire to do so, and she didn't return the feelings—she simply wouldn't come back at all.

I told Britt pretty much everything, but I didn't want to tell her what that thought did to me.

Britt, though, probably already knew. The hag.

She shoved my knee with her own.

"Mal," she said, quiet. "Your whole body relaxes when you talk about her. I've never even met her, but I'm half in love with June Davis just from the way you say her name."

Why *did* I even talk about June with Britt? How humiliating.

"She spends a lot of time on the road," I said. Even though I knew saying such a thing was admitting defeat to Britt. And even though I didn't care that June spent a lot of time on the road. The road was part of who June was. How could I hate it?

"I'm just saying," she said after a long minute of silence, wherein I made a determined plan with myself to never mention June to Britt again, "Pride feels like a good time to be brave."

And then she'd gotten up and left the table. I had dearly wanted to follow her and pummel her into the grass, but my knees hurt and it felt like too much effort at the time.

Brave.

Fuck my sister for implying I wasn't brave. Just as Olivia had implied. I knew Britt would never mean to hurt me the same way Olivia had hurt me—Britt had made her feelings about Olivia well known from the start—but damn if it didn't still hurt anyway.

I'd found the tickets online that night, after the barbecue. Hadn't gone out looking for them, but the ad had shown up in my email, and something in my brain had followed through without thinking about it too hard.

Although I'd spent the three weeks since then thinking about it *real* fucking hard.

I had paid to get the actual tickets rush delivered to me, so my grand gesture to the woman of my dreams would be more than an email confirmation. Brandi Carlile at the Gorge. I had no idea if June actually liked Brandi Carlile. She wasn't exactly a popular karaoke choice. Every now and then a bold bitch tried to sing "The Story," but even that was few and far between these days. So we hadn't discussed Brandi outright before, but I'd gotten to know the general flavor of June's tastes, after however many nights she'd sat through karaoke at Moonie's with me, and it felt right. Hell, even if I didn't know a thing about June's tastes, she was a dyke of a certain age. She was bound to like Brandi Carlile.

And there was nowhere better to see a show than at the Gorge. I'd only been there a handful of times, but I'd spent near every minute since clicking *Purchase Tickets* thinking about going there with June. Driving along the Columbia, crossing up into Washington once the land turned dry. Driving through all those high, sweeping golden hills that made my stomach jump into my chest a little, even though they were probably nothing to June after all the roads she'd driven. Finally arriving at the venue, in the middle of fucking nowhere. Staking out a spot in the grass. Watching the sun bleed over the canyon, the stars appear over the stage. Feeling small and big out there all at once, amongst the music and the open sky.

We'd get a hotel in Ellensburg. Pack snacks for the road.

It was a bit much, perhaps, for a first date.

But after years of only seeing June inside this dark bar, stealing brief moments with her between refilling beers and shitty well drinks, an epic first date felt earned.

And I wanted to know. We already had hanging out at a bar down pat. I wanted to know, if June said yes to spending time outside of Moonie's with me, that she meant it. That she was as road-trip-to-the-Gorge all in as me.

It was easier, though, to be brave in the privacy of my home.

Back here at Moonie's, June in her regular chair—god, it had been a pain in the fucking ass, shooing queers away from it all night until she'd finally shown up—those tickets in my pocket only made me feel like a fool. I didn't even know how I'd bring them up.

I was contemplating running back to the minuscule Moonie's office and shoving the tickets back into the depths of my bag, at least get the damned things off my person— my fellow bartender tonight, Victor, was actually competent, as opposed to some of the hires Lou made these days; he could handle the bar for a minute—when I was interrupted by Cher.

* * *

"Hey, you." Cher leaned across the bar and drawled to Mal in a deep timbre. Overtly, comically flirtatious. "Jack and Coke?"

Mal stared back, face blank. After a second, she grunted and picked up a glass.

I hid my face in my own glass, snorting down a laugh. Fuck, I loved her.

Moonie's was queer as shit, but normally in a quieter, weirder way. It wasn't a drag bar. It was, on its wildest nights, a one-to-two max drag queen kind of joint. But every Pride, at least a few dressed to the nines for us, usually only stopping in for a quick song or two before they carried on to brighter, flashier locales.

Like any self-respecting queer, I knew Mal was skeptical of Pride these days, its ever-increasing corporatization. Even though Moonie's was draped in rainbow flags tonight, both on the bodies of the people inside it and in the banners taped around the bar, advertising Smirnoff and Modelo and Coors Light, Mal was still dressed in all black.

I'd always had a soft spot in my heart for the weekend, though. Which was probably why I'd let myself have a third whiskey, last year. Sure, the parade wasn't really for us anymore. But I still remembered my first Pride. A small town queer, escaping to the city in June for the visceral, visual confirmation that I wasn't alone. It had felt revolutionary.

I suspected even Mal felt some kind of fondness for it. I knew, for example, that she was practically co-owner of this place at this point. She had told me before how she could pretty much set her own schedule, that management relied on her stability and would give her whatever she wanted. Well, other than better health insurance.

But still—every year. Even though she could easily get the weekend off. She was always here at Pride.

We were old and cranky, me and Mal. But it was still nice to watch people have a chance to let loose. Exactly as you were, or maybe more accurately, as you aspired to be. A chance, if you wanted, to be a cliché.

Like Cher, who was currently making her way to the stage, Jack and Coke in hand, to sing "If I Could Turn Back Time."

I propped an elbow on the bar, plopped my chin on my palm. Settled in to watch the show.

Because damn if clichés weren't the best, sometimes.

"That frat bro looking kid Cher's dancing up on right now?" Mal returned halfway through Cher's performance, leaning her hip against the bar and tilting her head toward me while she stared at the stage. "Name's Kai. One of my favorites since you were last here."

"Seems like he's one of Cher's favorites, too," I observed. Not that I could blame her. The boy was handsome.

"Yeah." A twerk of her mouth. "The kicker, though, is that he's with that miserable fuck over there." She nodded her chin toward a skinny white kid in the back with a mop of curly black hair, staring at Kai and Cher with a blush and a tiny grin. "Kiki said they were all over each other in the parking lot during that massive snowstorm this winter. Too busy sucking face to notice her walking to her car."

"Ah, young love." I took another sip of my whiskey. "Good for them."

Mal grunted and moved to take a customer's order.

But I was pretty sure it was a grunt of agreement.

She was still occupied with customers when Kai was called up to the mic next, still breathless from dancing to "If I Could Turn Back Time." A dark red smear of lipstick graced his cheek from Cher's lips, a buoyant smile lighting up his face.

Yeah. If I'd ever had any desire for such a thing, I'd suck his face, too.

A second later, Moonie's reverberated with bass.

I laughed. The Pride vibes were really kicking in now.

Within the first thirty seconds of Robyn's "Dancing On My Own," half of the bar had spilled onto the dance floor. A minute into the song, as if inspired by the energy of the crowd, Kai had pulled the skinny kid with the curly hair out of his seat. The miserable fuck, Mal had said.

Except he didn't look miserable now. He sort of shuffled around Kai awkwardly, but he was laughing. They weren't dancing on their own at all. It was so sweet my teeth hurt.

"I hate when they stand on the chairs," Mal sighed, near once again. I followed the direction of her stare. A redheaded girl stood on a chair, whistling. "Someone's gonna crack a skull one day."

With another sigh, Mal lifted the bar flap and walked through the crowd. I watched her weave between the patrons, grab the girl's attention. The girl, of course, complied immediately, flouncing back into her chair with a blush and, I could tell from here, numerous apologies.

When Mal caught my eye on her walk back to the bar, she rolled her own before dipping back under the partition and moving on to the next customer.

She always had her eye on the room, Mal. Even when she was talking to me. Like how my eyes were always on the road when I was in my truck. Always on the alert for people about to make bad decisions.

They weren't our responsibility, the bad decision makers. But I knew me and Mal felt a need to protect them, all the same.

The bar was packed by then, and after Robyn, Mal was kept busy for the next forty-five minutes solid. Which was all right, of course. Gave me lots of time to think. To waver back and forth, again, about my plan.

It was probably a slightly irrational plan.

But I didn't want to simply ask Mal to come home with me. I'd seen enough of Mal in dark rooms. I wanted to *see* her, outside of this place. Wanted her to see me.

I didn't get lonely on the road, really. Didn't think you could survive the lifestyle if you did. For a lot of my career, I'd brought my dog Arlo with me. But even after Arlo passed away a few years back, loneliness only caught me by the neck sometimes. After a scare—I'd had my fair share of near-accidents and full-blown-accidents at this point along the line—or at the end of a particularly long slog, when my eyes were dry and my back ached something awful. Exhaustion did funny things to the mind. I'd developed strategies to deal with my demons, but sometimes even tried and true strategies couldn't compete with a stretch of endless asphalt in Oklahoma, when you would've given your left foot for a jolt of Moonie's serotonin.

And any time the loneliness hit me these days, the only person I really wanted to magically appear by my side in my rig was Mal.

My plan was the coast. A drive I'd done a hundred times before, that I could handle easily in my pickup in the dark. I didn't know how long after close Mal normally had to stay, but I figured if we got out of here by three, I could have us to Cannon Beach by four-thirty, five.

Right on time to see the sunrise.

No, I didn't want to ask Mal back to my place, like it was a casual, if long awaited, hookup. I wanted to watch the sun rise on Mal Edwards's face. That seemed like something worth being scared for.

"All right, everyone," Kiki yelled into the mic. "Help me welcome up Jonny!" With a wink, she added, "Y'all are gonna like this one."

And as with Robyn before her, a minute into Natasha Bedingfield's "Unwritten," near every seat in the main room was empty. Kai, his curly haired boy and their redheaded friend, twirling in a circle with her hands in the air. Lily and her partner with the subway skirt, bodies close, laughter on their lips. Cher had long departed at this point, but everyone else was there, a writhing mass on the dance floor. Like they were reaching for something in the distance, so close they could almost taste it. Something only they could let in.

And goddamn if I didn't get a little teary, watching all that uninhibited happiness, when that early 2000s songstress kept telling us to live our life with arms wide open. It was so silly and free. Goddamn Moonie's at Pride.

I would never tell a fucking soul, but I decided it for sure then. In the middle of "Unwritten." I would ask Mal to leave with me tonight. I would drive her to the coast, if she let me. I didn't know how much of Mal Edwards I deserved, how much she would let me have, but if she was open to it—well, I'd try. I'd try to live my life with arms wide open, with her, for this second half century of my life.

A singer named Sophia went up next, started singing "Nights in White Satin." Which was somehow hilarious, after "Unwritten." Everyone returned to their seats from the dance floor real quick.

I knew Mal would love it. She always loved the people who sang weird shit.

And sure enough, when she approached my end of the bar halfway into the song, her mouth was doing it again. The almost-smile she only shared with me.

"Bit of a change in tone," she remarked, leaning her elbow on the bar and turning to watch Sophia perform.

"A bit," I agreed. While the bar had clearly been confused for the first three minutes of the song, a few people in the crowd were starting to stand now, whistling and yelling for her. She had been pretty lost in the music until this point, in her own world, but she smiled a bit at the whistles, blushed a bit. Took an embarrassed but happy little bow at the end before returning the mic to Kiki. Mal lifted her arms for a hearty clap. It was all pretty great. This place was pretty great. Mal was the greatest.

"Hey," I said, before she could get called away again. I wanted to keep her here, now that I'd made my decision, her elbow close to my arm, her not-quite smile cementing my courage. "How's Britt been doing? With the spa expansion?"

Mal lifted an eyebrow in surprise, something questioning entering her eyes before she smoothed her face again, replaced it with her classic impassive look.

"Good," she said, turning to look at the stage, see who would be called up next. "She finally got herself another assistant."

Mal's sister worked for a resort outside of Sandy, up near Mount Hood. Accounting, if I remembered correctly. Mal told me all about Britt, that night last Pride, and had mentioned a couple months back how the resort was adding on a day spa. How it had almost doubled her work, without any increased wages or help from management. I had liked the way Mal looked when she'd talked about it. Like she was ready to march up the mountain and kick somebody's ass.

"Still deserves more money, but she's working on that. Anyway." Mal turned back to me, rapped her knuckles on the bar next to my empty glass, which had been empty for a while now. "Another?"

I grinned to myself. I'd made my fair share of mistakes behind the wheel in my career, but there was one I never made, especially after what happened with my folks. I never stepped into a truck with alcohol still in my system. And while there were still a couple hours until closing time, while I had decent tolerance and would probably be safe with my second whiskey, I wasn't taking any chances with Mal's safety.

"Nah." I pushed the empty glass her way. "I'll just take a water for now."

That surprise entered her eyes again, and I wanted to ask her right then. But I could see at least four customers waiting for her attention. And on the off chance she'd turn me down, I didn't want to have to slink off in rejection early. I was enjoying myself. Wanted to stretch this night as long as possible. I'd wait until last call, until we found a quiet pocket.

I had never been more excited to nurse a glass of ice water in my life.

THREE

I WAS GOING to kill Britt.

Ice clinked against the sides of the pint glass as I filled it with water for June. My heart thudded too loudly in my head, even above all the fuzzy noise around me: the queers shouting at each other at the bar, as if they weren't standing right fucking next to each other. The white kid at the mic, butchering some hip-hop song their friends should have advised them not to sing.

The back of my neck felt hot as I clicked off the tap, like it always did when I was embarrassed.

And in the back pocket of my jeans, two slips of paper burned a small, shameful hole.

It had been a dumb idea anyway, inviting June to a concert I didn't know if she'd even want to go to, possibly the dumbest thing I'd ever thought of in my life.

But I'd been pumping myself up about it anyway, ever since June walked in tonight. Had almost felt ready to go for it. Especially when June had just asked that question about Britt. We'd shared lots of snippets of ourselves over the years. Except other than last Pride, those snippets always seemed to happen on accident. When a song someone sang reminded me of some dumbass thing me and Britt had done once, and I happened to be standing next to June when the memory slipped in, and it felt right to tell her. Or when one of the questions I asked her about her time on the road hit home, elicited a brighter smile and greater detail in her response than usual.

June remembering that Britt was overworked by the spa, asking me outright about it—maybe I'd simply read too much into it. But it had felt more direct. Like maybe we were gearing up for a repeat of last Pride. Another chance.

Except then, half a breath later, June had made it clear she was getting ready to go. A good two hours before last call. I tried to make my face blank, my mind blank too, when she rejected her second whiskey. She always got a second whiskey. Last Pride, when she'd gotten a third, was the only time she'd ever deviated from routine. But she always got a second.

I wasn't sure what had gone wrong, what made tonight different, when it seemed like things were going the same as always. Wonderful, in other words. Maybe it had nothing to do with me. Maybe she'd gotten a text about a family emergency or something. Even though I knew she wasn't in contact with her family. Because we'd learned these things, in the snippets we let ourselves share. That June didn't talk to her family. That Britt was my best friend. That June was a transplant from Jersey, that I originally hailed from Texas. Even though it had been a while since I'd been back to my home state, and June never talked about visiting hers.

There was plenty we didn't share, of course. But it was still more than I knew about any of the other lonely people who trickled into this bar.

More than I knew about most people outside this bar, too, if I let myself think on it.

Whatever was going on with June tonight, though, the fact remained that if she couldn't even stay until last call on Pride, then I wasn't going to make a damn fool of myself.

I'd probably just take the tickets home and shred them.

No, I'd probably offer them to Britt.

I spent the next hour busy with customers, stubbornly and perhaps childishly sticking to the opposite end of the bar from where June sat, keeping Victor as a buffer between us. And weirdly, the longer June kept sitting there, slowly sipping at her fucking water, the more irritated I became. I had never felt irritated by June Davis in my life. It was the worst.

But what was the fucking game here? Why was she still here? Why was I so fucking annoyed that she was still here?

Maybe I was just cranky because it was reaching the time of night when I was *always* cranky. I liked tending bar, I did, even if Olivia never understood—and fuck, thinking about Olivia was not something I was about to fucking do right now—but I rarely liked it once the clock creeped past one a.m. When everyone got sloppier. When I had to cut people off, which I'd already done a few times in the last hour, which was never a pleasant experience. When the karaoke singers got screechier, more full of giggles, and it all got less entertaining.

I had just worked myself up so much about this night, thanks to fucking Britt. Had come close to something like hope when June showed up, full of her regular smiles. But I guess we'd just go back to our regular selves after tonight after all. Enjoying each other's company for a few hours a month. Which was fine.

After I could get the hell out of here tonight, after I'd

cooled down and stopped being so fucking annoyed by June Davis sitting at my damn bar with her fucking water, it would be totally fucking fine.

"Everyone welcome up to the mic Lily and Sam!"

I glanced up from where I was cashing out a check. Watched Lily in that cherry dress jump up to the dance floor, the nervous kid hustling behind her. *Finally*, I thought. I'd missed it, I realized, Lily kicking off the night like she normally did with that Carrie Underwood song. But it'd already been packed by the time she and her whole crew came in—which had expanded since her and the nervous kid's crew had melded together—and strangely, she hadn't been up to the mic once, until now. Just watching her and the kid walking to the mic felt like a reprieve in the past-one a.m. hellscape.

They grabbed their mics from Kiki, grinned at each other. And when Lily started singing about leaving her job in the city, working for the man every night and day, something in my chest lifted. Lightened. Well, damn. This was gonna be good.

I served someone a glass of wine during the buildup, but I turned back toward the stage right after. Let Victor cover anyone else who might've been waiting so I could watch the transition to the fast part of Tina and Ike's version of "Proud Mary," where the horns come in and everything gets all hectic and great. It was everything I expected, Lily into it at this point, loud and gorgeous, wiggling those fantastic breasts all over the place. Sam mostly stood to the side and watched her with a goofy look on their face, only jumping in for a few *rollin' down the river*s, a few *do-do-do-do*s.

But during that first real exuberant round of *do-do-do-do*s after the transition, they sidled right up next to Lily's side. And suddenly, they were doing this dance thing together, Lily and Sam, where they swiveled their hips and their knees jumped back and forth in sync, like a pair of flapper dancers or something, all as they continued to half-sing, half-laugh into their microphones.

They had *practiced* this.

A surprised laugh escaped my lips. No one else at the bar probably heard it; it likely didn't even make a sound, but I felt it bubble up from my lungs. Their table of friends was losing their minds. It was the most adorable thing I had ever seen.

And for a moment, in the split second after I laughed, this sharp slash of something else whipped through me. Jealousy, maybe. Even though that didn't feel like quite the right term. I certainly didn't want to be up there on the stage doing a hand jive. My knees would give out anyway, if I even tried, if I even wanted to.

It just took guts, I always thought. To be that bravely happy.

Whatever it was, it passed after a few seconds. I went back to simply watching the show. Taking a minute, before I returned to my job, to absorb it.

It was a nice reassurance, somehow. So what if I never asked out June Davis. I still had a roof over my head. A job where I got to watch shit like this, sometimes.

When it was over, and Sam and Lily returned their mics to Kiki, their cheeks were red, eyes bright. Lily stood up on her toes to peck a kiss on Sam's cheek.

I put my fingers in my mouth and whistled.

Lily's eyes found mine immediately. She paused on her way back around the table to her seat. I gave her a wink. Her mouth dropped open an inch, eyes widening, before she slapped a hand over her mouth and giggled. Sam pulled her down onto their lap, and she buried her face in their neck.

I could feel June's eyes on me before I turned. Because —oh, what the hell. My body had somehow migrated back over to her side of the bar during "Pride Mary." If there was one thing I always made sure I had control over, it was my body. I was apparently losing my mind.

I didn't want to face her. But of course I did anyway.

And June was smiling.

Not just her regular half-smirk, half-smile, but a full-blown thing, one that seemed to beam out of her eyes at me, behind those glasses. A completely different look, somehow, from the one I'd just shared with Lily. Complimenting Lily, making her blush, was fun. A lark.

June's smile said, *I know you.* June's smile said, *I love when you're happy.*

And for a second, I lost myself. I almost took the concert tickets out of my back pocket and threw them at her face. I almost climbed over the grimy bar onto her lap. Almost grabbed her hand and stuck her fingers in my mouth.

Instead, I schooled my features. Returned my butch bartender mask.

I should have simply walked away. But instead, I heard my mouth say, "What?"

"You *whistled*," she said, voice full of a mirth that climbed down into my gut. Calcified there into a hard ball, like a tumor.

"They deserved it," I said, and turned to help another Moonie's customer.

Because that was my job. That was why I was here.

June was no longer drinking. She didn't need me anymore.

I didn't know *why* June came to this bar, honestly. There

were other regulars who never sang, but they mostly sequestered themselves at the video poker machines in the back corner. Or they came with friends to shoot the shit and watch the performances.

But June always came alone. Always sat right there. Doing nothing but watching the room as she nursed a whiskey. Looking gorgeous. Making me want to do ridiculous things.

Victor gave the last call. I cashed out what felt like a million tabs.

And June was still here.

Ten minutes from closing time, something in me snapped. Only the most drunk queers remained, the bar emptying out by the minute. I'd have to kick out the hangers-on momentarily, but I had to deal with the most frustrating one first.

"Why don't you ever sing?"

I leaned both palms on the edge of the bar, arms held straight, my gaze at her straight, too. I wanted something from her I couldn't even quite explain, something unfair and irrational. People were allowed to come to Moonie's for any reason they wanted.

"Have *you* ever sang?" June asked back, nodding over to the stage with a slight smirk on her face. But I wasn't here for this game. She didn't get to know, until she answered my question first, that every now and then, me and Kiki busted out a tune after everyone else had gone home.

"Why do you come here, June?"

Her eyes caught mine then, the smirk dropping. Everything felt sharp between us, taut and honest.

"I think you know the answer to that, Mal," she said carefully. It almost made me flinch, when she said my name, just as it had felt aggressive when I'd said hers. And then: "I don't come here for the singing."

We held each other's gazes, her eyes steady behind those glasses, their thick dark frames. For a moment, the rest of Moonie's receded into the distance, a barely-there din. And then June's face softened, that half-grin returning to her face.

"Although I like the singing, sometimes. Mal." The slightest tilt of her head. "You want to get out of here with me, after you close up? I want to take you somewhere."

My throat closed.

"Might take me a while to finish up," I managed.

"I don't mind waiting," she said, smooth, unbothered. From the corner of my eye, I saw Victor walking around to tables, encouraging people to close their tabs. I couldn't move, my locked arms frozen to the bar. "Do you have to work tomorrow?" she added, which only increased the confused pounding in my chest.

I shook my head.

"So you're free for the next twenty-four hours or so?"

Her mouth twitched as she asked, like she was trying to fight her grin from growing even further. I shook my head again, fighting off my own facial twitches, struggling for calm. *Twenty-four hours.* I had no idea what June had planned, but she'd said she wanted to take me somewhere. It didn't sound like she was asking for a casual screw back at her place. Twenty-four hours wasn't quite enough for a trip to a concert at the Gorge, but it was close.

My heart thudded away, trying to reconcile my irritation and confusion of the last two hours with the new knowledge that maybe June and I were, once again, actually on the same page.

"Perfect," she said after my second head shake. "So you in?"

I only hesitated a second. And then I nodded.

She slid off her stool, taking the last sip of her water.

"I closed out with Victor a while ago. I'll be waiting in my truck. Take your time."

And without a look back, June slipped out the door.

FOUR

"YOU OKAY WITH A BIT OF A DRIVE?" I turned the key in the ignition as I asked, a half-second after Mal closed the passenger side door. I was nearly out of the parking lot before she'd even clicked in her seatbelt. Which was bad form on my part. My nerves bleeding in, as if warding off the possibility that Mal had only climbed into my truck to say she'd changed her mind.

Even though I'd felt remarkably serene, these last twenty minutes I'd been sitting out here alone, watching the last patrons stumble out the door, laughing with each other until their drives came. I only scowled occasionally at the ones who crawled into their own cars when they clearly shouldn't have. But overall, I liked sitting in the dark quiet in my truck, taking my time to mentally transition from the loudness of Moonie's to this, my favorite personal space.

It was always an adjustment after a long haul, coming back to my own ride, the old pickup feeling strangely small. And what I'd always liked about trucks was how big they made you feel. Like you were in control of a modest but high up part of the world. On the rare occasion I got stuck in a compact car, I felt unnervingly vulnerable, like the smallest object in the road could reach out and obliterate me.

A feeling somewhat like that crept in as soon as Mal Edwards was in my truck.

She shrugged as we pulled onto the road, toward MLK. "Sure," she assented to my question about the drive.

I glanced over at her as I guided the truck down the dark city streets, heading south until I could switch over to 26. She looked tired, her strong shoulders slumped against the back of the seat. She was gazing out the window, away from me. It was hard to read Mal without being able to see those electric eyes.

"Thanks," I said, adjusting my right hand higher on the wheel, my left hand lower and looser on the other side as I switched lanes to drive around a car whose almost-jerks across the line I didn't trust at two-thirty in the morning. I was grateful when Mal glanced my way after I spoke, an inquisitive arch to her eyebrow. I was facing forward again, eyes glued to the asphalt in front of me, but it felt tight in here, like I could sense all of Mal's movements anyway, everything crystal clear in the corner of my eye, even in the dim light. "For not turning me down," I clarified. "For coming with me."

Her eyebrow lowered. She shifted her gaze to focus straight ahead, matching mine.

"Come on, June," she said, quiet, the sound of a hard shell softening. "You know I'd always come with you."

I sucked in a silent breath. I hadn't known that, at least not for certain. Something about her saying it out loud, the first sentences she'd said since we'd pulled away from Moonie's, and in that voice, was the most shocking thing that had happened all night. Made my left hand shake, just the tiniest bit.

At the same time, it was very Mal. Straight to the point. And it felt like an echo of my own admission back at the bar, about how I didn't go there for the songs. Which had to be obvious to her, at this point, but maybe me saying it out loud had been as surprising to her as this moment felt for me.

Thinking of the bar shook something out of my head, though. I didn't go to Moonie's expressly for the karaoke, but that didn't mean music wasn't still part of our glue, me and Mal. It didn't mean I didn't have my own carefully prepared playlists for the possibility of something just like this: finally, only the two of us.

I fumbled with my phone at a stoplight. Brought up a playlist. When I put my foot on the gas again, Big Brother & The Holding Company bled from the speakers. And I could've been making it up, but I swore I felt both of us physically relax. The space between us finally loosening.

I had hoped it would feel like this from the start, being with Mal outside Moonie's, as easy and unfettered as it always felt between us there. Had been disappointed at the anxiety that had clutched at my ribcage for the last fifteen minutes since the parking lot. It made sense, I knew, that this spontaneous outing, this detour from our safe routine, would feel fraught at first. But I kept thinking about Freddy's, when I had planned this all out in my head, and hoped that it wouldn't.

It had been two years ago, if memory served correctly, that I ran into Mal at a Fred Meyer, the local grocery chain here. It wasn't my regular store, but I'd had an eye appointment down in Southeast, and it was right there, and I needed a few things, so I stopped in. And saw Mal Edwards in the condiment aisle.

I learned so many things during that day at Freddy's. That Mal preferred bread and butter pickles to dill, a fact which, for some reason, shocked me. That she preferred regular fucking Oreos over double stuf, a fact that actually made no sense whatsoever. Who didn't prefer double stuf? But I made such a stink over it that her mouth had twitched into that smile. She'd almost laughed. And immediately, I had wanted to make a stink about everything.

I learned that she looked even better, somehow, under the horrible fluorescent lights of a supermarket than she did in the dim of Moonie's.

I learned that hanging out with Mal outside of Moonie's felt almost weirdly normal. It felt simple, walking down the aisles with her, memorizing the brands and items she preferred, another list compiled in my head. But it had also felt like a shot of adrenaline had been spiked through my blood the rest of that day, far after we'd waved goodbye in the parking lot.

I learned that spending an hour in a supermarket with Mal was almost the most fun I'd ever had.

We'd never mentioned the meeting at Freddy's, at least not in a direct way. But I'd been thinking about it a lot since leaving Dr. Singh's office. Since thinking about doing this. Hoping that Freddy's had been a sign that it would always be like this between us, no matter where we were. Simple. Thrilling. Good.

But I guessed picking out yogurt together wasn't exactly the same as driving off into the night in the middle of Pride. And even Freddy's, I realized now, still had the shield of being a public space.

And honestly, especially since Arlo died, I wasn't super used to having another warm body in my truck.

It felt better, though, with the music, with each stop-light, each turn. By the time I merged onto 26, drove under the tunnel out of town, I felt as at ease as I did on my barstool at Moonie's. Better.

By the time we passed the merge with 217, barely a minute later, Mal was asleep.

It took me a while to realize it. But when we were almost done flying through the suburbs, I heard a little noise from her side of the truck. I could just hear it over Elton John singing about Levon being born on Christmas Day. It was almost like a hiccup? Or a snort? Something was happening in Mal's lungs, anyway, and when I glanced over, sure enough, her head had slumped toward the window. Eyes closed, mouth slightly open.

I stared straight ahead again immediately, as if I'd been caught doing something I shouldn't. Like cheating on a test, or seeing Mal Edwards sleep. But of course she should sleep. It was almost three in the morning, and she'd likely been working for ten hours. My body was used to being awake at random hours, but of course Mal was worn out. Something in me relaxed even further, knowing that Mal was resting, that there was no pressure on me to make this not awkward.

As we eased past the farmlands that edged the last suburb, though, I let myself steal more glances. She looked...well, like Mal, a small crease still present between her eyebrows, like she would be ready to blink her eyes open and scowl at any moment. But in a peaceful way, somehow. It was cute, and hilarious, and I had to bite my lip to keep from laughing aloud. About Mal's sleeping bitch face. About Mal in my truck. About the fact that I was driving her to the ocean.

It was still possibly the strangest thing I'd ever done.

But as the road unraveled before me, the lanes that stretched through suburbia narrowing to one as 26 wound its way into the trees and hills of the Coastal Range, I felt all right.

There was a reason long haulers liked the cloak of night. At least, some of us did. I'd take a clear stretch of dark highway over a traffic jam in the heat of day any time. Assholes swerving in front of my hood, making dangerous, impatient moves to crawl forward one extra inch.

There were inherent dangers to a road at night, too, of course, that even the most hardened of drivers couldn't deny. Things jumping out from the black—not just animals, but curves that bit harder than you expected. Tricks of the eye, the mind. The most dangerous of all perils: exhaustion, the human body denying even the most acidic cups of truck stop coffee.

Like all things in life, pavement at three a.m. was a balance of good and bad. You weighed your chances. Trusted your gut. Hoped for the best.

I didn't need truck stop coffee now, though. I took the curves of the road nice and easy. There was no rush here, no suits waiting to clock my miles. Just my headlights against the evergreens, the stars above us. My playlist went on. Mal kept making her funny sleeping noises. And as the night crept closer to morning, so did my wheels toward the Pacific. I circled 'round onto 101 South as Dusty Springfield sang about wishin' and hopin' and I almost laughed again, picturing what Mal would say if she woke up right now, glancing around and hearing this silly song. I imagined she'd eventually stare at me and say, "What the hell, June?"

But she didn't wake up, not as we coasted past Cannon Beach, saw the top of Haystack Rock looming over the water just as the horizon was changing from midnight blue to cobalt, that first glance of the ocean that still made my heart jump, even now. Even if it was different here than it had been growing up in Jersey. At the shore, you could see the Atlantic stretching out for blocks and blocks before you got there, a tantalizing, shimmery blue-green haze wide open in the distance. The Oregon Coast, by contrast, was shrouded in foggy hills, craggy cliffs, trees that blocked your view until you came to the right bend in the road, and bam—a shock of endless steel blue, right below you, the exact color of Mal Edwards's eyes.

It wasn't long after Cannon Beach that I finally pulled off into the small, sandy-gravel parking lot for Arcadia Beach. I had always liked this spot, tucked between the popular shores by Haystack Rock and the drama of Hug Point, just south of here. It felt too cute, or something, taking Mal to Hug Point, even though it was a fantastic place. But Arcadia was full of an equal amount of rugged, fascinating stone formations and quiet stretches of flat sand.

It always kind of felt like me.

In a few hours, its parking lot would be crammed full, as was every parking lot on the coast in the middle of summer. But now, at four-thirty in the morning, the only other vehicle around was a sad-looking RV camped in a corner. I pulled up a few spots away, my headlights shining against the wind-sculpted trees.

Mal finally stirred when I turned off the engine.

I watched her cautiously as she shifted in her seat, rubbed at her neck, eyes blinking once, twice. With the engine and the music off, the only things that roared now were the waves waiting on the other side of the parking lot and the renewed pounding of my heart.

"You brought me to the ocean," she observed, voice scratchy. Turning away from the window, Mal looked at me, an amused look awakening in her still blurry eyes. A lick of hope leapt in my chest. Maybe she didn't hate that I'd brought her to the ocean. Maybe this hadn't been a bad idea.

She arched an eyebrow. "Just 'cause?"

I tried to think of the right answer. One that wasn't just blurting, *because I love you.*

But the more I thought on it, the more Mal's assessment actually felt pretty spot-on.

Wasn't that what love was, really? Doing beautiful, funny things, just for the hell of it. Because you wanted to. Because the other person made you feel like you could.

"Yeah," I agreed with a shrug. "Just 'cause."

She turned away again, before I could witness her smile. She kept rubbing her neck.

"You okay?" I asked after a beat.

"Neck hurts," she said. "Back hurts." And with a small, rueful laugh, "I'm an old bitch who spends half my life on my feet. Everything always hurts."

I laughed in return. If that wasn't the truth.

And this admission of our shared aches and pains made any vestiges of nerves about this whole ridiculous affair, any phantoms that had built up in my drive through the dark, bleed away from my system. It suddenly felt like it was just me and Mal again, shooting the shit. As solid and reliable as ever. Didn't matter that we weren't at Moonie's. Felt almost natural that we were here, alone in a dark parking lot about to watch the sun rise behind a rocky coast.

There were advantages, though, to not being at Moonie's. New things I could try.

I'd put some old blankets on the seat between us, for the beach. I moved them out of the way now, throwing them on my other side as I slid over to her. She didn't make a sound as my knee glanced against hers. But when I reached my hand up to her neck, dug my thumb and forefinger into the skin there, under the collar of her black bartending shirt, a noise rumbled from her throat, and her eyes closed again. My glasses slipped on my nose; I shoved them back up with my left hand as my right moved up and down Mal's vertebrae to the base of her skull, slow and hard.

"June." She said it so quietly, like she had when we'd left Moonie's and she'd said she'd always come with me. Her shoulder sank down against my arm. Like she was letting go. Yielding.

I thought about Dr. Singh, and my body. About my unspooling, uncertain future. About starting my second half century right. I dropped my hand from Mal's neck. Used it to grip the back of the seat behind her instead.

And even though it was clumsy as hell, even though it made my own back hurt, I did something I hadn't done inside a truck in a really long time.

I climbed onto a pretty girl's lap.

FIVE

MY BRAIN WAS STILL a little foggy here, what with the only sleeping for barely two hours inside a moving vehicle after a longass shift thing. So I forced my brain to quickly collect the facts.

June had driven me to the coast.

June looked hot as hell behind the wheel of her truck. This was the easiest fact to accept; my cognitive tissue already knew it.

June had put her fingers on my neck, dug in hard and deep just like I liked, and made my body feel better than it had in months.

June was climbing onto my lap.

She smacked her head against the roof of the truck as she did so. "Shit." And then, when she raised her arm to touch the tender spot on her head, hit her elbow against the window. "Fuck."

I laughed. I couldn't help it.

June looked down at me and smiled. "I should've gotten you into my rig instead," she said. "More space. Oh well."

We were, in fact, two large women, probably too large

and too old to be doing this. But there were other facts coming to light in this surreal situation. June's weight felt good on mine, her thighs warming my own. She smelled like vanilla, which I'd only caught hints of in the past, competing with the alcohol and fry grease and dance floor sweat of Moonie's. It surprised me a little, the vanilla, but I liked it. It was still pretty dark out, but June's eyes were even darker here, right now, her glasses only inches from my face. And she was definitely about to kiss me.

"Wait," I said. My hands, which had naturally come to rest on those fabulous thighs on top of mine, tightened their grip, as if they could freeze the scene. June's smile dropped. She opened her mouth as if to say something, closed it like she'd changed her mind.

I took a deep breath. Collected the facts. June had taken the jump in asking me out, in bringing me here. I could use my words.

"I've thought about kissing you for a long time, June." I kept my eyes on hers. She swallowed, a twitch pinching her cheek. "And hell if I'm doing it for the first time with morning breath."

June's tense face collapsed in a laugh. Her own breath cascaded over my face, and it only felt lovely, but seriously, my mouth was a swamp.

"I do have mints, actually, in my glove compartment." She gestured behind her with a tilt of her head. "But my body can't twist that way anymore. And I can only complete this sitting-on-your-lap maneuver once every three days, approximately, so I might be stuck this way for a while."

"Hold on. I got it." Reaching my hands toward the glove compartment, I attempted to shift forward, wrapping one arm around June to keep her steady. Our bodies shoved together, my eyes just barely able to peek over her shoulder, my fingers stumbling toward the latch. June dropped her head, her cheek pressed against my scalp, another laugh tinkling into my ear.

"Mal," she said through her chuckles, "I do not care about your breath."

"Shut up." My hand searched through the clutter of the compartment. "I do. And I can do this."

Thirty seconds later, my fingers clutched around a small, cold metal tin. I gave it a shake, heard the mints dance around, and squeezed June even closer in triumph.

Except before I could lean back and throw a damn mint in my mouth, I realized that at some point in the last minute, June's hands had dropped from where she'd been holding onto the back of the seat. They were wrapped around me now, one draped around my shoulder, the other cradling my head. Her mouth still rested against my ear, breath hot.

The arm that had successfully retrieved the tin of mints fell limply to my side. My face was buried in her shoulder. And we just sort of...sat there a moment. This tight cocoon of a hug. I couldn't remember the last time I'd been this physically surrounded by another person. I wondered, bewildered, if I had ever felt this surrounded, this safe and wanted, with anyone. The facts I'd been collecting in my brain, trying to grasp at what was happening here, washed away like sidewalk chalk in the rain, leaving only a smudged palette of soft colors. Leaving only the feel of June's body and mine.

"Mal," she said again, her lips grazing the shell of my ear.

Hell.

Awkwardly, hurriedly, I shoved my hands between us to

get the damn tin of mints open. I threw one in my mouth, tossed the tin onto the seat, chomped on that thing like a motherfucker, and finally, finally, grabbed June Davis's face in my hands. I was abruptly wide awake, a fire burning in my belly. Embers I had forgotten could live there, rekindling.

I pulled June's lips down to mine like we'd been waiting five fucking years to do it.

She was warm, that one arm of hers still cradling my head, her lips sure and steady and gentle all at once, just like her. I'd never been a person particularly starved for physical attention. I liked it, when I got it, but it wasn't something I needed to survive. This, though—June—when her lips touched mine, when her mouth opened with mine, when we fell back the few inches to collapse against the seat again—

It just felt like home.

It suddenly seemed silly, that I'd been so anxious back at Moonie's, so unsure of June wanting anything like this. I didn't know it would happen like this, at the break of dawn on the coast in June's truck, but it didn't really matter to me, right then, where we were. It didn't matter to me, at that exact moment, if this was all we ever got, if this was just something June had dared herself to do on Pride weekend. All that mattered was how right and natural it felt, like something had slotted into place that had been hovering right at the edges for so long. And even if it all went away, even if June never showed up at Moonie's again after whatever this was was over, I'd always be able to feel it, still locked in there in my chest. I'd always know it was true.

I'd never be able to explain it, to Britt or Cam or hell, even to June. Or myself, really. But it felt special and lucky, this confirmation that June and I slotted together, like the way a thunderstorm felt when you were safe inside and didn't have any place to be, like the way I could guess my regulars' orders, like the way the first shoots of daffodils and hyacinths in the early spring soil felt every year. A satisfying gratitude, a touch of wonder.

June pulled back a minute later, rested a hand on my shoulder. Let out a long, quiet sigh.

"Wanted to do that a long time," she said.

"Yeah," I agreed, a bit breathless. "Me too."

"We should head down." She gestured toward the beach with her head. "Don't want to miss the sunrise."

"You are romantic as shit, June Davis."

A more irritated sigh as she reached over to grab the blanket. "Shut it, Mal Edwards."

Well, this was a delight. Calling each other by our full names. Which seemed way too simple a thing to elicit such pleasure in my spine, but there it was. Climbing inelegantly out of June's truck in the half-dark, laughing at ourselves as we stumbled. I didn't laugh a lot, in general, at Moonie's. Wasn't 'cause I hated the job; it just didn't often fit. It fit here, in the open air with June. It felt good to laugh with her here, no one else around but us.

Although maybe we weren't completely alone. I glanced back at the dilapidated RV in the corner of the lot as we strolled across the gravel, toward the dirt path that went down to the water. The dusty RV was probably abandoned, or simply somebody's home, but I didn't trust it. If anyone did anything to June's truck—if someone had been creeping on us during what just happened—I'd—well, I'd do something.

"Mal," June said, and even though I was still staring at the RV, away from her face, I could tell she was smiling. Like she was always smiling at me. The witch. "We're good. We're fine."

And—well, damn. When she said it, I believed it. Like there was some magic transmission in her voice that made my blood trust whatever she said. So I relaxed. And walked down to the beach to watch the sun rise.

After the short, zigzagging path from the parking lot, followed by the small set of treacherous steps that seemed the hallmark of every beach on this coastline, we were on the sand, walking toward the thunderous churn of the water. The beach stretched out on either side of us, wide, smooth, and open, surrounded by a backdrop of cliffs and forest. Safe.

June laid down her blanket next to a hunk of rock that jutted dramatically out of the sand, and we sat.

"Sunset would've been better." June shrugged. "But..." She looked away, toward the other end of the beach, but I caught the smile on her face anyway. "Didn't want to wait."

It was true. The sun was technically rising behind us, behind the cliffs and the twisted trees. But there was still something wonderful about sitting here in front of the waves, the horizon lightening by the minute, tendrils of the distant sun stretching out across the dark water. The rising sun at our backs cast shadows of the mountains behind us across the dark sand, slowly shifting, reaching higher, minute by minute.

It was subtle. But it was still wonderful, in its own way.

If I was a sentimental person, I'd say it felt a bit like us.

It was still chilly in the dawn, brightening horizon or not. Before I even so much as released a shiver, though, June was rustling out another blanket she must have been hiding under the other one, resting it over our laps.

I almost didn't know what to do with myself as she

tucked us in. I felt distinctly like I was being...wooed. I realized, fully, now that I was truly awake, that June had had these blankets carefully folded in her truck on purpose. And what she'd just said about not wanting to wait. She must have stopped drinking on purpose, back at Moonie's, to make sure she was awake and sober enough to drive us here.

June had come to Moonie's tonight with the purpose of wooing me.

I'd be damned.

I couldn't remember the last time I'd been wooed. Most people assumed I wouldn't want such a thing. Olivia certainly had. It'd been clear from the start that Olivia was turned on by my wooing her, and I'd filled the role easily. But it was...sort of oddly charming, having a blanket tucked over my lap. At least, when it was June doing the tucking. I wasn't sure if I would have let anyone else do it. But I liked it, with June.

We sat there for a few minutes, quiet, thighs pressing together, as the sky changed colors. It felt good, both the quiet and the thigh touching. Even in the din of Moonie's, we'd already established we were good at being quiet, I thought. Half the time on a June night, I'd simply lean against the bar next to her as we watched karaoke. Never felt weird, and it didn't feel weird here either. Although a person truly didn't need to talk here, anyway. The sound of the waves, the wind, was enough for the world.

A flock of seabirds landed on shore as the horizon started to really shine, a fuzzy orange haze burning away the dark blue. Moisture started to lift from the sand as the light hit it, a low-lying mist. In the far distance, a lone early morning jogger made their way down the other end of the beach. Otherwise, we were alone. June leaned back on her palms, elbows locked, the wind rustling her hair. The colors of the changing sky reflected in her glasses.

I should've kept the quiet a while longer, probably. But for some reason, the upper edges of the sky were still dark when I asked, "So what's after this?"

Honestly, I was only sort of asking, are we heading back to the city after this, or what. I wanted to know how much more of this experience I got to keep. But when June was silent, I glanced back over and saw her lips had thinned, the line of her jaw tense. I wasn't sure I'd ever seen June this tense.

And then she abruptly sat forward. Ran a hand through her rumpled hair. I didn't have enough hair to rumple, myself, but seeing June's even slightly mussed made me want to kiss her face off.

"It occurs to me," she said, "that I've assumed some things. So...I should probably double check, to make sure. Mal, you're not—" She squinted up at the sky. "You're not seeing anyone, are you? You don't already belong to someone else?"

I opened my mouth to answer, but she waved a hand through the air in front of us before I could, seeming flustered.

"Not that, you know. You should belong to anyone other than yourself. But, yeah. You know."

I almost laughed out loud again. I understood the sentiment, was glad June was respectful of my agency, but seriously. It was hilarious to me she was even questioning it, especially after what had just happened in the truck. I half wanted to shout it to the birds. Of course I belonged to June.

On the off chance, though, that this whole chain of events *was* simply a spontaneously good time to June, and she was only making sure she wasn't stepping on some other broad's toes for the day—I decided to play it semi-cool.

"No," I answered. "I don't belong to anyone else."

And then I realized that just about said it all anyway.

June's shoulders relaxed. She fell back on her palms again, fingers stretching out on the blanket behind us. A satisfied grin graced her lips. I liked seeing June smug.

"All right," she said. "Then to answer your question. I was thinking probably breakfast."

I lay all the way back on the blanket then, my head hitting the sand. Because sitting was killing my back, and I was calling the sun officially up, and I was going to breakfast with June Davis.

There was this dumb happy buzzing in my head, just thinking about it. I wished I could eat breakfast with June at Rosie's in Redding, California. I wished I could see all of her favorite places on the road, the spots that brought her small bits of joy. But I would take breakfast on the coast. I would take anything.

After a minute, June joined me, groaning as her back made its way to the blanket, shoulder bumping mine.

"We're going to look like two beached whales," she muttered.

"Good," I said. "Whales are majestic as fuck."

I couldn't see her face—I was staring up at the azure sky, its peachy pink edges—but I could somehow feel her smile.

"You said you weren't working today," she said after a minute. "You working tomorrow?"

I turned my head, lifting a brow. "Yeah."

"What time do you have to be there?"

"Four."

She made a little humming sound. "Good."

She lifted her knees, rested her hands on her stomach. "I may have gotten a hotel room for later, down the road a bit in Rockaway Beach. If you were amenable to that."

I shifted myself up on an elbow to stare at her. "No shit."

She shrugged, her flannel shifting against the blanket. "Might be awhile until they let us check in, but I figured we could both use a nap."

"I am amenable as fuck, June."

June closed her eyes and smiled. "Good," she said again.

I lay back down. Processed this new nugget of information a bit more.

"How long have you had the reservation?"

There was a pause before she answered.

"A while," she said eventually, cool and vague. "Figured if you said no, a night alone at the coast still wouldn't be a bad deal."

I stared at the cloudless sky.

I was being wooed.

And it wasn't bad.

It wasn't bad at all.

 *june*

SIX

"SO." Mal placed her forearms on the table, leaning over her mug of coffee. "Here's what I'm thinking. If we're doing this, we should go all in."

I raised an eyebrow as I lifted my own coffee to my lips. I felt like I'd been pretty clear thus far on being all in.

"Agreed."

Mal nodded. "Let's get it all out there over this breakfast. Share all of our shit."

"Ah." I placed my mug back on the table, ran a finger inside the smooth handle. I admired a mug with a handle. "Sure. You can ask me anything. I'll tell you anything."

I hadn't always been a super open person, in the past. Which probably explained my patchy history of semi-relationships. But Mal was different. Asking her to do this at all had been the scary part. Walking into the hotel room in a few hours might be a bit scary, too. Had to wait and see with that one. But telling her shit wasn't hard at all. I sort of felt like maybe I'd been ready to tell Mal my shit for years.

"All right." Mal looked straight at me. There were bags under her eyes, exhaustion pinching the corners. But the eyes themselves looked bright. Present. Piercing. "Your family. Why you never talk about them. Why you never go back to Jersey."

I nodded. Rather expected all that.

And I was about to open my mouth to answer when our meals came.

I leaned back as the waiter placed the dishes in front of us. Smiled at Mal's basic breakfast: eggs over easy, bacon, hash browns. Something deep seated and wonderful had lit in me when I'd heard her order it, exactly as I knew she would. I'd never gotten breakfast with Mal before, but I knew her order. It was one of the first things we'd talked about, god, years ago now, when she'd asked about my favorite diners on the road. We actually talked about breakfast food a possibly weird amount, me and Mal, but when I thought about it, good breakfasts made up most of my favorite moments in life.

It was like the world getting a little more colored in, being able to witness all the things I knew about Mal Edwards actually happening in real time, in front of me.

Me, I always liked trying something new for breakfast, depending on the city I was in, the special of the day. That was half the fun of the road, experiencing what the locals loved, even if you'd never actually be one of them. Which was why I had a smoked salmon benedict in front of me. It had been the most expensive thing on the menu, but if being out with Mal wasn't an occasion to get the most expensive thing on the menu, I didn't know what was.

Although, truth be told, it wasn't the first smoked salmon benedict I'd had on the Oregon coast. It was possible I was almost dangerously close to being a local here. But that discomfited me far more than the idea of telling Mal my Very Sad Past, so I wasn't going to dwell on it.

"My parents were alcoholics." I picked up my fork and sliced into the egg on top of my benedict. Its deep orange yolk—must've been local too—ran onto the plate. "Drove sloshed after leaving the bar one night when I was seventeen. Never made it home."

Mal chewed on a piece of bacon. Her face remained steady, not betraying a hint of sympathy or surprise. Even in this, she was everything I wanted. "I'm sorry, June," she said.

I shrugged. "These days, I can only think about what a relief it is that somehow they didn't hurt anyone else. Drove off the side of the road all on their own."

Mal picked up her own fork but paused before digging into her potatoes, a thought creasing her brow. "Sort of interesting, though," she said, "that you decided to spend your life behind a wheel, after that."

"Yeah." I picked up my coffee mug again. "Driving is one of the most dangerous things a person can do. Knew that even without my parents killing themselves. But the need to be on the move always wins out, in the end."

Mal nodded. Dug back into her breakfast.

"Somehow I finished high school after that, even though I was pretty fucked up for a while there. An aunt watched out for me, made sure I went to school, even though the rest of that year is sort of just a big blank in my memory. But once I got my diploma, didn't see much reason to stick around. Didn't have a lot of happy childhood memories. Even though—" I plunked my mug back onto the table, "—I actually don't harbor that many bad feelings about Jersey in particular. There are lots of good things about Jersey. I just wanted to see more."

I dug myself another bite of benedict. Chewed before I kept talking.

"Stayed in Virginia for a bit. Did some random shit before I started work on getting my CDL. Trucker's license, basically. Once I got that and started trucking, I tried out different spots around the country in my twenties, places where I stayed between trips, before I ended up here." I took another few bites, allowed myself some internal reminiscing about that decade of my life. The tiny apartments and sublets, the cities and the small towns I'd passed through: a month here, a few months there. The people I'd slept with. It had been a time, that was for sure. A decade I wouldn't be able to sum up over breakfast, even to Mal.

To an outsider, perhaps, I'd been pretty lost. But I'd been finding my way. Seeing things, experiencing the world outside the glass house of bad decisions I'd grown up in. The one thing I was determined not to repeat, that I'd learned good and hard from my parents, was being truly out of control. I didn't touch alcohol or drugs for most of my twenties; only started having a beer every now and then in my thirties, when I knew I could handle it. Added in whiskey—two tumblers of it every visit to Moonie's, to be specific—and prescription marijuana for pain in my forties.

No, I hadn't been out of control when I was young. I'd simply been wandering.

I thought, in my own way, I'd been happy.

"And when I got here—" I finally picked up the thread again with a shrug. "It stuck."

Mal's mouth twerked up then. "Yeah," she agreed.

Our meals were both near finished now, eaten in the silence of my reminiscing, in Mal's easy acceptance of the quiet. I finished my final few bites before I shoved my plate to the side and leaned in for my turn at questions.

"What about you?" I asked. "I know you're close with your sister. But what made you get stuck here?"

Mal took her time with her last bite, pushing her own plate away, picking her coffee mug back up and staring at me over the top of it.

"Honestly—" She took a sip, "—it's not that interesting. Not nearly as adventurous as yours. I hated Texas." Another twitch of her lips. "So I left."

When she didn't say anything else for a stretch, I almost laughed. Wondered if that was all she would give me. After being the one who started this conversation with that little speech about sharing our shit. But if that was all she had to say—well, it also felt remarkably like Mal.

But after another few minutes, she set her mug down, stretched out her neck. "I went to college in California," she started. "Made my way up the coast, I guess, after. I liked it here, so I stayed. And somehow, over the years, convinced my sister and brother to come up here, too."

"You have a brother? You normally only talk about your sister."

"Yeah, I'm closer with Britt. Cam's okay, too. A bit of a dumbass." Mal's lips tilted past smirk to full blown smile. "But we love him anyway."

The smile faded. "I did—I do—feel a little guilty that I tore all of us away from our folks. Didn't mean to; it just sort of happened. My dad passed away a few years back, but my mom's all alone now, still in our old town outside of Houston. But she has this group of friends, so. I guess it's all right. We should probably visit more than we do. Cam gets back the most. But I try to get back for Christmas, every other year or so."

I suddenly, desperately wanted to meet Mal's mom. I blinked with the surprise of it, how deeply I felt it. Couldn't explain it, didn't say it out loud, but I wanted to fly to Houston with Mal this December. See what the house she grew up in looked like. Meet the woman who had raised a person like Mal.

"I bet if you're all happy, she's happy," I said. Because the way Mal was talking, it sounded like they loved each other. And I knew that was how it was supposed to work, between parents and kids who loved each other. When addiction didn't get in the way.

"Yeah," Mal said. "I think you might be right."

"What did you study?" I asked. "In college?"

I didn't know why I'd never pictured Mal in school before. Maybe because I never went to college, sometimes I forgot that other people's young adulthoods looked different. I liked thinking about it now, though. Mal with a mess of books and papers in a fancy library. Staying up late, typing essays.

Disappointingly, though, Mal's shoulders hunched a bit, her spine hitting the chair as she leaned back. I could see her hesitating, the slight clench of her jaw.

"Civil engineering," she said finally, shooting me a look as she did. Her eyes were guarded, fiercer than they'd been ever since she'd woken up in my truck. As if in challenge. As if I would have something to say about this, her being a secret civil engineer, other than being supremely turned on.

I shrugged, at a bit of a loss. "So you're a smart bitch," is what I came up with.

And thank god, her mouth tilted again. "Yeah," she agreed.

"I already knew that, though," I added, and she smiled further.

"You did," she said. "But yeah. Always liked school."

Her face was doing a funny thing, now, the smile on her

face shifting to something harder to define, something I'd never seen on Mal's face before. Almost...sentimental, like she was disappearing into her own well of memories, just as I had done before. But it almost seemed pained. Like the memories were bittersweet.

It occurred to me, then. That Mal had always liked school, that she had a civil engineering degree. Yet she was a bartender at Moonie's. Had been for years. It was possible Moonie's was her side gig, that she had a day job during the week she'd never told me about, but I didn't think so. Mal told me about her life, and the only thing I knew of that existed outside of Moonie's was her garden, her cats, and her sister. There was some disconnect there, but one Mal clearly felt uncomfortable about.

It didn't bother me, telling Mal about my dead parents, but I didn't want Mal to have to dig into anything today that would bother her.

I reached into my back pocket, pulled out my wallet. Left my card pointedly at the edge of the table. It had still been pretty early when we'd walked into this place, too early for most tourists on a weekend at the coast, but it was filling up now. I tried to catch the eye of our young waiter.

"Ready for a drive down the coast?" I asked.

Mal breathed out, long and slow, before taking the last sip of her coffee. "Yeah," she said. "Let's do it."

* * *

Mal and I drove down 101, out of Arcadia and past Arch Cape, through the forest of Oswald West State Park. Around Nehalem Bay. We didn't talk much; I resumed my playlist on the stereo. But it was different than the drive here. It was light out, for one thing, the sky a brilliant blue, which wasn't always the case on the Oregon coast, even in the middle of June. And Mal was awake. Our windows were down, the wind rattling our skin, making the music almost hard to hear, but worth it for the salty smell of the sea.

By the time we reached Rockaway Beach, it was still probably too early to check in to the hotel, but I called anyway to see. Did a little sweet talking, which I was good at, after years of dealing with stressed vendors and grumpy warehouse managers and the suits at headquarters. And the hardened waitresses at all-night diners, and the cleaning staffs and front desk workers at motels along lonely stretches of highways. It was kind of funny, with how much time I'd spent completely alone on the road, how good I'd gotten over the years, simultaneously, at talking to strangers.

I ended the call. "They can get us in in an hour."

"All right." Mal sounded easy, but when I glanced over at her, the exhaustion that I'd seen pulling at her eyes since she woke in the parking lot at Arcadia Beach only looked worse. The woman had worked a busy shift and then gotten two hours of sleep, max. I winced.

"Want to take a walk on the beach?" I asked, wishing there were better options of things to do for her in this moment, in this funny little town, so different from the one of the same name back in Queens, the one The Ramones made famous. There was nothing punk rock about Rock-away Beach, Oregon. But I suddenly wished there was something, somewhere special I could take Mal. A massage parlor, maybe. Would Mal Edwards even walk into a massage parlor? Fuck. I was tired, too.

"Actually," Mal said, "Do you think there's anywhere here where I could buy some clothes? A fresh shirt at least?" She gestured down at herself. "I still smell like Moonie's."

A laugh burst out of me. I thought I'd planned this little adventure pretty well. But in retrospect, whisking a woman away from her home without warning had some drawbacks. Like a lack of clean clothes. And the funny thing was, I didn't know if there *was* a place here where Mal could find new clothes. There was only a pizza joint and weird beach shops.

"There's a Fred Meyer in Tillamook we could drive down to," I said. Even though I didn't really feel like driving to Tillamook. Now that we were here, parked across the road from the hotel, all I could think about was getting inside it.

Mal was quiet a minute. And then she said, "Remember that time we ran into each other at Freddy's?"

I smiled. "Yeah."

"I liked that," she said, and my heart about burst out of my chest.

"Yeah," I agreed. "Me too."

"Let's see what we can find here," she said, and I put the truck back in gear.

Ten minutes later, we stood outside a short building painted a garish variety of aquamarine. Plastic flamingos and seashells dotted the edge of the walkway. A neon sign flashed OPEN above the glass door.

Mal nodded approvingly. "Let's go," she said. As if preparing for battle.

It was 10:05 a.m. We were the first customers. At 10:06 a.m, Mal held up an XXL *Rockaway Beach, Oregon* t-shirt with a sea lion on it. "Done," she said.

"Hold up, hold up," I protested. Because now that we were inside this place—there was barely enough room for two dykes to move without knocking over a rack of post-cards—I was into it. I reached over to a display of sunglasses. Picked out a pair with bright red, star-shaped plastic frames.

Mal's eyes were wary as I placed them over her nose, fitted them over her ears. But she let me do it.

Her mouth was flat as I stood back to survey the results.

"No," she said, voice as stone-cold as her stare had been when she'd served Cher their Jack and Coke back at the bar.

I grinned so big I could feel it stretch my cheeks. I couldn't wait to kiss her again.

"Okay, so definitely getting these." I lifted the shades off her face and tucked them into my palm. "And maybe—" I threw a floppy straw hat onto her head, barely missing her arm as it came up to swipe mine away.

"Fuck you." She yanked the hat off and punched my arm. I bounced away, laughing. She was right. The hat didn't fit her like the glasses did.

"Consider, though—" Still backtracking away on my heels, I stopped by a rack of shirts. "This one instead." I lifted the neon pink tank top to my chest. *What happens in Rockaway Beach stays in Rockaway Beach*, it read.

Mal's lip twitched, finally, as she shook her head.

"No," she said again. "But I dare you to buy it."

I searched through the rack for an XL. "All right."

"And maybe this?" Mal held up a puka shell necklace.

"Mal," I scowled. "Don't be ridiculous."

By the time we checked out, Mal had added a zip-up hoodie, and I'd thrown in an Oregon Coast mug. I imagined if this thing didn't actually last longer than today, I could at least have coffee in this mug sometimes and smile.

We were quiet again as we drove back to the hotel, as we checked in at the front desk. As we walked across the parking lot toward Building C. I had the overnight bag I'd packed; Mal walked with her hands in her pockets and her messenger bag slung across her chest, the shirt and sweat-shirt she'd bought slung over her shoulder.

I swore I'd had the best of intentions when I called to ask about checking in early. We did both need a nap.

But as we climbed the wooden steps to the second floor of Building C, something started to pulse in my head, leaving me a little dizzy. Something that had been building since Mal let me climb into her lap, since my palms had cupped the back of her head, since I'd first tasted her lips. Since our thighs had touched while we'd watched the sunrise, while she'd stared at me with those icy eyes over breakfast, calm and steady and here. Since she'd let her fingertips brush mine, for just a second, every time she handed me a whiskey over the last five years.

"You got an ocean view? Jesus," Mal said when she walked through the door.

I dropped my bag onto the bed. Heard the door click shut.

And then I turned and pushed Mal against the wall.

SEVEN

I WAS unprepared for June's hands on my stomach.

I was unprepared for all of it, really—the view of the fucking ocean through the sliding glass door to the balcony; June being all playful at that store, making me feel like a kid; me and June being here at all. And when she turned and pushed me against the wall so suddenly, I felt just like I had in her truck. Both like I'd been waiting for this forever, and like I was a teenager again, taken off guard by the idea of someone wanting me, the idea of physical intimacy. I'd always known what I wanted with Olivia, or I guess, more accurately, what Olivia wanted from me. Taking charge had always felt good. And now here I was, approaching fifty, and I barely knew what to do with my arms when June trapped my body with hers.

The truth was, I had been so happy to simply be around June the last few hours. To listen to her talk, to feel the solid, physical presence of her body next to mine. I thought I maybe would've been happy for the rest of my life to just exist with her.

But then she kissed me, and I remembered again. That I

didn't quite care how we did this. That we could have more than just existing. Because I burned for her.

She had my face in her hands, cradling my cheeks like I was precious, like she always handled me somehow, even though we'd technically barely touched before today. It was only the second time I'd kissed June, but it already felt almost shockingly familiar, soft and heady all at once. Her glasses kept bumping against my face, until she tore them off and threw them behind her onto the bed. Which I mourned a little—she looked so fucking hot in her glasses —but I suddenly realized, as I blinked at her after the break in our kiss, that I could see so much more now, here in the daylight, centimeters apart. More than I had been able to see in the dark of Moonie's, more than I'd been able to fully absorb in the half-awake, near-darkness of her truck hours earlier. The crow's feet that surrounded her eyes, so many fine lines there, testaments to the years gone by of June Davis, her smiles and frowns and every time she'd squinted into the sun. The faint slivers of gray inside her brown hair. The faint freckles, the small moles along her neck. A slash of sunlight crossed her face as she crowded me in again, and it lit up the brown of her eyes like chest-nuts over a fire.

I was aware, as her mouth met mine again, as I opened to her and our tongues tangled, as I let my eyes fall closed, that her fingers were making their steady way down my shirt, unbuttoning one careful button at a time.

But when her hands touched the soft expanse of my belly—I almost shouted. My body lifted on a gasping inhale instead, just as telling, my mouth yanking away from hers.

June's hands didn't linger on the sensitive skin of my stomach long, those lithe fingers now moving toward the zipper of my black jeans.

"This okay?" she asked, almost as breathless as I felt. "You okay?"

God, this felt dirty, up against the wall like this. It was the middle of the fucking day.

I nodded. And when she didn't move any further, gave my verbal consent. "Yeah, June," I huffed out, sounding almost irritated, almost like myself again. Even though I wasn't irritated. I just wanted her to touch me so fucking bad. "Fuck."

She smirked. It made my own limbs finally take action, a hand rising to her face to brush against the wrinkles deepened by that smirk, to grab the back of her head and pull her mouth back to mine as she snuck a hand into my jeans, rubbed her fingers over my underwear.

"Fuck," I said again, into her open mouth, spreading my legs so she could have better access. God, just that felt so good. Her tongue found mine again, sloppy and hot, a noise rumbling from the back of her throat into my mouth.

"Mal," she huffed over my lips as her hand slipped inside my underwear. "You are so fucking hot."

A grunt escaped me when her fingertips first touched my clit. I tried to tilt my hips forward, push my pelvis into her palm, communicate, *yes. Keep going. Just fucking do it.* I'd never really been good at communicating during sex, but I felt wild just then, blood thrumming everywhere, a way I hadn't felt in years. I wanted June to fuck me senseless.

But she didn't, not yet, pulling her hand back, bringing her other up to palm my breast through my bra while she re-focused her kiss. Don't get me wrong, that felt decent too, but fucking A, it wasn't enough. I swore I'd been about to fall asleep in June's truck a half hour ago, but ten minutes inside this hotel room and suddenly I'd never been so turned on in my life.

Eventually, I reached down, pressed her hand hard against me again. Moaned in relief.

"Fuck, June." My vocabulary had become extremely limited. "Fuck."

She increased the pressure on my clit, the speed of her circles, and I let my hand fall back against the wall, a weak attempt to keep myself steady. It was almost too much, the pleasure too sharp and near the surface, when she slid her hand down further and worked a finger inside.

I groaned my approval. That. That was good.

After a few slides in and out, she worked another finger in, a flash of discomfort for a second, and then we were golden. Her mouth moved away from mine, trailing to my ear as our breaths came harsh and heavy in the quiet room as she fucked me, as I pushed against her, looking for the friction of her palm on my clit, over and over.

"June," I said, my voice this shaky whisper I was too gone to feel self-conscious about.

Her whole body shuddered against mine, her rhythm faltering for a second.

She opened her mouth against my neck, trailed her lips across my skin. "If you only knew," she said, right under my ear, "how many times I've imagined you saying my name just like that."

"Years," I heard myself say, nonsensically.

"Years," she agreed.

"Close," I said a minute later, and she nipped at my neck with her teeth.

I felt frustrated for a minute, as I always did when I was close, not sure if I'd be able to make it there, wanting to claw my hands through June's skin, gnash at her clothes with my teeth, anything to make me feel not-helpless.

Until June took my earlobe in her mouth and sucked

while she kept up the hard rhythm of her hand and then I actually was helpless, in the best possible way, the tremor starting in my clit and shooting up through my belly, my muscles tensing and then loosening. Liquid and hot and light.

She stopped exactly when I needed her to, removing her hand and pressing her forehead against mine.

I wanted to say *fuck* again, but felt I'd already used up my quota, and also I was busy catching my breath.

"Good," June whispered. And yeah, that felt right, too.

I kissed her again, when I finally felt a bit more myself. And with a grunt, I lifted my body off that wall and walked June back until I could push her down onto that bed. Obviously.

I felt a little more in my element here, on my hands and knees over June, and I was still running on endorphins from the orgasm, so pushing that flannel off June's shoulders while I kissed that mouth felt easy now. Smooth. Who cared that it was the middle of the day and I was running on fumes. They were fucking-June-Davis fumes now, so I'd run on them all damn day.

June lifted her arms out of the flannel just as easily, reaching upward after she did so to snake her hands around my back, scratch her barely-there fingernails down my spine, which *ahh*, felt so fucking good. I was about to implore her to take off her t-shirt too when my senses kicked in. I sat back on my heels, away from her delicious fingertips, and took in the view.

I wanted to see June's tits eventually, of course, but the way she looked right now, in that tight white t-shirt she'd been hiding under her flannel? No, she was keeping the t-shirt on. I was going to fuck her just like this.

I made quick work on her pants and underwear until I

was exactly where I was meant to be. Between June's thighs.

I ran a hand down one thigh once I was there, taking a moment to breathe. To stare at her lovely mound of dark curls. Make a plan of attack. "Do you like penetration?" I asked.

"I don't need it," she answered, and then, "Oh god, is it okay I didn't ask you before I—"

"Oh, I liked it," I assured her. "June, you could've done anything to me in that moment and I would've liked it."

When I glanced up her body toward her face to see how she was feeling, I swore the flush on her cheeks wasn't only anticipation, but a blush. The way her mouth was twisting, trying not to seem too pleased. I wanted to bite that smirk right out of her lips. Not because I didn't like it, but because I did. But I was already down here, and I wasn't limber enough to get back up to her mouth without my knees protesting.

I ran my hand up her thigh again. I wanted June to tell me what she wanted.

After a moment's hesitation, June seemed to get it. She threw her arms over her forehead. "I just want your mouth," she said.

I'd figured as much, from the small noises she'd made when I'd ripped off her pants, when I'd moved down between her legs. But it was still hot as hell to hear her say it.

I settled in on my elbows, grasping her thighs. Was almost at my destination when she made another funny sound: almost a whimper, almost a laugh. Whatever it was, it made me pause, look up at her again.

Her arms were still thrown over her forehead. But she

stared down at me from underneath them, from underneath her heavy, half-closed eyelids.

"God, Mal," she said. "I could come just from the sight of you down there."

"Well." I considered this, letting it buzz pleasantly through my blood. "That does take a bit of the pressure off."

She laughed at that, a laugh that was cut off when I put my mouth on her clit.

I didn't know how much I'd missed this. The taste of it, the feel of it. The intimacy of it. It didn't feel dirty anymore, me and June, together like this. And I felt a little more settled, a little less swept away, now that it was my turn to focus on her. More grounded, able to take in every single noise June made in her throat, every twitch of her body. The way she ground her teeth into her bottom lip, let one hand fall from her head to twist the sheets between her fingers.

It didn't always work for me, being intimate with someone, but I always knew it would with June. I just hadn't been able to picture the exact details, until now. And now they filled me up, guided my tongue, escaped me in moans against her heat. She was relatively quiet, except for those little noises and the harshness of her breath. Until she got close, which damn, I was almost disappointed by. I should've held back. Made her work for it. Except then she said, "*Fuck*, Mal, fuck, don't stop," and god, I couldn't deny her then. I squeezed my hand into her hip, stretching my fingers up under that t-shirt, my other hand still gripping her thigh as I increased the speed of my mouth. She was loud when she came, this sharp shout before this high-pitched breathy wheeze as she shook. It was incredible, and a little funny. It didn't fit her at all, the woman who only ever drank whiskey at my bar, who had never been afraid of me even a little bit, sounding like a Disney princess when she came.

I hid my fade in her thigh to smother my laugh.

I planted some kisses on that thigh when we'd both calmed down. Slowly made my way up the bed to flop down at her side. Goddamn, it felt good to lie down.

We lay there for a few minutes, the rise and fall of June's chest slowly evening out. I took in the details of the room, the shells and twine above the desk. Took in the details of June's skin, the sun spots along her arms.

"Well," I said eventually. "Happy Pride."

June laughed, one arm still over her head, the other thrown over her stomach. And then she kept laughing. She laughed so hard, I thought she might roll off the bed. I almost felt prouder of making her laugh like that than I had making her come.

"Hold on," she said after a while, once she'd gotten herself together, although her voice still sounded breathless and silly. She stumbled out of bed, slipped her underwear back on. "I should've changed first."

She lifted her arms, ripped the t-shirt off while I watched from the bed. I only had, like, three seconds to admire the swell of the tops of her breasts that peeked out above her sports bra when she picked up something from the floor and wiggled into it. Something neon pink.

"What do you think?" She gestured at the *What Happens in Rockaway Beach Stays in Rockaway Beach* tank top. Which was just as tight as the white t-shirt had been.

I threw a pillow at her head.

"I think you're goofy as hell."

She picked the pillow up as she got back on the bed, pummeled me right in the stomach with it.

"Ow!" I protested. "Jesus."

"I think it's really going to complement my wardrobe."

"Definitely."

She settled next to me again, a hand behind her head. Our leftover laughter settled down, too. I started to get drowsy.

"What's next?" I asked. Just like when I'd asked at the beach after the sunrise, I really only meant it in the most basic terms—were we going to order a pizza now? Take a shower? Did June have other plans in her head for this ridiculous day?

Once the question hung in the air between us, though, I started to truly want to know the other answer. The one we'd been hinting at, dancing around, since we left Moonie's last night. That we'd maybe been dancing around for far longer than that.

"Well," June eventually said. "I have some weed. Was thinking we could smoke some and watch the waves for a while."

Maybe the other answer could wait for just a while longer, then. Because I couldn't argue with that one.

"That sounds literally perfect, June."

She smiled at me, that wonderful June smile, and fumbled for her glasses, still lying at the edge of the bed. We each made a trip to the bathroom and rearranged ourselves, June slipping her pants back on, me re-buttoning my shirt. I threw my new Rockaway Beach hoodie on; June put her flannel back on over the neon pink tank. Which was almost funnier, somehow. She really was a goof, that June.

We sank into the cheap plastic deck chairs out on the small balcony. June had brought out a small portable speaker she'd had in her bag, placed it near the railing and hooked it up to her phone before rolling the joint.

"Never used to smoke," she said as she did. "But I was

prescribed it for my back pain a few years ago. Can't use it when I'm driving, but when I'm home—" She took a drag before she handed it off to me, settled back in her chair. "It's not bad."

She smiled at me again, watched me take my first hit before she looked out at the ocean. The breeze ruffled her hair.

And even though I'd probably always known it, all I could think at that moment was, god. She was really something.

And she liked me.

She might have even loved me.

And maybe I loved her right back.

EIGHT

WE WERE QUIET A LONG TIME, out there on the balcony, sharing a smoke, listening to my songs. Watching the ocean.

If I had to rate it, I wouldn't even have to think on it. I'd had more exciting days, perhaps, back in my wilder days. But today would definitely be in the top three best days of my life.

"Ooh La La" was pouring out of my speaker now, the jangly, familiar acoustic guitar soothing my system even further than it already was. I'd always liked the song. But as I listened to the chorus now, the lyrics about wishing you knew all you knew now when you were younger, I discovered, somewhat to my own surprise, that I disagreed.

Maybe it was just the marijuana, or the post-coital endorphins that were making me feel so sentimental. But that nostalgia that'd hit me at breakfast came roaring back.

And looking back at it all, I thought I rather liked the way I'd found myself here. Sitting in front of the ocean with Mal. Feeling sure about who I was and what I wanted. I had been green and transient for a lot of my life, but no, I wouldn't have wanted to be wiser when I was younger. That girl who'd left Jersey all those decades ago was broken but brave as hell. I was proud of the fight.

I knew it was easier now that I actually had Mal by my side, that she'd said yes to everything so far, but it seemed a little silly now. That I'd been so scared leaving Dr. Singh's office that day.

Maybe of all the things we went through in life, getting old was the luckiest of them all.

"So." Mal broke the silence eventually. "We dating now?"

I took a drag of the joint, held it in my chest along with my silent laugh before breathing out.

"Is it weird if I feel like we're sort of past that already? Even though we've never been on a date?"

Mal huffed out a half-chuckle. "No. No, that's what I was thinking, too."

"Guess spending five years staring at each other inside a bar is enough lead in."

"Hey, I was always working." She yanked the joint away from my hand. "You were doing most of the staring."

"You liked it, though."

"Fuck yeah I did." She took a long puff. "I would've dated the shit out of you, though," she said after a moment. "If we met when we were younger."

I shook my head.

"Nah." I waved her off when she offered the joint back to me. "I mean, I'm sure you would have. But I wasn't really built for dating when I was younger. I would've fallen in love with you and left." I stared out at the crashing waves. "For most of my life, leaving's been the only thing I was really good at."

Mal made a vague noise of dissent.

"I don't know," she murmured. "I mean, I know you're always leaving for your job. I know I never quite know when you're gonna show up. But I don't know." I looked back at her. The sun shone on her face, made her standard steely expression seem golden and warm. "Still feels like you've been the most consistent part of my life, these days."

I stared at her for a beat before taking the joint back and turning toward the ocean.

"Yeah," I said. "Same."

"Although." I glanced at her again out of the corner of my eye as her voice turned thoughtful. Tentative. "Can I ask you something?" I nodded. "Why now?" A slight pause. "And why did you leave last Pride?"

I reached forward, put the joint in the ashtray on the railing. Something tugged at my gut. Shame. Surprise, maybe. It was vulnerable of Mal to ask, and Mal didn't show vulnerability very often. Which meant it must have actually hurt her.

Shit.

"I was too much of a coward last Pride," I admitted. I was suddenly glad we were talking about this. I wanted to talk about all of it. Let five years of tension escape out of my system. "I didn't want to lose you, and I didn't think I deserved you."

Mal made a sound of disbelief in her throat.

"I'm gone half the time, Mal. More than half the time. You deserve better than that." Before she could protest, I went on. "Except...I turned fifty last month—"

"What the hell, June. I didn't know. Happy birthday."

I laughed a little. "Yeah. Anyway, my doctor told me that I probably need to retire soon. What with this job wrecking my body over the decades, apparently."

Mal nodded. "Relatable."

"I'm hoping I still have a year or two in me." It sounded wistful, leaving my lips. Because it was. I wouldn't miss the suits. But I'd miss the road. "The turning fifty thing spooked me, though. Made me realize I was tired of waiting, of not showing you what I felt. That I need a next act." I shrugged. "I'm yours, Mal. And I don't know what you want that to look like, if you want to go back to just seeing each other at Moonie's after tonight, or if you want more. I'm still afraid I don't have enough to offer you, but..." I bit my lip, struggling now to vocalize the future I wanted. "But I guess I want more than Moonie's."

"How much more than Moonie's?" Mal's voice sounded...I didn't know. Uncertain. I tried not to let disappointment show on my face before I answered.

"However much you'd give me, Mal."

She was quiet for a long time. Long enough that I started envisioning future mornings, alone in my apartment, staring sentimentally at my Rockaway Beach mug.

I almost jolted in my seat when Mal finally spoke again.

"Here's the thing, June." She'd sat straighter in her seat, shoulders squared. "I'm just a bartender. I'm only ever going to be a bartender. I need you to know that."

I turned in my chair to stare at her.

"Mal," I said slowly. "I'm sorry, but—what the hell are you talking about?"

She wouldn't meet my eye, jaw clenched as she stared ahead at the beach. She released a sigh through her nose.

"My last relationship was with this woman Olivia," she started. "We dated for six years. I thought we were endgame, you know?"

I nodded, even though I didn't. I'd never dated anyone for longer than six months. The only endgame I'd ever

351

wanted was with Mal. And it'd taken me almost a half-century to find her.

"She was this real boss femme." Mal's lips gentled, that small smile threatening to appear again. I tried my hardest to not want to pummel this Olivia person. "Hot as shit."

"Sure," I said.

"She worked in advertising downtown, and she'd make comments sometimes, about seeing jobs I might want to try for. And I'd always be like, come on, Liv, you know I don't want that anymore. Because I did actually use my degree for a while, in my twenties, but—" Mal shifted in her chair. "I didn't like it. It wasn't what I expected, even though my professors in college had tried to warn me about what it would be like. I wanted to do science, build things, and it was all paperwork and permits and politics and fucking *waiting* to accomplish anything and—" She shook her head. "It was also a lot of pressure. What if the things we built failed? Killed someone? And I hated sucking up to other people in the office, the whole professional thing. One of my bosses was this racist, sexist, homophobic dick, but he'd been there forever, so I knew no one was ever going to do anything about it, and it ate at me. I was never meant to exist in an office, I think. Which made me feel like I was just being a whiner about the whole thing. But I hated not being myself."

I nodded. This was the longest I'd ever heard Mal talk at once, and I was fascinated. Certainly understood what she was saying. It sounded fucking awful.

"It was Britt who finally convinced me I could quit, that it wouldn't mean I was weak if it was making me miserable. Started bartending soon after that. I liked it. I could be myself, and leave at the end of the night and not have to bring any of it home with me. It was good money. Not as good as engineering, obviously, but the one good thing about that horrible engineering job was that it'd already made me enough to buy my own house, pay off some of my student debt. Which was fucking lucky," she added after a slight pause, "considering what the housing market's like now. And student loans, for that matter."

I nodded again. A nightmare.

"Anyway, so by the time Olivia came around, I was real settled, but she kept trying to convince me I'd just had a tough time at a shitty firm, that there were lots of other options for me. And I'd try to tell her I was happy doing what I was doing, and she'd eventually sigh and say I know, I know, and we'd kiss and make up and it was good."

Mal paused again here, and I stared steadfastly at the sea. Trying not to picture whatever *good* entailed for Mal and Olivia.

"But—" Mal breathed out. "One day she gets this job in Seattle. Wants me to go with her. And I don't know, maybe if she'd phrased it differently...but she said, this'll finally be your chance, to get out of that fucking bar. She had this whole list of jobs for me to apply to up there, wanted to work on my resumé. And I was like, maybe I don't want to get out of that fucking bar. Maybe I don't want to work on my fucking resumé. Maybe I don't want to move to Seattle."

Mal shrugged.

"So she left. Honestly, she didn't even seem all that sad about it, when she realized I was serious."

I waited a minute, to make sure she was done.

"Mal." I struggled to keep my voice even. "Tell me not to drive to Seattle and do something bad to Olivia."

Not that I ever would. Seeing how my mom and dad treated each other—how they treated themselves—had

353

made me despise violence from an early age. But I felt the sentiment, anyway, on a deep level.

Mal huffed out another half-laugh. "That's exactly what Britt said. Man, Britt is going to love meeting you."

The anger left my body then, replaced by something warm and unexpected filling my chest. I hadn't thought about that yet, for some reason. Meeting Britt. Maybe because I'd never gotten close enough to anyone else in the past to meet their family, to be introduced to siblings and friends. But I was already imagining it, just as I had imagined flying to Texas over breakfast, when Mal had talked about her mom. Pictured hanging out with Britt. And Cam. And whatever other friends Mal wanted to introduce me to.

It had just been a really long time. Since I'd had a family.

I cleared my throat, shifting my knee back and forth. "Mal," I started again, "you know who you're talking to, right? I'm a truck driver, for fuck's sakes. I'd be yours whether you were a bartender or a CEO." I paused. "I like you more as a bartender, though."

Mal laughed quietly again, but it was natural this time. A real laugh.

"Yeah. I know."

"I'm just saying. It turns me on that you're good at what you do, that you care about that fucking place. It's a good place."

Mal snorted. "I don't care about it *that* much. Management is shit."

I smirked. Let it slide for now. "What I mean is, I only care about what makes you happy, Mal. And anyone who doesn't is a piece a shit."

"Yeah." Mal sighed. "I just...I don't know. Had to say

something anyway. Which is embarrassing, probably, but whatever."

"Nah, I get it." I picked the joint back up, took another drag before offering it to Mal again. She took it. "Someone fucks you up, it lasts a while."

She took a long puff before nodding.

"Okay," she said, voice confident again, all Mal. "Now you know that I'm fully a bartender. And I can tell you what bullshit it is, the you not having a lot to offer me thing."

My shoulders tensed.

"I want more than Moonie's too, June," she went on. "But like I said before. I don't care that you're gone so much."

"Maybe I do," I said quietly. "You deserve—"

"Listen," Mal cut me off. "I've been thinking on this since I woke up in your truck. Maybe us being together doesn't have to look like other relationships." She paused. "Shit, June. Did you really think I'd need you at my every beck and call?"

"I—" I scratched at the back of my head. Shit. She was right. Mal didn't need a keeper. I'd just—

"Not that I wouldn't *want* you at my beck and call," Mal clarified with a grin. "But honestly, June, after Olivia left, I sort of got used to being alone. I like being alone, most of the time, these days." She shrugged. "It suits me."

"Yeah." My voice came out rough. I felt both comforted and confused. "Me too."

"It'd be nice," Mal said, voice turning thoughtful, "to have your number now. Be able to check in with you while you're on the road." She smiled at the thought, a real smile. "But even that, I don't need, if you don't want checking up on. I'm good at waiting for you, June."

I didn't know what to say.

"Hell." She squinted out at the beach. "You could even sleep with other people, if you wanted to, while you're away. As long as you came back to me."

I blew out a breath. "I don't do that much these days."

"Aw, come on." She turned her head to smirk at me. "I bet you meet lots of pretty waitresses on the road."

Goddammit. Mal Edwards was making me *blush*.

"Well," I said. "The same would go for you, then. God, Mal. I'm sure you have endless choices, at Moonie's."

She shook her head, sharp and quick. "I don't sleep with my customers." I held my tongue, but she must have heard my silent laughter anyway. "Ah, hell." She rolled her eyes. "You don't count."

I let my chuckle escape.

"You could, though," I said. "Fair's fair."

"No." She settled back into her chair, shoulders easing. "I stand by what I said for you, but I'm good."

A memory from when I first walked into Moonie's last night resurfaced.

"All right." I turned in my chair, grinning. "That woman from last night who you said sang 'All Along the Watchtower,' in the corner with the tank top. One of the best things you'd ever seen, you said. You're telling me if she came on to you, you'd turn her down."

Mal let out a low whistle, but her eyes were grinning, too. "Out of my league."

I put a hand to my chest. "I'm wounded."

She rolled her eyes again. "June. You're out of my league, too."

I laughed out loud. God, this woman was so full of shit. She was out of all of our leagues.

But then Mal shifted a bit in her seat, stuck her hands in

the pockets of her hoodie. That uncomfortable look came over her again.

"I'm actually...really not attracted to that many people. Normally have to get to know them a little first." Mal shrugged. "You're the only person I've been attracted to in five years, June."

Ah. Okay. "All right." I nodded.

"You shouldn't let that influence your choices though," she said with an awkward wave of a hand, before she stuck it back in her sweatshirt. "I trust you, and what, you know, you said."

"That I'm yours?" I grinned again. I wasn't used to someone making *me* blush, but I liked the look on Mal.

"Yeah. That."

"Good."

I almost told her she really didn't have to even worry about it, that I didn't plan on sleeping with anyone else now. But after I thought on it a minute—well, probably shouldn't look a gift horse in the mouth.

I turned back toward the ocean. Took in a deep breath. It was good, I knew, that we were talking about all this. And I was glad—more than glad—that Mal was good with how things were. But I knew I had to put it all out there, before we truly started this thing.

"What I'm actually—" My voice cracked a little, and I stopped, cleared my throat. Tried again. "What I'm actually most scared about is what happens when I *stop* being gone all the time." I bounced my knee. "I'm used to the road, Mal. I'm used to being alone, too. I don't—" I spread out my hands in front of me. "I know my GP's right. I can't keep going forever. But I don't know what I'm going to do when I'm not trucking anymore."

Mal surprised me then. She reached out and took my hand.

She didn't say anything, just wrapped our fingers together. Rubbed her thumb along the side of my palm. Even though we'd just done what we'd done in there, inside the hotel room, we hadn't done this yet, not even while we were watching the sun rise. It felt good.

"Fuck," I said. "I'm going to have to find a hobby."

And then I laughed. The joy of it spread, nice and slow, through my bones.

"Maybe you could move in," Mal said, and the laugh faded out of my mouth as I looked at her. She looked calm, serene. She glanced back at me and shrugged. "You could fix all my shit. I'm actually pretty bad at house shit. I like the *science* of fixing shit, just not the actual...fixing." She laughed a little at herself. "And my house is pretty old. You could remodel my bathroom."

I laughed along with her. God, that sounded...wonderful.

"All right," I agreed. And then, furrowing my brow, trying to be serious about it, I shared the only other thing I'd thought of. "I know engines, too. I was thinking I could learn some more about detailing, too, maybe. Refurbish old trucks."

I realized Mal was laughing even harder now.

"What?" I frowned.

"June," she laughed. "You are such a fucking dyke."

I dropped my hand from hers to shove her in the shoulder.

"Fuck you." But I was laughing too. "Fine. What are *your* hobbies, Mal Edwards?"

She only hesitated a second.

"I like embroidery," she said. "Cross-stitch."

I froze, staring at her.

"You're fucking with me."

"Am not." Mal sounded indignant, frowning at me. I'd never been happier in my life. "Fuck off, June. It's calming as hell."

I loved her. I loved her so much.

"And gardening," she added, still a little huffy. "Even though you already knew that." I nodded. I did. And then, more annoyed than ever, she said, "I can't believe I showed you my roses that night, last Pride, and you still left."

My smile dropped an inch. "They looked like great roses," I offered.

"You're goddamn right they are," she said.

"I'll make it up to you," I promised.

Mal made a small, approving hum. "I know you will," she said, quiet. And then, "You know, June, you can still go out on the road, after you retire."

I raised an eyebrow. She gestured toward the water. Toward the world outside this balcony.

"You can still travel. Go places. Be restless when you're tired of being still. Just without anyone tracking your miles. Only reporting to yourself."

I rubbed a hand over my mouth, stared out at the ocean. I wasn't a big crier, but my eyes felt hot, right then. It sounded better than I could imagine, honestly. And it wasn't that I hadn't thought that same thought, myself.

But it had never made me feel as assured, somehow, before, as when Mal suggested it now. It had only left me feeling a little hollow. A little tired. I'd already been so many places. Maybe I really did need settling down, for once.

"Would you go with me, sometimes?"

"Of course I would, June." Her voice was soft now. Tender. The pressure behind my eyes got worse.

Yeah. That felt different. The idea of being restless with Mal. When I needed to.

"All right," I said. "Okay."

We were quiet again then.

I watched the waves roll in. The children playing in the sand below us. Felt the drugs wrap around my brain, seep into my muscles.

Time stretched. I felt wondrous and grounded; tired and awe-inspiringly lucky.

And then, at some point minutes or hours later, "Ain't No Mountain High Enough" came on my speaker.

I felt the grin stretch wide across my face before I could stop it.

"Hey Mal," I said.

"Hmm?"

I looked over and realized Mal had maybe been sleeping. She blinked at me, eyes blurry. I cheesed even harder.

"You remember when you asked me what I would sing, if I ever sang, back at Moonie's?"

"Yeah."

"It's true that I never came to Moonie's to sing. But I did picture something else, every time I was there."

Mal lifted a sleepy eyebrow.

"I liked to picture dancing with you."

The smile that curled onto Mal's face was one I'd never seen before, even after our post-sex high, even throughout this miraculous day. This smile was marijuana and just-woke-up inspired, no room to hide. Slow and unfiltered. The first time I'd seen Mal look as soft on the outside as I knew she was on the inside.

"Yeah?"

"Yeah. Not like the queers at Moonie's normally dance, but." I stood then, taking a moment to grab the railing and gather my balance as the blood rushed to my head. After a second, I straightened my back, stretched out my neck. And held out my hand.

"Mal Edwards," I said solemnly. "Would you dance with me?"

Mal stared at me.

"Here?" she said. "Now?" She looked over at my speaker. "To this?"

I laughed at that. "Ain't No Mountain High Enough" was highly danceable, of course, but it was almost over by this point. I was sure my phone would shuffle to something more typically me next, something slightly melancholy, something I dreamed of holding Mal Edwards to.

And as if, once again, the universe was watching out for me, what shuffled on next was "Into the Mystic."

"Yeah," I said softly, hand still reaching out in the air between us. "Here. To this."

Mal lumbered up then. I dropped my hand so we could both push our plastic chairs into the corner of the small balcony, one stacked on top of the other for optimal room. I turned up the volume of the music a few clicks.

And then I wrapped an arm around Mal's back. Tangled the fingers of my free hand into hers again. Pressed my cheek against her cheek. And slowly but surely, we swayed, shuffling in a small circle to Van Morrison while the sea breeze swept across our skin.

NINE

WELL, this was ridiculous.

I mean. It wasn't *bad*, shuffling around this little balcony with June. But it was definitely ridiculous. On our third or fourth slow turn, I saw a dude a few balconies away, staring at us. He nodded when he caught me staring back, lifting the beer in his hand as if in greeting.

"That dude's looking at us," I grunted.

June merely hummed against my cheek. "Seems cool," she said. And annoyingly, he did. On our next turn, I saw he wasn't looking at us anymore, simply leaning on his own railing, looking out at the beach. "Maybe he's a Van fan, too."

I huffed a small laugh. A few seconds later, June's arm that was wrapped around my back tightened slightly.

"So," she started, voice tentative, "say I get good at fixing up old trucks and remodeling your house, when I retire. And we travel, sometimes."

I nodded, my nose brushing against her hair.

"What if it turns out we *are* better at being alone? At having distance?" I felt her swallow, the working of her jaw against mine. "What if when we're actually around each other all the time...we annoy the shit out of each other?"

I tightened my own arm against her spine. Clearly June needed some last reassurance on this. I had to make it clear.

"It's true," I said slowly, "that I like being alone. But with you...it's different. Like we can still be alone, but together."

I felt her nod, small but there.

"And we don't actually have to move in together, you know."

"No," she said immediately. "My apartment's a piece of shit. I want your old house and your roses."

Jesus, June was romantic. It kept throwing me off. I couldn't believe I was fucking dancing with her while we were having this conversation. I made myself focus.

"All right, then. We could have separate rooms, if you wanted. You could just knock on my door whenever you wanted to get off."

Thank god, this made her laugh.

"No," she said. "I would definitely want you in my bed every night."

I grunted my agreement.

"All right, then. In that case, just tell me to get the hell out of your face whenever you need room, June. I'll do the same."

"You promise?"

"Scout's honor."

I felt her body ease against mine.

"Okay," she whispered. "Good."

The song changed then. "Into the Mystic" transitioned into an old cover of Bruce Springsteen's "Atlantic City." June let out a little laugh against my scalp.

"What?"

"Just love this song," she said. A moment later she shifted her head back, lifted my hand, the one holding hers, to her lips. Kissed the side of my wrist. Swayed me around the balcony a little harder.

Romantic as shit.

"I never actually spent that much time in Atlantic City, when I was a kid," she said, smiling at me now as we shuffled around the worn wooden slats. "But I did take quite a few trips to Asbury Park. Wrong Bruce album, but, you know."

"Yeah?" I blinked at her, grateful for this return to reality. I had almost floated away there for a second, what with the wrist kissing and the wind playing with June's hair. And all that weed we'd smoked. I was definitely blaming the weed.

"Yeah. The concert hall there was epic. God, the whole place was epic, really, the boardwalk, the Stone Pony down the street. But Convention Hall is this old ass building right on the beach." June shook her head, a sentimental look on her face. "It was kind of gritty, you know, like everything in Jersey is kind of gritty, but it was also...I don't know. Our version of regal." She grinned a lopsided grin. Her glasses did that signature shift on her face. "My childhood was pretty shit, in general, but god, I saw some good shows in Asbury Park." She looked out at the water. "I haven't been back in a long time. But I can't say I wouldn't go back to Jersey to see a concert at Convention Hall again."

I stopped whatever weird sway-shuffle we were doing. Dropped my hand from her back.

"Oh." I brought my hands to my head. June frowned.

"Hey," she said. "Everything all right?"

"I forgot," I said.

I turned and walked back into the hotel room, leaving June confused behind me.

I had to stop and steady myself on the dresser when I stumbled inside. Shit. I had felt safe, steady, wrapped in June's arms, but now that I was moving on my own again, the joint hit me full-force. Fuck. I hadn't been stoned in a long time.

Okay. Focus. I could do this. June had done all this for me. I couldn't believe I forgot.

I rifled through my bag. Attempted to walk back out to the balcony in a straight line.

"Here." I shoved the tickets at June's hands. I squinted into the distance. God, it was bright out here. I wanted to hide my face in her face again.

June stared at the tickets for a minute, the slight crease in her forehead slowly fading.

I realized I should be saying something.

"Um," I said. "Your plan was this, apparently." I gestured around us. "My plan was that." I nodded at the concert tickets. "If you want to go. If you're able to go, if you're not on a job."

June was still staring at the tickets. But a grin was on her face now.

"I love Brandi," she said quietly.

"Oh," I said. "Right." Guess I should have confirmed that. "Good."

"I love The Gorge," she said next.

"Fuck," I said. "Who doesn't?" I was so stoned. She was still wearing that pink tank top. I was going to lose it.

"I love you," she said.

"Oh," I said again.

"You bought me concert tickets," she said, looking up

365

from the tickets to look me in the eye before I could say anything better back.

"You brought me to the ocean," I said. "You win."

"That's true." She looked down at the tickets again. "I do win."

Then she stuck them in her back pocket. Wrapped her arms around me again, started our shuffle-sway back up, easy and smooth. Thank god. It was entirely possible I would have fallen into the railing if she hadn't.

"I can't wait," she whispered into my ear. I also couldn't wait. To take a really long nap, soon. To order a pizza from that place across the street. To fuck June again. To bring her to Cam's next barbecue. To have her remodel my bathroom. Oh my god, she was going to do such a good job, I already knew it. I really lucked out here, somehow.

She squeezed me even harder. Sighed into my ear. She kept doing breathy things at my ear like that, I'd move the fucking her again thing higher up on my list.

"This song," she said, and I realized the song had changed again. I wasn't sure I recognized it. It felt like the only thing I'd ever recognize again was how it felt to dance with June. "'Holiday Inn.' Elton John," June filled in, as if she'd heard my thoughts. "I listened to this song—this whole album—over and over again, when I drove away from Jersey for the first time, when I was eighteen."

I'd learned so much about June in the last twenty-four hours. I felt lightheaded with it. Wanted to hear her tell me things about her life for the rest of my own.

"I love you, too," I said, belatedly. I added, "I feel like I've maybe been in love with you for a long time."

"Me too, Mal," she said. I tried to listen to the song harder, all the strings, Elton John's young voice. Pictured

June driving away from Jersey to it, taking charge of her own life. "Me too."

Things all mixed together, after that. The end of the song, the song after that, the sound of the waves crashing on the shore, the seagulls calling overhead. The heat and softness of June's body next to mine. The color of the sand and the water, the color of June's smiling eyes, a kaleidoscope of earth tones and strong, steady things. When she eventually took my hand and led me back inside, I could only think one thing. That this was what it actually felt like, then.

Endgame.

I couldn't wait to tell Britt.

i didn't sign up for this

A BONUS MOONIE'S SHORT

SOMETIMES, your girlfriend dumps you in Switzerland.

If you're lucky, it'll be right before Christmas.

To be specific, it just might be the day before you were set to go skiing in the Swiss Alps. As a Christmas present from said girlfriend.

And maybe Nicole didn't expect me to still go skiing in the Swiss Alps without her, but you know what? Fuck it. You only live once. I will never in my life be able to afford a day like this again. And sure, it's possible I've never touched a pair of skis before, but I'm an adaptable person. I'll figure it out.

Exhibit A: I've already successfully navigated the train to the right station, where I then boarded this cable car that lifted us right into the fucking sky. It swings back and forth above all these craggy mountains and fields of white, while rich white people hug their skis to their fit bodies and laugh with each other like it's normal. They are all carrying so much equipment and wearing so much bright, insulated clothing and acting like they are not hindered by it at all.

Which, fine, might all be a tiny bit disconcerting, as this swinging cable car is *not at all normal,* and I am wearing long underwear, jeans, Doc Martens, and one supremely puffy coat Nicole bought me on our first day in Thun. Apparently, my decade-old Columbia jacket wasn't up to snuff for winter in Thun, even though I had wanted to protest that my jacket was one of the highest quality garments I owned. I'd braved the Columbia Employee Store to get it, back when I lived with Jinwoo and they got free passes to it all the time through their work.

I wish I could text Jinwoo right now. *Look where I am, dude!* I'd text with a photo of the blue, blue sky through the window of this flying death trap, if I could afford international texting. *At the top of the world! It's like I'm a god!*

To Nicole's credit, the supremely puffy coat is also supremely warm and comfy. It has a big hood fringed with what is probably legitimate fur, which I should maybe feel bad about, but it is so soft against my face, so efficiently hides my mess of dark hair I haven't brushed in two days, and helps me feel protected from all these strangers around me who have so clearly done this before. It made me feel protected when Nicole bought it for me, the way Nicole's gifts often made me feel: unexpected, out of the ordinary, a bit Too Much, but when I gave myself up to it—luxurious and safe.

The cable car shudders to an abrupt stop.

I watch everyone else depart before I move, to avoid getting whacked in the face by their fancy skis or poked by their skinny poles in the tiny space. When I step out onto the walkway, I breathe in deep. Let it out slowly through my nose.

I'm in a tiny village at the top of the world. The buildings are made of warm, worn wood, but other than their sturdy presence, everything is glittering white and blue. Like *Frozen* for adults. Just inhaling the crisp, thin air makes me feel like a healthier person instantaneously, someone who eats organic vegetables and exercises on a regular basis.

As opposed to someone who spends their days mainlining Diet Coke while hunched over a steering wheel and nights shoveling in mediocre fries at a grimy karaoke bar.

I deserve this.

Or maybe I don't; maybe no one deserves this; maybe everyone here should be donating their money to feed children and get people abortion access instead. But Nicole's already paid for it, and I'm already here, so I wander until I find the equipment rental chalet and successfully communicate that I need, you know. Everything.

Luckily, Nicole already knew I would need everything, and pre-paid for it somehow with our tickets, and extra luckily, the Swiss bro who helps me doesn't seem to judge my jeans or Doc Martens too harshly. He has a thick, reddish-brown beard and smiles constantly and speaks to me in fluent English without asking, even though I hear him switch to German whenever he talks to the other ski rental chalet employees. My favorite thing I've learned about Switzerland so far in the less-than-a-week I've been here is that it has four official languages. Four! What a sexy country. What a truly confusing place to be dumped.

Liam's smile does disappear, however, his blue eyes narrowing at the corners in concern when he surmises this is my first time doing any of this.

"And you're here alone?"

"Yeah, it'll be fine. Don't worry about it."

"Have you signed up for a lesson? Our instructors tend to book up—"

"No." I wave him off. We hadn't booked an instructor, because Nicole was supposed to be my instructor.

It's possible I had been fantasizing about Nicole being my ski instructor for the last month, ever since she'd sprung the idea of this trip on me at Thanksgiving. The thing about Nicole is that even though she's leagues richer and more worldly than me, she was never condescending, never made me feel dumb for something like not knowing how to ski. I'd pictured it a thousand times, how her hands would be firm on my sides as she positioned my body the right way, how she'd lean in, her breath warm on my neck as she gave me pointers, her voice sliding into that slightly deeper timbre it took on when she was explaining something she was an expert on, authoritative and sexy and kind all at once. How she'd help me into my ski boots, cradling the arch of my foot in that way that always drove me wild; how her pale cheeks would go rosy as she laughed in the cold; how I'd ask her to order me a hot chocolate at the lodge and it would inevitably be the best hot chocolate I'd ever tasted, because she always knew the right things to order, the finest purchase for any occasion, and how later, I could slip my cold hands under her warm sweater and—

"Here's the key to your storage locker."

I blink at Liam, who's waving a small key with a resigned, disappointed look on his face, like he's seen the likes of me before. I want to tell him that it's not pure American arrogance that makes me think I can conquer the Swiss Alps without experience, it's simply that I can't afford a ski lesson, or anything else Nicole didn't pre-pay for. And I don't plan on actually *conquering* anything, anyway. I would like to be moderately successful at not dying on a gorgeous mountain today, and my medium-level confidence in achieving that is half heartbreak making my brain make poor decisions and half a very Kiki-specific level of stubbornness.

But it's busy in here, and Liam has things to do, so I take the key and don't explain myself any further.

He helps stuff my feet in the hard-as-rocks ski boots, makes sure they fit properly. I stash my bag and Docs in the locker before tromping out the exit, finding a quiet bench to lean my borrowed skis and poles against. I have to give Liam credit; lack of belief in me notwithstanding, he gave me an outstandingly pretty pair of skis: sunshine yellow and turquoise, swirled together in an abstract pattern across their shiny surface. And best of all, a neon pink pair of boots to accompany them. All of which is much more my style, really, than my eggshell-white puffy coat. The clash of unnaturally vibrant colors in this naturally resplendent place makes me feel at least 10% more myself.

What *doesn't* make me feel more myself is actually walking in my beautiful pink boots. Because these things are like, military-grade hard. People who are into predicting the apocalypse and building bunkers must be super into ski equipment, because these babies aren't going to let my ankles move a single inch. They also seem to be permanently angled forward a few degrees, which makes me walk sort of strangely hunched at the knees. When I look around, everyone else seems to have adopted this gait with ease, so I attempt to do the same. Even though I feel goofy as hell. I feel another urge to text Jinwoo. More accurately, I wish Jinwoo was *here*. I wish Mal was here, to give her unimpressed, cranky opinion on everything. *You think my knees are gonna do that all day?*

But no. I don't need my friends here. I can do this on my own. I am an independent woman, and I am not going to go back to the too-fancy villa Nicole told me I could stay in for the rest of our trip and cry over being left alone in a foreign country the first time I ever actually visited a foreign country. I am going to snap these shiny pink bombproof boots into these skinny ass skis, and—

Oh my god, I did it. I snapped the boots into the skis. *Boom.*

Tentatively, I slide my feet forward and backward. Even more tentatively attempt to lift a foot in the air, step to the side. It all feels odd, but—

I am on *motherfucking skis.*

I didn't have much trouble getting into them, I haven't fallen on my ass yet, and I am on *skis.* In the *Alps.*

And while it feels strange, it's a fun kind of strange. Particularly lifting my feet and clomping around, which I proceed to do in a funny little circle, laughing a little to myself as I do. It feels like I've grown two long, slightly dangerous extensions of my body, like I'm some kind of new badass creature emerging from the wilderness.

I grab my poles next, experiment with pushing myself toward a large, open area where people are milling about, testing their skis, chatting with each other. It's a bit tricky, actual forward motion, figuring out the balance between pushing myself forward with my skis/legs and adding momentum with my poles/arms. I hit myself with the poles more than anything else, but still. Gliding through snow on skis is rad. I shouldn't be surprised, really, that skiing is cool. All the stuff rich people get to do is cool.

I navigate myself around the clearing for a while, attempt going down a tiny hill off to the side, where—okay, I totally fall at the bottom when I realize I don't know how to stop. But I figure the first fall is also important. I know how to fall now, and get back up! It doesn't feel *great*, falling on my hip in the freezing snow, but at least the prospect of falling feels less scary now.

Eventually, I push myself over to a large trail map. And this I do fully understand. I spend half of my life reading maps in the car; I've always been good at navigation. And Nicole prepared me for this part before we left Portland, going over the different symbols that signify easier slopes versus more difficult ones, the similarities and differences between North American and European ski maps. I am looking for a little blue circle, and I see one...there.

I turn a few times, taking better stock of my surroundings now that I'm more comfortable on my skis. I just need to get to the top of this very tall mountain to reach the start of that blue circle run. Which means I have to get on that ski lift over there.

I start toward it, my medium-level confidence in full swing. I can take a ski lift. Nicole had warned me about the perils of rope tows, but this is one of the more standard ones with seats that lift you up in the air. I am super good at sitting.

Except as I get closer, and witness more clearly what is happening at the bottom of the ski lift, a different feeling enters my gut. A feeling that says, loud and clear: *okay, but hell no.*

Because the lift doesn't stop? To let you on? Those wooden chairs just swing around this rickety track and you just...jump on? With skis?

Which, okay, as I watch the smooth, continuous journey of Swiss skiers making their way up the mountain, makes sense. Having to stop the machine every two seconds to let on new passengers would probably be real inefficient. Like the least fun Ferris wheel ride of all time. And everyone seems to be handling it with aplomb. Maybe it's not actually that scary.

I get in line.

My tummy gets more and more upset as the line crawls forward.

And when it's my turn, I simply...can't.

The chair meant for my ass flies on by.

And the next one.

The person behind me says something very angry sounding in German, like even angrier sounding than normal German, and I bolt away, shouting English apologies. The only bit of grace the universe has for me is that somehow I don't fall straight on my face as I do so. I *almost* do, the top of my ski catching on a patch of snow and my ankle doing its valiant best to twist inside of its prison, but somehow I catch myself with a pole and keep moving.

I stand off to the side, heart pounding, wind singing in my ears.

It's just that, you see, if you *didn't* sit properly in the moving chair—if maybe the chair just scooted you forward instead, or your ass didn't make a good landing and you fell off—a few feet past the loading zone, the snow just...drops off. Into a cliff of snowy, rocky Alps-ness.

It seems like a poor setup, is all I'm saying. And while I wanted to have a day of independent adventure, I do not want to actually die here.

I'm not sure how long I stand there. I psych myself up a few times to try again, but annoyingly, each time, my body refuses to listen.

"You all right there?"

I jump. The rumbly voice appeared in my eardrum out of nowhere, and it belongs to...a tall, attractive person standing right across from me. They have short dark hair sticking out of a sage green beanie, light brown skin, thick-rimmed glasses. Ski goggles are situated on top of the beanie, and my first thought is that I want to see the goggles situated over their actual glasses, because it would look weird and funny and, in the past, before Nicole, I have tended to be attracted to weird and funny people.

My second thought is that their accent sounded distinctly American. And seriously, fuck our country, but in that moment, it felt almost surprisingly comforting. Like when you smell a specific scent you hadn't smelled in ten years and suddenly feel like crying.

"I can't do it," I blurt out after a prolonged moment of awkward silence. "The chair lift."

The person glances back over their shoulder toward the lift.

"Right," they say, and wow, that truly is a good rumbly voice. "I kind of gathered that. Your first time?"

I nod, cheeks heating despite myself. I had expected to possibly embarrass myself today in front of myself and myself only, not in front of a hot person with a sexy voice and two pairs of glasses.

"And..." They glance around the clearing. "You're here by yourself?"

"Nicole dumped me!" I shout at the hot stranger, like a very sane person. In my defense, the air is very thin up here and it's highly probable I'm not getting enough oxygen. "She was supposed to be here, and she knows how to ski, but I thought I could try by myself anyway, but I need to get up the dumb mountain to try, and—"

I gesture toward the lift with a ski pole.

The stranger stares at me for a moment.

"I'm Maya," they eventually say, and hold out a hand. "She/her pronouns. I promise you you can get on the ski lift."

I attempt to shake her hand, which is ridiculous, because I'm wearing my warmest mittens and Maya has thick ski gloves on, so it feels sort of like rubbing two oven mitts together, but it's nice anyway. I think.

"Kiki," I say. "Also she/her. And that's a big promise to make. I could be the worst ski lift rider in history. You don't know."

"I know they whip around the corner kind of fast, but they do slow down for you to get on. You just have to go for it."

"Okay, but hypothetically," I counter, "say one tries to

go for it and then gets cold feet halfway through, and the chair just shoves one out over that cliff."

Maya grins. She has a slightly crooked canine. It's a very cute grin.

"There are attendants who work the lift. They won't let you die. They can stop it if you fall off. I'm pretty sure there's a bright red button that says, Do Not Let People Fall Off the Cliff. It happens all the time."

"What? No! I can't make them stop it! People are already judging my jeans!"

It's possible I've gotten a little self-conscious since being yelled at in German.

Maya tilts her head.

"They do rent ski-appropriate clothing at the shop, you know, if—"

"I didn't know if Nicole paid for that!" I'm shouting again, feeling only more panicked at Maya confirming this clothing blunder. Liam *had* pushed me to get other stuff, in his gently concerned accent back at the shop, but I only knew for sure that Nicole had paid for skis and boots and poles and I didn't want to look like a fool who couldn't afford snow pants.

Because even though Nicole had left me use of the villa, if I *did* stay in this country for the next four days—which I imagined I would have to, being that changing plane tickets at the last minute also costs money—I had sort of expected Nicole to pay for most of our food. Since she normally paid for most of our food. So I had to be careful with every Swiss franc, now.

"I'm wearing long underwear!" It would be helpful, some part of my brain knows, if I could stop shouting embarrassing things to this attractive woman. I just need her to know that

I'm not completely unprepared for the conditions. Disappointing Liam *and* Maya feels like a bad start to the day. "Two pairs! These jeans are like, real tight with all these layers. I had to unbutton the top button, actually, but figured no one would notice beneath the puffy coat. Anyway, I'm good."

I breathe out and hang my head over my poles. I...need to calm down.

"How tight are they?" I look back up to see Maya frowning. "The jeans. Can you do this?"

She lifts a foot, separating the back of her skis so they make a V. She then squats down, tucking her poles under her arms so they stick out behind her. She has a serious look on her face. She looks...very silly. I definitely want to touch her face.

"Sure," I say, distracted by the confusing mix of panic and shame and attraction and gratitude I feel at that moment. Because while I am absolutely embarrassing myself in front of Maya, I am beyond grateful that she is talking to me right now.

I told myself I was ready to do this adventure by myself, but the truth is making itself more apparent by the second. That in fact, all I want to do is cry.

"Show me." Maya straightens and gestures toward me. "If you can't hold that position comfortably, you won't be able to make it down the mountain."

"Um. Okay."

I make the V. I squat.

"I'm good," I promise Maya as I un-squat myself. "These are my stretchiest jeans. Buttons are just evil."

Maya raises an eyebrow. But she smiles, too.

"What run are you hoping to hit once you get over your fear of the chair lift?"

"The Lynx. The blue circle one."

Maya nods. "All right then." She gestures over her shoulder with her chin before she swings her skis around. "Let's go."

And just like that, all my other confusing emotions are once more wiped out by fear.

"Come on," Maya says again. "The Lynx is a good one. I'll go down it with you."

"Oh." I am filled with relief at this idea, but don't know how to express it, what with the terror. "That's nice. You're nice. I like your goggles."

Maya grins again.

And then she skis toward the lift.

After a beat, my legs allow me to follow, which I take as a good sign. I even manage to stop myself next to her without crashing into either her or the person in front of her. I'm slowly learning the power of balancing my weight, leaning this way or that to achieve what I want. Like staying upright and not injuring others. A tiny portion of confidence returns.

"Remember," Maya says when it's almost our turn. "You just have to go for it."

I swallow. Follow her lead. She jets out to the loading zone, and somehow I find myself next to her. And then—

And then I sit my ass on a flying chair, and the safety bar is secured over our laps, and we are going up, up, up.

"Holy shit," I say.

Because...we are at the top of the world. We are literally soaring over snow-capped trees.

And it is dazzling.

It takes my breath away for one remarkable second, the snow and the sky and the towering mountains on all sides. They are terrifying, rugged and impenetrable, at the same time that they are reassuring somehow in their solid magnificence. I am not unfamiliar with gorgeous mountains; the Cascades are my home now, but still...I have never experienced anything quite like this.

"Yeah," Maya says, and her voice is quiet, a bit of that sandpaper tone made smooth in awe. "Pretty incredible up here." After a moment, she bumps her shoulder with mine. "Told you you could do it."

"Yeah." I smile. "You did."

I take another few seconds to take in the views before I return, slightly, to my senses, my blood pressure lowering, my brain working more efficiently. And once it does, it takes stock, fully, of the fact that I am flying at the top of the world with a complete stranger.

Which...is kind of great, actually.

I'm *good* at talking to strangers. I spend half of my life talking to strangers.

And clutching onto something I'm good at feels like a solid idea right now.

"So," I start. "What brings *you* to the Swiss Alps by yourself? Unless you're not by yourself, and your friends are hanging out at the lodge while you're taking pity on me."

Maya had been staring off at the passing scenery, but she turns her gaze back to me.

"Nah," she replies. "I'm by myself, too. I..." A troubled look enters her eyes, her nose doing a cute scrunchy thing before she sighs. "I got pissed at my job. So I quit. And came here to clear my head. But hey, look," she continues before I can cut in, even though I have a lot to ask about this job, and the kind of person who goes to the Swiss Alps alone to clear their head. "I should tell you that the scariest part of a ski lift is actually getting off of it."

"*What*?" I tear my eyes from her face to stare back

ahead, and oh *shit*, we are almost at the top. I do not like this news, one bit.

"Yeah, but listen, just follow me and you'll be fine. The most important thing is that you jump off at the right time and then *keep skiing* away from the lift, so it doesn't hit you in the ass and you're not in the way of the next people getting off."

"Uh." My blood pressure is back to panic levels. "Sure."

We near the landing zone and the safety bar lifts from our laps.

"Just scooch up," Maya instructs, loudly, over the whir of the lift, "and—go for it!"

I launch myself off the seat, heart in my throat, and try to follow both Maya and my own skis. Which I accomplish for about three seconds, until the tip of one of my skis runs over the other and then I am tumbling, comically, until I am flat on my back blinking at the bright sky.

Luckily, I have veered off to the right of the tiny hill that slopes away from the lift in my fall, leaving me—I hope—out of the way of other skiers. Unluckily, I am probably still in full view of all of them.

"Well." Maya leans over me, blocking out the glare of the sun. "That could have gone better, but it also could have gone worse. You all right?"

I open my mouth to answer, and realize the wind must have been knocked out of me, because it's hard to draw air into my lungs. Maya must realize this, or see the panic in my eyes, because she reaches down a gloved hand and squeezes my puffy-coated shoulder.

"Hey," she says, voice softened again, the amusement in her eyes fading to a reassuring calm. "Hey, you're okay. Just take a second. Anything hurt?"

I shake my head, blinking up at her. The constriction in my chest eases.

"No," I'm able to say after a minute. "I think I'm okay."

"Good."

And after another minute, I realize her hand is still on my shoulder, a thumb running idly over my coat, and I am just staring at her, studying the tiny moles on her right cheek, the strong set of her jaw, her dark brown eyes behind her glasses. And—and shit, I am a huge bottom, and her hovering over me like this is really working for me. Which is probably not exactly what I need today.

I force myself to sitting with a groan. Maya's hand drops.

"Oh," I say when I see my left ski sitting on its side a few feet away. "I didn't even realize that popped off."

"Yeah, skis are good like that." Maya stands from her hunched position, grabs the ski for me and plops it next to us on the snow. "Keeps you from breaking your ankles. Come on."

She holds out a hand. Hauls me up like it's nothing.

"Here." She guides my hand to her shoulder. "Lean on me and snap it back in."

So I do. I shake out my legs, try to make the embarrassment fade.

"This way." Maya nods over her shoulder again before she skis away. My breathing still isn't completely back to normal, but I follow anyway, trying not to notice how smooth Maya looks in her skis, how natural, how attractive it somehow is, even though we're all basically lumps in too much clothing up here. Still, I am glad I'm following her particular lump. That I'm not alone.

A feeling that is only amplified when I stop where she has stopped.

"*This* is a blue circle?" I ask, incredulous.

Because holy *shit.*

"It's a blue circle in Switzerland," Maya replies.

I am going to die so hard.

Maya looks my way. She's placed the goggles over her glasses now, and yeah, ugh, I am *into* it.

"You really haven't skied at all before? Did you even try the bunny slope before heading for the lift?"

"I didn't see a bunny slope!" I protest. "I looked on the map!" I absolutely would have chosen the bunny slope if I had seen one. It sounds adorable.

Maya shakes her head before looking back down at the hill before us.

"They don't always call it that in other countries, and even the bunny slope here would be..." She shakes her head again. "I probably should have asked more questions before I helped you onto the lift. But we're here now, so. Practice the V again."

She does the same serious squat she did at the bottom of the mountain.

"Just do this, the entire way down. But make sure the tips of your skis don't actually cross, like they did when you got off the lift. Widen the V any time you start to go too fast. Don't head straight down; try to veer side to side across the slope, without getting in the way of other skiers if you can. And if you start to get tired, just go off to the side and sort of gently fall on your side. We can rest as much as you need. I'll lead and you can follow the whole way down, okay?"

The whole time Maya has been talking, I've watched other skiers glide past us, swishing their way down the mountain, their knees and skis leaning side to side in tandem, fluid and straight ahead, this way, that, like I've seen in the Olympics, like it's nothing.

None of them are squatting in a wide V.

"There's no way this is going to be fun for you," I say. "You don't have to do this."

"Maybe," Maya says easily, straightening. "But I also really don't want you to die, and you very much could here."

I swallow. Because this is...very accurate.

The path of the wide slope is clear, shaped by snowbanks on either side. But beyond the snowbank to the right is just...open air. A freefall drop into the craggy expanse of the surrounding world-famous mountains.

I understand it would probably take away from the aesthetic, but you'd think the Alps could really invest in some guardrails.

"I'm scared," I say out loud before my brain can stop me.

"Understandable," Maya says. "But the V will get you down."

I feel like there has to be some kind of sexual innuendo in there, but I'm too rattled to be immature about it.

"We could also go back to the lift," Maya adds, "ask them if you can ride it back down. That also happens all the time."

"No." I shake my head. I'm here. I have to do this. "Promise you won't let me die?"

Maya nods. "Promise." And even though I hardly know her, I believe her. She has the presence of a grizzly searching for fish in the middle of a stream, which I mean in the hottest way possible: strong, sturdy, observant, even as the world rushes around her.

She says, again: "You just have to go for it."

I take a deep breath.

And I do.

I hold in a scream as gravity kicks in, the incline of the slope hurtling me downward even as I squat and V my skis for all I'm worth. It makes sense almost immediately, the V, even as the momentum makes my leg muscles screech in alarm. I feel how easy it would be for my skis to cross, for the V to yank my legs all the way apart and turn into the splits instead, how I have to balance my weight continually to make sure it doesn't happen. I still don't fully understand what to do with my poles.

Maya skis just a few feet ahead of me, and I follow her path across the slope, a gentle diagonal, until we reach the other side. She does a neat little turn, her skis snapping together as she comes to a stop. Except—except I don't know how to do a neat little turn, and I ski more or less directly into her.

She's ready for me, though, an arm reaching out to barricade my chest, somehow bringing me to a stop. The wind has been barreling around inside my ears, along with the drum of my heartbeat—it has to be ten degrees cooler up here, and I'm wishing I had earmuffs or a hat and, fine, snow pants—but I hear Maya's gentle, delighted laugh, slightly muffled through the neck gaiter she pulled over her mouth before we started down the slope.

She pulls it down now and she's smiling at me, like she's proud, even though we have only skied approximately twelve feet.

"That was great!" she says. "You didn't fall! Most new skiers would have fallen there. You must already have a good sense of balance. Now just situate your skis around, and we'll ski that way—" She points to the terrifying snowbank on the other side, the one with no safety net beyond it —"and then turn to ski this way again. Slow and steady, all right?"

I nod, too breathless to say anything else.

I manage four more full turns before I can't take it anymore.

"Maya," I call out as we reach the scary snowbank side once more.

She turns to look back at me, snapping those skis in another snazzy stop a second later.

I reach her and, partly to stop myself and partly out of physical necessity, fall into a pathetic heap on my side.

All I can see are the edges of my fur-lined hood and the white of the snowbank in front of me, but I hear Maya's laugh, can sense her movement to my side.

"Thighs hurting you?"

"They are *screaming*." The last ten minutes of my life were essentially one perpetual squat, and if it was not already clear to Maya, I am not an athlete. The V is probably saving my life, but the V also fucking *hurts*.

"Yeah, mine are, too. Let's take breaks every few turns."

She's on the snow next to me now, leaning back on her elbows, looking weirdly casual about chilling on the side of the slope while the rest of Switzerland wooshes past us.

"Tell me more about this shitty job," I say once my breath has recovered enough.

Maya looks down at me, and even in the glare of the sun, I see one of her eyebrows raise underneath her protective layers. She looks back out at the slope.

"It's dumb," she says. "I was a social media manager for this outdoor recreation company. I was good at it. I liked it, even though it was a lot of work, but in a way that's weird to explain to other people. They're like, oh, you get paid to post on Instagram, how hard. But you actually need the skill set of like, ten departments to do it well. Anyway." Consciously or not, her shoulders have crept toward her ears as she's talked. I lift myself up off the snow to hear her better. "I spent the last year working on this campaign, raising awareness about local environmental justice initiatives. We got a shit ton of followers, raised a lot of money and volunteer hours for good causes. Totally in line with our company's actual mission. I met a ton of really cool people doing cool things. I was proud of it. And then..."

All at once, Maya's shoulders drop, her back slumping. I've only known her for thirty minutes, but I feel in my gut that it's a posture that's all wrong for her. Makes me want to fight whoever made her spine bend that way.

"They gave all the credit to my marketing manager. Gave him an award for it and everything. Even though I had run the whole entire thing."

I suck in a harsh breath between my teeth. "Fuck."

"Yeah. And the thing is—" Maya crunches some snow in a glove. "—I know this kind of stuff happens all the time. I shouldn't have been so hurt by it, but I was. I really thought I'd scored a job that was exactly where I was meant to be, doing something worthwhile, and then it turned out to all be bullshit. And once I get pissed about something..." She trails off, letting the snow drop from her glove as she looks away. "I have a hard time letting it go. Not my finest trait. So yeah, I quit. Even though it was probably immature. And I came here because I grew up on skis, back in Utah. I always feel at peace when I'm in the mountains."

I could see that. Other than the terror of having to get down this slope, I remember how I felt when I first stepped off the cable car. I imagine it's even more peaceful when you know what you're doing.

Maya bites her lip. I can sense she's hesitating, contemplating whether she should continue.

"But it was probably dumb, too, running off here

instead of just looking for another job. Especially dumb because traveling while trans and brown is always a risk, and traveling alone, internationally…" She pounds a fist into the snow, once, twice. "But luckily, it's worked out all right so far."

"I'm glad," I say. "And for the record, quitting that place that fucked you over and then coming here by yourself all only sounds badass to me. Not dumb at all."

"Thanks," Maya says after a minute, voice soft again. She clears her throat. "Anyway, thanks for listening to all that. Guess I'm still having some feelings." She turns her gaze to the granite-filled horizon. "So what's the deal with this Nicole?"

I groan. And push myself up, off the snow and back onto my skis, because if I don't, my muscles will lock up and I'll make Maya be stuck on this slope all day.

"Nicole is a topic for the next break."

I make it six switchbacks this time before my legs collapse again.

"How much longer until we reach the lodge?" I ask dramatically, throwing an arm over my face.

"I'd say we have accomplished…" Maya looks up and down the slope. "Ten percent."

"Oh sweet Jesus." My legs are going to be reduced to mush by the time I make it to the bottom. Maybe Maya will carry me to the lodge.

Not that I should be imagining such things.

I drop my arm and squint into the sky.

"So, Nicole."

"You don't actually have to talk about it if you don't want to," Maya interjects. "Sorry. I can be kind of nosy."

"No, it's okay." I find I want to talk about it. And since I can't contact any of my actual people back home, for now it's Maya who gets to hear it. "We had only been dating a few months when she invited me here. But who's going to say no to an all expenses paid trip to Switzerland? And the first couple of days were amazing. We're staying at this fancy place that makes me feel like I'm the princess of Genovia."

Maya laughs.

"But then she says an old friend happens to be in town; asks if I'm okay getting dinner with them. Because I guess when you're rich, that's a thing that can happen. Just happening to both be in Switzerland." It occurs to me as I wave a disbelieving poor-person hand at this that Maya might be rich, too. As I assume everyone on this mountain is richer than me. But even if she is, she feels different. Like she would also think this whole scenario was wild.

When I glance at her, I notice her laugh has faded to a grimace. As if she knows what's going to come next.

"And when we get to dinner, it turns out this old friend is actually an ex."

"Kiki."

Maya's tone makes an unexpected laugh burst out of me. Because now that I'm saying it all out loud, yeah, it *is* obvious what's going to happen next.

"An *old* ex, like some girl she'd met during summer camp when she was a teenager. But dinner was like, fine? The woman seemed nice, and I didn't feel like a third wheel, at least at first. But I could tell, as the night went on, that there was some kind of vibe happening. And the next morning, Nicole tells me how seeing Aja again has made her realize how long it's been since she's felt how she did when they were together—"

Maya snorts.

"And how, even though she likes me, she knows she

won't be able to stop thinking about it. That it wouldn't be fair to me."

A louder snort, one that makes my mouth twitch.

"That she wants to find that feeling again. So she left."

"So she left," Maya repeats, voice flat. Pissed off, maybe. "She left you in the middle of Switzerland?"

"She's letting me stay in the villa."

Maya shakes her head.

"Queer women should be outlawed. Or at the very least, not allowed to be around their exes."

"Yeah." I hang my head, feeling a strange combination of embarrassment that Nicole left me, in Switzerland, because she simply didn't like me enough, and relief, somehow, that Maya is snorting about it.

"That's some weak ass, selfish, immature shit. I'm sorry, Kiki. You didn't deserve that."

I smile. "You hardly know me. Maybe I'm a horrible person who did deserve it."

Maya shakes her head again.

"No, you're not, and you didn't. It's easy to tell these things sometimes."

If my cheeks weren't frozen, I think I'd have blushed.

"Thanks."

"Man. Your thing is way worse than mine. No wonder you were so determined to hurl yourself down this mountain."

"I don't know. I think yours is worse. Mine is just one person being shitty; yours is like, a whole chain of command of shittiness."

"Yeah, well." Maya gathers some snow in her glove again, throws me a small grin. "Let's not have some queer sadness Olympics, all right? Let's just get down this mountain."

She lets the snow fall before she stands, extending her hand.

I smile as I take it.

But no matter how I fight it, that smile wobbles a second later as I watch Maya ski away.

Because even though I know she's right, that what went down over the last forty-eight hours *was* some weak ass shit—I am still really, really sad.

"They should have a speaker system out here some-how," I say when we've accomplished another five percent of the mountain, trying to get myself in a better headspace. "You know, pump·out some tunes as a means of encour-agement."

Maya laughs, loud and rumbly. "What kind of tunes would you *pump out* right now if you could?"

I tilt my head, contemplating, until I laugh at myself, too.

"I spend a majority of my life listening to people sing their favorite songs and suddenly the only thing I can think of is Beyoncé."

There's a long pause before Maya responds. And oh no. If Nicole dumped me *and* the woman I'm currently being charmed by turns out to be a Beyoncé hater, this truly will be the bleakest holiday season of my life.

Thank Beyoncé Maya eventually says, "I think Beyoncé is always a correct answer. But what do you mean, you spend your life listening to people sing?"

"I'm a KJ. Karaoke jockey. I press buttons on a computer in this weird dive bar while drunk people yell into micro-phones." I stretch out my arms in front of me. "Pretty impressive stuff."

But Maya's smiling.

"Is being a KJ a full-time gig? Or do you do something else on the side?"

"I'm a food delivery driver during the day. For Grubhub?" I bury my face in my mittens. "God. I can't be surprised Nicole broke up with me. It made no sense that we were together."

And it hadn't, from the start. It started at Moonie's, where I KJ. Of course it did. So many bad decisions started at Moonie's. And while I was plenty used to patrons hitting on me there, something about Nicole felt different. Maybe because she was sober, so I knew it wasn't simply the alcohol-soaked impulsivity karaoke brought out in people that made her smile at me. Maybe she felt different because she and her friends so clearly didn't fit in at Moonie's, but she was the only one in her group who didn't seem to care.

"Why?"

I blink over at Maya, lost in my thoughts.

"Why what?"

"Why didn't it make sense that you were together?"

"Because...I work for Grubhub and a dive bar? And she can afford villas in Switzerland?"

Maya makes a low noise of disapproval.

"It sounds like hard work, working all day and night. Do you like it?"

"I mean." I drop my hands, my brain struggling out of self-pity mode. "I don't *love* working two jobs, no. And both can suck sometimes, in their separate ways. But...overall? Yeah. I think."

Maya's quiet. The kind of quiet that feels comfortable, non-judgmental. Like she's giving me space to continue.

"I like being on the move and talking with people. I knew I'd never survive an office job, at least not happily. And in both jobs, there are regulars you get to know—

restaurant workers, people who come to the bar a lot. And it's kind of nice, you know?"

"Yeah," Maya says. "I get that."

"Although—" I hesitate. I'm veering into oversharing territory—something I tend to do—making Maya my therapist instead of a kind stranger helping me down a mountain. But the longer I'm up here in the thin air, surrounded by the purest scenery I've ever seen, the more it feels like we're in some kind of magical safe haven. A safe haven where, sure, it's possible I could die or at the very least, pull about five muscles, but where I can say anything I want and Maya will probably go with it.

For the first time since we flew into Zürich, being in a different country, where no one knows me at all, feels like a gift.

"It's weird. Sometimes, I feel like I spend my whole day talking to people. Like there are all these people I know, through my deliveries or the bar or some other way. And it makes me feel good. Connected, you know? But then sometimes..."

I bite my lip.

"Sometimes I realize how shallow most of those relationships are. I have a couple of close friends, but most of the people I talk to all the time—they don't actually *know me*, you know? Like I couldn't call them up in the middle of the night if I was feeling sad. And whenever I think about it too much, I don't know if being an adult feels so incredibly lonely to everyone, or if I just haven't figured it out right."

I look away. I have officially rambled too much. Ran too hard with this safe haven. And yet, my mouth opens again a second later.

"Which is why it's nice, you know. To have someone

who wants to *know me*, at least for a while. Someone like Nicole. Even if she did end up being selfish and immature."

"Yeah, Kiki," Maya says, and her voice comes out soft and gruff all at once. "I get it."

I'm the one who stands up first this time. I brush packed snow off my ass. Cold wetness has seeped to my first layer of long underwear by this point, but I'm trying to ignore it. I fear if it seeps to the second layer, reaches my skin, there will actually be nothing to hold me back from crying.

"Anyway," I say. "Thanks for listening."

"I know we're just focusing on getting down this mountain right now," Maya says, still on the ground, voice velvety and slow. "But just so you know. I would want to know you. If I had the chance."

She stands, and I feel that blush try to make its way to my frozen cheeks again.

"Goo Goo Dolls," I blurt as she adjusts her poles.

She pauses, looks at me.

"I think that's what I would want to hear right now, if they had speakers out here."

Maya's mouth cracks into a skeptical smile. "*Goo Goo Dolls?*"

I shrug, laugh a little. Because if Maya *did* know me, she'd know this morose, sad Kiki isn't really me at all. I can't wait to eventually shrug her off, be loose, fun Kiki again.

"Being on vacation always makes me feel nostalgic. Like I'm a kid again or something. So yeah. I would kill to hear some *Dizzy Up the Girl* right now."

Maya laughs, and I ski away first.

* * *

"Here's what I think," Maya says a few rest breaks later. I'm laid out flat on my back, arms out at my sides. Maya's assured me we're at least halfway down the slope now, but I am gassed. I'm probably good on exercise now for the next, say, ten years.

"Yeah?" I say when Maya doesn't go on. I flop my face toward her, half of my vision lost to the puffy coat. She's leaning slightly forward, goggles pulled back onto her hat, a serious look in her eyes. Like she's been building up to whatever she's about to say.

"How many more days are you in Switzerland?"

"Four."

"Okay. I think you should spend the next four days having sex with like, a bunch of hot Swiss people."

I burst into laughter. Maya grins, still serious, but also a bit...mischievous.

I like this look far more than I should.

"That is," she adds, "if you're into sex."

"Oh, I'm into it." I snuffle out my laughter. "I'll work on that."

"Good." She nods in approval. "You deserve it."

She leans away from me again.

I bite my lip, bending an elbow to rest my head under my wrist.

"Here's a question you don't have to answer," I say before I lose my nerve. I sense Maya's eyes swivel back my way. "What's your favorite part of sex? If, you know, you're also into it."

Maya releases a phlegmy noise that I interpret as part snort, part laugh, part cough.

"Talking more openly about sex is one of my New Years resolutions," I add, as if this will soften the blow of my question. True fact: it's actually been on my New Years resolutions list for the last three years. And I fail rather spectacularly at it each year. Maybe I can get a jump start on it this year, in the Alps with Maya. "My favorite part is right after," I mow on when Maya doesn't say anything. "When I get to lie back with my feet tangled in the sheets, tired and tingly and naked."

Maya coughs up some more phlegm, but I'm pretty sure it's mostly-laugh-phlegm now.

"I would argue that doesn't count," she says, "if it's after the actual act."

"Oh, it totally counts." I wave my other arm in the air in emphasis. "The best part of a soccer game was always getting orange slices after. It's all part of it."

"I think it's more accurate to say—" Maya finally looks over her shoulder at me, an eyebrow raised behind her glasses in amusement. "—that the soccer game ends when the whistle blows."

"*Psshh*. Sex and soccer are hard work. The rewards afterward are the whole point."

"And you're saying—" Maya twists toward me, leaning an arm on her raised knee, "—that the reward isn't the orgasm, but when you're just lying there doing nothing afterward."

I don't even think about it. "Absolutely."

Maya laughs, another loud, full-throated one that forces my gaze away from her, squinting into the sky to school my reaction to it.

"I…" Maya shakes her head as her laughter fades, steering her face back toward the horizon, though her body remains tilted toward me. "My favorite part is the build up," she says. "You know. Just making out, and all the… rubbing of things."

I can't help myself. I burst into my own laughter, and

Maya smacks me in the side.

"Shut up. I'm trying to answer your question here."

I swallow my giggles.

"I know. Thank you. Please continue."

Maya yanks a hand out of one of her gloves, scratches at the back of her head, under her hairline. A surprised breath gets caught in my throat at this new glimpse of skin—the squared off nails, painted a pale pink, the thick knuckles—this peek at how Maya looks when she's stripped down, a person with curves and vulnerabilities. Not an insulated lump on a ski slope at all.

"The lead up always feels the best," she continues. "I could make out for hours. Orgasms are fine and all, but it's like...when you get to the happily-ever-after in an enemies-to-lovers romance, and it feels good, but you really kind of want to just go back to the beginning of the book, when they were always arguing and there was all this hot tension all the time. That tension is the good shit."

I stare openly at her now.

"You read romance novels?"

"Yeah. I only got into them a couple years ago, but—" Another scratch, under her chin this time, before she shoves her hand back into her glove. "They're an amazing escape after a long day of work or like, the world being really shitty. Plus..." That small mischievous grin again. "Some of them are real hot."

My grin mirrors hers as I shove both hands under my head and squint back up at the sky.

"So in conclusion," I say after a minute, "you and I both hate orgasms."

"Fuck 'em," Maya says, and I can hear that grin inside her voice. Warming it. Shaping it into familiarity, like we've joked with each other for a hundred years. Another laugh bubbles in my chest, and it takes me a moment for it to really sink in. That all the laughs I've laughed over the last ten minutes have been real, easy.

Happy. If only for a small moment.

But it's a moment I likely wouldn't have found all alone up here, without Maya. The kindness of a stranger.

This stranger, specifically.

"They're actually not bad, though," Maya adds after a minute, and I laugh again.

"Yeah," I agree.

Maya shoves herself to standing.

"It's good to know that lying still and doing nothing is your kink now, but the resort *will* close at some point." She smiles at me as she sticks her poles in the snow. "Let's go."

I almost point out that she *told* me we could take breaks, and that lying still and doing nothing should be *everyone's* kink, but also: she's right. The longer our breaks stretch, the more my muscles start to seize up whenever they get back into their goddamned V. I force myself up with a groan—it's a good thing I have use of the villa, because I am going to lie on that opulent white couch inside of it for the next four days—and follow.

Skiing down the mountain now is both easier and more exhausting, my body more used to the repetitive motions, my body more ready for it all to be over. But as we turn a bend in the slope, as the lodge and the accompanying chalets at the bottom of the mountain come into view, tiny but visible, something aches in my chest.

I've been selfish, stealing all this time of Maya's. She could've skied ten more runs, at this point, on her own. It'll be good to release her from babysitting me when we reach the bottom, to go our own separate ways. The right thing to do.

But even if I know all that—I still don't want to say goodbye.

"Easier question this time," I say when we're resting once more. Maya eyes me warily, like she doesn't trust me anymore, and it makes that happy laugh want to bubble up in my chest again. "What's your favorite place you've ever skied?"

Maya's shoulders relax, and she leans back.

"I know I'm probably biased," she says, "but I'd probably still say Utah. Although this—" She gestures around us with her chin, "—is pretty incredible. I've also been to some unbelievable places up in the North Cascades, in Washington. And I always like Central Oregon. Mount Bachelor, Hoodoo."

I know Utah isn't *that* far away from Oregon, but it still makes my heart beat a bit faster, hearing her mention places even closer to Portland. Picturing Maya jetting down slopes just a few hours away from me, back home.

"This is my first international trip," she continues, "although I've always really wanted to get to Chile. They've passed some okay laws recently about gender stuff, so." She shrugs. "Maybe one day."

"I hope you get there," I say, and wish I could say more. About how I wish she didn't have to worry about personal safety when she's chasing the thing that makes her feel free. How I wish she didn't have to worry about safety, ever.

"Speaking of travel," I add after a beat, for some inexplicable reason, "your family was okay with you coming here by yourself for the holidays?"

I want to hit myself as soon as the words leave my mouth. What kind of queer person am I? I know family can be a touchy subject.

But Maya doesn't appear bothered, answering easily.

"I made a decision a few years ago to not go home for big holiday gatherings. My immediate family's cool, but some of my extended family is...not. Considering my family's super Catholic, missing Christmas is definitely not looked upon favorably, but..." Maya shrugs. "It's better for me."

I make a noise of understanding in my throat. "Still sucks, though."

Maya shifts a little, one of her skis scraping against the snow.

"Yeah. Sometimes I'm proud of myself for setting up a boundary, and then other times I'm like, wait, why am I letting them push me out? I deserve to see my mom's Christmas tree. But I know it's for the best. Even if my uncle or my brother-in-law don't actually say shit, my anxiety over what they *might* say, especially as I started transitioning more, became kind of out of control. Plus—" Another ski scrape across the snow, intentional, playful this time. "I have a bunch of friends back home who don't spend the holidays with their blood family either, or who don't celebrate the holidays at all. We always end up doing some dumb, fun shit together, and it's cool, making your own traditions."

I nod. "Absolutely."

"What about you? Was your family okay with you being whisked off to Switzerland for the holiday?"

I shrug.

"All my family's back in Michigan, and I normally can't afford plane tickets from Portland more than once every few years anyway, so they're kind of used to me not being around. Not that they're happy about it. I think my mom definitely felt Nicole should have spent her money on flying me back to the Mitten instead of this, but." I smile. "She knows I'm going to do what I want to do."

"Yeah."

"I'll have to figure out how I can video chat with them from here somehow, on Christmas, and that will be enough. Well, not enough. But you know."

"Yeah. I know."

We don't talk at all on our next break. A break I understand is likely our last, as the lodge looms closer and closer below us. As if we've been slowly zooming in on a camera lens. It feels like the most intimate moment of all between us, the silence stretching in between the wind in our ears and the din of activity below us.

Everything feels incongruous inside of me.

It's been one of the worst days of my life, in one of the most beautiful places I've ever been. It's been one of the best days of my life, alongside a stranger I feel like I've already somehow known forever.

My chest suddenly aches to ask Maya the stay-up-all-night, text-all-day questions you ask when you're falling in love: what her biggest dreams are, her favorite memories. Whether she's a morning or a night person, how she takes her coffee, when she fully embraced that she was trans, her first kiss, where she most likes to *be* kissed. Her fears.

But I know I'm probably misreading the situation, wrapped up in the moment and the magical mountains; my bruised, just-dumped brain and my sore, exhausted body creating a storm of illogical emotion. That even if I wasn't misreading things, none of that would be appropriate right here, right now—a simple blip of time wherein Maya chose to be kind when I needed it.

I didn't sign up to be alone in Switzerland at Christmas.

But this, right now, is probably one of the greatest gifts I've ever received.

That should be enough.

"All right, Kiki." Eventually, Maya breaks the silence and pushes herself up. I'm probably imagining that her smile looks a little sad.

"Let's finish this sucker."

She doesn't wait for me this time. Doesn't patiently lead the way for me in a measured V. Maya swishes down the slope, legs and skis tight, her body and the snow melded together in a dance, and I stumble forward onto my skis after her.

I dare myself to stand a little straighter as I approach the bottom, even as my legs protest. I'm not fully out of the V, but enough that I accelerate faster than I have before, the cool air battering my exposed cheeks. I feel the wobble of my skis, the strain for balance, the increased risk of falling flat on my face.

It's exhilarating.

Maya's waiting for me at the bottom.

I release a tiny scream as I approach, adrenaline pulsing through me.

And then—

Well, I still haven't quite figured out how to stop.

I scream my way into a tumble at Maya's feet. Not to get too full of myself, but I feel it's my personal best.

Through my beating heart, I hear Maya laugh.

"Holy shit," I wheeze after she helps me up. "Maya. Thank you, and I'm sorry. Please let me buy you a hot chocolate in that very warm and inviting-looking lodge as a very miniscule way of repaying you."

Maya doesn't answer. She holds eye contact as her

smile slowly fades. My stomach twists, adrenaline turning sour.

"Kiki," she eventually says on a small sigh. "I don't think that's a good idea."

"Oh." *Fuck.* "Right, of course." I tighten my grip on my poles, look anywhere but at her face. "God, I've already wasted so much of your time; I'm sure you want to go hit all those black diamonds or whatever—"

"Kiki," she says again, voice quiet and commanding and chilling in how immediately it makes my eyes snap back to hers.

I would let this woman absolutely ruin me.

"It's not that I don't want to get a hot chocolate with you. Just..." She blows out a breath, lifting her goggles to rest on her beanie before she looks back at me, clear eyed behind her glasses. "If I go in there and get a hot chocolate with you, I will want to do much, much more than that with you. But you were just broken up with, and you need some time. I don't want to be a quick Switzerland rebound you fuck and forget. But—"

She pauses, and my heart thrums in my throat.

"You might not even be interested," she amends, with a slightly nervous swallow that makes me want to lean forward and kiss her neck, "but I was wondering if you might be interested in getting together sometime, whenever you're ready, back in Portland."

"Wait." I frown. "Portland? But you live in Utah."

She bites her lip, eyes unreadable.

"I'm *from* Utah. But I've lived in Portland for ten years."

"But—" I sputter, my mind tripping on itself. "Oh."

"I thought, when I first saw you," Maya says slowly, sweeping out a hand, "that you looked vaguely familiar. But I didn't quite believe my own hunch, because how weird would it be to see someone I knew, here in Switzerland?" A grin kicks up the corner of her mouth. "I put it together when you talked about being a KJ."

Something in my brain explodes then, a fireball of *what the fuck*. It's followed by a trail of smoke that sounds like Mal laughing.

"You've been to Moonie's?"

"I'm a queer person living in Portland, Kiki. Yeah, I've been to Moonie's. I mean—" Her lips twist. "I'm not a huge karaoke person. But I've been dragged there with my friends a few times." Her head tilts as her grin turns into a full-blown smile. "You know everyone who goes to that bar is a little bit in love with you, right?"

And maybe I did know that. But it still sends a flush through my entire body to hear Maya say it out loud.

"Well, you or that bartender," she amends after a beat. "But I always say, why not both?"

She throws me a look, that mischievous one, and I laugh.

"Mal's taken now, you know. Tell all your friends."

Her grin doesn't abate. "Duly noted."

I breathe out, taking this all in. I feel like I'm high. Maybe I somehow accidentally got high.

"Okay. So say, if I did want to meet up in Portland..."

Maya bites her lip again, then pats her pockets.

"My phone is in my locker. Do you—"

I shake my head. "Mine's in my locker, too."

"Well...since it might be easier to remember than my number, my username on Instagram is pizzzamaya. All one word, three z's in pizza, which I know is dumb, but just pizzamaya was already taken. M-A-Y-A."

I smile. "Pizza Maya?"

She shrugs.

"Once a month, my friends come over and we make homemade pizza at my place. I always make the best ones."

I know, if I take a step back from this moment, that Maya's right about us not stepping into that lodge together. Nicole broke up with me less than forty-eight hours ago. I'm still pretty messed up—confused, and angry, and sad—and I've never been a person who jumps from relationship to relationship.

It's time for me to return my skis to Liam.

But there's another thing I know, in this moment.

Nicole taking me to fancy restaurants, to vineyards I'd never heard of, to countries I'd never been to—it had made me feel special. It had all been fun.

But Maya's kind of fun is a fun I already understand. One I already know, deep in my bones.

I think of the villa in Thun, waiting for me, spacious and gorgeous and lonely.

"And say, Pizza Maya," I start, staring at her brown eyes behind her glasses, her slightly chapped lips, "that I respect your respect for my space. That I don't want to fuck and forget you either. But maybe...maybe a couple days from now, I get tired of being alone in a big ass villa in Switzerland. Maybe I really don't want to spend Christmas in that villa by myself. Say I want some company, and want to see this really great woman who helped me not die the first time I tried to ski."

Maya studies me for a long moment. And then she skis forward, just a bit, so her skis rest alongside mine. So her face is inches away.

"If that's all true," she says as she removes that glove again, "I'd say what I always say."

Her hand reaches up. So softly I almost don't feel it, she cups my cheek. Runs a thumb along my cheekbone. Her fingers, having been cocooned in her thick glove, are warm against my cold skin. They rest there for a lingering second before she delivers her parting shot, before she pushes away and skis back to the chair lift, leaving me with a grin and a pulse of hope in my heart.

"Go for it, Kiki."

acknowledgments

Thank you to every person who read drafts of anything contained in this book: Manda Bednarik, Piper Vossy, Jen St. Jude, Kate Cochrane, Chandra Fisher, Matthew Broberg-Moffitt, Sossity Chiricuzio, Maiga Doocy, Meryl Wilsner, Briana Miano, and KT Hoffman.

Thank you to Em Roberts for your beautiful covers of the novellas, and to Kelsey Bowman for your kindness and talent in creating the cover of this collected edition.

Thank you to everyone who has read, loved, and supported this series; it truly means so much to me.

Thank you to Sam and Kerri for surviving the Swiss Alps with me.

And thank you to Katie, Manda, and Kathy for being my karaoke ride-or-dies.

a tribute to dive bars & queer karaoke

A BRIEF ESSAY ON THE INSPIRATION FOR THE MOONLIGHT CAFÉ

On an industrial stretch of Columbia Boulevard in Portland, Oregon, near the intersection with MLK, sits a squat building with barely any windows. Currently a strip club, its nondescript facade and gravel parking lot mirror any American dive bar meant for the working class, a world away from the brighter, hipper restaurants and bars the Portland culinary scene is known for. For many a year before its current strip club iteration, the large roadside sign out front read *Chopsticks III: How Can Be Lounge*. A sign by the door featured a drawing of the iconically cheerful face of its owner, David Chow.

I wrote *Sing Anyway* a few months into the height of the COVID-19 pandemic. It spilled out of me over the space of a few days; it remains the fastest I have ever written anything, the most fully absorbed I became in a world for a concentrated period of time. Our lives had become so insular, those days; I had become so used to focusing on surviving with my family through the little routines of our suddenly quiet life. It became easy to forget that none of it was normal, that our lives had once been Not This.

And then one day I remembered karaoke nights at Chopsticks III—the complete antithesis of quarantine. Loud, crowded, sloppy, unsanitary.

Community with strangers.

Sam and Lily's story came naturally: a celebration of memory, a bittersweet therapy. A processing of what once was.

I grew up in a small town without queer bars; I hardly had a knowledge of their existence. Even in college, when I came out and lived in a large city, I simply wasn't the dancing-in-packed-bars kind of queer. I wished I was, sometimes; even now, I feel wistful for bars I've never visited, dances I've never danced, queer history I didn't grab a hold of.

We did discover one bar in Boston, though, a sunken, narrow-roomed space off Tremont called Limelight, where I at least learned that singing to your favorite songs on a stage full of your friends was, well, the best. (Sam and Lily lamenting about that guy who always sings "Pour Some Sugar On Me" in *Sing Anyway* is a nod to an unfortunate old tradition at Limelight.)

I can't remember the first time I visited Chopsticks III, years later on the other side of the country, but it was, shall we say, different from Limelight, which had fancy lighting and fancy drinks and a cover charge at the door. Chopsticks III was the kind of dirty, dimly lit bar one could find anywhere.

Except once the karaoke started, things always got fucking weird.

Weird enough for even me to feel safe.

When Chopsticks III announced its abrupt closure in

2018, the *Portland Mercury* described the joint thus:

> Chopsticks III had a very particular, enthusiastic following, that was at once supportive, competitive, and open to wild experimentation in the art of karaoke. The crowd was a welcome mixture of old-timers, hipsters, drunks, lesbians—a virtual rainbow of bar diversity that's hard to find in other parts of the city.

Very particular, indeed. Much of my descriptions of Moonie's in this book are taken straight from Chopsticks III. It didn't purport to be a queer bar, but queer people found a space there anyway, among the other odd assortment of folks who felt comfortable there. And once the karaoke got flowing, everyone, no matter how different we all were, just...fit. At least for a few hours, at least for the night.

In particular, I don't think I've ever been in another room—before, or since—where there were regularly so many trans people. Where it was never a big deal.

For many years of my late twenties and early thirties, there were two places where I felt perfectly happy and queer and at home. One was the general admission fan supporter section at Portland Thorns games—a topic for another book—and the other was Chopsticks III: How Can Be. That feeling—of being perfectly happy and queer and at home—was one I never fully understood as something I'd been missing, until I felt it.

There was a glittery Happy Birthday banner behind the stage, Chinese zodiac placards along the wall; the fries and the Chinese food were mediocre but we ate them anyway. There were singers and KJs you recognized, that you got excited for, if you went there enough. It wasn't the quality of the performances that made the karaoke so good so much as the passion and diversity and shared nostalgia behind them. (Fully into our Chopsticks III era, we once visited a friend in LA who took us to karaoke there. It only took a few songs from actually musically talented people to learn that karaoke in LA was...not the same as Chopsticks III.) The bathrooms were absolutely atrocious.

The *New York Times*, in a 2013 article about Portland karaoke, described Chopsticks III as "the kind of awful nightspot where if your watch was broken, you could keep time by the diminishing height of the melting heap of ice dumped in the urinal in the men's room." They went on to describe the randomness of the singers they witnessed, from a group of puppeteers who brought their puppets with them to the mic, to a "guy who looked just like Dick Butkus." I don't like you very much these days, *New York Times*, but at least your 2013 description of Chopsticks III was point on.

In *Our Favorite Songs,* I snuck in a reference to one of our favorite Chopsticks III regulars, Hollywood. In real life, Hollywood was an elderly Black man who would wander into the bar late at night, maybe around midnight or so, when things would be really hoppin'. He always had on a colorful, full suit, dapper as hell. He'd sing James Brown—the same thing every time—and absolutely kill it. And then he'd walk right on out of the bar again.

I sat at home during the pandemic and I thought: I miss that kind of shit.

A Chopsticks III night was always a big group outing, for a birthday or New Years or Pride; you never knew exactly who was going to show up or how the night was going to go.

I took my mom, once, because she loves music and is a beautiful singer. In my misguided mind, I thought she might like it. We walked in early, as we normally did; there was exactly one other group already there. A group of clearly already-inebriated women, doing explicit things with each other on the dance floor while wearing very little clothing, oblivious to the fact that no one else was there and that the sun had barely set. "It's not always like this," I quickly tried to explain to my mom and her husband.

Even though, of course, that wasn't actually true at all.

They sat very politely, watching me and my friends drink too much and sing very badly, before they left, and sometimes I wonder what they said to each other on their way home.

Sorry, Mom.

* * *

Another night, when the karaoke was in full swing, a woman got up to sing and I gasped, leaning in to our table. "That's Tina Kotek!" My table stared at me blankly. I was real into local politics at the time; apparently I was the only one who knew she was our (openly queer) speaker of the house. She was still dressed in lesbian business casual, like she had come straight from the Capitol. *Gay politicians!* My brain thought in glee. *They're just like us!* My immediate recognition of her remains one of my proudest moments of nerdery. (Unfortunately, I cannot for the life of me remember what she sang, but it was something very cute and thoroughly noncontroversial and her table of friends was very excited about it.)

Kotek has since worked her way up to the very top of state politics. Whether I agree with her on every issue or not, whenever I see her on TV, I smile and think, *I saw you at Moonie's.*

* * *

Sing Anyway was the first thing I ever published; I was exceedingly nervous to do so. I sent a draft off to two sensitivity readers that I found via Google, to help confirm I wasn't fucking anything up too badly; both were complete strangers.

The queer reader I found to help me with Lily's fat rep also happened to live in Portland. When I mentioned Chopsticks III as the inspiration for the story, they emailed me back right away to say, oh, I know that place! They told me a story: they had visited years ago with the person they had just started dating, who sang a perhaps accidentally vulnerable rendition of "In Your Eyes." *We've been together for eleven years since then*, they said, *so yeah, I have a soft spot for that place.*

At the time, it felt like such an incredible (and hilarious) coincidence, a piece of kismet that helped give me confident to press Publish.

Now, after a few years experience with what can happen when you actually share your stories, I only think: of course. Of course.

* * *

Although we never visited, Chopsticks II also met its demise over the last decade, a memorable building on East Burnside that, like so many old Portland establishments before it, was razed to make way for condos. Chopsticks I still exists; we visited once and it's decent, but lacks the camaraderie and queer-home-in-an-industrial-wasteland vibe of NE Columbia.

Now, the closest thing we've found is Escape Bar & Grill, which has similarities to Chopsticks III in that it's in a truly bleak part of town—far north Sandy, near 205 and the airport—and a really great blue-collar queer karaoke vibe. It actually advertises itself as queer friendly, full of the rainbow flags that never once appeared at Chopsticks; the dance floor is smaller but still welcoming. The bathrooms are single stalled, gender neutral, and spacious; when Lily pictures dragging Sam into a bathroom and banging against the wall in *Sing Anyway*, I was definitely picturing the bathrooms at Escape. Nothing sexual should have even been contemplated in the bathrooms of Chopsticks III. (And I refuse to accept any reality to the contrary.)

I often blended the two in writing Moonie's, as memories from both spots often mix in my memories now. The inspiration for Mal came from a butch bartender at Escape, who made good drinks—at her own damn pace—and never smiled at me once. I love her; please don't tell her I sent you.

While still in business, I haven't been back to Escape since the beginning of the pandemic, either; it's still a level of human closeness that hasn't felt safe to breach. I *have* sung with some loved ones in a private karaoke room, and while these are still fun, and I totally understand how social anxiety would make these a preferred night out for many, they can't compare to what we found at Chopsticks III. What generations of queer people have found in dimly lit spaces across geographies, across red states and blue states and any borders at all.

A place where, at least once in a while, we can all feel a little less alone.

also by anita kelly

Love & Other Disasters

Something Wild & Wonderful

How You Get the Girl

about the author

Originally from a small town in the Pocono Mountains of Pennsylvania, Anita Kelly now lives in the Pacific Northwest with their family. An educator by day, they write romance that celebrates queer love in all its infinite possibilities. Whenever not reading or writing, they're drinking too much tea, taking pictures, and dreaming of their next walk in the woods. They hope you get to pet a dog today.